TERRAGNATA

AND THE HEIR OF THE EARTH

C. D. MACKENZIE

To anyone who fell in love with a Dragon.

And is still burning.

PROLOGUE

ULTIMATE SACRIFICE

"*N*eferti," a distant voice called my name.

"Neferti," it repeated, the sound echoing off what had become the caverns of my blank mind—not hearing, not seeing, not processing. All I knew were my baby's green-brown eyes, staring up at me. Innocence would have been an incomplete description of what they held. Her eyes were a clean slate; full of potential, yet empty of any true course.

"Neferti," the voice said again, and this time the rasping tenor of the words snagged my attention. I looked up to find myself not in the mahogany room alone with my newly born baby but surrounded by the Elders. A group of husked bodies—feminine, decayed, and all but forgotten. They looked more like reapers of death than the powerful enforcers of fate I knew them to be.

A sinking feeling crept past the exhaustion gripping my bones. "Why do you visit me?" I croaked, my voice still raw from the screams of labor. "I am no one to you."

The group smiled at me, but their eyes drifted almost unwillingly to the tiny body, still wet with afterbirth, squirming in my arms.

The chamber was humid; perspiration from my heated pushing

clung to the air. Yet a shiver kissed my skin as if the surrounding sea itself had risen to flood the room.

"No," I shook my head, pulling her into my chest. "She's nothing, she's an innocent."

"Do you know what day it is, child?" The voice that spoke sounded even more ancient than the decrepit vessel it came from. She stepped out from behind the group, which parted for her as she approached my bed, jet black hair floating behind her. Distinct milky gray eyes trained on me.

The Rexi Prima. The First Queen Who Was a King. The Bearer of Cold Hearts.

I shook my head, a final whimper of denial, but of course, I did know the day. The sinking feeling turned to stone in my gut.

The First Queen smiled sadly, her sea-forged eyes foreboding of the little island we called home. "The Full Moon of the Creatrix, my dear. You remember how you conceived, don't you? You made a great sacrifice in Her honor. You prayed, asking for a drop of Her blood, in exchange for yours. Such a prayer I imagine you thought symbolic, but to a God in Her temple—well, it is not. You are holding a child of the Earth, dear. The One we have not seen in a thousand years."

I squeezed my eyelids tightly, wishing the Elders would disappear, praying they were a hallucination brought on by the sharp pains of birth. But I knew her words, knew of the cursed legend that gave our land its prosperity. "It can't be her," I whispered, choking on my protest. "She is not the daughter of a queen."

When I opened my eyes once more, they were gone, save for the Rexi Prima.

She shook her head, long black hair flowing in the still, thick air as tears streamed down her face. "You must name her as she is. You know what a name is to a child of the Mother. It will be a conduit and could very well mean her survival." She remained silent for one endless moment, like she feared being overheard. Her dry lips parted, and she mouthed the words, "I'm sorry," over and over again, her image slowly fading. And she was gone. I could not tell if she had apologized to me, or to the blinking, sleepy eyes that rested in my arms.

My daughter squirmed again, making a gentle sound—a squeak that would melt even the coldest of hearts. But a chilling intensity speared into the softness her noises inspired. "Don't worry," I whispered, brushing my lips to her head. "I will do what it takes to keep you safe."

PART I

ARGENTION

CHAPTER ONE

SHADOW DREAMS

I was burning.

I was burning—and the fire hadn't even touched me yet.

Flames licked, ebbed, and flowed like living creatures, twisting—no, contorting to touch me. Shadows danced within them, and I swore I saw faces of pain peering up at me.

I backed up a step. And then another. My spine collided with a pole. I whipped around to face my obstacle, the object I'd need to break through to run from the fire.

But it was a man, not a pole. A man who stared down at me, his eyes glowing. His features were hard to make out. I could only see his eyes, so close to my own they reflected my nearly engulfed figure. I whirled again to see those burning shadows rear as if they were one unified cobra, ready to strike. They lunged, and I struggled back, trying to move, but the man wouldn't budge, and they were close, so close, I tried to scream, but it died in my throat—

I woke, gasping at the crisp air of my cool, shadowed room. Moonlight flooded the piñon floors, soothing my pounding heartbeat as I refocused on the surrounding reality. On the hills faintly illuminated past my window. On the small washbasin set across from my bed. On the familiar woolen blanket tugging on my skin.

Home, I was home. Safe.

I let my head fall dramatically back into my pillow.

I heaved a sigh, the soft light of the moon lulling me back to sleep.

I'd definitely been reading too many novels.

———

THE DREAM STUCK to me like an invisible oil the entire next day. I rose, like I always did, to start a fire in the kitchen.

I hesitated that morning. The idea of seeing flames felt oddly nauseating. But my mother would be up soon, and I knew baking could not be done without a fire.

I stared at the flames, entranced, searching for the shadows that visited me in the night. But the logs burned harmlessly, as they had the morning before and the morning before that.

"Oh no. It's finally happened. She's gone mad."

The flat joke snapped my gaze from the stove.

My brother Danson sported a crooked grin, crossing his arms. "Should I call the healer? Brilliant, actually. A claim of insanity might be the only thing that could get you out of Spring Day."

"I'm not that desperate," I muttered, rolling my eyes. Though I hid it, I cringed within at the mention of our town's upcoming match-making event.

Danson's brows rose. "Oh really? I've seen you do far more to avoid the Argenti male population."

"That is because the Argenti male population is full of leering brutes," I snapped, shooing him away from the kitchen. "Shouldn't you be waking Javis? Shifts start in a half hour."

My eldest brother flashed his winning smile and backed away, hands raised. "It's no secret you've been unimpressed with the other members of my sex, but I'm just saying, we're not all that bad. Maybe it's time you branch out of your normal... circles. And try to breathe a little less... fire."

I pinched the bridge of my nose, exhaling with a loud sigh. "I'll take that into consideration."

He was gone with a wink, dragging my youngest brother—eyes half-open—through the front door of our log cabin.

They would head to the mines, my father in tow. Our town, Argention, made its living primarily through silver mining, a trade my whole family participated in. My father and brothers mined the silver, and my mother and I worked it. We worked it so hard that it sometimes left rashes on my skin. It was a grueling process. Melting, cooling, hammering. Melting, cooling, and hammering again. Coins, jewelry, beads, serving dishes, and more were all sold by the townswomen to travelers and merchants.

We rarely kept our wares, not needing the finery, but occasionally one trinket made its way out of the selling basket. On my eighteenth birthday, almost two years ago, my father bade me select my favorite of my mother's creations. A small dragon—devastatingly intricate in its carving—hung around my neck ever since.

My brothers had teased me endlessly, calling me *firebreather*. It was somewhat of a masculine choice, I supposed. Not a flower, nor a heart, nor a simple shape. But it seemed powerful, a feeling rarely afforded to the young ladies of my village. My mother had smiled knowingly when I'd chosen it, as if she'd fashioned it for me in the first place.

"Are you just going to stare off into the distance, letting the garden wither away, or will you be getting on with your chores this morning?" My mother's sharp voice, lined with weariness, cut through the room. She appeared, tying an apron around her waist. "The plants won't water themselves, dear."

I nodded, not complaining for a moment about the upcoming ache I knew would line my arms after my thousandth trip to the well. I tugged on my mud boots and woolen jacket, inhaling the scent of the smoky stove before ducking out the door.

I was home. I was safe, at home.

I only wondered if that was all there was to life. If there could be more.

AFTER MORNING CHORES, it was my duty to drop off all new silver creations and a fresh basket of my mother's jams at the seller stands in the market. The elderly women who weren't strong enough to work the silver maintained the booths on behalf of the town. They might not have been strong enough to work physically, but they haggled mercilessly with the merchants who came to trade their exotic foods and new fashions for Argenti silver. My father always grunted when he saw those merchant caravans cresting the Argen hills, making the descent into our valley. I never knew if his grunt meant approval, for they bought the silver he and my brothers mined, or if it meant a sort of silent regret since he and my brothers would have to return to the mines the next day.

But today—something felt different at the market. The cobbled roads, humble shack stands, the smell of roasting nuts and fresh bread were all the same. But a thickness filled the air that raised the fine hairs on my arm.

A familiar face greeted me as I handed over our wares to my mother's most trusted seller. "Fine day," Miralvda remarked, gesturing to the general hustle of the market and gleaming sky.

I nodded, fondness blooming in my chest, settling my unease. Miralvda—one of the elderly in town—never gossiped, never pried into who I would choose to match with on Spring Day. I would have picked her as our seller every time, had my mother not thought it imprudent. We had to maintain a bench of trusted partners—it was risky to play favorites.

"You seem chipper this morning." I smiled as she thumbed each piece of silver, inspecting our work. "I think it's some of her best—"

Something shoved into me, and I stumbled forward, nearly

toppling the table. Before I could catch myself, strong hands guided me back to stand.

I pivoted, pulling myself out of the stranger's grip.

"Apologies miss. It's rather crowded in these stalls, and I *am* rather large."

Indeed. I was staring at quite possibly the largest man I'd ever seen.

Miralvda's eyes shot back and forth from us as if she'd launch herself between me and this wolf.

"N—no problem," I stammered, looking at the man. He pushed back the hood of his black cloak, revealing a face so carved it almost looked gaunt. It would have been unfair to describe him as anything but beautiful. Eerily so, his beauty seemed impossible. His eyes were as blue as deep water.

"May I help you with something?" Miralvda's tone sharpened into something harsher than I'd ever heard her use with a customer.

The man's head inclined slightly. He inquired about her selection of silver cuffs when I saw them. A collection of men scattered throughout the crowd—the largest men I'd ever seen, just like the one before me, with angled jaws and black cloaks drawn low over their faces. They were not akin to the usual types I saw at the market: scraggly old traders, pompously dressed capitolites, or young adventure seekers. I knew at once they were all together, even though they were dispersed throughout the market, some examining goods, some meandering quietly, some surveying the crowd.

I couldn't take my eyes off them. Were they soldiers? They weren't in uniform, at least no uniform I'd ever seen before. And how could they all be so *impossibly* large?

"Terra," my best friend Gia broke my trance, appearing by my side. Her empty basket indicated she'd already dropped off her mother's goods.

"Are you finished? We could walk back together." She pointedly ignored the man next to us, who was shooting me a glance every other second.

I exhaled, relieved. "Yes, let's." I gave Miralvda a nod, who returned it in kind. Gia just linked our arms and steered us away from the table. We slipped out a small side exit next to Miralvda's stand.

When we were far enough, I let out another breath. "Did you see those men?" I asked, hushed. "The huge ones, with black cloaks. Sprinkled throughout the market like... ants."

Gia shrugged, the motion lined with a slight tension in her shoulders. "Foreigners, most likely."

I shuddered. "They gave me the strangest feeling. I couldn't wait to get out of there."

Gia gave me a sidelong glance that could have been mistaken for an eye roll. "You just want to get back to whatever novel is currently tucked under your mattress." She grinned, deftly changing the subject. "Matthias, was that his name? The broad-faced knight with long waving locks of gold and washboard abdominals?"

I threw her a glance of equal amusement. "You would like to know, wouldn't you?"

Two and a half miles stretched between our homes and the town center. Gia's cottage was past mine, up the hill, but still opposite the forest. I loved my home, I did. But the past year or so... I'd been having dreams of grander lands, palaces filled with sparkling gowns and smoldering candles. Ships sailing fast over open ocean. They weren't always pleasant. No, like the one the night before, sometimes the dreams were terrifying. But each morning I woke, it felt like something was yawning inside of me.

I squeezed my eyes shut for a moment, as if my view would change upon reopening them.

When I did, I only saw the familiar trail home.

"You okay?" Gia's face held genuine concern. Leave it to my best friend to never miss a thing.

I shrugged, shaking my head. Shaking free the fantasies and thoughts of a world beyond our small town.

"I'm just thinking about Spring Day tomorrow. I'm nervous, that's all."

But I wasn't thinking about Spring Day at all, I was thinking about what came after. The safe and predictable life of domesticity prescribed to a girl of my age. It wasn't that I didn't want it. The promise of my own house and a family to warm it didn't sound *bad*. But something about the thought of that life beginning *now,* manifesting so soon—

"Nervous? Well, of course you are! It is your first, after all. I'd be concerned if you weren't. Especially given Mav will be in attendance." Gia gave me a small, knowing smile.

Her comment earned a healthy cheek reddening from me. Gia was three years my senior, and while she did not qualify to attend Spring Day due to her spoken-for status, her brother, Mav, did.

"I don't want to talk about Mav right now." I tried and failed to lighten my tone. "It's not that I don't love him fiercely, you know I do. But I—I don't think I'm ready." A fabricated image of me perched on a ship's bow, wind rippling past my face, appeared in my mind.

As always, a sudden pang of guilt followed the fantasy. Mav would make a fine match. Everyone considered me lucky to have his interest.

"You two were so close when you were young," Gia protested quietly. "You played together endlessly—so much I even felt left out for a time. And the other girls say he's not terrible to look at..."

It was true, Mav was one of the more handsome boys in our village, athletic and strongly built. He had the same features as Gia, clear eyes set amidst pale skin, chocolate hair, strong brows, and dark sweeping lashes. He was good-natured, quick, and close to me in age —nineteen, nearing twenty. I spent countless hours with him in the hill grasses and forest creeks until our mothers finally pulled us apart for propriety's sake. It was then I was forced into the open arms of Gia, to make a *more appropriate* friendship. And although she preferred gossip and hairstyles to trapping frogs for further study, we became great friends.

"And," she continued, "we'd be double sisters. How could you not want that?" Her clear eyes questioned me, penetrative as they always were. I fixed my gaze on the path ahead, shading her from any guilt crossing my face. We had talked about it in our younger years, rejoicing in the possibility that we would cement our friendship in sisterhood. But back then, I couldn't have imagined leaving Argention. And now...

"At least help me with my hair." I poked her in the ribs, hoping my diversion wasn't as obvious as it felt. "You know I'm complete rubbish when it comes to styling."

Gia squeezed my hand. "I wouldn't miss it. Tomorrow, one hour before sundown. And you better be washed when I get there." She practically skipped away as I veered off the path and towards home.

Our small cottage was nestled at the edge of a thickly wooded forest, which butted up to the foot of the Argen hills. My father and brothers had built it when we'd moved to Argention from Lahar. I was only eleven or twelve then, but I still remembered the care they'd used to stack planks of piñon on one another. The precise angles of slanted edges met at a point each time, resulting in a geometrical pattern mirroring the layers of mountains.

I crossed the small field before my cottage. The uneasy feeling from the market, which had grown silent on the walk home, spread wide again in my gut. I reached the front door and spun around, half expecting to startle something or someone. But I only saw Gia disappearing over her hill. Nothing strange, nothing to validate the turmoil coiling in my belly.

I shook my head, dismissing whatever dramatics were being cooked up by my imagination. Too many novels, indeed. Stepping into my house, I attempted to will away any intrusive thoughts. Despite the valiant effort of my logical mind to puncture holes in that building shroud of intuition, I could not rid myself of the sinking feeling that someone—or something—was watching me.

"Well, look who's home late, with not much to show for it," my brother Javis said when I walked in with my market basket half full of Mama's jams. I faced discerning eyes. Her work with muddled fruit was unparalleled, and we almost always sold out of her ingenious combinations of rathumby and bullionbur, gallonberry and clove.

"What distracted you today, dear sister? Laying in the meadows with Gia, daydreaming of your first Spring Day, perhaps?"

Talk like that to a sibling would have earned me a smarting hand-print across my face from Mama, but Javis only got a sharp look.

"Our Terra isn't one for the boys, Javis," my eldest brother Danson replied. "I do not doubt that even if Mav *does* work up the guts to ask for a dance tomorrow, she will decline." Though he said it as a statement, the way his eyebrows rose made it seem like a question. For a moment my family stilled, even Mama kneading dough in the kitchen, and they all looked in my direction.

"As I just told Gia..." I emphasized *just* to make them understand how much I disliked repeating myself, "I have no interest in a husband right now. And frankly, since you two seem set on barreling down the path towards marriage, or at least accidental fatherhood, there may soon be no one here to help Mama." I said the last part matter-of-factly, making it seem like convenience formed my opinion, rather than a deep reluctance to sacrifice what tiny scrap of freedom I had and would surely lose when wed.

Danson choked on his drink. Mama gaped at me, probably for suggesting one of my brothers might unwittingly become a father out of wedlock. But before she could scold me, Javis quipped back. "That still doesn't answer our question, Terra, now does it? If Mav asks you for a dance, will you say yes, or will you say no?"

"Boys, leave Terra alone and go help your father chop wood. Terra, bring me what you didn't sell in the market today. And for the gods' sake, can someone set the dammed table," Mama said, fully recovered from my comment.

A few moments later, I did earn a smarting mark on my cheek after the boys had gone outside. But I could have sworn the corner of her mouth quirked up as she turned back to her kneading. It soothed the sting.

Dinner was short—not quite unusual with three miners at the table who wolfed down food quicker than a late December sun fell behind the mountains. The boys and Father spread themselves out in front of the fire in a post-meal stupor, while Mama and I tended to the dishes. We worked in silence, as usual, but something hung in the air. Something she wanted to say, but didn't, which was unlike her. She rarely guarded her thoughts.

Later that night, long after I'd settled into bed, I used a sliver of moonlight peeking through my bedside window to read. I was lucky to have my own room—a result of having no sisters. My brothers were more than happy to sleep side by side in front of the fire in the main room. It was a position they likely would have found themselves in most nights regardless of having their own rooms, given the exhaustion in their bodies and the ale in their bellies.

I sighed into my novel's crinkling pages. Matthias, the blonde warrior-prince-knight-hero, had just slain a magically mutated wilde-beest, standing up from its mangled body only to find himself surrounded again, by wolves. He took on the predators, one by one.

C'mon, Matthias, I cheered silently. I shuttered my eyes from the page, imagining myself greeting him once the battle finished. I was his long-lost maiden, found at last, appearing from a supernatural mist. The spell that had kept me away was broken, now that he'd defeated that gruesome beast. We embraced intimately, pulling back only to examine one another. We'd barely looked at each other a moment before a straggling wolf, somehow un-slain by Matthias, leaped out of nowhere, raging red eyes trained on Matthias's neck. But I was quick, too quick for the wolf, raising my hip dagger to its throat before it could bite into my returned love, making me the hero—

I jolted at the sound of my father's footsteps outside. I quickly tucked my book between the sheets before he crept into my room. He sat down next to me, and though I did not stir, he spoke.

"You do *not* have to accept his offer tomorrow, Terra. It is your choice. But you must understand the gravity of the situation. Spring Day may seem routine and archaic to you, but to Argention it's a proud tradition. A dance means you will be entering into a promise with him. A promise that you will be courted with the intention of marriage. Do not make a promise you cannot keep.

"I have little to give you in this world, Terra, and this world will take more from you than it will share. But if there's one thing I ever say that you remember, let it be this. There is a little voice inside of you—something old and knowing and of the universe. It is not the thoughts that swirl in our minds or the stories we tell ourselves, but rather a deep wisdom that lives in our gut. This is your intuition. Seek it out, and it will be your guiding compass. If you don't know what decision to make, it will lead you. If you are blind, it will see for you. If you are afraid, it will be brave. Should you feel alone one day, remember, you are not. Because *it* is there."

And with that, he gave my hair a loving stroke and got up.

I released a shaky breath. *Did Father just tell me to refuse Mav?* No, he loved Mav like a third son, and some days more than his own, depending on what mischief my brothers had gotten into.

But the words he didn't say were the ones that struck me. Words I'd heard from everyone else in my family, from the other ladies in the market, from the traders in the square. From my teachers and the seamstress and the patrons who bought my mother's jams. Hell, even Gia had implied it.

You may never do better than Mav, Terra. He's a good one, Terra. He will love you. He will be true to you. You would be stupid to turn him down.

The thought reverberated through me. Every single day. One that a small voice, coming from somewhere within me, refused to accept.

CHAPTER TWO

THE OUTSIDER

The morning of Spring Day was very apropos of its name, with clear skies, chirping birds, and too much pollen. The season incarnate.

Despite the weather's optimism, dread weighed like bricks on my chest.

I had known Mav my whole life. I knew he would be a kind and gentle husband. It wasn't the idea of him specifically that made me feel like oxygen slipped from my lungs but the idea that I would blindly tether myself to him for life. How did people rejoice in such commitment with no knowledge of the world? The finality of it sat unsettled in my stomach like curdled milk.

Such thoughts, mixed with the uncertainty stoked by my father's words, plagued me all day. From morning chores, through breakfast and mid-day weeding, all the way until I found myself submerged in water, washing the grime from my skin in wait for Gia.

"Terra!" A voice sang through the cracked window to my right. I hoisted myself up, fists clenching on the sides of the tub, to see Gia marching down towards the cottage, carrying what looked like a sherpa's pack. I giggled to myself. At least if I was going to be dressed up like a doll, the right person for the job would be doing the dressing.

Gia burst through the door a few moments after I rushed to put on some clothes. My room wasn't big, but it offered enough space for a small bed, a tub, and Gia's heap of supplies.

She furrowed her brow at me. "Your hair is still wet."

I just grinned back at her. "You only asked me to be clean."

Two hours later and well past sundown, I donned my best dress, which Gia had modified to hug my waist tighter and push my chest upwards. The fit flattered my figure, which was a contradiction of soft curves layered over a muscled body. I had never been called petite like Gia—I was average height for a woman and blessed with a strong build. The forest green color complimented my coloring, Gia said—calling to the thin ring of green around my irises.

She piled my butterscotch hair on top of my head with such vigor that tears sprang from my eyes as she worked. Somehow, curls, twists, and beautiful braids fountained from the point on my head where all the hair gathered. She left out strategic wisps, framing my face, and adding a hint of mystery. I never quite knew how she got my soaking wet hair to look like the locks of a goddess, but she had a talent for such things.

We both stared into the small mirror in my room, and she squeezed my hand. "You look radiant, Terra of Argention. Any man would be lucky to win a dance from you tonight."

Though the thought of dancing with anyone snapped my attention back to the collection of stones that were taking up residence in the bottom of my stomach, I exhaled and met her gaze. "Thank you, Gia. As always, your work is pure sorcery," I breathed, attempting a smile I knew didn't quite reach my eyes.

I opened the door to the main room, with Gia in tow, to find my family sitting by the fire. Javis gave out a low whistle and Danson smacked him on the back of his head with a laugh.

Mama sprung up and said, "You look beautiful, darling." My father, and escort for the evening, rose as well. He wore his finest silk-spun jacket. He said nothing, his dark eyes shining.

"Doesn't she look just gorgeous," Gia crooned.

"She looks nothing like us," Javis remarked.

This earned a scornful look from Mama. "Shut your mouth Javis. Just because Terra is blessed with my family's genes and you are not, does not give you cause to talk such."

But he was right. My brothers' dark eyes and hair matched my father's, and their sharp cheekbones matched my mother's. Freckles and soft edges defined my face, and my blonde hair called after no one. "I had a blonde aunt and three cousins," Mama went on, "all of whom Terra resembles strikingly."

"Terra, are you ready?" My father cut in.

I nodded, my voice not reaching my lips. I may have been simply Terra of Argention going to a match-making ceremony, but I felt more like Matthias. Headed into battle.

———

THE GATHERING WAS SMALL, given our village boasted only two thousand strong. It took place on the sixtieth day of Spring each year. Qualified attendees included all unmarried or not-promised men and women, aged nineteen to twenty-four. It was a great honor to be promised in the first year and a great shame to turn twenty-five with no match.

The process was simple. A man would ask a woman to dance, she would accept, and they'd dance. As long as the Matron—our glorified match-maker—approved, they were on their way to a several-months courtship and eventual marriage.

Spring Day took place in the town square, close to the market. The air was warm enough to energize, but cool enough to draw people together. I wondered if that was why the ceremony always occurred sixty days into Spring; it was good weather to yield a high crop of matches.

We stepped out of the small buggy pulled by our old mare Gallonberry, and my heart fluttered upon noticing the dancing underway. Girls and boys lined up facing each other, one gender on each side, performing traditional Argenti step dances. The boys, or... men, I supposed, kicked their heels together in the air and spun around, while the women faced their right or left sides, palms touching their female partners while they circled one another. The line dances always fascinated me. Men peacocked, and women batted their eyelashes in flirting. One line responded to another until it ended in bows and curtsies. The men and women retreated to their respective sides, where the women waited with hopeful eyes, and the men busied themselves with anything they could find. Usually, refilling their ale cups.

As far as I could tell, no promise dances, which consisted of one-on-one touching, had yet begun.

I searched my father's face for any sign of what he said to me the night before. "Please, can't you stay for the ceremony?"

He smiled and shook his head. "Terra, you know I can't. Not requiring my presence signals your readiness for the next phase of life. No matter what happens, I am so proud of you." I had little time to respond, to even contemplate confessing my plans to leave Argention. For he transferred my palm straight to the Matron behind me, and the battle began.

THE MATRON SMELLED of strong brandy and foreign perfume, likely bought with the taxes she collected from the town for her match-making services. I trusted her less than I trusted my old mare to make it up a steep hill.

"Time for your metamorphosis," she sneered. And then she

turned to project to the gathering. "Our next guest is Terra of Argention, aged nineteen, daughter to mine worker Ravello and jam-maker Katalana. This is her first Spring Day, and she is now eligible for invitations."

As is custom with new bachelors and bachelorettes, the Matron led me to the middle of the square. The men and women had stilled upon her words and formed two separate lines again, but this time not for dancing. Every woman's opening entrance resulted in a grand ordeal, given it was the men's first chance to ask her to dance. For the most desirable women, there could be several men on one knee signaling their intent. If more than one did so, the Matron would pick whomever she deemed to be most suitable. Then the woman could accept or decline. If there were no men, the Matron would deposit the girl at the end of the women's line and the dancing would resume.

Men only typically knelt, from what Gia told me, if competition was anticipated. If a match was publicly speculated, like mine and Mav's, the man might ask afterward, in his own private way. He would have little concern that another would try to compete.

"The first chance to ask for Terra's dance is now," the Matron boomed. "As we pass each man, he will have the opportunity to kneel. She will not decide until we have passed each and every one of you."

I let my gaze lift from the ground and settle on the two long lines of decorated bodies. About forty men and forty women made up each side. My throat felt like I'd swallowed hay, and my heartbeat reverberated throughout my body. I'd always thought of myself as brave, ready to tumble down a hillside or jump over a wide, rushing creek. But here, I stood frozen.

The Matron nudged me forward at my low back, likely to straighten my spine, as well as spur my advance, and the procession began. I was torn between looking the men in their faces to project strength or withholding eye contact to avoid encouraging any unlikely desires. What I settled on I can only imagine looked like erratic head jerking, but if it deterred any suitors, it was all acceptable to me.

The crawling pace of my walk made me acutely aware of being picked over by every woman sizing me up with her nose in the air, and every man sizing me down as he looked at my neckline. Eventually, at about halfway, I saw Mav's face at the end of the line. I had to admit, I felt relieved to see him. He placed a fist over his heart, the Argenti gesture of comradeship we used to perform during make-believe war as kids. I expected him to look at me without an ounce of stress in his body—his default demeanor was an almost unnatural ease. But I sensed an unfamiliar stiffness in him.

He was worried. *Why? Does he know of my plans?*

Two heartbeats later, I noticed movement in my left periphery. Then, the Matron halted. Why were we stopping?

I stilled, as it seemed the world around me had. A man lowered himself to one knee. The blood drained from my face. There was a man on his knee, and it wasn't Mav.

It was the man from the market. His pushed-back hood revealed coiffed blonde hair. He looked to be late into his twenties and peered up at me with those eerie blue eyes, a sinister leer on his face.

A feeling like spiders running along my skin swept up the back of my spine.

What in the gods' names is an outsider doing here, let alone kneeling for me? My jaw dropped, but no words formed.

"Rise traveler," the Matron spoke for me. "What is your name, why do you request Terra of Argention's hand, and what think you to give in exchange for a daughter of Argention?"

Dowries were not necessarily custom amongst the Argenti, unless one's daughter was so sought after that a match could only be determined with a sum in gold (not silver, of course, we didn't need silver). However, they were absolutely required if an outsider kneeled for a daughter of Argention. The town and family would have to be compensated for the loss of a healthy, breeding-aged woman. It had only happened three times. Ever. All three of those requests were for women whose beauty had been so renowned and captivating that travelers spread stories to other villages and kingdoms. Young dukes or princes had come searching for a pliable and striking country wife, instead of the power-hungry courtiers lined up for them.

I harbored no delusions of my beauty. I was neither ugly nor breathtaking. Which begged the question—why would an outsider come for *me*? He would've had to know our matching traditions. Hell, he would have had to have *known* me.

The man stood, shadows crossing his face from the flickering firelight. He towered over me at an unnatural height. He would have even looked down on my father and brothers, who were considered taller than most.

"I am the lumberer Fayzien, of the offshore Kingdom Wahaca," his voice almost sang. "I would like to ask Miss Terra of Argention to dance by way of formally courting her. I can offer the village of Argention her weight in gold as a dowry."

The Matron snorted. "How could a lumberer have so much gold? And even if you did, why would you want to spend it on her?"

I glanced down the line at Mav. His eyes darted from the man and locked with mine. He tapped his heart with his fist again.

The stranger examined his immaculate nails, seemingly annoyed. "I am a favored lumberer of the king. He pays me in kind. I have come here to find a bride, and I noticed Terra selling jam in the market. She is the one I want." He looked at the Matron once more. "If you do not trust my word on the gold, you need only to look behind you."

Not much of an answer about why he chose *me*, but then the Matron turned around to find several of his men holding large sacks, undone at the neck, revealing the shine of gold.

The Matron's mouth spread wide. "Very well. Your offer is acknowledged. You may kneel once more." A sinking realization hit me—the Matron would be able to choose which match she viewed to be the most suitable.

You still have the power to decline, Terra.

My heart pounded so violently that it took shape as a ringing in my ears. The man called Fayzien seemed to notice my unease, his interest turning predatory as he resumed kneeling. A hint of a smirk held more promise of cruelty than romance, and I knew something was very wrong.

The Matron tugged me after her. I should have been relieved no other surprises presented, and that, in the end, only Mav knelt with the stranger. But relief felt inaccessible, as my plan to politely decline Mav's offer in private had become priority number five hundred. The first four-hundred and ninety-nine priorities would be to stay the *hell* away from that blue-eyed man.

After what had been about five minutes, but felt like an hour, the procession finished. We turned around to face the two lines, and the Matron spoke again. "As is the Argenti custom, I have made my decision about the most suitable match for Terra. In this tradition, the man I choose will ask Terra to dance, which signals a request for a formal courtship."

The Matron took a breath, to play up the drama of the moment. "The man I have chosen is Fayzien of Wahaca."

My heart raced faster, though I had expected this. Of course, she would choose the option with a price. I looked at Mav and gave him a reassuring nod. I would not accept the outsider's invitation to dance, which was my right.

"But this situation is one of delicacy," she continued before I could get a word in. "As a profound offer has been made by an outsider. No viable courtship can be conducted across sea-separated kingdoms, and as such, Fayzien of Wahaca has proven his commitment and dedication to Terra of Argention with a more than fair bride price. I hereby remove Terra's burden of choice to accept or deny Fayzien's request and dismiss the required courtship. I pronounce Terra of Argention and Fayzien of Wahaca betrothed, and as such, demand full dowry payment in kind, to be accepted by me on behalf of the people of Argention. Fayzien of Wahaca, do you accept the terms of your betrothal?"

Fayzien didn't bother meeting the Matron's gaze. Triumph lined his irises as they swept over me, from head to toe, sending a spear of terror through my spine. He rose and bowed with the grace of a wildcat moving through tall grass, assessing its prey. "I accept."

"You can't do that!" Mav shouted. But the Matron paid him no mind. She was looking at the bags of gold loaded at her feet. And when I searched the crowd for support, I saw only the same thing. Their attention was not upon Mav, nor the strange man, nor me. It fell on the bags and bags of gold.

I looked back at Mav. His mouth formed an unmistakable word.

Run.

CHAPTER THREE

ESCAPE HATCH

I ran out of there like a cockroach fleeing a freshly lit torch. One foot after another, weighed down by heaps of skirts, I ran towards the forest. The town road wound around it, but the quickest way home would be through. I needed to reach my level-headed father and sharp-tongued mother. They wouldn't let a stranger take me from my home. And, surely, they had some say in it, since I was their daughter. Cursing myself for even thinking of leaving my family, I glanced back.

If Mav had run after me, he no longer held my trail. The group of black-cloaked men, however, seemed to follow at a leisurely pace, hoods drawn. My skin prickled with fear, but I drew comfort as I neared the forest. It was my childhood playground, a safe haven, and I could easily lose them. As I turned my head to face forward again, I saw a flash of blue eyes and blonde hair. But before I had time to register a hand held out in front of me, I flew with sudden force up into the air. I landed with equal violence on my back.

I wheezed, trying to reflate my lungs after the impact, my brain not processing the unnatural way in which I was flung off my feet. The blonde man hadn't even touched me! I fluttered my eyes open, revealing my vulnerable, horizontal position. I clenched my fists, filled them with dirt, and pushed myself up to sit. As I lifted my gaze for the second time, I locked eyes with the bluest set I'd ever seen.

The man extended a hand to me, revealing a pale forearm brushed with light blonde hair. His open palm seemed delicate, no trace of roughness left by the household work I'd grown accustomed to. Nor of the hard labor of lumbering, I noted. Everything inside me screamed to resist his offer to pull me up, but I could not. My thoughts felt like eels I tried to catch with wet fingers, my focus seemed to pulse in and out, nauseating me. As if the motion was not my own, I extended my hand, my body betraying me. *No!* The touch of his fingers was both comforting and wrong, wrong, wrong.

On the short journey from sitting in the dirt to standing, I felt a breeze tickle everything from my stomach to my toes. My eyes shot down. My gown was gone. Save for the small silver dragon pendant hanging from my neck, I was utterly naked.

I looked up to see the man staring at me—a smile forming on his face. He still held my hand, which felt overly warm and uninvited. But I couldn't break his stare, nor could I determine how I lost my dress.

As my slippery thoughts tried to re-form, a searing heat brushed my fingertips where they met his. I wanted to scream, but I couldn't move, couldn't speak. The pain lessened, and the heat traveled up my arm, caressing me in a possessive, alarming way. After it passed my shoulder, it tightened around my neck just so slightly, as if to remind me it was there. Tears slipped down my cheeks as the heat advanced on my chest and circled my breasts, taunting me. I knew then I was being violated—in some strange, impossible way. His eyes had gone from hungry to ravenous. But even in my delirious and pained state, I had the vague impression his desire was more cruel than carnal.

I battled to get the words out. "What do you want from me?"

An almost imperceptible shadow crossed over his simmering grin. "Well, first of all, I believe you owe me a dance."

The man led me into a twirl and laughed as if he was playing his favorite, most hysterical game.

My face grew hotter, wetter. I felt utterly exposed and trapped, unable to move.

"But more importantly," he continued, pausing our dance, "I am here to complete my queen's task, sweet Terra. And honestly, I didn't think you would run. Lost good money on that, I might add. I have never had the pleasure of experiencing rejection from a young human maiden. It is a rare occasion to find myself surprised, and I have to say, it was to my supreme delight."

Queen? Of where? "What could a queen possibly need from a miner's daughter?" I asked, tears continuing to streak my face. "There must be a mistake. I am no one. I have nothing!" I breathed out the last part, a silent scream. My heart blared so loudly I could feel it ring in my ears, but I could not move.

"In time, you will see you have more to give her than you may wish. Now, I must take you home," he said.

This is my home! I wanted to yell.

The heat continued to roam southward. Though my mind was saturated in a fog of pain, my feet called to me, begging me to run. I could not break his gaze, but my left hand throbbed, drawing my attention to it. The throb was more acute—more pounding—than the searing heat I'd felt in my right when Fayzien touched it.

The new pain grew so intense that it became a heartbeat in my chest, in my head, in my whole body.

The tension in my left hand came from the dirt I'd forgotten I was holding. Not from my strained fist, but the dirt itself.

Not just dirt. Earth.

The word "Earth" rang in my head like a call to prayer. The pulsing seemed to have an upward direction, as if it wanted me to raise my clenched fist. On instinct, I battled to comply, bringing my hand level with the man's face. The faintest sign of confusion flickered in his eyes as I opened my palm.

The Earth leapt from my hand, hitting him with an unnatural

29

force that knocked him several feet back and to the ground. His grip on me released. My jaw loosened at the absurdity of the act, but I gaped only for a split second before the dirt beneath my feet pushed me towards the forest.

I ran at a pace I had never reached before. The Earth seemed to lift my feet faster, propelling me forwards. I no longer followed any trail I recognized, though I had wandered every nook and cranny in our small forest countless times. A path opened up, shrub and brush parting like curtains as I flailed through the trees. I wanted to pause, to check if the ludicrous assistance I seemed to be receiving was the conjuring of my mind. But I did not. I had not a second to spare.

The unfamiliar path led me to a stone bridge across a creek. Cut with gallonberries on both sides, I recognized it as the place Gia and I picked earlier that week. Across the bridge was home.

The path seemed to be diverting me away from the bridge, but I did not acquiesce. Home was close. I jumped and scrambled over bushes and roots alike until I hit hard stone. I heard a humorless cackle and turned back to see the man. He stopped several paces away from me, arms extended out to opposing sides. He breathed heavily, his cloak was torn and riddled with brambles, and his golden hair was in more disarray than someone like him would ever allow. But his grin spread wide, gleeful. I felt movement beneath my feet and looked down to see water swirling beneath the bridge. I blinked. The river moved impossibly—not in a current pattern at all. It moved as if... it were alive. My eyes snapped back to him, his arms open. *Was he...?*

I tried to take another step, but the water built to the point of crashing over the bridge. Two steps later, and the river *erupted*. A wave swept over my head, nearly taking me down, but I steadied myself on the railing and pushed forward. The water was a rising tide, raging as if to wrap around my waist and whisk me away. The frigid moisture clung to my bare skin like a sodden woolen dress, and I knew my feet would lose grip in a matter of moments.

I looked up for any sort of help, desperate. I spotted a lone vine that hadn't been there a moment ago, dangling from a tree that curved over the bridge like a crescent moon. Despite the cold, my legs launched me high enough to grab hold of the vine. As I did, it flung me out of the water and across the bank. Onto the other side of the river.

I shot a glance backward at the man. It looked like he was *gliding* towards me over the river, which inexplicably had become a tormenting sea. Despite my acute disbelief, pure adrenaline pushed me forward, and I continued to run until a massive rodent hole opened up before me. The rodents of Argention grew to the size of the pigs. When I was a girl, I used to play in those long tunnels, and was smacked senseless for coming home head to toe in dirt. But right now, I had no time to question my instinct. I took a deep, steadying breath and jumped feet first into the hole. As I slid down, I thought I heard the opening close behind me.

I BARRELED through the tunnel until I landed in what appeared to be an underground cavern of sorts. Despite the raw sting that coated my skin from the fall through the Earth, I could only think of the blue-eyed man. *Fayzien.* I squeezed my eyes shut and shook my head, the impossible image of a man walking on water plastering itself to the back of my eyelids.

"This can't be real," I whispered aloud, looking around. "Is any of this real?"

But as much as the last hour had felt like a nightmare, I was fairly certain I wasn't dreaming. Forcing myself to focus on the escape, I took in my surroundings. It was a large enough space for me to stand nearly upright. The tunnel I'd fallen through opened into the space from the ceiling behind me, and three other tunnels forked out of the cavern in front. One seemed to slope down further, possibly to another network of caverns below. The two remaining tunnels stood opposing one another. From my vantage point, one went left and one went right.

I flipped a coin in my mind and chose left. I couldn't allow myself to overthink things. After twenty minutes of crawling on hands and knees, I ended up in a smaller cavern with even fewer viable exit options. I squeezed my eyelids together, willing the hot moisture of frustration to stay behind them. Turning around to try the other tunnel, I moderated my breathing—in and out—as I crawled. Moments after entering the other path, I realized conventional crawling wouldn't work. I resorted to pulling myself forward one forearm at a time while my lower body dragged behind me. A painful activity, particularly when naked. Which I still was.

I gritted my teeth, biting the inside of my cheek to keep from crying out at the searing cuts of gravel against my unprotected skin. By the time I reached the third cavern, my body was a masterpiece of dirt, grime, and blood. It felt like battle armor.

The third cavern had one large tunnel, wide enough that I could walk through hunched over. I marveled at the size; yes, moles were large in Argention, but these were beyond practicality. The tunnel opened up as I made my way, eventually feeding into the mouth of a cave shielded by a canopy of vines. The clear night sent the moon-light streaming through. I pushed the curtain of vines to the side and breathed in the evening air—the scent of the Argen forest pines, spruces and firs with creeping moss coats and sprawling twisted roots. My forest. The foliage had breathed into my blood my whole life. The place I loved but had felt compelled to leave behind. It was still my home.

I steadied myself. The position of the moon told me the end of that day had just passed. It was likely about an hour past midnight. It took another hour of running in circles, wandering around surpris-ingly unfamiliar canopies and rock fields, to get my bearings. At first, I was hesitant. Hiding behind trees, throwing paranoid glances over my shoulder. But my mud-skinned body and dirt-matted hair gave me a comforting camouflage. Eventually, when I became convinced no one was following me, I concentrated on finding my way home.

It was easy enough, once I found a landmark I recognized. Each brush of that wood had its own feel, its own heartbeat. Each breath the forest took helped point me in the right direction. After another hour, I reached the edge of the trees, just a few hundred yards away from my cottage. Candles were burning, a soft glow in the windows.

They must be worried sick about me. A familiar pang of guilt emerged, sharp in my stomach.

Determined not to walk through my front door stark naked, which would surely embarrass my father and brothers as much as it would me, I crept silently towards the house. We had an old cellar a few dozen yards away from the cottage, used mainly for old storage and dry goods in the winter. A tunnel connected it to a crawl space beneath the main room, a function my father added for retrieving supplies during cold winter nights. I knew my father had left some military wear from when he trained to be a soldier in his youth. I had played in the clothes as a child, imagining myself a war hero. They were nothing more than simple camouflage trousers and a jacket, but they would do better than mud.

I tugged on the cellar door and descended into the space, shutting it behind me. I pulled on my father's pants and buttoned his coat, both of which hung awkwardly snug on my curved body. When I turned to leave, I heard a faint, alarming sound from the tunnel opening. I stilled to listen. The thick round stone that served as the door in the direction of the cottage muffled the noise, but I heard it again. The unmistakable sound of a woman's cry.

I moved faster than I could think, shoving the first stone to the side and sprinting through the tunnel. The cries mixed with screams and continued to amplify, turning my insides cold. By the time I reached the end of the tunnel, I shook almost uncontrollably, a sinking feeling about who those screams belonged to lodged in my gut. But I attempted to calm myself—in and out went my breathing. *Slow is smooth, smooth is fast,* my father always said. I ran my fingertips along the circumference of the second stone and loosened its seal. Working my fingers through the crack between the tunnel and the stone, I found purchase on the door. I nudged it, tipped it forward, and lowered it carefully onto the ground.

As silently as I could, I slid on my stomach into the dirt crawl space until I was underneath the main room of our cottage. The wailing remained relentless, and figures came into focus as I rolled onto my back to face upwards. I looked into my house through the small gaps between sweet-smelling piñon floorboards laid carefully by my father years ago. I was looking straight up at the outsider.

CHAPTER FOUR

TWISTED VINES

*I*t wasn't his eyes I saw this time. I stared at the bottom of his shoes. They were black leather boots, unremarkable in every way, save for some sort of crest imprinted on them. A goblet of twisted vines, a distinction I did not recognize, but more screams ripped my mind away. The cries belonged to my mother.

He held her by the shoulders, and judging by how her cries had turned to sobs and my interaction with him earlier, his grip was not gentle. "Where is she?" he yelled. "What have you done with her?"

"I don't know," she whimpered. "She didn't come back, I swear. I don't know where she went."

The man seethed. "If you can't tell me, Katalana," he growled, "you know I will have no choice but to kill you, too. Thus is the will of the Rexi." The synapses in my brain responded slowly to that comment, not understanding. My eyes darted around the room, but from my angle, I couldn't see anything other than what the slight crack between floorboards revealed directly above me.

"Why?" she said, some strength coming back to her words. "We did everything you asked of us, everything! I raised her as my own daughter, I loved her as my kin. We all did. She hasn't been discovered. How is death the reward?"

I froze. My world spun like I was a globe on an axis, carelessly slapped by a child. She spoke as if she knew the man, as if she owed deference to him. My mind reeled, and I almost didn't notice the dripping from a few panels to my left.

Blood, a steady drip of it. I pressed my hand into my mouth hard and bit, stifling a scream. Was it Papa? Javis? Danson? The tears were coming freely now, and it took every bit of strength I had not to cry out. I swallowed the bile building at the back of my throat. I resolved to act. I needed to get Mama out, fast.

It was like the blue-eyed man heard my thoughts. One crack and she fell to his feet. Her auburn hair slipped through the floorboard cracks and ticked my forehead.

One of her eyes, already glazing over, met mine. It widened slightly. And then blinked three times.

Mom. I mouthed the word.

Another crack, and she was gone.

Everything stopped. No. *No, this cannot be happening.* I squeezed my eyes shut. I lived in a small, peaceful mining town. Every bit of what I just saw was nothing more than a horrible nightmare. I would open my eyes and wake with a sense of dread, in my own bed, ready to live another day of my boring, safe life. But when I opened my eyes, I only saw Mama's lifeless face. Bile rose up my throat.

The tears came steadily then, rushing out and down my face and pooling on the ground around me. *Was it my desire for freedom that brought on this hell?* The foreigner Fayzien shouted commands I didn't register. He stomped around the cottage, ripped doors off cabinets and overturned furniture. He even murmured some strange sounding words that clattered in my head, throbbing in a way I'd never experienced. But he didn't move my mother's body and look down through the floorboards. It was as if her final act of dying was to save me, whether she planned it or not.

I don't know how long the blue-eyed man and his companions were there. It was clear he killed my entire family. I contemplated showing myself so he could kill me, too. But, I was terrified. Mostly that he would do something worse than only ending my life.

So I stayed frozen. I stayed frozen for so long, I felt I had always been still. Exhaustion came over me, exhaustion from the day, from running, from crawling, from holding in my tears, cries, and vomit. When I woke, quiet darkness commanded the house, and he'd gone. I tried to move, but I couldn't, as if my limbs were wrapped tightly against my body. A strange round shape cocooned me, fibrous to the touch. *Tree roots?* I felt around myself. They had sprouted up from the ground. I was readied for burial, dressed in dirt and laid in a birch tomb. But why? And how? Those questions dissolved the moment I remembered. My family was dead. And I had done nothing to stop it.

If anyone came to check on us, I didn't hear them. I was no longer thinking. I was wrapped in root, moss, and all the Earth's matter. I didn't attempt to move or understand how the Earth had come to wrap itself around me. I waited for what I believed—and maybe even hoped—would be my eventual death. I prayed I would wake up to see my family again, smiling at me with open arms.

———

REALITY STRUCK me awake with the sting of a slap.

My eyes flashed open to the sound of footsteps and hushed voices above my head. For a moment, I forgot where I was. When I looked up, Mama's body was gone, and I wondered if I had imagined the whole horrible ordeal. But through the gaps in my make-shift pine bough cocoon, the blood stains on piñon told a different story.

All at once, my protective shield felt like a cage. *Out, out, out.* The voices in my home were new, different to the ones that had wreaked havoc however many hours before. I didn't know if I could trust the new voices, but I wasn't thinking straight. Only instinct controlled me as I released something guttural, something between a cry and a grunt. I raised my arms from my sides, expecting a struggle, but the sharp branches parted away from my hands, as if in deference to me.

The people in my house shuffled around looking for the source of the noise. The walls of my birch tomb were tight, too tight, and I couldn't breathe. I slammed the heel of my palm above my head and into one of the floorboards. It broke easily and one more hit brought me to standing, half in the crawl space, half in the main room. The intruders' eyes were wide and jaws loose, staring at a girl caked in several layers of mud, blood, and filth. I must have been quite the sight.

As my pupils adjusted to the daylight, I nearly laughed at the absurdity of my impulsive move, but the flicker of humor died as quickly as it surfaced. Fayzien did not stand among them, nor did the black cloaked men who'd been at Spring Day. I was careful to be quiet, placing my palms on the floor and hoisting myself up, one foot at a time. I counted six of them, three men, three women. They were not Argenti, and I saw no familiar faces. I exhaled, an instinctual calm I didn't recognize washing over me.

A woman with silver hair and a lined face stepped forward. "Terra, I am Jana," she said, placing two hands on her chest, miming her words. "Can you understand me, Terra?"

My head nodded on instinct, but my eyes narrowed. She knew my name. Just as Fayzien had known my name on Spring Day.

"I am here to bring you somewhere safe," she said, hesitating a moment. "Do you recognize me?" she whispered.

I had no recollection of the woman's face, but her presence seemed friendly. Barring, of course, that she maintained the company of what appeared to be henchmen or warriors of some kind. But if she was using some sort of trust-building tactic on me by acting like she knew me, it was *not* going to work.

She took another two steps forward, more urgently this time. "We don't have much time. We must go now," she said, holding a hand out for me. I extended my hand as if to place my palm in hers. Instead, I snatched her wrist and yanked the woman towards me, shifting my body to the side as I pushed her into the three people standing behind us.

It was all the distraction I needed. In a flash, I darted through the space she had stood and I was out of the house that no longer served as my home. My diversion worked. No one followed me as I raced back into the forest, darting from rock to root to lessen my tracks. To Gia's. I had to get to Gia. I had to make sure she was safe.

But less than a minute after entering the trees, something firm crashed into me from behind, taking me down to the ground.

I braced for the fall, somehow directing myself toward a patch of soft grass. Lightly tanned, muscled arms framed my vision on each peripheral. The hard point of a knee pressed into the small of my back, pinning me down. I let out a wheeze of pain from the hard impact, and the pressure on my back softened. It was the space I needed. I shifted my weight just slightly, giving myself enough leverage to flip onto my back and knock the knee away.

The terror that had a firm grip on my mind loosened. Like the blue-eyed man, my attacker was unnaturally large, with features that seemed to be cut from glass. But he wasn't as unsettling as Fayzien; his face was warm and had a soft golden hue. And his ears... they came to sharp points, unlike any ears I'd ever seen. But all of those details were nothing compared to his eyes. Set behind thick curling lashes, they were an unnatural green, like smoldering emeralds.

His brows furrowed, and I snapped back to the present moment. He heaved, like he was winded. I immediately tensed and tried to shove myself backwards.

His body stiffened in response to mine, and he grabbed my wrist, pulling me up. He stood a head taller and clearly outweighed me. His broad chest hadn't stopped heaving, and I knew it was my best chance to run. I pulled myself close to him before he could react and sent my knee straight into his manhood.

Surprise flickered on his face as he keeled over, huffing in pain, but didn't release me, the pressure of his fingers still hard on my wrist. "You know, this would be far easier if you didn't play little warrior," he grunted out.

The deep tenor of his voice sent a shock through me, but I didn't let the feeling breed hesitation. I twisted my arm in his and maneuvered to hold on to his wrist. I yanked hard, putting one hand on his shoulder and using my other to bend his arm behind him. Then I jammed the heel of my foot into the back of his knee. That made him falter, dropping to the ground, and he released me. I blinked in shock at the efficacy of the move. But before I could turn to run, he swung a leg around, sweeping me off my feet. I fell face first into the dirt and a wash of heat ran through me, my cheeks reddening.

I rolled over my shoulder and found him standing once again, staring at me.

"Pretty clever move, especially for a country human. I wonder, where did you learn to fight someone three times your size?" he asked, his tone challenging.

A country human—*what odd specificity*. And his question rang through me, like I had the answer sealed in a box my mind couldn't access. I shook my head slightly, refocusing on my adversary. I stood and raised curled fists to each side of my ears.

An amused smile spread over the man's face. "*Bellatori* wants to dance, eh? Well, I never refuse when a lady asks for a dance." With that, he lunged. He jabbed, I swerved. He hooked, I ducked. I blocked only when absolutely necessary, conserving my strength. I was in a cold focus, landing a few blows to his unguarded ribs. How *did* I know how to fight? It felt effortless, like my muscles remembered something I did not.

The man watched me with a wild intensity as we "danced." He seemed hesitant to strike me and unaffected by the punches I made to his gut. Eventually he landed a hit on my jaw, which left me staggering back, spitting blood. He made a move to seize me again, and I let him think my moment of vulnerability was his triumph, wobbling back towards a lone aspen as he grabbed me. I flipped my grip on his wrists once more and twisted them behind his back. He was far too strong for me to hold, but I used his weight as momentum. I let him fall into me, let his struggle collide with my strength as I pivoted and forced him forward, slamming him into a nearby tree.

He collided with it headfirst. I let him slump to the ground and took off running once more.

I ran full speed to Gia's. Dusk set, and Gia's was the only place I had to go. My association with Gia must have posed great danger to her now, with so many looking for me. I approached her house on light feet, triple checking for anyone on my tail. Crossing my fingers that she would be home, I tapped a pebble three times on her window, our private signal to meet at our favorite maple, just a few paces into the wood and out of sight.

IT TOOK TEN LONG, dread-filled minutes before I finally heard Gia's distinct footsteps. The sound of her approaching sent a wave of relief over me and I exhaled, not realizing I'd been holding my breath.

"Terra? Is that you?"

I stepped out from behind the large trunk, letting the moonlight cast shadows on my face. "Oh, the gods, look at you, where have you been!" Gia cried as she embraced me. "Mav told me what happened at Spring Day. I can't understand it. The whole town looked for you everywhere, including that stranger—Fayzien."

I grimaced at her words. The mere mention of Fayzien's name gave me chills.

"Eventually, they all assumed he found you and you left with him. But I knew you wouldn't have gone willingly without saying goodbye... and I went to your house, and everyone was gone, and blood stained everything and, oh, Terra, I was so worried," she babbled.

But she stopped when she noticed the tears streaking my mud-soaked face. I couldn't hold it in anymore. Now that I felt an ounce of safety, I let them come, in loud heaves. She held me as I sobbed and

41

sobbed, eventually pulling me into her small lap on the ground. And she sobbed too, her wailing rivaling mine. For she realized what I had lost. And she realized what she had lost too, for her betrothed had been my brother Danson.

LONG AFTER OUR TEARS DRIED, the sun had set, and we clung to each other like we were all we had left. I guess that was true. Gia was all I had, at least. Eventually, I pushed myself up to sit.

I rested my head on my knees. "I'm so sorry Gia," I mumbled. "They killed him because of me. I don't know why, but they were looking for me and, and I just..." I trailed off.

Gia sat up and faced me. "Terra, it is not your fault," she said softly, squeezing my hand. "Do you know what they did with his body?" she asked, a moment later, tears re-forming in her eyes.

I shook my head. "They were all gone when I came out. I was... I hid in the cellar when he killed Mama, and I couldn't—" I choked, unable to finish my sentence.

"You don't have to say anything now. Let's get you cleaned up. You'll sleep with me tonight," she said, clearing her throat, ready to push forward as she always did. I felt my broken heart swell with appreciation for my resilient friend.

"Gia, I can't. There are more of them, different ones. I lost them in the forest, but... I think they'll keep coming. If I go to your house, I put your whole family in danger. I put you in danger. After everything, I can't. I can't," I whispered.

"What do you mean, more?" She furrowed her brow. "Who are they? What did they look like? How did you lose them?"

"I have no idea. One acted like she knew me, but I've never seen any of them before... I fought one of them off and then ran straight here."

"*Fought* one of them off?" I nodded and Gia's brows pinched together. "How on earth would you know how to do that?"

"I don't know. It all happened so fast." I shook my head.

"If you don't stay here, where will you go, Terra? Are you planning to live in the forest for the rest of your life?" she asked, a sharpness creeping into her tone. "Do you really want to leave the only people you have left? And what about Mav?"

"There are questions I need answered," I mumbled, a thrumming pain starting up in my head from hours of crying. "The man said a queen was looking for me and he mentioned something called... the Rexi. Maybe, maybe I could take one of your father's maps, and then just a bit of food, and I could head to the Great Library in Lahar. I've heard it has books about all sorts of things. Maybe I could find—" I whipped my head to the forest. "Did you hear that?"

Gia's eyes focused on the blackness, and she sniffed the air but said nothing.

"It sounded like someone stepping on a twig," I added, my gaze following the direction in which Gia looked. And then a slice of pain seared my mind, turning everything black.

CHAPTER FIVE

NEW CHAINS

I found my wrists and ankles chained outward to stakes in the forest ground when I awoke, twilight unfurling around me.

The events of the last few days roared back, dread punching me in the gut with such intensity I had to choke a cry down.

Dead. My family. Gone. Not a nightmare.

And Gia?

Against all instinct, I stilled my breathing, coaxing it into the rhythmic sound of someone asleep. I recognized the group from the cottage earlier bustling around, but I didn't think anyone noticed I woke.

If Gia was still alive, I would find her. I would not lose her. Could not.

"I told you we should have just leveled her right away," a male voice said, somewhat hushed, somewhat familiar. "Her magic might be dormant, and her memories gone, but she is still the Earth Daughter."

A soft snort came from one of the younger females. "Me thinks someone es jest a wee bet embarrassed that he almost lost a testicle

44

teh an untrained nineteen-year-old human," she said, extending the word human as if to add insult to injury. Her accent was thick, sharp.

"You and I both know she is many things, but human, and untrained for that matter, are not any of them," the male replied with more bite than before. That word again, *human*. I knew his voice now —it belonged to the man I fought in the woods.

"Ezren, Leiya, silence. Both of you," a third voice said. "I was clear: no magic upon initial contact. The poor girl just had her family slaughtered by that maniac. She deserved us to come to her in peace and at least *try* the easy way."

"So what now, then?" another voice asked.

"We will attempt the cleansing. Regardless if it is successful or not, it will be her decision whether to stay or go."

I opened my eyes, panic at this 'cleansing' overriding my plan to eavesdrop. The male called Ezren turned to me first. There they were, emeralds on fire. Again, my mind went blank under his searing stare. It felt as if those eyes could burn me from the inside out. He blinked, pulling me back to the present moment and the state of my body. My hair was a matted tangle of mud, my body still slathered in filth. I turned my face away, heat rushing to my cheeks. "What did you do with Gia?" I demanded, refocusing on the important facts that I was kidnapped, in chains, and my best friend was nowhere to be seen.

"She is safe," the older woman, Jana, replied. "No harm came to her—nor to any of the other humans in your village. We simply calmed her mind and told her to go home and back to bed."

I weighed her words. She seemed genuine, but then again, she was also a kidnapper.

"Why have you taken me?" I rasped, panic bubbling as I pulled on the chains with little effort. I was well and truly trapped with these strangers. "What have I done to be your prisoner?"

"Terra, we are here to help you, truly. I swear on the lives of those I love. If you cooperate, we will unchain you and explain everything."

I detected no deception, but these were the words of a captor.

And I didn't have many loved one's lives to swear on anymore. "Who the hell are you people? And what is a cleansing?"

"You have some memories trapped in your mind that we need to free, and I can do that through the cleansing. It will make sense after. I promise," the silver-haired woman replied.

I remembered an account of Lahar healers using hypnosis to help trauma survivors recall repressed events. Many cases did not end well, with more than one instance reported of the patient clawing their own eyes out.

Didn't seem ideal.

"Afterwards, you will let me go?"

The leader exhaled. "If that is your wish."

"Will it hurt?" My words were whispers that seemed to echo through the forest clearing.

I didn't need to see Ezren's searing stare to feel his eyes on me.

"Yes," the leader Jana replied. "I will do my best to be gentle and to block your nerve endings from pain. But memory recovery and magic emancipation are no simple tasks, especially when the memories and magic have been buried for as long as yours have."

Magic. Magic was a fantastical concept, a tool for conceptual metaphor in storytelling. It was also the creed by which some religious fanatics claimed to live. We had a group on the outskirts of Argention, necromancers, or Deathspitters we called them. From what I'd heard, they fed off small mushrooms that grew into late winter and made minds turn mad. No one took them seriously.

Maybe these were a different breed of religious enthusiasts. The cleansing sounded an awful lot like a cultish purification ceremony. Something to scare children. I pulled on my chains once more in a futile attempt to improve my position. "Please, just let me go," I whispered, wincing at the pitiful sound of my words. "I am no one. I've done nothing."

Jana exhaled. "Terra, only half of that statement is true. I cannot explain the rest unless you let me help you. Please, let me help you." Her words floated over me, casting a warm stream of sunlight. I felt my resistance lighten as if a weight lifted from my chest, agreeableness its replacement. Agreeableness, along with the knowledge I wasn't going anywhere before they finished performing whatever the cleansing was.

I pressed my eyelids together, defeated, a numbness sinking into my skin. Whatever it was couldn't be worse than waking up and remembering the life leave my mother's eyes.

I could live a hundred lifetimes and never forget that image.

"Just get it over with."

They removed my chains, which, according to the older female, were silver and thus... magic dampeners. Whatever that meant. I considered attempting another run for it, but my body clung to the ground, leaden and heavy, sucked dry of any energy.

"Terra, we'll have to hold you down with our own hands. I cannot use the chains, and I have no rope with me. Do you understand?" Jana asked.

I understood that I smelled like piss, blood, and dirt, and was about to have strangers' hands all over me. *Not the first time I've been violated this week.* I remembered the blue-eyed man leering at my naked body. Doing something I could not comprehend, but knew was inappropriately intimate.

Some small, broken part of me hoped it would hurt.

That it would wipe away the stain of the past few days from my skin, my soul. That it would be more painful than the pain I'd just awoken to, if only to give me some small reprieve from the crushing loss settled on my chest, threatening to swallow me whole. I begged for a distraction.

"Fine." Small tears escaped down my face, pooling in the creases of my mouth.

Two women, one young and one middle-aged, took each of my wrists, pinning them down with all their weight. Two men did the same with my ankles. Jana folded her legs on each side of my head, framing it, her knees light touches on my shoulders, a palm cupping my cheek.

"Your power, your magic, rests in here dear," she said, placing the other hand on her own gut. "Right now, yours is hibernating, shall we say. Someone made it very comfortable there, like a bear in perpetual mid-winter. It will not want to come out and will *certainly* not want your mind to be cleansed. Though the pain will likely be in your head, most of your *fight* will come from there," she said, gesturing to my torso. "Ezren will hold your abdomen down, is that alright?"

"If I said no, would you let me go?" I let out a humorless chuckle, knowing the answer before I spoke.

Jana sighed. "What I meant was, well I just meant, I could have one of the females switch positions with him, if it bothers you to have a male—"

"Just please get it over with," I whispered, my eyes still shut, tears creeping out of them. A pair of knees settle somewhere between my parted legs with what sounded like a pained breath. I hoped it was Ezren struggling to breathe due to a cracked rib of my doing. The thought made a ghost of a smile caress my mind.

Warm hands pressed on my lower belly, sending a new terrifying jolt through me. I blinked my eyes open again, and it took a moment for the welled-up moisture to clear. His flaming green stare loomed just a foot away from mine. He looked scared too, which, though strange, comforted me... as if I was not alone in my fear.

Jana began. She first rubbed my temples. After a minute of massaging, she pulled her hands out and away from my head, tenting her fingers like something still invisibly connected them to the temples they had touched. Then her energy became chaotic. One moment she swirled her fingers in the dirt beside me, another moment she chanted with her arms open. Another I felt her hands on my scalp. I almost laughed aloud at the insanity of it all, but the pain soon came.

When I was fourteen and fell off the thick curling branch of an ancient oak thirty feet above the ground, I thought I had known pain. I shattered nearly my entire ribcage. The healer was shocked I'd lived. I thought I knew pain when my brother Javis dropped a boulder on my hand, or when father didn't come home for three days following a mining accident, or when I saw Mama's body slump to the floor of our cottage.

But I had not known pain like this.

Pain that made my body turn white hot. No build-up, no crying, or whimpering, just searing hot pain that made my body want to contort, sweat, scream. It felt like she was taking a man's dulled shaving razor and using it to scrape out every corner of my head. Every nerve ending I possessed mirrored the pain, culminating in my gut, as if to highlight how my mind was ultimately connected to it all.

I screamed and screamed until my voice went raw, my body thrashing against hands that kept me pinned to the dirt. If tears or prayers or pleas left me, I don't remember them. Eventually, my whole body went limp, and darkness claimed me once more. I drifted away, praying I wouldn't wake up this time.

I woke on a warm feathered cot with a pounding in my head. I squinted through my eyelids, light peeking through a small window to my left. I felt I'd dreamt a thousand dreams but could remember none.

Unease pressed itself upon my lungs as if I'd forgotten something important.

The memories followed.

Matron. Stranger. Mav. Running. Hiding. Mama. Gone.

I squeezed my eyes shut, water dripping from their corners. How many more sleeps would I have to endure, waking up to a world where my family no longer existed?

I lay there, sinking into an internal pit of darkness, content to do so indefinitely. But the urge to relieve myself eventually won. I pulled off the covers and found myself in a woman's dressing gown, free of the dirt and grime that had previously decorated every inch of my flesh. My hand flew to my throat—the familiar feeling of a small pendant resting on my clavicle sent a wave of comfort through me. I touched my hair. It was clean, too—someone had made an effort to de-mangle it. Someone who bathed me... while I was unconscious.

I sat up too fast, dark spots peppering my gaze. I steadied myself on the bed frame and swung my feet to the ground. It felt good to be clean after what I'd been through. But even that pleasant thought sent a staggering ache through my body, for how could I afford even the smallest happiness when my family was dead?

I made use of a chamber pot positioned in the corner. Someone had left a tray on a small table next to the bed, a cup of water, and a large, buttered piece of bread. Though I had resolved never to eat again, my body betrayed my will. My mouth watered when I sank my teeth into it.

My caretakers had also been kind enough to leave me a change of clothes: simple trousers, boots, and a loose-fitting linen shirt. The small gesture was comforting, but another wave of grief washed over me when I realized it meant my father's military wear was likely gone. What would I have left of him? Of my family?

I sat again on the bed, working up the courage to open the door, wondering what awaited me outside. Wondering whether or not Jana spoke true when she said all would be explained. So far, her promise to treat me well seemed kept.

I loosed a breath, padding over to the door. I peeked into the hall. Just Leiya sat there, cross-legged on a stool, sharpening her knife—surprisingly nimble for such a tall woman. She had cropped fire-red hair and a warm face peppered with freckles and faint smile lines. She possessed the same pointed ears I'd noticed on Ezren. She looked formidable, and I had the distinct impression she'd seen the days of battle.

"Finally, the princess hath awoken," she said mockingly, without looking up from the blade. "Have a nice sleep, did ye?"

"How long was I out for?" I asked, rubbing my eyes.

"Oh, only about three days," she replied.

I shifted on my feet. "So, did *you* bathe me?" My eyes narrowed.

That made her look up, "Nay, Ezren ensisted he do et. He es the best wi' hair, anyway." My expression must have been a mix of intense terror and confusion, because Leiya burst out laughing. The terror faded from my face, but such horror remained that she said, "Oh come on now, jest a wee joke." She rolled her eyes. "If yer done pissin yer pants over a wash, do ye thenk yer up fer a walk?"

LEIYA LED me out of what turned out to be a small inn with a few bedrooms and a cozy tavern on the first floor. Jana had let me rest in the homey dwelling to recover from the cleansing, but requested I be brought to her camp several miles away right after waking—or so Leiya said. The moment we stepped outside, it was like walking head-first into a stone wall. Instinct stopped me in my tracks. The wall that I had 'run' into was made of an overwhelming surge of light, sound, smells. I bounced back, nearly falling on my hind.

She caught me by the arm and said, "Slow down lass, yer senses are gonna have a right time catchen up. Ye walk steady now an' breathe deep. Big enhale an' exhale. That's et. Take et slow an' leave yer hand on me arm."

The inn stood lonesome on a tree-lined coach path, and other than that, there was very little to help me identify our location. And even if more clues presented themselves, I'm sure I wouldn't have seen them. I was too busy taking in a new spectrum of color—a field of light that shone more vibrant, more varied than I'd seen before. Sounds blended together like notes in a song, making them less discernible. Odors, putrid and delightfully fragrant, mixed together, making my nose wrinkle.

The tree to my left bowed, and nausea bubbled in my stomach. "Leiya, I'm hallucinating," I choked out, my eyes darting around.

"Et's called settlen," Leiya explained. "Yer gonna feel right off for a few days, as es with any cleansen, but the settlen es quick enough. Ye got more magic than most, so et could take a bet longer. An' I've heard ets a bet harder for Wetches than Fae. But settle ye will all the same."

Magic. That word again. And Witches? Did I hear her right through her thick brogue? Her explanation made little sense to me, but my body was still too absorbed with grappling its staggering transformation for me to voice my confusion. I took enough away from her comments that I knew the sensory overload was not permanent.

"See ef ye can feel the life around us, the forest," she probed. "Maybe et well help."

Her words held no meaning, but a deeper voice urged me to listen. I slowed my breath, and gave myself over to my senses, my legs continuing to move where Leiya led me. And then there it was—a buzzing jolt that flowed through me.

"What do ye feel?" Leiya asked.

"I-I'm not sure how to describe it. It feels... like the fabric of life."

I had always been in tune with the forest. My whole life it sang a song to me that I felt like lifeblood. But now, it was different. I knew, somehow, I could sing back. And it would listen. It would bend and obey. And it wouldn't *really* be bending or obeying, because it was a part of me. The lungs don't obey because the mind consciously commands it. They move with the body's intention. And that's how it felt. Like the heartbeat of the forest was my own.

It took us almost an hour to reach the camp, and the walk was tedious. I felt like I'd been put into someone else's body, which made doing anything, even walking, foreign and clumsy.

Eventually, we came upon a large camp of tents with people buzzing about. It looked how I imagined a war camp would, but far less dire and without the stink of death in the air. Many sat outside their canvas shelters on beautiful woven rugs, drinking from shining goblets, smoking from long pipes, and playing cards. "Who are these people?" I muttered, the words forming under my breath.

Leiya must have heard me, for she eyed me and said, "Wetches like their fancies, eh? I remember me ferst time at a Wetch camp. Looked like a bunch a' rich folks on holiday. Thought them Wetches were soft, needin' all these comforts and such. But no, them Wetches are tough as any Fae warrior. They jest like to travel en *style*."

"Witches," I repeated, dazed. Maybe I really was going crazy.

"Now look," she grabbed hold of my arm and stopping me in the middle of the camp. "Yer gonna be right confused when everythen es explained to ye. Ye won't know what te believe and ye won't know who te trust. But ye hear me when I speak the truth right now. We are the only ones who can help ye get what ye want. Trust *that*."

I raised my gaze, staring up into Leiya's hazel eyes, feeling a limpness in my own. "And what is it you think I want? My family is dead. I have nothing to want for."

"Yes, yes ye do. Whether ye want et now, or later, ye want revenge. And ye won't be able te think straight again until ye get et. And even then ets a coin toss. But ets yer best shot at moven on, and we're yer best shot at getten et," Leiya said.

The word revenge sounded dirty to my ears. But it stirred something inside me—something primal. The word burned in my chest where it had been cold and dark before.

It felt good to burn.

CHAPTER SIX

OLD MEMORIES

*L*eiya led me to a small canvas tent in the middle of camp. She pulled back the flap, revealing several long dining tables, serving stations, and even elaborate candle fixtures. I gaped at the warrior—the tent should have fit one or two cots inside at the most. She only gave me a nod and motioned me through the threshold.

Magic.

Jana sat at the middle of the table rather than at the head, and everyone seemed to angle themselves towards her. The other woman I had seen before, the one from the cleansing, sat to her left. She appeared younger than Leiya. And smaller, though that wasn't difficult to accomplish. The two men that held my feet during the cleansing were there too, one averaged height and lean, the other that looked like three of Leiya put together. I wondered if they were related.

Jana rose upon my entrance. "Welcome, Terra of Argention. Please, have a seat," she gestured to the spot directly across from her at the table. I did, feeling as numb as I had before Leiya's 'revenge' speech kicked up something inside of me.

Guess that was temporary.

"Friends, Terra has been through a great deal. May I request the room while I read her in?" Everyone hurried out except Leiya, who remained standing behind me. Eventually, Jana tilted her head back and Leiya too retreated.

"Well, you look much better." Jana offered a soft smile. "Without all the filth on you. I imagine it feels good to be clothed and clean for the first time in such a while. Are you hungry? I can get you anything to eat. I am happy to call for a—"

"Am I your prisoner?" A genuine question. Not that I cared terribly.

Jana sighed. "No, Terra, you are not my prisoner. I just have some things I need to discuss with you. And you can ask me all the questions you like. If you still want to leave afterwards, well, that is your choice."

The cold, empty place in my chest took shape into something harder. "Who are you, why do you know my name, and why did that... man want to take me away?" I pinned her with my stare. "And why," I said softly, choking on the last part, "why did he kill my family?"

Surprise flickered across her face. "Do you still not remember anything, child?"

"Remember *what?*"

Jana rubbed her temples. "The cleansing is a fickle process. It may take several days for your memories to come back. You likely need to still your mind and quiet your new senses in order for that to happen. For now, I will fill in the blanks. But I must warn you—this story will not be easy to hear."

I clamped my teeth together to keep them from chattering.

"Your family, the ones you called mother and father and brother, were not your kin. Of course, you grew up with them, so you should always call them yours, but your father did not seed you and your mother did not bear you. The blood of your brothers does not run in your veins."

"Stop," I whispered. *Maybe I shouldn't listen. After all, she could be making this up—*

"You were born in Nebbiolo, a Witch queendom isle far east of here, to a Witch mother and a Fae father. Your father raised you from a young age in a Fae kingdom called Viribrum, after your mother died in Nebbiolo. He was a famed warrior amongst the Fae, and you showed unbelievable promise as a young Faerie in training; many thought you would one day follow in his footsteps and join the ranks in protecting the kingdom."

I wanted to cover my ears and shake my head in disbelief, but it felt like she put color and sound to the muted dreams of a long sleep. *I had lost not only one mother, but two?*

"How is any of this possible? Witches? Fae? Am I truly supposed to believe these fabled creatures exist—that *magic* exists?" But even as I questioned her, the words tasted stale in my mouth. The tent alone told me enough.

Jana extended her hand. An ornate dagger appeared, resting in her palm, out of thin air, and then vanished once more. "You should know that Witch and Fae exist, because you sit amongst them. You, yourself, are one of them. One of us."

My eyes widened, catching on her hand where the dagger laid a moment before.

"Around your twelfth year, a budding power revealed itself. Fae blood mixed with Witch blood doesn't necessarily result in a potent combination, often they dilute each other. But in your case, the opposite occurred. Fae magic from your father strengthened the Witch magic from your mother. The combination gave you what we call Earth magic. It is very rare, you see, for someone to be able to call upon the Earth. Air, Fire, yes, they are common enough. Water? A bit rarer, and requires great strength, for the element is dense, but it is not unheard of. But Earth? It comes once a millennium. The Earth is the closest thing to calling upon the Mother—the creator—herself."

"And you think I can... call upon the Earth," I said flatly. "To what? Make it do my bidding?"

Jana lips set in a firm line. "I know you can."

I let out a sound between a huff and a laugh, but Jana did not relent. "When your power revealed itself, many in the Viribrum took notice. Your gift was too rare, too difficult to hone in Fae land. Your father, Viturius, knew you would need Witch training to control such a power. You set out to leave Viribrum and return to your mother's country, Nebbiolo, for schooling. On the way, you and your father were ambushed. And I'm sorry to tell you this, but he was killed." She paused, her voice beginning to tremble. "And you were taken— though we didn't know it at the time. Months after it happened, one of the ambushers was caught and confessed to taking part in both your deaths. So for the last seven years, despite your body having never been recovered, everyone in both the Fae Kingdom of Viribrum and Witch Queendom of Nebbiolo has presumed you dead," Jana finished.

I shook at the thought of losing another parent, however foreign, the recent memory crawling up my throat, threatening to shatter my questions into irrelevant pieces.

But I needed to know more. I needed to know *something* that could explain why all this was happening. "Why now? Why did you come for me *now*?"

"A group of us always held suspicions over your death. We've been tracking a known associate of the ambusher who was caught. The search went on for years. Once we located him in remote caves of the Safroy Mountains, it didn't take long to recover the truth about how you never died, and where you were hidden. This was only a few months ago. We came as fast as we could."

"Why don't I remember? I had a real childhood in Argention. I had a family. As real as you sitting across from me right now... Or at least they were." Heat pricked my eyes, and it took all my effort to shove the wave of loss down—to not let it consume me, rob me of the truth.

"The male who coordinated your abduction is a very powerful Witch. He cleared your mind of previous memories and replaced them with false ones of an early childhood. He found a town full of silver that would dampen your power and trap the magic in you, hindering it from presenting and preventing your Fae body from maturing. This is why I had to perform the cleansing on you—to release such power. And he paid a human family to look after you. You know this man, Terra," she said, using my name as if it were tender to her.

Him.

The man who stripped me naked. The man who murdered my family. A family he supposedly gifted me.

All of a sudden, the burning feeling Leiya offered me returned. It rolled through me, swallowing that wave of grief. Shame, loss, fury— all churned together into something ugly, scarred, emboldened.

For the first time in my life, I had a thought so frightening, so vile, it pierced through my sea of fear and anger.

I will kill this man.

The sentiment should have terrified me. I'd never come to blows with another being physically.

It didn't.

In fact, it soothed me. It eased the grip wound so tight around my lungs—ever so slightly—letting me take in more air than before.

I wouldn't have gone so far as to say I could breathe normally again, but hey, it was a start.

I met Jana's amber gaze, which simmered regally. She had soft gray hair, braided in a crown that piled on top of her head. She wore an acorn pendant around her neck—which seemed to pulse and move with its own energy. I would have thought twice about it, had the new fantasy taking root in my head not distracted me.

"Fayzien of Wahaca," I ground out.

"Fayzien of Nebbiolo," she corrected. "We still have not confirmed why he took you, though I speculate he thought you, an Earth Witch, would threaten his position in the Witch queendom. Why he didn't just kill you right away is still a mystery to us all."

I blinked, trying to slow my thoughts, attempting to sift through them for the memories that had supposedly been unlocked. But I only heard the buzzing of camp, louder than it should have been, and a steady thrum in my blood—demanding that of Fayzien.

The chaos in my mind stilled a moment. "If he went through all the trouble of planting me in a human family... why did he come back? Surely, the goal was to keep me hidden." My nostrils flared. It was a flaw in the story, a crack that sent adrenaline straight to my gut.

Is she lying?

Unless... my heart sank. "Did someone in your ranks tell him you had found me?"

At this, Jana looked down, not able to meet my eyes. "To that question, I don't have an answer. Fayzien arrived in Argention three, maybe four, days before we did. He was far gone by the time we reached your cottage, so we could not confirm if his return to Argention was related to our quest to find you... but... the timing is conspicuous. I have interrogated all who knew about our mission, and I have sensed no deception."

"So, if you had never come for me," I said, my voice shaking, "he wouldn't have, either? I would still be home, my family alive." I reached for that well of fury I was nurturing but met only darkness. *If they had only left me alone...*

Jana remained silent, as if weighing how to respond.

Her carefulness only angered me more, for she'd been utterly careless when the cost was so high. I stood, knocking my chair back. "How can I trust a word you say? You are the reason my family is dead." I meant to yell, but choking on tears, my voice came out barely above a whisper.

A flash of genuine pain crossed Jana's face. "Terra, truly, I am so sorry about your human family. I told you all this would not be easy to hear. But you have to know, I—"

I didn't hear another word from her, as I spun on my heels, feeling a sudden claustrophobia in the room, hating the way she said *human*. They weren't just humans, they are—were, my family. I needed air, needed to breathe—

I took off towards the canvas door. But out of nowhere, two males appeared in front of me. "Jana, we found—" The loud smack from my head-on collision with his companion cut him off.

I had been moving too quickly to stop, blinded by too many tears. My nose hit square on the man's chest, which was shrouded in a proud breastplate of some unforgivable metal. A broad hand wrapped around my waist, spread out on my lower back, steadying me as I rocked on my feet. I looked up to surprised eyes of blazing green, peering down at me through thick curling lashes. I blinked, and he must have sensed my dizziness because he held on to me for a moment longer than he needed to. His body tensed as he sucked in a breath of surprise.

"*Bellatori,*" he said, his eyes falling on my upper lip. All of a sudden, I felt our bodies pressed together. I raised a hand to my face, and the sticky sensation of blood coated my fingertips.

No one said a word as I shoved Ezren to the side and continued my bolt towards the door.

THE FOREST WAS ALL I knew, and Jana's talk about the Earth calling to me was the only thing that made any real sense. I ran through camp back the way Leiya had led me, eventually meeting the carriage road. But I didn't go to the inn. Without thinking, my body turned towards the trees, the buzzing from before threading around me in a beckoning song.

It told me to come.

I moved as if in a trance, my limbs slow and heavy. Every step into the wood breathed air back into my lungs, bit by bit, until they were full enough I could exhale. A thick scent of *life* coated my nostrils, sending a fizzing sensation to my head. Once, at sixteen, I'd snuck a bottle of sparkling wine and guzzled it down by the creek with Gia. The sensation of being drunk had made the colors of the setting sun deeper, the smells of wet meadow heavier.

I felt drunk again—this time, on the forest itself.

It was a comfort that sent me deeper into myself, yet further away from my body. A salve to the pulsing grief that felt like arrow-shards in my belly, in my chest.

Continuing to meander, I let my fingers brush over moss and bark and stone. The touch tingled in a way that hadn't before. I had always sensed an energy in the outdoors, but this seemed different, almost like a current of lightning. I felt as if I could reach out and grab it, risking a shock.

After the gods knew how long, I found myself sinking onto a slab of granite bordering a riverbed. Not bothering to wash the now dried blood from my face, I let my feet fall into the snow melt. I sat there, hollow, unfeeling to the freezing water soaking my boots. The song of the forest died down. The buzz wore off. And I wept. I wept for my family, for loss, for death. I wept for the lies and for the truths. I wept for myself. For the simple place in the world that I never wanted, but was robbed of nonetheless.

At some point, my blank gaze settled on the running water, watching the curls and ripples dance over obstructions in the stream. I looked, numb, not really seeing. I thought about the memories Jana had probed. I could see them, some of them at least, but from a distance. The first images I guessed were my sire, Viturius. He looked stern, the picture of a warrior, drained of warmth. His expression lacked the kind and loving smiles I earned generously from my father. Images of drilling with him came back. They appeared in the water, glimpses of hand-to-hand combat, repeated under his instruction until the young girl of twelve could gain some sort of advantage over him.

More swirls of color and motion flashed. A boy with golden-rimmed purple eyes and a devious smile. A gravel pit, a sword in my hands, a girl with white-blonde hair as my opponent. The memories came as quickly as they went, and eventually, I let my eyes close, opening my mind to them, no longer needing to see them projected in a reflection.

The faster they passed, the more my head ached. The memories seemed to race to get to something, to show me some final part, the apogee of the story. I saw Viturius's muscular arms hoisting me into the back of the horse-drawn cart, covering my body with a heavy cloak, bidding me to sleep. I saw a castle fading into the distance. I saw the sun setting in the west, as I looked out from the cart headed south. I felt my eyes—the tired eyes of a child—droop, the image fading to black. The last thing I saw was waking to a halted cart, looking up at two blue sapphires set in the same gaunt face I'd encountered in Argention days before.

I knew with chilling certainty that Fayzien was my abductor. At least Jana wasn't lying about that.

CHAPTER SEVEN

REBEL PRIDE

I stayed by that creek a great while, far past dark, until the moon rose high enough to cast silver echoes on the water. The truth in Jana's story was undeniable after my memories came back. Much of my life remained missing, but I remembered enough. I remembered the Fae—the point of their ears. I remembered the magic of the Witch. I remembered living in a grand house adorned with servants, blazing fireplaces, and countless rooms. I remembered my father, a stern disciplinarian who laughed seldom but, when he did, lit up a room. The glossy memories Fayzien had provided me of an early childhood dissolved, replaced with flashes of the Fae world.

I rose after my long meditation and followed the distant sounds of a bustling camp. My pace was unhurried, and I used the time to collect my thoughts. I had more questions for Jana. Though I knew the truth in her words, and I appreciated no one tailing me after I left, I couldn't shake the uneasiness that coiled in my gut—as if she withheld something from me. Remembering my father's words, a lump formed in my throat.

Listen to the little voice.

The words rang out in my head, as if he'd spoken them aloud. I pressed my lids together, warm liquid leaking past the barrier.

I'll try, papa.

By the time I reached the camp, the noises I'd followed were just above whispers. Fires had burnt down to embers, light snoring sang through several of the tents. I entered the meeting room, a familiar tension of tiredness weighing on my eyes. My gaze snagged on a note left on the long table, with "for Terra" inscribed on the front. It read:

> If ye are reading this note, ye've decided to return to camp and will need a rest spot. Ye can bunk en me room while I'm out on watch tonight. Ets number nine, four down from the right of the big tent.
>
> -Leiya

I breathed relief, fatigue overcoming my instinct to confront Jana. I found Leiya's tent, empty as promised—the size of the interior matching the exterior this time. I didn't bother taking off my boots—I just fell face-first onto the firm cot and pulled a thick woolen blanket over my head.

I WOKE to broad daylight shining through the cracks in the tent. At first disoriented, I squinted and saw Leiya had left me another chunk of bread with two heaping slabs of butter and a steaming cup of something. I relaxed into the hardness of the cot, unflinching to the torture of remembering. I supposed I'd become numb to it—my new normal. This normal where I woke, and my mother, father, and brothers didn't. The scent of the blanket calmed me. It was piñon and the forest after a summer rain. It smelled familiar, of home.

I ate the generously laid breakfast, tidied my bloodied face with the washbowl next to the cot, and set out to find Jana.

She perched where I'd seen her last, at the middle of the long table in the main tent. Ezren sat next to her, wisps of dark auburn-hinted hair falling in swirls on his forehead, over strong eyebrows, his face turned down to a map. His elbows rested on the table, forcing the curving, hard lines in his well-muscled arms to bulge. The male that had appeared with Ezren out of thin air the day before sat on Jana's other side. He looked small-bodied with deep brown skin, cropped hair, and ink markings climbing up his neck. Leiya stood behind them, predictably sharpening one of her long knives, of the curved variety this time.

"So you came back," Jana said, without looking up from the map. "At least thank Ezren for unknowingly lending you his bed last night. Though I know not *why* you chose his tent over the one I provided you. Did you find your accommodations inadequate?" she asked, lifting her gaze to me with raised brows.

My mouth fell ajar, and my eyes shot to Leiya, not missing the reddening on Ezren's pointed ears. His face remained turned down, steadfast on the map. Leiya, of course, shook almost uncontrollably in silent laughter, fueled by my aghast reaction. She must have replaced whatever instructions Jana had left me with her own.

"I, uh, well, I didn't know that was his tent," I ground out, feeling a distinct heat crawl up my neck and into my cheeks. "It was empty when I went in, and I was exhausted..." I trailed off, my eyes trained on the table. "Apologies, Ezren. I hope I didn't put you out too much last night."

When I looked up again, he was staring at me, and it was all I could do to keep the flush from my face. Those *eyes*, they were a live flame and seemed to burn straight through me.

"You can sleep in my bed whenever you want," he replied, to which my chest constricted and my eyes widened, and he realized the error in his speech. "No, not whenever you... meaning, not in that way. I just meant, I didn't mind..." Ezren didn't finish, because Leiya and the male that looked like her had burst out laughing. This got a few other members of the room giggling, too, until Jana rolled her eyes and said, "Enough. We have work to do."

Mortified, I took my seat, resolved to remain silent until the reddening in my face subsided. Ezren rolled his shoulders back and tilted his head to each side, cracking his neck as if to shake off the exchange.

"We should send scouts more frequently now," Jana said. "Given Fayzien will be looking for us. I'll need reports daily, rather than bi-weekly. I know that will be hard, and we will have to coordinate a rolling schedule of some kind. Everyone will have to do their part."

"I volunteer to scout," Ezren cut in. "I could do two routes weekly, with Dane, which should help the fliers a lot. I'll leave and return always under the cover of night, or heavy cloud-cover."

"Absolutely not. That is much too risky. I shouldn't need to remind you. Besides, I require you here. Someone must continue Terra's training," Jana responded.

"Is not Leiya fit for the job?" he asked. I noticed a stiffening in his neck.

"Leiya is better suited to scout, as I just said. But please, do let me know if Terra's training will be too much for you to handle," Jana bit out.

Ezren cleared his throat, and his eyes flickered to mine for a moment. "It will not."

"Good. Dane will handle the magic side of training; coordinate with him. Leiya, assemble your top choices for a scouting crew and report back to me at half past. Dismissed." Everyone got up in response to her commands. I did the same.

However, I made no move to exit. I only stood, silent. She waited until the last of them exited the tent. "I continue to scent distrust on you, Terra," Jana said. "You are not yet schooled in controlling your emotions. What can I say to alleviate your doubts?"

"Who are you? What is all this?" I asked, gesturing to our surroundings.

Jana smiled, prepared for the question. "We are a coalition of representatives from all three kingdoms: Viribrum, Nebbiolo, and the Witch Kingdom Drakkar. Everyone here desires peace amongst our three nations, regardless of species. More than just Fae and Witch live in our lands—Elvens, Gobles, Sprites, Weezins, and other lesser Fae live amongst us. We promote tolerance of all."

The unfamiliar names of new creatures washed over me. Questions for later. "And why are you all here—together—for me?" I was a famous warrior's daughter, so that gave me *some* importance. At least enough to warrant a small team for my rescue. But an entire camp? That seemed odd.

"Tensions between Viribrum and Drakkar have been invigorated, I will say, ever since your abduction. Though *we* now know Fayzien kidnapped you, the Viri King and Nebbiolon Queen publicly blamed Drakkarian operatives for your presumed death. The king has been using your disappearance to stoke the public's desire for war. Many of us have banded together in opposition of this and have searched for a way to cool the tensions for years, unsuccessfully so. But when we discovered you were alive, we... we finally had hope. If the Viri King and his subjects find out you live, it may just be enough to hold off the looming war."

Coalition. Banded together. Opposition.

My eyes narrowed. "You're rebels."

Her smile didn't reach her eyes. "The Viri King might call us that, yes. Not quite how we see it, though. We do not use violence to further our cause—only in self-defense."

Her words scratched something in my mind.

"When Fayzien tried to take me, he said his queen commanded him. Who is his queen, and what does she want with me?"

Jana flexed her jaw. "He was referring to Rexi Neferti, Queen of the Witch Queendom Nebbiolo. She commands Fayzien. He is her Manibu—the closest advisor to the Rexi. He acts on her behalf in ways she cannot. But he is delusional, Terra. He believes all his actions, even the most unspeakable, are sanctioned by his queen."

"Why not kill me, all those years ago, when he murdered my father? Why go through so much trouble to keep me alive and place me in Argention?" It was almost as if he *hid* me there. As if he *wanted* to keep me safe.

She shook her head. "I do not pretend to know the mind of a sociopath. Perhaps he was protecting the option to use you to his advantage in the future."

"And you think by simply showing everyone in Viribrum and Drakkar that I am alive, it will stop a war? Why would they care about me, especially if I've been gone for seven years?"

"Your father, Viturius, though not expressly warm or affectionate, commanded love from his fellow Viri. He became famous, you know, a celebrated war hero. There are stories sung of his quests. He fought in many great wars over his lifetime, ensuring the safety and rise of the Fae people. And you were considered a daughter of Viribrum, Terra. Daughters are rare, and so precious to the Fae. Your return to Viribrum would right a grave wrong," Jana said, her eyes alight.

Her unexpected soft tone struck a chord. "Did you know him, my father?"

"Yes, I did. In my youth we met on our travels. He'd already been blooded—a distinguished soldier by then. We didn't always see eye to eye, but he was good. Dying to protect you, there is no cause he would have deemed more noble." Her face shone with something like pride and sadness.

The little voice nudged me. I chewed my lip. It didn't appear I had many other options than trusting Jana.

I exhaled. "What do I need to do?"

"Come to Viribrum with us," she said, relieved by my question. "No one can deny you are the seed of Viturius. You have his bright eyes, curved nose, and heart-shaped mouth. You are proof that Drakkar did not sanction your death. It may be enough to ease tensions and prevent war. And besides, it *is* your home. You will be safe there, from Fayzien and anyone else that might want to hurt you. You have relations in Viribrum, too, a few cousins, aunts, and uncles.

And your father's estate, which is rightfully yours. You can have a home again."

Whether she knew it or not, the word *home* gave me a tendril of hope. I wanted to cling to it like a lifeline; I wanted to imagine days filled with purpose and evenings filled with laughter. But I couldn't, not really. The ones I'd loved were gone. My birth-sire was gone. I couldn't return to Argention, not without alerting Fayzien and endangering Gia or Mav. Gia would wonder about me, I knew. She'd never get the truth of what happened or where I went, and that would hurt. But she had her brother and her family. She would be cared for and safe.

I, however, was utterly alone—save for the fire that burned inside me, driving the cold emptiness from my chest.

Revenge. That was my lifeline.

I blew out a breath. "I will accompany you to Viribrum. But I need your word. I need your word that you have not lied to me, and never will. And I need your word that no matter what happens, you will ensure the just punishment of Fayzien of Nebbiolo for the murder of my family. Human and... not." I expected to hear my voice shake, but the words came out smooth and cold.

Jana only nodded, her face solemn, but her eyes shining with something that almost resembled pride. "You have it."

CHAPTER EIGHT

BROKEN MIRROR

"*Magic, well... She is a fickle thing,*" Dane explained with wrists clasped behind his back as we meandered through the canvas camp toward the forest. Roughly my height, Dane had dark skin, a broad mouth, and wore his hair shaved close to his scalp. Most uniquely, faded swirling tattoos snaked up his neck, growing towards his face like flames. The Witch had not been present at my cleansing, but he seemed to be one of the closest to Jana, and he intended to teach me the ways of my element.

The absurd thought of magic generated by my own hands made my eyes roll, but I quickly remembered dirt exploding from my palm in defense.

I swallowed, my heart racing, refocusing on Dane's lesson.

"Some call upon Her with words. We call these spells, of course. It's the most reliable act for us Witchfolk. They allow specificity and control. We achieve simple tasks with cantrips: a single word or short string, usually the same backwards as forwards, a palindrome if you will. These take little energy, but some repetition to master. Here, let me show you."

He paused and extended his hand. "Navid divan," he said, and an apple appeared in his palm. He held it between his fingers, rotating it to prove its realness. My expression softened at the trick. So small, yet another confirmation that the reality I had always known was changing rapidly.

"There is always a balance that must be restored, or maintained, when it comes to magic. This apple did not appear from nowhere, you see. It is not to say I snatched it out of some poor sap's hand to present it to you. But, somewhere, there is an apple tree not yet in full bloom. It will grow one less apple because of my little cantrip. What is the harm in that, you might ask? To which I would reply, none that I perceive. Now, what if I dumped a thousand apples at your feet? Well, maybe that tree would die. Again, it seems like a small consequence. It is, after all, only one tree out of millions. But I assure you, there are times when the consequence is more than the death of one tree."

"And... everyone has magic?" The unsaid question hung between us: *I have magic?*

Dane shook his head, hands still clasped behind his low back as we walked. "I would say about half of Witchfolk can tap into Source —that fabric of life that weaves between us—with only a small subset able to wield an element. Some Fae have powers, but theirs are single manifestations of Source. Like a knife or a sword—their powers are a tool with a purpose. These powers can be quite vast but are limited to that utility. This is why they cannot portal, unless they specifically possess traveling magic. Witch magic is more... flexible. Like a multi-purpose tool. We can spell—we have mastery of all Source. We typically are more limited in power, and I suppose that is nature's check and balance, but the variety of what we can do with that power is far more vast."

"Portal..." My mind drifted to his instant appearance in Jana's tent the day before, Ezren in tow.

"Yes, folding oneself through space to hop from one place to another instantly. Quite convenient, quite taxing."

I chewed my lip, not sure I ever wanted to experience *folding oneself.*

"As I was saying, spelling only requires mastery of Source. What is less common, say maybe one in several thousand magic-blessed Witches, is the ability to call upon the elements. Water, Air, or Fire. For Element Witches it is not terribly difficult to ignite this call, as the elements are extensions of themselves. However, control does not come easily. I've seen entire villages lit aflame by the hand of a green Fire Witch attempting a simple task, such as roasting a suckling or warming a bedroom. So, while your training will consist of some cantrips and a few practical spells, control of your Earth power requires immediate attention."

I let out a breath. I'd agreed to train with Dane and Ezren, given Jana seemed to believe it was highly dangerous for my magic, now unbound, to roam free inside me. Still, I was wary.

"How do you know for certain that I have Earth magic?" I could feel the vibration and purr of the Earth more clearly since the cleansing, but nothing else. *Shouldn't I innately feel such a power?* "And if I do, how would you know how to train me? Jana said the last Earth Witch lived a millennium ago."

"Certain things are unmistakable to the schooled eye. I suspect Jana is not wrong about your power, and I can feel a tangible amount of it coming off of you. But soon enough, our suspicions will be validated or denied. As for the training, I am a Fire Witch. Earth is living, and in a way, so is Fire. It will be different but not impossible for me to train you. I have half a century of experience in the art of control."

I gaped. Half a century? He looked a mere few years older than me. I would have guessed not a day over twenty-five. "Dane, how old are you?"

"Seventy-one," he said, amusement flickering over his expression. "We Witches don't live as long as the Fae, but certainly age as well." His coy expression was almost endearing.

I stopped in my tracks then. "And how long will you live?"

"I am in my mid-life, or nearing it," Dane explained. "Witches have a fixed lifespan, though we didn't always. Unless we're killed or die of some incurable ailment, we live for one hundred and fifty years, only aging visibly like a human would in the last two decades. Fae live far longer. The oldest Fae is more than thrice that age."

I remained still, the camp bustling around us, Witch and Fae alike moving in preparation. "How long will I live?" The question came from my lips of its own accord.

"That, I cannot say. You are part Fae and part Witch, making your lifespan somewhat mysterious. I have known mixed breeds to live as long as Fae, but I have known some to pass at the one-hundred-and-fifty-year mark. The scholars have postured the idea that it's related to which bloodline is stronger," Dane said, attempting to begin our walk again.

I placed my hand on his arm, drawing his eyes to mine. "How old *am* I, then?" In the past week, everything in my world had turned upside down, so it would be fitting to learn my age was a lie.

Dane's gaze softened. "You are nineteen, just as you have been told. Faeries and Witchlings mature similarly to humans. First bleed for females is typically between the twelfth and fourteenth year. But once fully matured in all the human woman-like ways you might think of, the aging will slow. You will appear as you do now, save maybe a bit more angle in your face, for a great many years."

I relaxed, allowing him to continue our journey towards the forest. At least I didn't find out I was forty-five. I fell silent, and he droned on about the characteristics of Fae versus Witch, something about the history of the distinct point of Fae ears. And, even though my ears were human-like and rounded now, it wasn't fully indicative of how I would appear for the rest of my life. My mind wandered, a million questions percolating. How old were Ezren and Jana? Soft creases lined the Witch's face, gray streaked her hair. She must be in the last few decades of her life.

"And of course a Witch would never shift," Dane said. "For that is a very specified manifestation of magic, again—why Fae have *specific* shifts. It's said that some Witches, back in the old ages, mastered universal shifting. You can imagine the implications of *that*. They were hunted, their children were hunted, and their children hunted. It became highly frowned upon for Witches to shift, though I suspect some have maintained this practice in secret. Unnatural, in my opinion. No Witch, even half Witch, should degrade themselves like that, flying around in bat-like form or something else... dreadful." He shuddered.

I pulled my eyes away from the nearing trees. The woods always drew my gaze when I found myself lost in thought. Gia fondly called this directional shift entering Terra's world. I looked at Dane sidelong. "What do you mean, *shift?*"

He sighed, clearly exacerbated. "Terra, I will not have my efforts to train you wasted. If you don't deign to listen, I won't explain again. You're mistaken if you think there are no other demands on my time."

I did my best to look apologetic. "I'm sorry Dane, it won't happen again."

This earned me an eye roll. "Now Terra, lying isn't becoming on you."

WE WENT DEEP into the forest, allowing the wood to grow thick and guarded. Dane thought it would be best for me to make my first attempt at calling the Earth somewhere remote. We came upon a small clearing with moss-covered rocks, tall grass, and a few lone oleander shrubs. Large oaks surrounded the meadow and tangled roots framed the area, which was littered with wildflowers; delicate daisies and lilac colored chicory, coneflowers and milkweed.

Dane beckoned me forward and knelt in the center. I followed, letting my knees sink into the dirt beneath the grassy surface, facing my teacher.

"Terra, listen now, for this first lesson will be the most important. The Earth calls to you—I see that plainly. And it has for many years. And for many years, though not intentionally, you have denied your nature. When you finally call back, the power will be like releasing a dam. As Element Witches prepare for battle, we spend months hoarding our power, allowing it to build up within us. When we finally call to it again, attempting to command that power is akin to curbing a large swell of the ocean. In a word, difficult.

"You will feel an immense rush. You will have no control at first. It will try to claim you, using your body as a channel. You cannot let it. I will guide you in gaining control, but you must open your mind to me. You must trust me. Can you do that?"

Despite the warmth of the spring day, a shiver shot down my spine. I wanted to shake my head at his caution. Dirt had leaped off my hands, yes. Not the most incredible power. Beyond the memories that returned to me in a trickle, I knew in my bones that my connection to the Earth was different. I could discover the way home through dense canopies when others could not. My hands blindly found their way over branches and tree-knots, letting me out-climb Mav every time we raced to the top of an old maple. And I could coax a bloom from a dried seed better than anyone else. Somehow, I'd always known my relationship to the Earth, to living, breathing things, was special.

"Could I hurt you?" I chewed the inside of my cheek.

"I know how to protect myself from novice error," he said with a cheerful grin. "Anyway, someone has to guide you through it. Can you trust me?"

"Yes." And to my surprise, I meant it.

"Close your eyes," he instructed. "Open your palms. Feel the energy calling to you. Envision every root and tree and blade of grass as you. You live in them, and they live in you. They are your spirit, your lifeblood. And you are their commander."

I did as he said. I felt out to them, as if the roots of the nearby oaks were extensions of my fingertips. I reached out slowly, gentle and exploring in my touch. A small current, no more than a spark, formed in my mind's eye. I extended my forefinger to it, intending to give it a small brush.

Within an instant, the power flowed into me like a massive wave, dousing me from head to toe. But the wave didn't just coat my skin, nor did it brush me with a gentle buzz. It penetrated my being. I couldn't tell if it flowed into me or out of me—it might have been both. And it felt good, *so* intoxicatingly good. The vulnerability and grief and despair that had been lurking beneath the surface, threatening to bury me with every breath, were gone—evaporated, as if they'd never etched cruel markings into the shape of my soul.

I had the Earth, or rather it had me, but I didn't care. Dane's words floated past me, barely registering: 'resist,' 'control,' and then my name, over and over again. I didn't feel his hands on my shoulders, shaking me back and forth, trying to wake me from a trance. I didn't hear Dane screaming in horror at what unfolded around him. I didn't see the Earth erupt in reaction to my touch—flinging rock and soil into the air in an uncontrollable tornado. I didn't smell the burning of huge oak tree limbs, incinerated by Dane as the debris flew towards him.

I felt only the current of power, unwavering and completing. Healing.

Whole, whole, whole.

I knew I was submitting to the power. I knew it could kill me, as Dane had warned. But I didn't care. The hole in my chest, ripped open when my family was murdered, no longer gaped. It no longer threatened to swallow me with every breath I took. I was burning. Everything was burning. And I was whole.

A fresh wave of magical ecstasy reverberated through my veins, igniting my every nerve. And then a loud *boom!* sounded, vibrating across the land. I didn't feel the ground shift beneath me, severing— opening up as if an angry god had just split the world in two, mirroring the feeling in my chest. I just knew I was falling through a crack in the land.

Power thrummed through me as I fell, weightless, deeper and

deeper into the crevice. I didn't flail through the air—I only wondered how deep I would fall before I met certain death. Some distant, numb part of me stretched wide, opening its arms, welcoming the end. The euphoria from the surge of power had subsided and I just... didn't want to go on. I didn't want to wake every day, tortured by the descending grief and adjustment that followed *remembering*.

But then, out of nowhere, a tight grip squeezed at my midsection and I was snatched from the free fall, my descent reversed. I looked down to see claws, no—talons—clutching my stomach. Up and up we went, the crevice beginning to close behind us.

Perhaps my magic can split the Earth, but not hold it open for long.

It was a race, it seemed, and the huge flying creature carrying me was determined not to lose. I couldn't see above me, for a large scaled body blocked my view, but below us the Earth folded in on itself at an accelerating speed. I knew we wouldn't win. I stared at the dirt as it enveloped us, swallowing our bodies whole.

I SHOULD HAVE DIED—I figured the rubble would crush us instantly. But it held us, a pocket of air lining my body. The beast struggled against it and I sensed my rescuer had no special sheath. I was resigned to staying there, allowing whatever air I had to run out. Tears escaped down my cheeks as I thought of Mama's face. My father's warm touch. Javis's devious smile and Danson's hearty laugh. Close. I was so close to seeing them again, in whatever form the gods had in store for us. In that moment, I felt them. I felt their presence, so close to the edge of death, beckoning me forward.

After a few moments of peace, a pain stabbed in my chest. As if my heart was being ripped from my body. I shrieked in surprise, the scream echoing in my small bubble, ringing in my ears.

The sound—or maybe the pain—woke me from my trance, and terror swelled. I could no longer sense my family reaching out for me across the edge of life. I searched, desperate for that sense of warmth.

But I could not feel it. I pictured my mother's face, eyes alight. *Survive, daughter. The Terra I know does not give up.*

Her words echoed, and I blinked, unsure if her voice was in my head or somehow spoken out loud. But I was alone in the dark bubble —and I knew what she told me. She told me to *try*.

I closed my eyes again, reaching out to the power. But this time when I saw the pulse of the Earth in my mind's eye, I did not touch it lightly. I grabbed it, holding fast in my grip. "Release," I whispered.

Light pierced the darkness and the ground opened up once more, revealing a yawning depth below us. And then we were falling again, and I realized the beast had lost consciousness. Somehow, its talons remained locked around me and I hit them wherever I could get purchase, desperately trying to wake my would-be rescuer. I screamed until my voice went raw. We plummeted toward what appeared to be the bottom of the crevice, and I could do nothing to stop the impact. Hysteria bubbled up my throat, the realization I didn't actually want to die sending a bolt of panic through my spine.

I'd commanded the Earth to release us, hoping to save myself and my rescuer. Ironic, that it would lead to our ends.

"Gods save us," I whispered, bracing for the looming collision.

But it wasn't the gods who saved us. A moment later, we took flight.

THE BEAST SHOT out of the ground as if catapulted into the sky. My eyes darted around for Dane, but we were moving too fast for me to pick anything out of the smoking debris that littered the previously flowered meadow.

I hung limp in the creature's talons as we soared up and up, away from camp and past the edge of the forest. I hadn't asked where we were, and I didn't recognize this land. *Far enough from Argention, then.* We passed treetops and mountains capped with creamy white glaciers that turned into rolling green hills. The sun's bright light reflected off the snow, and not a cloud dotted the blue sky.

Mere minutes later, an endless body of water came into focus, and the creature began its descent. The flying beast dropped me, none too gently, on the sheer cliffs bordering the coastline, covered in lush foliage and with no forest in sight. Only a field of boulders to my right and the steep drop-off to my left were visible. For a terrible moment, I thought it would fly away and leave me there, stranded.

But the creature just circled around, adjusting its approach for landing, which let me see its full form. The animal had a scaled body with imposing webbed wings that spread out longer than four of my cottages combined.

Dragon.

The rear talons that had held me collided with the ground, the impact reverberating through the plain, nearly throwing me off balance. The towering beast lowered its head, which was dotted with menacing spikes that ran down its spine in two lines. When my gaze met its face, I went ice cold.

Emerald green eyes, blazing on fire.

CHAPTER NINE

BURNING EYES

*T*he pendant at my throat seemed to sear into my skin. Staring into the Dragon's eyes was like looking at the hottest part of the fire, at the glowing coals that weren't quite red, but weren't quite blue. The coals that burn the watcher's eyes, watering and drying them from the smoke. It sat so still, pinning me with its stare, barbed tail swishing from behind.

Maybe it's true. Maybe the ancient gods really are divine immortals. Perhaps this is Raingar the Magnificent, from the fables we were told as children. Maybe I have gone crazy, and magic is real, or maybe I'm dead after all.

But I didn't feel dead; I felt unsettlingly *awake*. Those eyes were the same as *his*, save for the pupils, which were slits instead of circles.

The Dragon continued studying me, but not with the level of recognition I would have expected from a rescuer. In my trance, I advanced a step and raised my hands slowly, exposed. But before I took another step, something caught in my peripheral—a brown blur rushing towards me. The sun reached its mid-point, and I had to shade my eyes, but the blur came into focus as a spotted falcon. It transformed mid-air, and Leiya landed gracefully in a crouch with one hand on the ground. I gaped. She wore battle dress, with two long scimitars strapped to her back. I had seen her sharpening her blades many a time but not wearing them in anticipation of use. The thin, curved blades looked menacing on her strong frame. And a cold focus gleamed in her eyes, which were fixed on the Dragon.

The Dragon's body tensed but remained still, as did Leiya. "Terra," she said coolly. "Slowly walk backward an' move behind me."

My confusion intensified, but I moved, slow steps at first, my hands still in the air. "Is that not Ezren?" Had I mistaken those eyes? Or misunderstood Dane's lesson on Fae shifts?

"Aye, but nay will he thenk as Ezren. We need te move before he shefts."

"What do you mean?" I whispered. "You changed and are just as you always are."

"I dunay have time fer thes! Get yer hind behind me. Leuffen well be here soon."

Her demanding tone sent a regrettable bolt of stubbornness through my body. "What's wrong with him? He just saved my life. Why would he hurt me now?"

Apparently, the Dragon who was and wasn't Ezren didn't like my raised voice, however subtle. He gave out a sharp cry, head angled towards the sky, talons scraping at the ground like a horse preparing for battle.

Shit.

No way could we stand against a Dragon. Unless Leiya slew it with a well-positioned strike of her blade. Which I guessed would be a fatal blow to Ezren. The options did not seem optimal.

"Terra..."

The Dragon screeched again, breaking into a lumbering charge, only taking a few steps before shifting. It happened in an instant, the change occurring with a twist of the air. And then Ezren, armed with two scims of his own, barreled towards us. I would have laughed at the obscenity of it, but a blood thirst raged in his eyes, sending a chill down my spine.

He did not recognize us.

"Ah, fer fucks sake, Terra," Leiya growled. "Get yerself behind me, and when the bloke's distracted, get yerself a fucking weapon!"

Her tone rang clear enough. I leaped far behind her, my eyes not leaving him. Leiya bent her knees in anticipation, crossing her arms over her shoulders, and drew the pair of gleaming blades from her back. Leiya was only a few inches shorter than Ezren, and from what I gathered, equally skilled in combat. But he had an edge to him—a fury I hadn't seen before.

And then he was upon her.

Scim collided with scim, and flashes of steel whipped around too fast to track. Leiya landed a few blows, but so did Ezren, and his were harder. I searched the ground for anything I could use as a weapon. I stumbled over a small boulder I hadn't seen before, as if the stone rolled out to trip me. I picked it up, feeling its weight. Heavy enough to do damage, but not too heavy to be unusable.

I slipped the dirt-stained shirt over my head, silently thanking whoever had left me clothes for thinking to include a brassiere. I laid the linen unbuttoned on the soft grass and tore a single strip from the hem. I placed the rock in the middle of the shirt, gathering up the fabric and twisting it around the stone. I tied the rock in place with the torn strip and gave my make-shift bolas a few good swings. The small boulder stayed steady in place as I whipped it through the air by holding the sleeves. I had no idea if it would be effective, but it would have to do.

I looked back to Ezren and Leiya. They continued to do battle, and I knew I couldn't swing my weapon with any accuracy while they danced. I held it behind me and crept towards them, preparing for my opening. Ezren knocked one of Leiya's swords to the side and landed a firm kick on her middle that sent her flying a dozen feet back. She landed with a thud, her other scim ricocheting out of her hand. She groaned, the wind knocked from her lungs.

With his back to me, Ezren approached Leiya. I ran toward him, not making a sound, wondering what I would do if he turned his blades on me. But before I could consider the potential repercussions, I whirled my weapon with as much force as I could muster.

The inelegant blow landed with a crack on his left shoulder. From the impact alone, I could tell it was a considerable strike. One of his scims dropped, and he turned to me in a wild fury, but half bent over. I was ready for him. Swinging up diagonally, I sent the boulder into his abdominals. He fell on hands and knees, releasing his other blade, wheezing. I sprinted over to Leiya, who still struggled to get up. I extended a hand, pulling her to stand. She swayed on her feet.

"Stay here. I'll run towards the boulder field and lead him away," I whispered to her.

Her eyes widened, and she shook her head. "No, Terra. Can't. Leave. Ye," she choked out.

I spun and took off. Ezren stood again but still without his blades, his palms pressed into his thighs, heavy breaths escaping him. I shot past him, denying him the chance to grab me. I felt a comforting assistance from the ground, giving the slightest spring to my step, pushing me faster and faster. The Earth was on my side. Despite the circumstances, I smiled.

But he, too, held an advantage. The strong Dragon blood must have still been pumping through his veins. How long until his strength waned?

I ran away from the coastline, maybe a hundred yards off, towards the expansive field. Boulders, large and small, dotted mossy green grass and granite rocks towered next to slabs of flat stone. If I made it, maybe I could tire him out, weaving through the obstacles.

One of his steps cracked a nearby branch—he was gaining on me. I barely reached the edge of the clearing before Ezren tackled me to the ground. I gritted my teeth and rolled him off, ending my fall in a small crouch, weapon still in hand.

Thank the gods he didn't have his scims. He faced me, expression untamed and wild. He was a disheveled mess, tendrils of sweat-soaked dark auburn hair dancing down his forehead and his shirt half ripped, revealing the definition in his chest. I swung my bolas in a figure eight, building the momentum. He pounced, and I aimed for his head, hoping to land a clean knockout. He ducked and then rose again. My weapon veered toward him again, nearly of its own accord. He leaned back, allowing the bludgeon to glide past, grabbing the neck of the cloth, ripping it from my hands.

The force pulled me into him, but he pushed, shoving me into the sheer face of a nearby megalith. I collided with it, back first. I would have slid down the stone, sinking to my feet, but Ezren was upon me, his body pinning me to the wall. I had to jerk my head upward to look up at him. The brutishness remained on his face, but he looked down at me with an animal desire that was not the same bloodthirsty expression he had given Leiya.

I froze, my throat tightening. The scent of male sweat and piñon lined my nostrils, and the rise and fall of his chest grazed my own. His forearms framed my head, flush with the rock, as he dipped his face to mine. Up close I could see his pupils remained in his Dragon form—vertical slits, almost like that of a cat, rather than circles.

Sweat dribbled down the sides of my face as we both panted. Droplets of blood clung to his scruff. I freed my hand, ready to twist and send a sharp hook into the ribs I knew I'd broken with my bolas. Before I could, Ezren took my cheek in his large palm, his thumb grazing the bottom of my jaw, and he tilted my head back and to the side. He shuttered his slitted eyes and ran his tongue up my neck to my temple, tasting the salt of my sweat and sending a tremor through my body.

His fingers found my neck and squeezed, his teeth snagging my earlobe.

A whimper escaped my lips, and my heart pounded so violently I thought it might explode. The sound stilled him for an instant. His body remained taut, loaded with tension. He turned my face back to his, and I opened my eyes, unaware I had closed them. His pupils were the circular kind again, set in a bed of emeralds on a face now filled with pure terror. His gaze shifted down my front, an almost undetectable linger on the space where my shirt should have been.

"Terra," he breathed, saying my name for the first time to my ears like a prayer, his hand still cupping my cheek.

I didn't have time to answer, for a deadly strike to the back side of his head knocked him away from me, a strike delivered by Leiya with the hilt of her blade.

I remained flush with the boulder, aghast. Leiya wiped her forehead with the back of her wrist and said, "Well, let's get thes fucker tied up."

Leiya had some rope tucked under her leathers. It seemed she had expected things to go about as they had. I helped her bind his hands and feet together.

I retrieved my shirt, now torn and decorated with blood and grime. Untangling it, I fastened what buttons were left after the whipping it delivered.

"Leuffen will be here soon, ye can rest en the meantime. He wilna give us any trouble now." She gestured to Ezren.

I wrapped my arms around myself and nestled into the curvature of a soft boulder. The sea breeze felt warm, but a shiver danced over my skin. I grazed my face and winced; a small bruise must have been blooming on my cheekbone. I shook my head to clear the tears that were forming. Too much was happening too fast; I couldn't keep up. One more thing to add to the list of things I didn't understand, didn't know how to process.

Less than an hour later, Leuffen arrived with a small cart. We loaded the still unconscious Ezren into it and made our way back to camp. It had only been about a fifteen-minute journey by flight to the coast, but the trip would be much longer on the way back, Leuffen informed me. We would be lucky to make it before nightfall.

Our pace was slow due to the colorful, varying beatings Leiya and I had sustained. Finally, I looked up at them, dazed. "Why? Why did he want to kill us?" I turned to Ezren's unconscious body in the cart. He wouldn't wake for hours. Leuffen ensured that with a dose of an unfamiliar herb concoction.

"Eh, well, he's a wee bit unusual, fer a Fae," Leuffen replied. "Sheften' takes a lot from all a' us, that's why ye rare see us fightin' with magic after a sheft. But Ezren here, well, et gives him somethin' too. A thirst fer blood, ye see. Dragon shefters have never been known fer their control."

"The last known Dragon shefter lived a millennium ago," Leiya continued. "At the time, they were common. Dragons as a species were, too. But they were tools a' war, ye see. Violent beasts, aye, but remarkably controllable under the right command. Many Fae and Wetch alike sought out Dragons and Dragon shefters for battle. Eventually, the animal species became so brutal they wouldna' breed and died out on their own. As fer the Fae, they were terrified a' being used as tools a' battle again, so they dispersed. When Ezren's shape was discovered many years ago, his master at arms sent hem away from Viribrum. He didna' want Ezren te fall te the same fate as many before hem."

"How exactly does this make him violent beyond recognition?" I probed. "Is that just the curse of the Dragon?"

"He shefts very rarely—ets too risky fer others te know his form. When a' Fae doesna spend time en their form... well, et makes the sheft very hard te control, akin te yer power. And even a practiced Dragon shefter would be dangerous, fer they have many millennia of battle bred en them. Et takes several hours for Dragon blood te clear his veins after a sheft ef he doesna have a Wetch controllin' him."

"Why did he save me, then? How could he, if he has no control?"

Leiya sighed. "That, I dinna' know, lassy. We all felt the Earth move when ye split et en two. I was with hem. But how he knew ye were en trouble, I dinna' know. He just took off flyin'. Must've had such a straight mission, so even hes Dragon mind knew he needed te grab ye. Now the whole camp's aware we have a Dragon shefter, I 'spect."

I considered her words as we walked, remembering the last few days. "And why did he volunteer for scouting? If he can barely control his shift?"

Leuffen chucked. "Good question. That dinna' have much more te do with anythin' but pride, en me opinion."

"Well, te be fair," Leiya reasoned, "he *can* be controlled. Dane has flown hem a time or two fer such missions. Was drainin' from what I gathered, fer the both a' 'em. Had to be spellin' the whole time, Dane did."

There was another question, one I didn't want to ask, but couldn't quite keep in. "Has he..." I trailed off, unsure of my phrasing. "Is it usual for him to become dangerous in that... that male way?"

Leuffen looked bewildered. "What're ye referrin' te?"

Leiya ignored him. "No. I've seen hem change a dozen times, many a' them brutal, but I've not seen that. He'll be feelin' right sorry about et tomorrow."

"What do ye lassies mean?" Leuffen asked.

"Ets none of yer business, ye oaf," Leiya responded at the same time I said blankly, "He licked my face."

Leuffen huffed out a sound of disturbed surprise. After that we were silent again, both of them afraid to speak, I thought.

WE MADE it back to camp by nightfall. Though everything looked the same, a sense of restlessness hovered over the group, like they anticipated a move.

Jana ushered us into her personal tent. From the outside, it appeared to be the standard tent size and triangular shape. The inside spread circular and wide, though, with a large bed frame, dining table, and other chamber furnishings—nothing like Ezren's tent.

We laid Ezren on her bed. She extended her hands over his face and midsection, murmuring. His eyes blinked open, and he shot upright, wincing.

"For the gods, Leiya, you couldn't have gone easy on me, eh?" he said, clutching his abdomen.

She gave him a weary look. "I'd usually be embarrassed te admit thes, but yer injuries are mostly Terra's handiwork," she said, a smirk forming behind her words.

I stood the furthest back, somewhat blocked from Ezren's view by Leuffen's large stature. But I saw him freeze, eyes searching the room. The burning emeralds landed on me.

A ghost of a smile flickered across Ezren's face. "Why does that not surprise me?"

I could stand only a second of his searing gaze before I cleared my throat. "Jana, where is Dane? I'd visit him, if I may."

"Six tents to the left of here. He is resting now. The healers have been with him all day. You can sit with him if you like."

I nodded. I had prayed on the walk back that Dane was unharmed, but alive was better than dead. I darted for the exit, feeling the urgency of leaving that tent before it threatened to swallow me whole.

CHAPTER TEN

HUMAN HEART

$\mathcal{I}$ peeked my head into the sixth tent. The inside also contrasted with the deceptively small exterior frame but less so than Jana's. A young Witch, one of the original six that had taken me from Argention, sat in a large chair next to Dane's bed, his limp hand in hers. She looked young, maybe fourteen or fifteen at the most. Light strawberry hair exploded around her unmarked, round face. She shot up from the chair upon my entrance, stumbling into a half curtsy.

"I'm sorry your—ehm, m'lady."

I cocked my head at her formality. "Sorry for what? I'm the one owing an apology." My gaze lingered on Dane's bruised body. Bandages covered half his head. Large and small cuts, all sparkling with a fresh coat of salve, decorated his arms.

I shifted foot to foot at the threshold of the tent. "Is he—did I..." I nearly choked on bubbling guilt. "Will he be all right?" I asked, my question more of a plea.

"Yes, m'lady. He was caught beneath some rubble after, er, the Earth split. But it seems the boulders pinned him in such a way that protected his vitals. What luck for two boulders to fall precisely against one another—as if to prevent the other from crushing him? Almost... holding each other up. We Witches aren't easily broken, you know. He gave us healers a run for our monies, but nothing we couldn't handle in the end."

My face heated with shame, regardless of whether my power or luck had protected Dane from the falling debris. But the healer's voice was soothing. I sensed she was much older, for her foggy gray eyes told a different story than the rest of her appearance. They weren't quite sad, but they were heavy with a weariness that is only earned.

"May I sit?" I asked. "Only if it would not bother you."

"Oh no, I'd love the company. You *are* the talk of the camp anyhow, a celebrity. My fellow healers would scorn me if I didn't take the opportunity to investigate the newcomer," she winked at me.

I sat in the chair opposing hers. I knew the healer meant her words in humor, but I still felt she told the truth; if I shared something interesting, word would get out. A wave of exhaustion passed over me, and I let my head rest on the back of my leathery perch until it tilted upwards, my eyes unfocused on the canvas ceiling.

"What's your name? I presume you know mine, since I'm so famous." My words came out with more of an edge than I intended. It had been a long day.

"Sanah," the girl replied smoothly.

"Sanah," I repeated, turning her name over in my mouth. "What is the origin?"

"It is Nebbiolon, and not a terribly uncommon one at that. I believe the word for it is dew." She paused, cocking her head in thought. "Specifically, it would translate to the condensation that is left after the fog rolls in."

"It's pretty." I couldn't think of more to say.

We were silent for a moment, and I blew out a breath. "Nebbiolo, Drakkar, Viribrum. All these places that are supposedly my heritage, all I've never heard of." I sat up, some energy returning with my percolating thoughts. "How is that possible? Before all this, I focused on my studies, and I read voraciously. I read more fiction than not, yes, but my geography wasn't awful. I have *never* seen those places on a map, *never* read about some... princeling or adventurer finding their way there. Nor have I heard of the Fae or Witches beyond fables. How?"

Sanah leapt to her feet, and began rummaging around Dane's tent.

"What are you doing?" I asked, not bothering to move from the chair. "Wouldn't Dane object to you tossing over his belongings?"

"In my professional opinion, no he would not," Sanah smiled to herself in a way that made me feel like I wasn't in on the joke.

"Ah, here!" She slid a dressing cabinet ajar and pulled a long tube of parchment from behind it. "I knew he had a map lying around."

Sanah knelt on the ground, smoothing the parchment out before her, using a few odds and ends, a rock here, a bottle of herb liquid there, to weigh down the corners. I crouched beside her. The map was certainly not one I had ever studied. It looked like a version of the one I knew, but much, much larger, with my version shrunk and shoved west. The familiar piece was warped somehow, squeezed narrower.

"There." She pointed to a small illustration of hills in the upper left corner of the map. "You know these well, the Argen hills. And there, there is Argention."

My chest tightened and then went vacant as my fingers brushed against the spot. I bit the inside of my lip to keep the heat from my eyes. Home. So much smaller than I'd ever thought.

"These are the human lands you know of; see the Kingdoms of Teyzen, Laharam, and Salamiere." She showed me with a trace of her fingers. "And there. You know these mountains, don't you?"

"Yes," I breathed. "The Adimon Mountains. After those..." I trailed off, furrowing my brow at the continuing depiction of land. "Where is the Endless Ocean?"

"The Endless Ocean is what human eyes see looking east from the Adimon range."

What human eyes see... meaning—

I blinked. "It's... a glamor?"

Her brows peaked, encouraging. "Yes. A glamored barrier to keep the human and magical realms separate. If a human were to cross it, they'd become confused and face a strong desire to return home. No one knows when it was created, though there are myths and fables that claim its origin."

"And it's always been this way? Separate lives—worlds—for the Fae and Witch from humankind?" I whispered, the reality of just how little I knew about my world washing over me.

"As far back as my grandmother can remember, yes. You have never crested those mountains, at least not in your human life, I take it?"

"I scarce ever left Argention."

"What do you remember learning about the Endless Ocean?" Sanah asked.

"Strange tales, none really substantiated—but just as you explained. Travelers who got the idea to explore the Endless Ocean seldom returned. And if they did, they did so changed, confused. None in Argention left to explore it, but we are not the seafaring kind. Though, I did hear a tale from a wanderer once..."

I paused, remembering aloud. "He said the most peculiar thing—mentioning Fae, actually. I thought he was just another madman returned from the Endless Ocean, but now..."

"What did he say?" Sanah probed. I closed my eyes in concentration, willing the memory forward.

"Those who can survive beyond the barrier have more than power in body, but power in spirit. It is true, both are needed, but one aspect the rarer. Those who dwell there for their whole lives have both, but also neither, for they seldom find themselves tested. It is the interloper, the challenger, that has both advantage and disadvantage. For she sees the ways of the Fae and the Witch, maybe even comes to live by them, but she never forgets the human heart. Hers is a heart that will never grow cold."

I opened my eyes to find Sanah staring at me, something unfamiliar on her face. I supposed the recitation was strange—it shocked me that I even remembered the whole thing. But before I could say more, she shook her head. "Sounds like a human with a scrambled head."

Everything I'd known had been turned over. Now, the wanderer's message felt more pregnant with meaning than ever.

But Sanah moved on, leaving my confusion in her wake. "We are headed to Valfalla, the capital city of Viribrum. Your father's homeland, remember? Nebbiolo is off the coast of Viribrum. See here." Sanah pointed to an island. "That is where I am from. You, too, were born there."

"The Witch queendom."

She nodded.

"And Dane?" I looked at him rather than Sanah, his chest rattling as it rose and fell. Even with medicine, he must have been in immense pain.

"He is Drakkarian." Her words came out heavy.

My earlier conversation with Jana came back to me. *The Viri King and Nebbiolon Queen publicly blamed Drakkarian operatives for your presumed death. The king has been using your disappearance to stoke the public's desire for war.*

"So any love between a Nebbiolon and a Drakkarian would be frowned upon... given the... tensions," I ventured.

Sanah released a hollow laugh. "Try forbidden, not frowned upon."

Interesting. "Is that why you're here?"

She gave me a sad smile. "It *would* be nice if we could be together without giving up our families. It may be naïve of me, but I believe in a better world. An ambitious goal that starts with one small step. One you can help us take."

Nausea roiled in my belly. These strangers' faith in me still felt far-fetched and misplaced. What if my return to Viribrum didn't make things right? What if they were wrong and showing my face wasn't enough to quell whatever tensions were brewing?

I swallowed the doubt—tamping it far down—and instead pulled on the little thread of fire that laced itself around my heart. *It doesn't matter. Only Fayzien. Justice matters.*

I rose. "Sanah, thank you... for the information."

"How's he doing?" she asked as I made my way to the exit. I knew she didn't refer to the patient beside her.

I shrugged. "I think okay. When he changed—back to his usual form, I mean... I've never seen anything like it. He was... an animal that had lost its mind. Rabid," my eyes grew glassy, recalling Ezren's feral expression, the beast that was trapped within him, begging to be let out. I chuckled. "You would think the craziest thing to me would be seeing his Dragon form. That seemed a lot more natural than what came after." I shuddered.

Sanah sucked in a breath. "Terra, you should try to stay away from Ezren. It's not my story to tell, but he's... troubled, I would say. I know you may feel indebted to him for saving your life, but I would keep my distance if I were you."

I dipped my head, unsure of how to respond. Though its exact meaning was vague, her warning didn't shock me. Ezren's eyes alone seemed dangerous.

"Thank you again for your lessons tonight, Sanah. It was nice to meet you." And then I set out to find a bed.

I WOKE on the cot provided to me, this time verifying the tent belonged to no one else. I slept without dreaming, exhausted from the events of the day. Rolling over, I saw Leiya's familiar shorn fire redhead bent over, examining the point of her blade.

"Good morning, watchdog," I croaked, my voice hoarse from a deep sleep.

At that, she grinned. "Yer quite a self-important lassie, hey, te think I've been watchin' ye all night. Nay, I've jest been here a few minutes. Yer to report te Jana immediately."

I opened one eye to regard her, still adjusting to the morning light. "I agreed to accompany you all to Viribrum, not to be at Jana's beck and call."

Leiya rolled her eyes. "Et es about Fayzien, lass. She needs yer help te... assess hem as a threat," she said, her tone soft.

The name turned my insides to ice and my throat to ash. I closed my eyes, willing away his image. "All right."

When I walked into the tent, everyone sat at the long table. Except Ezren. He stood at the far end, one arm in a sling, the other resting on the back of a chair. He seemed to be positioned as far from the entrance—or from me—as possible.

"Good morning, Terra," Jana said. "Please take a seat."

I obliged.

"I promise to ask this of you only once. Given yesterday's events, we are worried that Fayzien will be notified of our location. The Earth splitting was likely heard and felt widely by anyone with Fae hearing. We have already stayed in this location for several days too long. In order to move safely, we need to know everything about Fayzien's goals and plans. Could you tell us about the night he came to Argention? I know this will be difficult, given what he did to your family, but it is crucial to spare no detail."

The room's attention turned to me. I hadn't bothered to wash after falling into the crevice, and the subsequent battle on the cliffs. I swallowed, my skin itching. I had no desire to remember the events Fayzien brought to Argention, let alone in front of a group of strangers.

Leiya laid a comforting hand on my shoulder. I looked up at her, and she gave me an almost imperceptible nod.

"I'll try." My voice sounded distant to my own ears like I was separating from my body to prepare for reliving the horror.

"I first noticed Fayzien in the market the day before Spring Day. Spring Day is a matching ceremony for the young people of Argention. He'd been with four other men, all hooded and as large as he. I didn't see him again until the following evening when he made a claim for my bridehood. Given the amount of gold he offered, the Matron accepted his price without providing me my rightful chance to accept or reject his proposal.

"I ran home, hoping my parents would reason with the Matron. But he caught up to me." I paused, my eyes closing at the memory.

"He stood in front of me, and suddenly I was on the ground, my clothes missing." Heat traveled into my cheeks upon discussing my nakedness with strangers. "He did something to me then. I am not sure what, but it hurt. He only touched his hand to mine, but I felt him; I felt him inside of me. As if he traveled into me through my fingertips. And went everywhere," I whispered. My gaze remained fixed on the table, unmoving.

"Terra." Jana's face softened, her tone too gentle. "Would you say he sent his magic through you? Does that feel accurate?" Her words resonated.

"Yes," I breathed. "It does. The sensation hurt, like a... burn weaving through me."

"And he went everywhere with his magic?" she asked, her voice low and steady. Her eyes traveled to my womanhood.

I nodded, my tongue coated with disgust.

I ventured a look at the group, shame thick in my throat. Shame that only grew thicker when my eyes landed on Ezren's back, moving through the opening of the tent.

I stared at the flap for several moments.

He left.

Mortification was a cresting wave, breaking on my cheeks, leaving a trail of heat in its wake.

Jana cleared her throat, and I looked back at her. "R-right," I stuttered, shaking my head. "Where was I?"

"Fayzien sending his magic through you, dear. Will you be able to finish?"

"Yes." I said, wanting to get the rest over as quickly as possible.

And I did. I told them of our following conversation, of how Fayzien said he acted on behalf of his queen, how she had some mysterious use for me, and how he had expected me to go with him willingly on account of his *beauty*. I told them of my escape, how we battled on the bridge. I told them how I made it back to my cottage, how I crept through the passage to the crawl space under our living room.

"I hid beneath the floorboards, watching Fayzien scream at her. It happened fast—she was standing one minute, shaking, afraid. And then she wasn't. And I did nothing to save her." I whispered the last part, pressing the jagged part of my nail into my palm to keep the tears from flowing. "After that, I just laid there, hoping I would die too. That somehow I would go to whatever place she did."

"Terra, there is nothing you could have done," Jana said, her voice firm yet tender. "You have to know that."

Even if my rational mind agreed, my heart wasn't prepared to listen. Her words floated past me, skimming the surface of the dark black well those memories lived in. I nodded absently and continued. I told them about the Earth, how it closed up around me in what I'd thought was a coffin, but now seemed to be a shield. About how I woke to the sound of their voices, confused and afraid.

And then I was done.

Jana tapped two fingers on her lips. "Interesting that he could not track you. He should have been able to, given he sent his magic through you." She shook her head and rose. "Thank you, Terra of Argention, for your bravery in telling us your story." She placed a hand over her heart, touching the necklace she always wore. "I promise to you, on my Siphon, this sacred bur oak that feeds my power, I will aid you in obtaining justice for Fayzien's wrongdoing to you and your family. In front of my council, I swear this." And then she hinged at the waist and bowed to me.

Leiya cleared her throat behind me. "I, too, swear," she said, her eyes bright. The rest of the room rose, repeating the words in an echo of promises.

My chest swelled, and I beamed in awe at their gestures. I rose, placing my hand to my heart, a bizarre sense of camaraderie descending across the tent. Though I was still unsure if they could keep their vows, I sensed a truth amongst the group—even amongst those I didn't know. As if they felt Fayzien's wrongdoing against me was a wrongdoing against them, too.

"And I swear to journey to Viribrum, to aid however I can in your attempt to prevent the death of the innocent Fae and Witches of Viribrum and Drakkar."

———

I LEFT Jana and her advisors to discuss strategy. I made my way back to the coach path, eventually reaching the creek I had found a few days before. I removed my tattered shirt, filthy trousers, and bloodstained boots, and stepped into the frigid water. It stretched only about a dozen yards wide but deep enough that it reached the middle of my stomach while standing. I lowered myself, and the water flowed around me, covering my head.

I stayed there, under the surface, for as long as I could bear. I let the cool water wash away the memories that hurt and bring in the ones I'd forgotten. Maybe it was the stillness—but more glimpses came. Images of my birth father across the dinner table cutting into a piece of well-prepared meat, a teacher reprimanding me for reading a novel under my desk during lessons, playing in the dirt with the golden-purple-eyed boy. The memories were full of ample treats, tutors, and nannies—I was comfortable in my previous life, in a way I hadn't been in Argention. It made sense if I truly was the daughter of a famed warrior. But everything felt hazy. The images were soft, like gauze. Details of them were clear—I saw the purple-golden eyes of my young friend as if I stared into them in the present. But who he was lingered on the tip of my tongue, as did the remaining pieces of the puzzle I felt were missing. Eventually, I saw a woman, beaming with a gentle roundness in her face that matched my own.

An abrupt disturbance in the water pulled me from my peaceful exercise. Strong arms yanked me up, air filling my lungs once again. "What the hell!" I half yelled, half sputtered, annoyed at the interruption and rough handling. I brushed the hair from my eyes, expecting to find Leiya frowning over me. But I was staring at wet linen, stuck to the curvature of a heaving, tanned male chest.

The rage boiling on Ezren's face took me aback. "What?" I demanded, meeting his anger with my own.

"I came to apologize for yesterday, *Bellatori*," he bit out, maintaining a guarded control in his voice. "But I see you are just hellbent on killing yourself. I suppose my first rescue wasn't sufficient?"

I gaped, stunned at his audacity and cavalier tone. I forced my chin upward so that I could meet his eyes, even though we stood so close I could feel the steam roll off his body.

"How *dare* you assume what I do or don't want after what I've been through." My words were deadly quiet. "Do you know how it feels to stand by and watch your life, and everyone you love, being ripped away from you? To be violated in a way you couldn't even understand, helpless to stop it? To watch the life leave the woman who raised you, who loved you, who cared for you when you were ill, and shared in your joy and your pain? Do you know what it's like to know you did *nothing* to stop her death, and that you'll never see her smile again, never hear your brothers laugh again, never feel the comforting touch of your father again? I suppose you do *not*. So how dare you reprimand me if I wanted to die." I paused, letting the heat of my words settle on him. "And for the record—I never tried to kill myself. I just didn't fight the Earth splitting."

Ezren's eyes flashed down at me with a look that was both softer and harder at the same time. They snagged on my dragon pendant and his gaze turned molten before dragging back to my face.

"Actually, Terra, I do know."

"You do?" Though a small part of me stumbled within, my tone was haughty, and I maintained my stare.

"Let me guess," he purred, those green eyes practically glowing. "It feels like a hole has been gouged into your chest? Like you've been flayed, ripped open for the world to see, vulnerable to whatever or *whoever* wants to tear into you. The grief is so overwhelming, it might just rise up and swallow you whole, which might even be a mercy, because you'll never be forced to wake, remember, wake, remember, wake, remember—ever again."

Whatever mask of indifference and anger I'd been maintaining shattered. He shook his head, almost in disgust.

"I lost my father when I was very young, barely fourteen. What I remember of him is cruel and difficult. I never knew my mother and lived a life largely in hiding. I found love again—once, but she, too, left me. I've been abandoned by every person I've ever loved. So yes, I know the pain of being utterly alone in this world, powerless to do anything about it."

The glimpse into the warrior's past—the reasons for his frost and distance—fissured my hard exterior, letting shame seep through the cracks. I'd judged him, so lost in my own pain, I couldn't imagine another's suffering. And he'd *seen* me, described exactly how I'd felt. "Ezren, I'm so sorry—"

He looked away, uninterested in my apology. "There is no difference between not fighting for life and wanting to die. You didn't just lose control of your power... you submitted to it. You let the Earth mirror your internal world—mirror that hole in your chest, ripping wide and swallowing you whole. You could have killed Dane."

At that, I flinched, which seemed to cause his cold mask to slip once more. His eyes did not let go of mine. Awareness of him hit me —of every outline of his chest and abdomen, defined by his wet, clinging shirt, rolled up at the sleeves. I could see the veins that danced down his forearms, invigorated by the clenching of his hands at his sides. His jaw was tight, flexing at the hinges to make it wider, the angles of his face even more dramatic than they already were. His waved hair dripped down his forehead in a tousled male way. He looked like a true warrior. All of that couldn't compare to his eyes. I almost tasted their flames; the heat of his gaze threatened to burn me from the inside out.

Maybe that's why Sanah called him dangerous.

Something traitorous tingled in my low belly. I ignored it, forcing myself to loosen an exhale, turning to climb out of the water. He remained silent for a few moments longer, unmoving from his position while I dressed.

Ezren released a breath as if he'd been holding in air the entire time we stood close. And then he spoke, breaking the silence that frayed my every nerve. "I'm sorry for the cliffs. Leiya told me what happened. I'm sorry I hurt you, and I'm sorry for... I am sorry for the other thing, too. I've never done that before, and I'm truly horrified at the thought of it," he said, his voice low.

My cheeks flushed as he spoke, my fingers fumbling with the buttons as I faced away from him.

"I'm not sorry for saving you. You have immense power, but you have no idea how to control it. I understand that. Believe me, I do. And I also know what it feels like to have blood on your hands from a lack of control. You have to be smarter—stronger. If you treat your power and your life carelessly again, you might do something you'll regret."

I waited a few moments before speaking, my arms wrapped around my chilled body, his apology and warning lingering in the air.

I turned to face him. "How did you know I was falling into the Earth?"

Surprise flickered over his face.

"What do you mean, *how* did I know?" he asked, cocking his head.

I sighed. "I mean, how did you know I was in trouble? Everyone heard and felt the Earth split, but how did you know that someone, or that I, was falling through the crevice and needed to be saved?"

His eyes remained alight. "Terra, you called for me."

CHAPTER ELEVEN

MUSCLE MEMORY

I called for him. I stood there stunned for a moment, not comprehending his words. I opened my mouth and then closed it. Thinking better of continuing *that* conversation, I turned and ran, leaving Ezren in the water. Rogue thoughts bounced through my mind. *Did I call for him aloud? Or in thought?* I certainly didn't remember releasing a cry for help.

I made it back to camp in much less time than the trip out, searching for Leiya. I needed something to do with my idle brain. If I wanted to find Fayzien and prevent a war, I had to get involved in the meetings Jana held. I needed to learn more about these people, or rather non-people, their kind, their motivations and capabilities.

I needed to *not* think about the Fae male I just left in the creek.

The camp was not as I had left it. People were buzzing around, but the tents were gone. Fae were sharpening blades, Witches were grinding powders on stones, or boiling small pots over various fires. I found Leiya with her ax in her lap, a sharpener in hand.

"When are we leaving?" I asked.

She regarded me with one eyebrow subtly raised, then looked

back down at her blade. "Yer scent es very overbearin' right now, Terra."

I gaped at her, horrified, and sniffed my underarm. "Okay, well, I tried to clean myself in the creek, but I had no soap, and this place has no proper bath, and there's no—"

"That's not what I meant."

"Then what do you mean?"

She just chuckled. "Well, when a female, eh, feels the pull te another, ye know the one, deep en the low belly, she gives a scent, te call the male, or female, te her. Ye have a very strong one, now. Ets a wonder ye canna smell et, because ets stuffin' me nose right up."

Heat rushed to my face, my mouth hanging ajar, and Leiya just laughed. "Ye shouldna worry, lass. The smell es, well awful te me, but from what I've heard, the right male or female well feel the need te feast en the scent like a traveler needs water en a desert," she said, a mischievous look in her eyes. Then she cocked her head at me. "Ye know, I actually thenk I smelled et on the cliffs before I knocked Ezren en the head. But I didna thenk too much about et, I was a wee bit focused on somethin' else at the time."

I shut my gaping mouth and turned on my heel, leaving her deep chuckle and the scrape of her ax behind me.

I found Jana surrounded by Fae and Witch alike, accepting her orders. I approached her, self-conscious of whatever odor I was apparently omitting. But if she could smell it, or if anyone else could, they did not comment. Jana picked me out of the crowd and waved me over.

"Terra! Good, there you are, dear. We have to move today. We will do most of our traveling by night, on horseback. Given the Fae cannot portal and we Witches can only take one passenger at a time, we'll conjure mounts. Fae with flight or long-distance enabled shifts will shift, except Ezren of course. How are you with horses?"

I cleared my throat. "Em, descent, I suppose."

"Excellent. You will ride in the middle of the caravan, next to Dane. He'll be in the medic cart." She paused and snapped thrice, and Sanah appeared out of nowhere next to her, as Dane and Ezren once had in the meeting tent. I marveled at the trick; there seemed to be a mist descending off her skin as she transitioned from a blur to a clear image in the blink of an eye. "Sanah will show you to a horse and accompany you and Dane. Leiya will fly above, and Leuffen will take his cougar form by your side. Sanah, make sure to get blinders for the horse's bridles. You know how the beasts start at Leuffen's shift."

The afternoon passed in a haze. Sanah put me to work preparing the horses with supplies and loading Dane's cart with blankets, pillows, and crates of dried herbs or pre-mixed potions. When the sun began its nightly descent, we set out for Viribrum—the Kingdom of the Fae, and my supposed childhood home.

I chose a sturdy jet-black gelding with a long, waving mane and a diamond of white on his forehead. Blackjack, Sanah called him. He gave an anxious prance when I mounted him, but I laid a soothing hand on his neck, and he quieted.

"Why do we go by night?" I asked Sanah, daunted by the impending sleep deprivation.

"It's much harder to be found at night," she replied. "No wandering traveler will spot us, nor one of Fayzien's Witches on look-out. The horses and shifted Fae can see perfectly well, so they will guide us. Even those in Fae form should be able to see okay. Your Witch heritage doesn't do you any favors with sight, but you'll likely be able to see better than I, given the Fae blood you also have in your veins."

She was right. I'd never thought about it, but I'd always been able to see better than my brothers in the dark. On this clear, crisp evening, the moonlight served as enough of a guide, and it shone through the occasional openings in the sky as we rode northeast through the dense forest.

The entire camp was not privy to our route—Jana preferred to keep that intelligence to her council. But Sanah told me we were heading to the southernmost border of the North Sea, a week's journey by horse caravan at night. Our pace would be slowed by the limited dark hours—summer approached, which meant longer days and shorter nights. Then, Jana and her advisors would decide whether to cross through the Adimon mountains or go by boat through the North Sea. They deemed both treacherous, and it would be a grueling expedition.

Eventually, in the early hours of the morning, before the light crawled its first fingers up the horizon, we found a clearing and set out to make a small camp. Sanah left my side to attend Dane, whom they had immediately moved from the cart to a tent. We were forty strong, so the camp was tight, and quarters were close. My body ached from the long ride, but everyone else hurried around me with purpose, unloading here and setting up there. I felt awkward and out of place, waiting for directions no one else seemed to need. I wandered about, attempting to look busy, aware of every suspicious glance thrown my way. What did they think of me? Did they think me some pathetic rescue? Or an unremarkable, surprising key to stopping a war?

"Terra!" A familiar voice came from behind me. "Yer with me tonight. Just me luck, bunkin' with the stinker," Leiya said, more friendliness in her tone than her word choice suggested. She steered us to a tent on the eastern edge of camp, guarded on all sides but one, for escape access should we need it. Our tent was of equal proportion on the outside as the inside—just how the Fae liked it, or so Leiya said. Only Witches with sufficient power to distort space slept in the luxurious accommodations.

We settled into the hard cots, canvas draped over our heads, wool laid over our bodies. "Leiya, can I ask you something?"

"Oh gods, are ye gonna require a bit of pillow talk?" she replied.

I ignored her retort. "Is... is it likely that Fayzien will find us?" *Will we get a chance to kill him?*

She paused, releasing a low exhale. "Yes, et es. He likely heard the Earth splet, and we still didna know ef he left a bit a' his magic en ye. The Wetches have been usin' every ounce a' magic they can spare te conceal us, ye see, from findin' spells and such. But he, well... ets a good sign he hasna found us yet. I know ye'll want te take yer revenge —but he es one a' the most powerful Wetches living today. I wouldna recommend et just yet."

"You all promised to help me bring him to justice," I growled. "Wouldn't it be better if he just... showed up here?"

Leiya snorted. "I dinna think so. Fayzien doesna show up unless he has some advantage—leavin' ye en the defensive. He's calculated, cunning. He es not te be underestimated, Terra."

She said the last words with a heaviness that hung in the small space between us. "Do you know him?"

Her lip curled. "Aye, no en mind, but en combat. He es a Wetch by training, but he es half Fae, like ye. And like ye, hes mixed blood didna cower at the combination—et made 'em stronger. He did a stint en warrior trainin' at Valfalla. He was me student."

I gaped. "You taught him?" The thought nauseated me.

"Aye. He wasna always as he es now. I recognized the potential for darkness en him, te be sure. But he was just a young male, a few years yer junior, when he came te me. Et was me hope te make him strong enough te beat et. I didna succeed."

"When was this?" I asked.

"Oh, about three decades ago. Maybe more." She offered no more, giving the distinct impression she'd finished with the topic.

"How old are you? And Leuffen? He is your brother, right?"

"Me an' Leuffey, well, we're a wee bit of Fae anomaly as well. He es not only me brother, he's me twin. That's a rarity for the Fae— twins. One Faerie babe es hard enough te get. We come from the north, near Panderen, but were selected to fight en the royal armies. They called us the prized warrior twins a' Viribrum," she snorted. "As for our age, we're close to a century—several decades younger than Jana. Though we don't show et, a course, since we'll outlive her by another lifespan or two," she paused. "And Ezren, ef yer curious, es the oldest Fae amongst us. He's past a Wetch's life, and though he doesna act like et, he certainly fights like et."

Tightness bloomed in my chest—and lower—at the mere mention

of his name. I fought to keep my breath steady, to reveal nothing of my reaction.

"Leiya, would you train me?"

"Train ye en what?"

"I know I trained to fight when I was younger. My muscles remember more than I do, but I am certainly not a warrior. And magic doesn't seem to be safe for me to explore at the moment... I want to defend myself, for if, or when, we meet Fayzien again. I want to be able to fight. Ezren was supposed to train me, but I'm not sure that's a good idea."

She waited a moment to respond, for what seemed to be contemplation or holding in laughter, and then said, "I have te scout durin' most a' the days at camp. But ye definitely should learn some skills en combat and the like. Leuffen will do et. Ye'll meet tomorrow, at high noon. He'll find ye," she promised, a hint of satisfaction in her voice.

I WOKE after a few hours of restless sleep, Leiya gone from the tent. The sun streamed in at a high angle, indicating the lateness of the morning. It had been just over a week since Fayzien blasted into Argention, since he'd turned my world on its axis. Just over a week since I saw the life leave my mother's eyes. Just over a week of remembering.

A week felt like a lifetime.

It was time for training, but I almost stayed there—weighed down on the small cot. It took a considerable amount of effort to force myself to rise and track down some food. I painted the image of Fayzien's face—cruel blue eyes sneering—to the back of my mind.

As I wandered around camp in search of Leuffen, something reached around me from behind. Suddenly, I was in the crook of a bulky arm, struggling for breath, my hands pinned behind me.

"Leuffen—What. The. Hell," I croaked out.

He laughed, a deep barrel from his chest, and released me. "Aye,

Terra, yer easy te sneak up on! Leiya told me te spare ye nothin'. I'm te push ye hard, like I would any other Fae. Canna ye handle et?"

I turned to him, facing his broad smile. "I'll certainly try."

On day one, my will was tested. He took me deep into the forest, away from our small camp, for 'conditioning.'

"Ye mighta been a lil' Fae warrior once, but yer weak as a fawn now. Ye need te build strength. Dinna worry, yer Fae blood will hurry along yer muscle build. Ef ye were trained properly en yer youth, which me thinks ye were, et should only take a few weeks fer ye muscles te remember."

At first, I ran. I ran carrying a pack full of rocks while he barked at me to go faster. I ran over logs and up small hills, through streams and thick brush. And he ran beside me, shifting into his cougar form, teeth barred and maw nipping to give me a fright, and back to his Fae form to add more rocks to my pack. The Earth gave me no aid while we trained, as if it knew the purpose of my running and wouldn't interfere. Once I'd soaked the fresh training clothes Leiya lent me well and good with sweat, Leuffen wrapped my hands in cloth. He brought me to a small sapling, no wider than a potato, and made me strike it. He bellowed at me to strike it again, in the same location, over and over. And I did. I didn't stop until I broke the sapling in half.

Throughout the afternoon, he alternated me from running and striking various hard surfaces, to ground exercises for abdominal strength, to climbing fear-inspiring rock crevices, to running again. He allowed me breaks to sip from a canteen, just long enough to ensure I didn't vomit, and then we started again. It ended when my knuckles were raw underneath the cloth, and my clothes were heavy with perspiration.

"To the gods," I breathed on our walk back, holding Leuffen's arm to remain upright. "Is Fae training always that brutal?"

He smiled down at me. "Aye, but et usually esna that long. Ye have a shorter window te rebuild strength than most. Dinna worry, ye'll feel like right shit tonight, but yer Fae muscles will heal quickly an yer strength will come weth et. If ye can handle et, I'd show ye the bow tonight, after we eat, but before we set out te ride again."

A small chuckle escaped through my lips. "If my arms can bear to spread the string, I'd like that."

THAT NIGHT I tried my hand at the bow, and though I struggled to hold it, my aim was decent in the dusky light. Afterwards, we rode until early morning, and I slept until midday. And then we did it all over again: him yelling at my muscles for several hours under the afternoon sun, and adjusting me with the bow or throwing knife in the early evening. It took little to improve my shot, for I must have been quite good at a young age, Leuffen mused.

On the fourth day, he said my muscles were progressing and prepared for combat training. Instead of pushing me with his words and feline growls, he struck me and sent me to the ground. I earned a smattering of bruises and cuts—highlights on my cheekbones, elbows, and knees. I learned fast to minimize our contact, to leverage my swiftness, to duck more than strike, and to let him tire out. He taught me combination moves—tricks to outwit his hits and gain an advantage. It was all about gaining the advantage, he said.

When we rode at night, I no longer noted my surroundings. I ran through fighting combinations in my head. By the sixth day we were actually sparring, set in a dance of our own, one where I knew some of his moves, and he mine. I surprised him, finding little openings to add my own unique tactics, an unexpected roundhouse here, use of our environment to gain favor there. We never used weapons, and I never went for his manhood. Leuffen called that desperate. I pushed off nearby aspens to gain leverage and slid away from his strikes in soft dirt and led him to unsure footing.

"Yer early trainin' es clearly coming back te ye," he said as we walked back to camp that afternoon. I grinned to myself, not knowing if he meant to reassure me or himself.

"Terra, Leuffy!" Sanah yelled when we approached the small clearing. "I found a small pond just a few hundred yards northwest of camp. Leiya already scouted it and said it's clear. Thank the gods, we finally get to bathe. I thought I would smell of horse permanently!"

We chuckled and followed Sanah through camp to her discovery. The late afternoon sun glittered on the water, and willows draped over the edge as if to kiss the surface. Other Fae and Witches were splashing in the water already, male and female alike, fully nude. I learned that Fae rarely shied from nakedness, and it seemed the Witches had adopted the same practice. I could tell them apart now —noting the slight difference in build. The Fae were generally larger, with ears that came to sharp points. The Witches looked more human-like, save for their eyes. Despite varying shades, their eyes were like that of the Fae—unnatural and striking.

Sanah ran over to Dane, who had gained mobility just yesterday. He perched on a large rock, dangling his feet in the water. I gave him a small nod, which he returned. We had spoken only pleasantries since the accident, and though Sanah said he would recover fully, I'd avoided bringing up that day with him. If he harbored anger against me, I would not blame him.

Leuffen shed his clothes and dove into the water, joining a rowdy gaggle of Fae males at the far end of the pond. I removed my boots and squatted next to the water, splashing my face—a heavenly act after the days of sweat that had accumulated.

I looked up again, surveying the revelry. Near Leuffen, at the far end of the pond, my eye caught on a Fae male standing half out of the water on the shallow end, his glistening back turned to me. I instantly knew it was Ezren by the broadness of his shoulders, and the ripples in his arms as he lifted his hands, running them through his hair. I indulged myself in the stare, letting my eyes linger on the long muscles that traveled down his back, ending with two little dimples just above where the water covered the rest of him.

And then, out of nowhere, a hard shove smacked into my back, and I went face-first into the pond.

I re-surfaced to see Leiya, still clothed in casual trousers and a linen vest, on the pond's edge, chuckling once again. "Didna Leuffen teach ye how not te let anyone sneak up on ye?"

I rolled my eyes at her and extended my hand up to request a lift out of the deeper end of the pond. And I suppose I had been rather humorless with her until now, because I caught her by surprise as I yanked her into the water with me.

This sent Sanah into hurls of laughter, and she jumped in. A moment later, we were splashing each other like young girls, basking in the novelty of play after a sleepless week. Leuffen joined in as well, taking pleasure in making Leiya the victim of our endless water torments. Eventually, Leiya held up her hands in surrender, which was fine with the three of us, for we were breathless from laughter. I felt joy for the first time in weeks.

We hoisted ourselves out of the water one by one, the warm spring air clinging to our sodden clothes and wet skin. As I climbed out of the pond, I felt the searing heat of emerald eyes trained on my back. And though I only caught his image in my peripheral, I could have sworn I saw a rare smile on Ezren's face.

CHAPTER TWELVE

WARRIOR BLOOD

That night, our ride was the shortest yet. Leuffen and I had grown close in the last few days, and my fast progress had transitioned us from teacher-student to near peers. He continued to instruct me, but in time I shared some tricks of my own—moves that had either come back to me from previous study or were inventions of my imagination. Despite his size (his palm could encompass an entire side of my face), I had bested him several times.

Warrior blood, I guess.

"Ye'll have te start trainen' weth Ezren, lass. Ye fight smart, and there isna warrior that fights smarter than that bloke. Plus, ye'll have te get te a point where ye can fight us both at once," Leuffen said to me with a wink during our evening ride.

My body sang in response to the idea of fighting with Ezren. It itched for contact with him—there was no denying it now. I became aware of whenever he was near, every nerve ending responding to his presence or lack thereof. And though I continued to ignore Leiya's comments, I grew too tired to deny it to myself.

But we had not spoken once since our exchange in the creek, and he seemed determined to ignore me. As tempting as it was to test his resolve, I resigned myself to reciprocating his behavior. I suppose it felt easier—safer—that way.

"Is that really necessary? Shouldn't I be moving on to learning the way of the blade? If my returning memories serve me right, I once was quite formidable with a scim. For a twelve-year- old, at least."

Leuffen only chuckled and said, "Aye, then. I'll try an' find ye a sword once we make camp."

We were nearing the coast of the North Sea, and Jana prepared to stop at some distance from it to plan the next leg of our route. The scouts had yet to pick up any sign of Fayzien or his men, but caution was in abundance, Sanah told me. The decision of whether to travel by land or by sea to Valfalla—the capital city of Viribrum—would be made tonight, with preparations beginning at first light. If we crossed the sea, the Witches would need a full day to magically craft a sufficient ship.

We set about forming our tight camp, everyone moving efficiently in rehearsed synchronization. My eyes stung from the lack of sleep, and my muscles ached from the constant breaking, tearing, and rebuilding. But I saw a definition in my arms and unfamiliar lines of tension on my abdomen that weren't there before. In another triumph of the week, my appetite had finally caught up with that of the Fae. Leuffen certainly took advantage of it, forcing extra portions onto my plate whenever he could.

After camp was readied, the council gathered in the meeting tent, candles ablaze with Dane's Witch Fire illuminating the dark early morning. I'd been welcomed into a strategy meeting for the first time, and it did not come easy. They only allowed me in after much arguing and advocation on the twins' part, though they did not share who opposed my attendance, or why.

Jana stood at her usual place in the center of the long wooden table, with Sanah and Dane adjacent to her on each side. Ezren sat at the far end of the table, looking broody. The usual resident council members occupied the rest of the ten seats. I stood behind Leiya's seat, determined not to seem out of place.

Jana began. "We have until dawn to decide about traveling to Valfalla. Land, or sea? Over the past several days, I've heard arguments for both routes, and many valid points. I want to hear everyone's vote before deciding—either path will pose significant risks. Parson, please begin."

Jana sat, and Parson rose. He had been the other Fae male present at my cleansing. He stood at my height, with light brown hair pulled into a low bun at his neck. He was rarely present, for he was always scouting, Leiya once told me.

"My argument is for travel by land," Parson said in a low and gruff voice, and I realized I had never heard him speak. "Travel by water when being hunted by a Water Witch is madness, if you ask me. He will always have the advantage. Any warrior knows not to enter a battlefield where his opponent has the advantage." He ended his speech there, sitting once more. I got the feeling he was not a male of many words and would not speak again unless addressed.

"We won't have material advantage if we go by land either," Dane cut in, staying in his seat. "We will be moving *much* slower than by ship, and we'll be heavily exposed. The North Sea is known for thick fog, which could be intensified by some of our Air Witches. By sea is the prudent decision."

"Of course, we have an advantage in going by land," Leiya pointed out. "We have a bloody Earth Wetch."

"Not a trained one," Sanah said firmly, not meeting my eyes. "She can't control her power at all. Asking her to call to the Earth would bring more risk than advantage."

"She's progressed well en warrior trainin'. Perhaps her misstep en callin' her power had more te do weth her teacher and the fact that she'd almost died days before," Leuffen growled back at Sanah. "Not te mention, she likely hadna' finished settlin'."

"Nearly killing Dane is a *misstep?*" Sanah's voice remained level, her brows raised. My throat tightened at her comment. She did not seem angry—only fair—though I wouldn't have faulted her for the former.

"And I suppose *you* could teach her to command an element, Leuffen?" Dane jumped in. "Yes, that makes perfect sense. The Fae brute knows best about an Earth Witch's ability to control such a potent force. Perhaps you wouldn't be so quick to defend her if she had nearly killed *Leiya* in the attempt to call her power."

Leiya launched back at Dane with a sharp retort about not being easy to kill, at which point I stopped listening and turned my focus to the lick of a candle. The flames flickered and the tension rose. Eventually, everyone talked over each other, and the chaos level of the tent escalated. I glanced at Jana, who was staring off into the distance, silent, as if her mind drifted elsewhere, analyzing some alternate solution.

"Oh, for fuck's sake, shut up," Ezren cut in, slamming his hand on the table and rising to his feet. The room quieted. Whether in deference or surprise, I could not tell. When he spoke, his voice was low and even, the trained tone of a warrior. "You're all talking about Terra like she's not here. Someone at least get her a gods' dammed seat." He avoided my eyes as if they would incinerate him. Parson stood and motioned me to take his chair next to Ezren. He seemed more than happy to fade into the background of the room.

"Jana, could you safely assess Terra's ability to call her power? Perhaps by conducting a test of some kind?" Ezren asked, his voice measured and his gaze trained on Jana as I walked over to his side of the table. His words seemed to pull her back into the room.

"I believe there may be a way," she said. "And I will do it regardless of if we go by land or sea." She turned to me. "You will need to face this part of yourself, dear, whether you wish to or not."

I slid into the chair next to Ezren, conscious of my body position in relation to his, where my feet fell under the table, where I placed my hands. I nodded in response, but images of flying branches and a tornado of debris flashed in my head. I looked at Dane, still cut and bruised, regarding me as if I was a bubbling volcano about to erupt at a moment beyond prediction.

"If it doesn't work, if there is no way for me to control it, I mean, could you re-bind the magic inside me?" I asked, turning to Jana.

"It could be possible," she considered. "But it would fight me, of course. I would need assistance, and it would likely be as painful as the cleansing, if not more so."

"I would help you, Jana," Dane said, eyeing me suspiciously. "Should it be necessary."

"Et should be out a' the question," Leuffen bellowed. "Ye weren't there Dane, but et was a right awful theng. I've seen suffering en me life, but nay like that. Ezren had te cover her whole damn body wi' hes te keep her from thrashin' so hard she'd injure herself. We canna allow et."

"It is not our decision." The quiet but firm comment came from the Dragon-shifter seated on my left. He looked at me now, his blazing eyes searching my face. For what, I did not know. It was the closest I'd been to him in a week, and I could feel a heat radiating from him.

I didn't dare move as he leaned back into his seat, his attention cast toward the group once more.

"I'll do my best to learn to control it. But if Jana deems me to be incapable, I *will* take the necessary action to keep everyone safe," I said, nodding to Jana.

At that, the discussion of "if by land or by sea" continued to unfold. Eventually, the council settled on a two-pronged approach. Jana deemed it the wisest course, though some opposed dividing our forces. A ship with over half the group would go by sea as a decoy for Fayzien, tempting him to gain advantage on the water. The best Fae warriors and battle-tested Witches would occupy the boat to fend him off long enough before he realized I was not on board. By which time, the smaller group, my company, would have already navigated through the Adimon Mountains. If all went according to plan, we'd be well on our way before Fayzien resumed his search for me. Then, the sea-faring group would slip into the Viri port of Panderen under the cover of night and wait for us to make the remainder of the journey together.

The Fae warrior twins were assigned to the ship. The idea of them fighting Fayzien on my behalf made me nauseated, and I wondered how they would defend themselves against a Water Witch on the sea.

"Didna worry, lass," Leuffen said to me with a wink after the meeting ended. "Fae have some magic too, remember? Ye just havna seen et yet. We'll give hem a run for et, promise."

Sanah was also assigned to the ship, given she was the most skilled healer and they expected to need her abilities. Jana would lead my group, along with Ezren, Dane, Parson, and a few others not on the council. Twelve of us—three Fae, six Witches, and one half-breed, would travel on horseback through the Adimon Mountains.

I was bleary-eyed by the time we all stumbled out of the canvas structure, looking for cots on which to catch a few hours of sleep before preparations began in the morning.

I was so exhausted I hadn't noticed a Fae warrior approach me from behind. Any trace of sleepiness vanished when Ezren pulled me behind a tree, out of the torchlight, out of earshot from the rest of our group.

"You don't *have* to bind your power. There will be another option, a different way to keep everyone, and *you*, safe." He bent his head close to my ear, so close that I could feel the hot air of his words against my skin. My chest constricted. "You don't want to spend a lifetime denying something that is you. Trust me. It's painful, and it will eat away at you, bit by bit. The Earth will always call to you, whether you run from it or not. Rebuffing your nature brings only suffering."

I opened my mouth to ask why he'd cared or what pain he'd suffered—but before I could utter a sound, he was gone, stalking off into the direction of his own tent.

Leaving me in the heat of a moment that had fled as quickly as it arrived.

I ROSE EARLIER than the rest, no sign of life at camp except for those posted on watch. I found a clearing a few yards off and began my drills. I ran through the different combat combinations I'd learned the past week, picturing an opponent before me. Occasionally, a lone aspen became my adversary, taking the brunt of my beatings, the calluses that had formed over my knuckles protecting them from abrasions. I longed for the weight of steel in my hands. The feeling of power and the strength of it had come back to my memory. I swung an imaginary blade, whipping it around with force, fantasizing about the chime of metal on metal.

"Did ye really thenk I'd let ye train all alone this mornin'?"

I jumped, startled by Leuffen's voice floating out from beyond a tree.

My mouth turned up in a smile at the gentle-faced, unarmed warrior, and I wiped the sweat from my brow with my forearm. "Well, if I'd waited for your lazy ass, who knows when I would've started," I chirped back.

Leuffen let out a deep chuckle and then charged at me. We fell into a familiar combat. He tried to pin me in his signature position, with my back to him and my throat in the crook of his arm, his other hand placed on the top of my head to show he could snap my neck with ease. I didn't let him. I was too fast when he tried to grab me, and I snapped the edge of my hand against his throat. He bent over and gasped for air.

A throaty chuckle came from behind me. "I think it's time you let me take over, Leuffen."

I whirled around to see Ezren making his way towards us at a casual pace, his hands clasped behind his back. The morning sun glinted in his soft waves, burnishing the dark auburn locks. His eyes were practically molten, purring with a royal green hue that I could have sworn glowed like the sun hitting his face—even from several yards away. The tips of two swords peaked out from above his shoulders. One of the hilts cased an emerald, casting prisms of light.

"She requires a blade, anyhow. And I happen to have two," he said, his eyes still fixed on Leuffen, who'd resumed a standing position.

Leuffen furrowed his brow. "We're en the middle a' sparren'."

Ezren smirked. "From the looks of it, the two of you were no longer sparring by the time I arrived."

Leuffen made to protest again, but Ezren cut him off. "Why don't you go back to camp and grab your blade, mate? We can show Terra a few tricks for fighting two-on-one."

Leuffen hesitated a moment longer, looking agitated at the hijacking of his training. He eventually glanced at me and nodded. Just like that, he turned and jogged off into the wood.

I eyed Ezren. He watched Leuffen until he was gone before turning back to me.

A familiar heat bloomed on my face in reaction to his predatory gaze. "How long were you watching us?"

He sauntered over, keeping his hands clasped behind his back. "Long enough to assess Leuffen's training of you," Ezren said lightly. He unsheathed his blades, tossing the Emerald-less sword in my direction. It landed in my hand with some heft.

"Its size may be a little awkward for you, but it's better than nothing." He shrugged.

I turned the blade over in my palm, admiring its weight and gleam. I clasped it between two hands and buried it into the side of a nearby fallen tree.

The blade cut deep in the dead wood, and the power of it reverberated back through the hilt and my intertwined fingers. I yelped at the backlash, my hands screaming in pain. The sword stuck out of the fibrous trunk. I glanced at Ezren, who was chuckling. I shook my head in mild embarrassment and tittered. He went over to the tree and yanked the weapon from its base.

"Well, your first lesson will be proper grip. These blades can't cut straight through surfaces like solid wood, even if the wood is rotting. They can cut through flesh, sure enough, but if you ever hit anything harder than that and don't have the proper grip, well," he winked, "you will feel it."

My cheeks heated further.

"Eventually, you'll fight one-handed, and maybe even with two blades, like Leiya and I do. But for now, place your dominant hand at the bottom of the hilt... yes, perfect. And your other above it, touching, like this."

He took it easy at first, demonstrating the various blade positions and how to properly make contact. But once he realized I could keep up, the pace quickened. He was faster than Leuffen and equal in strength, despite Leuffen's enormity of size. He knocked the weapon from my hand numerous times, critiquing the vulnerability I allowed when holding the sword at a certain angle. Before I quite realized it, we were sparring. Metal against metal, I spun around to meet his every move, to block his every hit. I was on the defensive, but I could tell I was making him work harder than he expected.

"Your training has come back to you a little." Ezren huffed, jumping back, barely missing the tip of my blade.

I whirled around, bringing a knee to the ground so that I could continue my swing from a lower vantage point. He blocked the risky move at the last second.

"Only a little?" I asked, looking up at him from below my eyelashes, our blades still connected.

Ezren stepped back and let me rise, laughing at my feigned innocence. "Tell me something—about your human family."

My brows pinched together as I sprung for his unguarded left side, and he parried, pulling us into a sequence of strike and block.

"Don't try to distract me." I whirled on him, sending a kick to where his midsection should have been. But he was too fast, and my foot struck only air. He took advantage of my stumble and pulled me into his body, sword pressed to my throat.

His warm voice tickled my ear. "I would never." His mocking

tenor was low and sent vibrations into my core. He paused a moment longer, relaxing his grip. "I want to know, really."

I pushed his armed hand away, resuming the fight stance. *Ezren one, Terra zero.*

"Alright." I sighed. "How about a question for a question?"

A beaming smile spread over his features, and my heart stumbled. *Focus, Terra.* I gripped the hilt of my blade harder.

"I accept." He faked right and went left, but I'd been watching his feet and was prepared for it. I struck his blade back, nearly knocking it from his grip, but he recovered and whirled on me.

"Were they good to you?" His question was devastatingly genuine, and I paused a moment, considering.

Had Mama hit me for disobedience once or twice? Had she created nights of unpredictability when she turned to drink? Had Papa never intervened?

All yes. But... "I felt very loved," I whispered.

He softened at my answer, and I lunged. He was on his back foot, and I took advantage of the poor stance, whirling myself around him. I had to stand on my toes, but *my* blade found his throat this time.

He stilled.

I could have asked him a million things. Should have. But what popped out of my mouth was beyond my control.

"Why did you lick me?"

The body in my grip warmed, chest heaving.

"I suppose I thought you would taste good." His voice was so low I almost couldn't hear him.

"And did I?" I breathed, not daring to move a muscle.

He disarmed me with ease, in a blink, throwing my sword to the ground and twisting out of my arms. "Not your turn, *Bellatori*."

I picked up my blade, but before I could raise it high, his blade clashed with mine.

"Why," he huffed, "do you insist on putting yourself through pain?"

I hit back harder, gritting my teeth. Sweat formed on my brow, threatening to impair my vision. "I. Do. Not," my breaths and blows separating each word.

"Yes, you do." Ezren struck my blade with such force that my weapon flew from my hand. Irrational rage poured over me, at his better fighting or his patronizing words, I wasn't sure. Although he paused to let me retrieve the blade, I placed both hands on his wrist and slammed it into a nearby tree. His sword fell to the ground.

We were close now, and I tilted my head back to see the shock register on his face. I sent my fist towards his jaw, eager to land another blow and keep my advantage. But he caught my hand, his grip tightening around my fist. In one swift motion, he turned us, and I was the one pinned to the aspen, my hand pressed into the tree above my head, his knee jammed between my thighs, and our gazes locked on one another.

He dipped his head so that I could better see him as he towered over me. What almost looked like a sliver of guilt flashed across his emerald eyes. "You've built your strength, that much I can see, so a part of you must want to live. You have to learn to control your power, *Bellatori*. If you deny it, if you deny who you are, its hold over you will only grow."

Something white-hot—maybe anger, maybe not—flared in my chest. "You say all of this as if—as if you care," I spat. "Yet you have no reason to."

Conflict wore on his expression. "Terra," he whispered. There it was again—my name like a prayer. His eyes darkened, scanning my face, lingering on my lips, falling to my necklace. "A Dragon made of silver," he murmured. "Why?"

"My mother made it. They called me *firebreather*."

Ezren's fingers tightened around my wrist possessively, his entire body a bow loaded with tension. I squirmed in reaction, feigning escape from his grasp, pretending like a small part of me didn't revel in the friction.

"Is that why you're always so damned flushed?" His voice was a graveled heat wave, flaring across my skin.

Words evaded me; I could only breathe in desperate gulps of air, my body screaming for him to be closer. He cupped my cheek with his hand, his other still pinning my wrist to the tree. His thumb raised my chin, brushing it lightly, and I trembled at the silvery tingling that ran like lightning through my veins. My heartbeat grew so violent I thought it might jump from my chest.

I will turn to ash in this man's arms.

Unable to bear another moment of building, raging fire, I raised my free hand to his cheek to pull his face towards mine.

But when I did, I heard a loud and somewhat angry "Ehem" from Leuffen, who stood several yards away, ripping Ezren and me from our delicate little world. He pushed himself away, and my arms dropped to my sides. I looked at him, but he turned his gaze to the brush in the distance, his expression cold and removed. It was like I'd been punched in the gut, and redness spread even more across my face—down my neck. I lingered like that only a moment longer before I straightened, and Leuffen said, "Jana requires you, Terra."

I didn't look away from Ezren as I said, "Understood."

And then I sprinted back to camp.

CHAPTER THIRTEEN

EARTH DAUGHTER

*H*eat pricked my eyes as I ran towards my tent, which, praise the gods, had not yet been taken down. Leiya was still in the small space when I stumbled in. "What's the matter with ye?" she asked.

I shocked myself by half-yelling at her. "What does *Bellatori* mean?"

She looked genuinely confused, so I continued, choking on my words. "You make all these comments about Ezren and me or my smell, but half the time, he won't look at me, and the other half, he is calling me *Bellatori*, whatever the hell that means. I can't help, well my *body* can't help reacting whenever he's around, and I have tried to ignore it, and him for that matter, believe me—"

Leiya took me by the shoulders.

"Ye need te take a breath. Now sit."

I did, and she dropped her hands.

She cleared her throat, looking embarrassed, and sat on her own cot. "*Bellatori* comes from the old Fae word, *Bellator*. Et means somethin' like 'fierce little warrior.' As fer the matter a' ye an' Ezren... sometimes, I say things that I shouldna say, things that come te me mind and I canna keep en. I didna think these things would push ye te act, I was just jokin' really."

"Can you elaborate?" I asked through gritted teeth.

She examined her nails with unnecessary attention. "En me opinion, ye should drop the Ezren thing. Et'll do ye no good to pursue et. Fer so many reasons, Terra. Ezren es... well, he es dangerous, fer one. And he lost someone, very close te hem. He never recovered. He's unstable, like ye en a way, he can barely control hes power, despite livin' weth et fer a century and a half. Fer so many reasons I dinna think he can care fer ye, not really, nay en the way ye deserve."

I could feel the heat lingering in my face. Though I knew Leiya was trying to be kind, her words left me more humiliated and lonely than comforted. How could I be so naïve to think a century-old warrior would care for me? And even worse, how could I let myself get so distracted pining over him, when I should focus on seeking justice for my family?

I let out a clearing sigh and stood to leave. She grabbed my wrist, halting my exit. "Ye know, yer body es reactin' te him so because, ye never, well... ye know."

"What?" I asked in exasperation.

She released me, the devious Leiya-like smile returning to her face. "Ye never touch yerself, en the female way. Ye should, ye know. Et won't do te rely on a male fer pleasure. They rare know how te give et anyway." She laughed at her own joke and perhaps at my aghast face. "Make small circles around the tender place, at the top of where yer womanhood parts, usin' the ferst two fingers. Ye'll see," she said, miming the last part in the air. With that, she winked at me and left the tent, singing, "good luck," as she went.

Any temptation I had to explore her suggestion paled compared to the idea that one of Jana's minions could discover me pleasuring myself.

I rolled my eyes and set out to find the leader. She was in the meeting tent, addressing letters. "You sent for me?" I asked.

"Ah, Terra, yes. The Witches need until dusk to ready the ship. It takes enormous skill to build something of that nature safely. I have prepared a little day trip for us." She dipped a seal into a pot of wax and closed her final letter. If Leuffen had relayed the compromising position he found me in, she showed no sign of it.

She walked over to me and took my arm in hers. And then we were gone, the room disappearing from my view while everything in front of me turned black.

It could have been a moment or an hour. Time didn't seem to exist in the in-between, which is what they called it. My first portal was uncomfortable, unexplainable, and unnerving. But life is relative. It paled in comparison to what I'd experienced the last weeks.

We appeared in a meadow, Jana's arm still linked to mine. Nothing but the voices of nature reached us, and I relaxed, my nausea subsiding. Light trickled through the canopy above and an explosion of flower varietals dotted the greenery below. The place felt alive, and somehow, I knew it was no accident.

"Where are we?" I whispered, as much to Jana as to the place we were in.

"Somewhere far enough away to be safe, but close enough to portal," she answered, her words smothered by another voice flooding my ears.

Terragnata, it sang, a sweet lullaby, the musical calling of a siren. *Daughter, you are here. Here you are, as you shall always be.* The words rang in my ears.

"Terra, are you alright?" Jana asked.

My head snapped back to her, breaking my internal dialogue with the element. "What is Terragnata?"

"Where did you hear that?" she asked softly. I shook my head, unsure how to explain.

"It is what you were given, dear. Terragnata is your name."

My brows furrowed. I had no recollection of ever being called that.

Jana just grinned. "I believe it means Earth Daughter."

Figures. A question scratched at the back of my mind. How did my parents know to name me so, if my powers didn't present until well into my young years—just months before Fayzien had kidnapped me?

Jana led us to the center of the field, and we descended into the lush. The grass tickled my exposed forearms resting in my lap. "Why didn't we just portal to Viribrum?"

"We considered it, of course. But you would have had to travel with a single companion, given a Witch can only portal with one passenger at a time. And unless you are exceptionally powerful, the allowable distances are short, requiring rest in between. Those periods would have brought enormous vulnerability, just you and a Witch guardian. We deemed the strength of a large cohort necessary for this journey, which is why we plan to reunite with the ship crew before entering Valfalla. But no matter, we did not come here to discuss strategy."

I leveled my gaze. "Why *are* we here, Jana?"

Jana returned her own look of challenge. "Alright, Terra. I am going to link my magic with yours, to attempt some handle on it, should you need assistance in control." I chewed my cheek as she took my hands in hers. "There are many ways in which magic can be shared—through joinings, couplings, and other specific tactics. We will do a simple link. Witches can easily share magic upon physical contact. You must open your door to me, and I to you. Then, we can strengthen each other, or limit, should the need be."

I kept my eyes on the Witch, fighting to maintain a neutral composure. "I'm ready."

Jana took my hand in hers, and a familiar sensation of heat crawled over me. I yanked it back as if stung, and she blinked at me.

"S-sorry, let's try again." My breath turned shallow.

She lifted my fingers gently. The warmth began again, even more tepid and tender. I bit down on my lip, swallowing the rising panic as that sensation traveled elsewhere, ignoring the sudden feeling that I was no longer clothed and standing in front of a strange male.

Don't move, don't move, don't—

I yanked my hand back again, a strangled sound escaping my open mouth.

"I don't know if I can," I whispered, heat stinging my cheeks, a solitary, traitorous drop of water springing from my eye. "I don't know why it feels... so... unbearable."

"Because last time, this was not of your choice." Jana's words were not a question.

I swallowed, nodding.

"Let's take it at your pace." Jana gestured for my hand once more, and I gave it. "Just feel my touch for as long as you need. We are in no rush."

So we sat like that—for minutes, or longer—until my breath returned to its usual rhythm. "Let's try again." I forced a smile.

The Witch's brows raised. "Are you sure? We can take it slow."

"I want to learn control." This was *my* power. I would not let Fayzien or the memory of him take any part of it.

Jana smiled back. "Alright, now, try to send a hint of your power into me first, and once I feel it, I will return a slip of my own."

I did as she instructed, the act more intuitive than I expected. It was as if she waited for me—waited to embrace my magic in a friendly hug that returned her own. And when she did, discomfort still nagged, especially for the heartbeat it traveled through me. But after a few moments, our link completed, and the sensation faded.

"Doing okay?" Jana probed.

"Yes, I can feel it—our connection. It's not so bad now... just slightly foreign."

"Good. Now, let's try to activate your magic. This time, I don't want you to simply grab that tendril of power you saw before. I want you to perform a specific action of control *using it*. Imagine the soil between us. Life flows within it. Feel that life force. Make it yours. Accelerate the growth within it."

I am okay. I am safe. I will not lose control, not again.

I held her fingers in mine and looked down. A patch of dirt revealed itself. I closed my eyes once again, sensing the vibration of the Earth.

"Easy now, Terra. I've got you. Try to start with a single bloom— nothing more. And *relax.* Think of something that makes you feel calm to start."

My pulse hummed and I released one hand into the soil, the image of Leiya, Sanah, and I splashing in the pond painted faintly to the back of my eyes. The Earth was an extension, calling out, a soul yearning for mine in a way that was undeniable. I flowed a slip of my power to it, beckoning it to rise and give life. It bent to my will, or I bent to it, and a single sprout grew. I gaped at the sudden bloom, at the thrill of it—and adrenaline flooded my veins.

The sprout exploded, growing in thickness and height in almost an instant. It traveled up, up, upwards, reaching toward the sky.

And then the growth stopped, and my power was yanked back as if held by a leash.

"*Tranquilla,* Terra. I know you are excited—the release of power can feel... overwhelming. Thrilling. But you *must* relax and remain calm if you want your commands to be obeyed. If you don't want to lose control."

Jana breathed a cantrip, and the giant stock dissipated, a green mist blowing gently away from us. She narrowed her eyes at me. "Again."

I nodded, exhaling to calm my stammering heart. But the image of flying debris and Dane's unconscious body stuck in my head.

Jana handed me a palm full of dirt. "Visualize what you want—a single bloom from only here."

I blew out a slow breath, concentrating on the Earth in my palm. I fed another tendril of power into the dirt, focusing on controlling it. But instead of the Earth blooming into a small growth, it flew off my hand with speed, exploding into a visual cacophony of flower buds, blinding us for a moment.

I uttered an obscenity. "I can't do this."

Jana squeezed my hand, and I met her gaze. "Is this what you are telling yourself?"

I shrugged.

"Terra, you were *born* to do this. You can—and you will. But you need to relax and calm yourself. Consider it a dance between letting instinct take over and remaining active in the process. *Feel* your power and *believe* you can control it. If you doubt yourself, you will lose every time."

I closed my eyes, blowing out an intentional breath. "I can do this," I whispered. "I know what to do."

I cleared the fauna from the ground and again sank my fingertips into the dirt. When I let my power flow into the Earth, this time, it was with an exhale. I did not control, but firmly guided it.

A single sprout grew about six inches off the ground. I felt the desire for it to continue blooming, but my magic remained there, hovering all around it, calm but not quite retreating.

"Hold," Jana commanded.

And I did, the little green sprout bending in the wind.

"One more," Jana instructed again.

One more sprout grew in its place.

"Hold." It held.

"Again."

I repeated the process under her instruction—at least fifty more times—until a small patch of soft-sprouted grass rustled there.

"Excellent. Now, I want you to do the same again but with more power. Bloom the entire field, but *only* the field."

I grinned, ready to do what I could *feel* I was born to do.

Wild flowers sprang up around us; daisies, prairie smoke, and columbine, budding in the between and spiraling around our bodies, formed intricate structures that spread like fire across the clearing. The rest of the Earth responded to them, shifting, allowing the growth to shape them too. The forest moved in harmony, a synchronized dance. I felt the sway and the breath of it as my creation took hold of that meadow—and only the meadow. Despite the slight sensation of unpleasantness from Jana's magic, the unfolding beauty mesmerized me with a symphony of red and yellow and fuchsia hues, and the music it played seemed to sing only to me.

Eventually, the flowers became so enlightened they flew from their stems, forming a circular ring that landed on the top of my head. *Crown, crown for a queen*, I heard whispered amongst them. At some point, Jana asserted her hold and pulled my power back. But when she did, the meadow remained as it had been a moment before. In all my wonder, I did not see the tears that had crept down her face.

She beamed, her eyes shining. "It has been said that what we create may save us. What you create, Earth Daughter, will deliver us."

———

JANA BID ME to show her a few more single callings, at first still linked, and then without her power ahold of me. In the end, she was satisfied with my progress. We portaled back to camp, and she sent me to the woods to continue exploring. Now that I had a sense of control, it came more naturally. The rest of the afternoon, I let the others prepare for the journey and wandered through the forest to continue my familiarization.

My walk through the woods was slow and indulgent. I let every touch of my fingers on a branch or a mossy covering leave a trace of me. At first, I was a botanist—reveling in the ability to incite bloom, to see small leaves sprout before my eyes. I studied each movement, eager for the reaction to one small brush of my finger. Dane had told me if he called for an apple, then a tree would grow one less fruit in its season. But for me, it felt the opposite. Somehow, I knew if I called for an apple, the tree would grow one more. I gave life to the Earth, and it gave it to me, as two conduits. Which came first, I could not tell.

I had also been told the more magic Witches used, the more it drained them. According to Dane, that was why some would conserve it before battle. His logic made sense and explained why it poured out of me with no control upon my first calling. But each time I flexed my power, I felt more awake, more energized. Like an atrophied muscle gaining strength within me. Maybe it was because Earth magic, in its essence, is pure life, the blood that pumps through everything around us.

I came upon a small clearing surrounded by sequoias that were fifty times my height. The sunlight had dimmed to an afternoon hue, revealing the lateness of the day. They were ancient trees. I knew this not just by their height or the thickness of their trunks, but because their roots extended throughout the clearing in an intricate, entangled way, woven together over centuries of growth.

I approached one of them, its vast size casting a long shadow over me. I ran my fingers down its bark, resting my forehead on the trunk and letting my nostrils fill with the sappy fragrance. And then I heard —or maybe felt—the vibration of a language old and strange, yet new and familiar.

Terragnata, it rumbled.

We see you, Queen of Earth, Daughter of the Mother. You honor us, creating, creating, creating. Life trails in your wake. Let us honor you.

I started at the words, spoken aloud and yet not, but I stayed still for fear the slightest movement would send the voice away. And as I remained there, an image floated into my mind.

A gift from the Earth.

I shook my head, heat pricking my eyes, not wanting to accept what the trees offered. How could they sacrifice themselves for me? Why?

We have lived a great many years in this life, and the previous, and the previous to that. We do not die, but our form rebirths. Do not cry for our sake, child. Receiving honors the giver.

I nodded. *Indeed.*

Taking a deep breath, I knelt in the soil of a small clearing. I lowered my fingers to the dirt, the cool Earth engulfing them. I slid my power down, feeling for every root that ran under the ground nearby. I sensed a pulse of life and thanked them silently for their strength over many centuries.

I took hold of those ancient roots, pulling them up as gently as I could. The ground began to rumble and disrupt all around me. My magic flowed up and through their massive trunks, touching the trees' every nerve ending. The half a dozen sequoias around me swayed, destabilized. I raised my hands, holding their energy between my fingers. I thanked them once more, then flicked my wrists, wincing at what came next. A bellowing crack indicated the breaking of one of these foundations. They snapped in half one by one, pushing the next down like a falling circle of dominos. But when they fell, their roots rose to catch them, placing them on the earthen floor with a gentleness befitting their sacrifice.

I shuttered my gaze, letting the wood unfold around me, picturing the enormous battleship of a history book I had poured through as a girl, a ship used by the seafaring warriors of Salamiere on their expeditions. I imagined the trunks of the sequoias splitting into long planks. Held together by flowing tree sap, the planks formed a massive hull, thick and impenetrable, save for oar holes that lined the port and starboard sides.

A disturbance vibrated all around me, the ground shifting in a dizzying way. The soil beneath my knees gave way to hard wood, dirt sifting out. I knew I was being raised up in my creation, but I did not break focus. In my mind's eye, I saw the roots crawling up the sides of the ship to form a large, twisted mast at the center of its body. The smaller roots danced around and into the hull, and I allowed them to take any shape they pleased, for function or form. There was the till and rudder; roots braided together to create the steering capability of the ship. And last came the sails. Harder and more intricate, I imagined each fiber of discarded bark splitting into millions, floating in the air. After they stilled, I coaxed them together, weaving them in a cross-stitch pattern I'd learned from my mother. And between each fiber, I left a slip of my power. For strength, for guidance, and for bravery, I whispered to them. The sails settled on the mast, my work finished.

I kneeled on the elevated bow, facing the stern of the ship. It was imposing, beautiful, and *mine*. I beamed at the creation, my heart feeling fuller than it had before. A loud, slow clap broke my moment of silent pride. Leuffen peeked out from behind one of the still-standing trees. More invisible clapping ensued, delivered by the rest of the observers I hadn't known were there, until a crowd applauded.

I SWUNG my feet over the side of the ship and pushed off, my waist landing in the ready hands of Leuffen, my palms resting on his shoulders. He spun me around, his arms extending me into the air above his head. I threw my head back and let a laugh escape. He put me down and wrapped me into his chest. "Well done, lass," he said softly.

He released me, and more of the crowd approached. Few I had spoken to before, but everyone came to admire the ship, to "ooh" and "ahh," and pepper me with questions about my construction technique. Apparently, most of them had been there for the weaving of the sails. I was told it was quite the sight, millions of bark fibers floating in the air one moment and then converging into sails the next. I even heard a few snickers followed by a "Well, that beats Dane's handiwork" or "What a waste of a day that was."

But despite the comments, Dane came over to me after the commotion had settled down. He grilled me on the choice of wood, strength of the sails, and position of the till. It was the most he'd spoken to me since I nearly killed him. He seemed genuinely excited to talk now, a true lover of learning.

Eventually, Jana emerged from the group. "I suppose I should have shown you control earlier," she said lightly. "Late this evening, we will launch both ships. Under the cover of night, we will inspect them and deem them seaworthy or not. Before dawn, the chosen ship will be well on its way toward the northern port city of Panderen, and we will make our way through the mountains."

By the time Leiya, Leuffen, and I began walking to camp, nearly every member of our group had congratulated, thanked, or complimented me, save for one unmistakable pair of green eyes.

"Ye never said ye were a shipbuilder," Leiya exclaimed. "How'd ye even know what te put where?"

I shrugged. "I studied them as a girl. I studied many things, actually. I read whatever I could get my hands on. But I always loved ships. I used to dream that I'd sail one far away from Argention. Before, I only wanted adventure, to see more of the world, to be more than the wife of a miner." I shook my head. "Now, I'd do anything to go back to the way things were—to have my family again. I almost feel ashamed I ever thought to leave them."

"Aye," Leuffen said quietly. "Et isna 'till the things we love are gone, that we appreciate them so."

"Well, Terra, she's a beauty. What're ye gonna name her? She's gotta have a name, ef she's te carry us all the way to Panderen." Leiya winked at me and then bit into her daily apple. I paused, thinking, walking just a few steps ahead of my friends. And then out of nowhere, like a restrained synapse finally fired, it came to me.

"Casmerre," I said, the familiar name warming my chest.

At that, Leiya choked and bent over, heaving and spewing half-chewed chunks of fruit. Leuffen just stopped in his tracks, frozen. I spun around to face them.

"What? Is something wrong with Casmerre?"

Leuffen, who had gone to thump his sister on the back, turned to me, his face pale and unreadable. "Why that name, Terra?"

I shifted on my feet, uncomfortable with their reaction. "It was the name of my late Shepard in Argention. Maybe it's stupid, naming a ship after a dog, but he was fearless in water. Even when the snow melt made the rivers violent, he could always keep up in a current and had a steady direction. Why?"

They stared back at me like I'd grown a second head. But a moment later, they recollected, straightening. "We 'ad a parrot when we were young, ye see, beloved by our family, but he died when a dog named Casmerre ate hem," Leiya said. "The similarity a' name jest caught me off guard, that's all."

I caught Leuffen shooting her a quick glare. "Is that it?" I asked, cocking my head.

Leiya only cleared her throat. "Ets me turn te scout. I'll see the two of ye later."

I snagged her by the back of her arm before she shifted. "Leiya," I searched her eyes for whatever she was hiding. "Be safe."

She just blinked, and then twisted into flight.

THEY CHOSE my ship in the end. It was lighter, faster, yet seemingly more impenetrable, according to Leuffen. "And after all, Wetches do like beautiful things," Leuffen had said with a wink.

I prepared my saddle bags and fastened my bedroll to Blackjack's hind with a pat of his rump. We were downsizing now, no more carts to carry large canvas tents and cots. Jana wanted the ability for a quick escape, should we need one. The evening fell heavy when I finished, and the Casmerre was nearly ready to depart. I mounted Blackjack, and we made our way down to the water. We were still about an hour's ride from camp, but the ship crew's many trips throughout the last few hours had forged the path well.

Sanah stood at the helm, already aboard, and I waved to her, hoping she could see me on shore by the light of the moon's reflection. I didn't see a wave back, but I could have sworn she touched her

hand to her chest—and perhaps her forehead. Leiya soared across the
water in falcon form, returning periodically to give updates by coded
cries. Everyone seemed to be loaded, save for twelve riders on the
beach, waiting to send our compatriots to what we all hoped was not
their impending doom. I noticed Leuffen to the side of the shore, in
deep conversation with Jana. It looked near contention; though
inaudibly, he was raising his voice more than was usually in his
nature.

It ended with an abrupt turn, and he made his way to the last
remaining rowboat, shaking his head, seemingly in frustration. I
dismounted and ran to him. The splashing of my boots in the shallow
water gave me away. He turned to me as I sprang up to him, wrapping my arms around his neck. Leuffen seemed ready for it and
enveloped me in a hug. We lingered there, two friends, not ready to
say goodbye.

He lowered me and pulled me into him once more, my head now
resting on his chest. "Lass," he whispered into my hair. "Dinna worry,
we'll be alright." I gazed up at him, unsure if I could trust his words,
knowing he held back. But a sincerity shimmered in his eyes, and the
way he'd watched out for me the past few weeks made me feel
comforted. Safe, even.

"I know there's something you're both hiding from me, I can feel
it," I said, and he grimaced in reaction. "But it's okay, truly. I know
you'll tell me when you're ready. And I just... well, I can't lose anyone
else."

He looked in pain then, unsure of what to say in response.

I stepped back from him, letting his arms drop. "Can you call
Leiya to come here, just for a minute?"

He inclined his head. "Aye." And a few moments later, she soared
toward us, changing right before her boots hit the sand.

"Eh, Terra, what's thes about? Ye know et takes me strength te
shift!" Leiya said.

I took each of their hands in mine and closed my eyes. If they
objected to my power's touch, they did not say. I sent a small bit of it

into each of them with an intention. And though the language of Witch magic and spells had long been lost to me, somehow I knew to say, "protegere eos."

When I opened my eyes, a soft glow rippled off them, scarce more than for a moment or two. And before I could explain, Leiya placed a hand on her heart and bowed. "Thank you, Terragnata, for yer protection and blessing. Et es a great honor, one I dinna deserve. But know that I will always serve ye with the same intention, te protect and defend." At that, she flew off again, her falcon form spreading its wings and gliding up into the moonlit sky.

Leuffen still stared at me a moment, conflict wearing on his face. But before I could probe, he knelt on one knee, maintaining his grip on my hand. "Aye, Terragnata, there isna one I'd rather serve. Ye have me promise te protect ye, en every way I can." And then he kissed my hand gently and rose, before turning towards the Casmerre.

He hesitated a step, glancing back, turning air over in his mouth as he weighed his words. "Et may nay be my place, Terra, so please forgive me. But ets me strong sense ye should stay away from Ezren. The bloke's an asset en a fight, but he's got no control over hes power... en many ways. Ye best keep yer distance, so ye dinna get hurt." And then he was off, rowing towards the Casmerre. I sent one final slip of power to my ship, blessing it in my way and leaving a small carving of its name on the stern.

I jogged back to the horses, wondering the entire way what he'd meant by *serve*, if he'd truly said all he'd wanted to say—and how he knew my full name.

CHAPTER FOURTEEN

CRASHING WAVES

$\mathcal{W}$e rode across the open beach, watching the Casmerre sail off into the distance. I ran Blackjack as fast as he would allow, given the small loads strapped to my sides. The sea salt in the air stuck to my face and my hair whipped all around me. I cried out at the exhilaration.

But it was not a joyful time—not with the group as serious as they were. Jana's orders put Parson at my front, and Ezren at my back. They were my shadows, in case of any trouble. It made for a silent journey to the Adimon Mountains. Parson spoke rarely on a normal day, and even less when set on a mission. And Ezren acted like I didn't exist, despite his position as my personal guard.

So we journeyed like that, with Jana in the lead, until a few hours before dawn. We came to the base of the range's imposing peaks, outlined in shape by the lingering moonlight. Tomorrow our real journey would begin, Jana said. We set up a small camp, just large enough for the twelve of us, our bed rolls fashioned around two fires like petals from the center of a flower. Parson slept to my left and Ezren to my right. One of them was to remain awake at all times, regardless of who else in the group was on watch.

Ezren volunteered to stay up first. He wandered several yards out, putting a safe distance between us. His silence had become increasingly loud, and I didn't understand it. I wanted to hate him for how he humiliated me in front of Leuffen. I wanted to despise him for the rejection. My body didn't share the sentiment, however. I could still sense when he was around, like smoke from a fire. And when he wasn't, I was both relieved and agitated. I played various scenarios in my head. In one, I would get up, walk over to him, and ream him out for his mixed signals, strike him across the cheek even. In another, I would just reach up to feel the short stubble of his face in my hands and pull him towards me.

I did neither. I only lay there, awake with my thoughts.

At some point, sleep came. But it didn't last, and when I opened my eyes, Parson and Ezren had already readied their mounts. Someone set out a small bit of breakfast for me, a few pieces of cheese and berries laid on a cloth to my left. Parson, I assumed. I gobbled down the food, condensed my bedroll, and made my way to Blackjack. We moved with quiet efficiency, as if our first night in the split group crystallized our new reality. Dane's withdrawn demeanor struck me the most, for he usually commanded conversation. I shot a glance over at him—he was fixing his horse's girth in silence. He worried about Sanah, I imagined.

I finished preparing my saddles and then walked up to Parson. "Thanks for the food," I said, extending his intricately woven handkerchief back to him.

He cocked his head at me. "Sorry, Terra, but that's not mine." And then he stuck his foot in the stirrup and swung his leg over his horse without another look in my direction.

My eyes moved back towards Ezren, but he was busy examining the underpart of his beast's hoof. So I just tucked it into my saddlebag and did the same as Parson. The rest of the twelve followed suit, and we were off once more. This time, to summit a mountain.

Breath slipped from my lungs as the range came into focus. The peaks were jagged and terrifying, but all the more stunning for it. After a few hours, we gained the vantage of elevation and could see the miles and miles of thick forest that we'd traveled through. Wildflowers and growths that called to me lined the mountain paths. I flexed my magic more and more, no longer insecure about control. If a leaning tree blocked our path, I would direct it to let us pass, or if the foliage became overgrown, I would bend it so that the horses could move through with ease.

I also was instrumental in bolstering the food supply. I wasn't the huntress, of course, for I had no bow nor Leuffen to verify my skills with one. But I could sense where the safe mushrooms burrowed or where the sweet berries thrived. I took pleasure in the usefulness, especially given the scrutiny I faced. Either Parson or Ezren was required to accompany me on my foraging. Neither spoke nor addressed me, but I made them carry my sack of spoils.

On the third day, we breached the tree line on one of the peaks Jana intended to cross, leaving us exposed to the elements, and the gods knew what else. The peaks were more visible then, boasting hard edges and snowcapped tops. Although vegetation grew scarce, I still loved to look at their lines—dramatic, powerful, and utterly perspective-inducing.

Despite the lack of roots and branches, I could coerce the rubble into forming a small rock hut for us to spend the night in. Again, we lit small fires and arranged our sleeping mats in the usual way.

"The mountains are beautiful, aren't they?" Dane said, sinking into a bedroll, his positioned next to Ezren's.

I looked up at his distant eyes. "They do have a way of making you feel small yet large all at once."

"How does your magic feel in them? Sifting through the rockery, I mean," he asked.

Heat crept up my neck, either from the fire or the green eyes I felt trained on me as I answered. "It feels different. Still like the Earth, but not quite alive in the way of the forest or the brush. Like pure existence, which I suppose the mountains are since they are formed through so many years of rain and sun and snow. I can sense their might with my magic, but they feel much older and more magnificent than anything I possess."

Dane nodded at my musing and lay down, his curiosity gone. I too fell into my bedroll, and for the first time since our travels began, I didn't think about who would lie beside me or watch me all night.

I SHOT UP, a deep sleep still heavy in my mind and on my chest. Something had woken me. Parson was gone from my left, so I risked throwing a glance over my shoulder to Ezren. He lay there, asleep as I'd never seen him before. And he was breathing fast, short, like he was having an unpleasant dream. I closed my eyes, willing myself to go back to sleep. But he started to mumble, an unsettled stream of consciousness—not quite coherent words. He tossed and turned, his murmuring growing louder. And then I saw it, a ripple of green scales running down his face, his neck, and further south.

I swore under my breath. *Could he accidentally shift from being too worked up in a dream state?*

I crawled to him and gave him a gentle shake by the shoulders. "Ezren," I whispered, "Ezren, you're dreaming." He stirred, slowly pulled from the grips of his nightmare. "Wake up," I pleaded. His eyes fluttered open, sleepy at first and then wide with terror. For a moment, I thought he would push me off or attack. But he only shuttered his velvet eyes once more and let out a long breath, his body relaxing into the ground. I could have sworn I saw two tears escape down the sides of his temples before he pulled me into his chest, his hand on my mid back, gentle. My mouth fell open at the smooth and natural move, more familiar than he'd ever been with me. And maybe it was the shock—but I went willingly, laying my ear on his heart, absorbing its elevated beat. He fell back asleep, soft snores evidence of a more peaceful rest than before, and I wondered if he was ever fully awake to begin with.

Despite my acute awareness of our close proximity, it lulled me to sleep. The next time I woke, I was back on my own bedroll, with Parson asleep beside me and the fierce-eyed Dragon Fae nowhere in sight.

THE FOLLOWING FEW DAYS, Ezren continued to ignore me, but his energy seemed softer. I knew for sure it was him who left me food each morning, him who rolled up my bedroll if I went to relieve myself before packing my saddle bags. He always stayed near but never too close, and though part of me was driven insane by it, the other part of me relaxed into the routine. At least it didn't feel like the dead of winter in his presence. He was kind, but seemingly uninterested. Something held him back. I had to accept that.

"We will crest the top of the final peak today," Jana said to Parson while we rode. "After that, we descend toward the valley."

Parson only grunted in response. We were all weary from almost a week of riding through the steep, rocky cliffs. Jana wanted us to cross many miles south of the sea, to deny Fayzien the advantage of nearby water should we meet him.

I had seen glimpses of the Nameless Valley through small clearings in the trees or trail bends around the mountain. The vast arid landscape that I knew as the Endless Ocean actually *looked* like an ocean, in a way. The plain spread wide, barren of trees and boundless. Something struck me every time I laid eyes on it; the valley felt wrong... as if it dipped below the sea level, and I wondered if they withheld some detail about the place—a piece of the puzzle that was missing.

"Terra," Parson said, snapping my attention up. "Be on alert. This is no time for daydreaming." His eyes shifted to the warrior behind me, and I turned back on instinct.

Ezren's gaze narrowed on me. Over the last few weeks, I had done my best to resolve my mind and train my emotions to accept the Dragon as a neutral protector. But just then, the wind blew past him, sending his scent to me. Piñon and the forest after rain. I'd noticed his scent before, in a subtle way, but this time it hit me like a wall. I faced forward, my skin beginning to itch as the friction of the saddle beneath my womanhood became quickly unbearable.

Parson cocked his head at me, his nose crinkling. "Are you all right, Terra?"

I nodded, gritting my teeth, attempting to survive whatever bizarre reaction my body was having. Then his eyes widened, and he whipped back forward, the tips of his ears reddening.

I continued to breathe through the reaction, and eventually the discomfort reduced from acute to bearable. As we approached the Nameless Valley, the energy turned tense in our group. Ezren remained a bit closer and Parson a bit more watchful. Quiet chatter grew into sharp silence. I tensed, too, seeing each rock as a weapon, each tree as potential shrapnel.

We stopped to gather and hunt once more before crossing over to the other side of the mountain for our descent. It was Parson's turn to search for game, and Ezren's to hold my sack of berries and root vegetables. I could've just summoned them, but Jana insisted we conserve all magic, even when I argued that using mine made me feel stronger.

I searched for anything in the rock rubble that lived above the tree line. Finally, I found a patch of fungi that I knew would be delicious with whatever rabbit Parson caught, and I yelped with glee. Ezren dashed to my side at once, eyes wild in search of danger.

I just looked at him and laughed, shaking my head at how on edge he was. This seemed to irritate him, and he broke his silence.

"What?" he demanded, his arms folded across his chest.

His direct address caught me off guard, and it dawned on me how starved of his voice I'd been.

"Oh, now you speak to me." I snorted, turning back to the

mushrooms. He walked over and said nothing, opening up the sack for me to place my spoils into. His scent hit me again, and the itching on my body resumed. I clamped my jaw shut and only took small necessary sips of air until I finished loading the sack and stood.

He turned and made to walk away.

"What do you dream about, Ezren?" The words escaped me before I had time to process them. There had been more of his nightmares, and I always woke him with my touch. But I'd never stayed with him again like I had that first night. "It's my turn to ask a question."

The Dragon froze. After a few long moments, he took what seemed to be a pained breath and turned to face me. "I dream of your screams, Terra. I hear them, the ones from the cleansing, the ones from the crevice, over and over again. And I hear ones that I know you have not yet let out but that will come. And I wake, in terror, that I will be able to do nothing to stop them."

"Why?" I asked softly, feeling my face redden. "Why do you dream of me if you can't bear to speak to me? If you were so repulsed by my touch when Leuffen saw us?"

I could sense the stillness in him now, unmoving. "Not your turn." His stony expression gave nothing away, but a whisper of challenge laced his words.

I crossed my arms and shrugged my shoulders at him to go on.

His eyes danced. "Why do you think I dream of you?"

My heart thundered in my chest.

"That's not a fair question," I whispered, retreating a step.

Ezren took a step forward. "Fine. How do you *think* I feel about you, then, Terra?" His voice was near a growl.

"How you feel about me?" My breath hitched. "You barely look at me. You—you *left* when I had to *humiliate* myself in front of everyone by recounting what happened with Fayzien." I threw my hands in the air. "I suppose you're kind, but uninterested."

Darkness flickered in Ezren's expression. "No one has ever

accused me of being kind. And for what it's worth, I left that room so I wouldn't destroy it."

My chest flared, his comment burning yet... emboldening. "So, what is it, then? Are you disgusted by me? By your interest in me?"

"I had to create some space between us. There are reasons, good ones, that we can never be together in that way. It's not my place to say, but I *cannot* allow myself to feel that way for you."

My breathing grew deep and labored, my throat tight at the idea that my feelings were reciprocated.

"But do you?" I murmured, searching his eyes. "... feel that way about me?"

He stayed silent for a moment. "Of course I do," he rasped guiltily.

His simple answer was all it took to break the wall I'd built. I didn't care about whatever reason held him back. I prowled to him, holding his stare. We both held our breath.

"I've had *everything* taken from me. And the only thing I've learned is that *this*," I gestured to us and everything around us, "is fleeting."

And then I drank in his scent, letting it fill me up. The itching was so intense it turned into a heated buzz that settled on my skin and blurred my vision. His gaze sharpened as I lifted my hand to his unmoving chest.

"You have no idea what you're doing," Ezren ground out through his teeth, fighting the instinct to breathe. "Your Fae senses are returning to you as we near the realm, and you don't know how to control them."

I dragged my eyes up and down his body, letting my fingers travel down his abdomen. "Does it burn for you, too?" I whispered, not needing a response. That primal part of me knew the answer. He didn't move or say a word, remaining as still as stone. "Just breathe, Ezren," I said in a voice that sounded distant to my ears. I was all instinct now, guided by my growing Fae senses.

My fingers reached the top of his trousers, catching on the lip

146

where they were fastened. At this, he sucked in a short breath, an unintended reaction. But it was enough. He inhaled fully then, drinking the air as if it was the first time he'd breathed in an hour.

His pupils dilated into Dragon slits, his hand flying to my throat and clamping down firmly, but not dangerously. I let out a small noise, and the corners of his mouth turned up. "I've never been very good at control either," he murmured, cocking his head. "Always so damned flushed."

The sack dropped from his other hand, and his arm wrapped around my hips, pulling me into him. My body was one rhythm then, a drum that beat for one thing. His fist tightened into the tunic fabric on my low back and he brushed my bottom lip with his thumb. But he did nothing more, frozen as if waiting for my consent. So I pulled his face to mine, and his lips parted, meeting in a release of pent-up desperation.

We were two waves crashing into each other, swells that could not be stopped. He let out a small moan and placed one hand under my backside, pulling me up and into him, leading my legs to hug his waist. His other hand tangled in my hair, guiding my head in our kiss. My heart exploded. I needed him more than I'd ever needed *anything*.

Without meaning to, I let my power flow into him. He recipro-cated. It felt right, unlike what I'd experienced with Fayzien or Jana. I let my hands run everywhere, grazing over the ripples of his muscled arms and back. His body responded to my touch in more ways than just the male. And while we explored each other, our magics did as well. If mine was life and vibrance, his was the wind and light, wild and heated one moment, and a cool summer breeze the next. He moved us, pressing my back into a nearby boulder. I could feel the swell of him now, the hardness that told me irrevocably he wanted me. He ran his tongue up my neck, and a shudder went through me at the recollection of the last time. I unbuttoned my shirt, not breaking my kiss, eager to remove any barrier between us. But he stilled.

"Terra," he breathed into me. "Look."

All around us, rubble floated in small, soft, individual green glows. It looked like thousands of emeralds hung in the air, as if our magic had come together upon instinct, forming a life-size kaleidoscope right there on the side of that mountain.

He set me down and cupped my cheek in his hands, his pupils circles once more. "Not like this," he breathed. He pressed his lips to my forehead and stepped away from me, taking my hand in his and pulling me to follow him back to camp, our soaring emeralds falling gently down around us.

CHAPTER FIFTEEN

THE TRANSMUTATION

"Alright," Jana said, after we all re-mounted our horses. "We should cross over the peak in the next hour and be back in the Fae and Witch realms. Once we pass the tree line on the other side, we'll make camp for the night. Tomorrow, we send scouts to the valley. Should everything look undisturbed, we will descend at dusk, hopefully crossing the valley during the dark of the late evening. Understood?"

We all nodded and urged our horses to walk on.

As we made our way to the pass, an overwhelming sense that something was off clung to my every nerve. Not only did the bizarre and wild itching hit me time and again, but my head tightened, and my breath shortened.

I breathed through the itching spells and pillaged my canteen, determined not to let my sickness slow the group down. Blackjack whinnied and pranced as if he, too, felt the wrongness, or at least my unease. I dug my heels into his sides and swallowed my nausea, my eyes trained on the horizon.

At some point, Ezren may have asked me if I was okay, but I only jerked my head, focusing on getting through the discomfort. I survived the better part of an hour like this, relieved that we were about to cross the peak and make our way down the other side. If it was altitude sickness, descent would be the only cure.

And then it came into focus—the shimmering, faint glow of whatever magical barrier had been erected to keep humans in their realm, and away from the Fae. I could still see the valley through the blur—it looked the same as it had from the previous hundred vantage points I'd seen it. Close to the barrier, however, the vista was obscured by a slight sparkling haze.

I expected a sensation of tingling, or maybe nothing, as Blackjack set his hooves over the line. Instead, when my mount made his way through the webbed film, the pressure in my head became *searing* pain. My vision blurred, and I tumbled from the horse, screaming in agony. Everything hurt; it felt like the cleansing all over again, but without Jana's magic attempting to block some of the pain from registering.

Ezren leaped off his mount, crouching before me in an instant. "Terra, can you tell me where it hurts?"

I couldn't form words, couldn't do anything but cry out. I pressed my palms to my temples, signaling at the pressure in my head. Voices were all around me now, and Ezren yelled at the Witches to *do something, to fix it.* Dane tried to take my hand, but he yelped upon touching me, jumping back.

Although the pounding in my head was ruthless and unending, I heard Dane exclaim. "The bitch's power bit me!"

Ezren spat a frosty reply. "If I ever hear you call her that again, I will make sure that Fire of yours burns you from the inside out."

Then Jana's voice cut through my cries, which were now alternating between whimpering and screaming. "I think there must be a small part of the cleansing that we couldn't complete in the human realm. The spell must be trying to finish itself now. Ezren, can you see if Terra's power rejects you? It needs outside magic to fuel its working. I fear Terra's power is feeding on itself."

Tears streamed down my face, and I wished desperately to lose consciousness. "Please, stop it, Ezren, just end it," I begged, hysteria bleeding into my voice. A thousand knives shot through my skull, the pain reverberating down the rest of my body. I should have been numb or passed out, but it seemed the spell was determined to make me feel every slice, every ounce of pain. "Or just kill me if you can't," I whispered.

He pulled me into him, cupping my wet face and forcing my dull eyes to meet their antithesis in his. "You are a fighter, Terra. You need to help me, so I can help you. Can you do that?"

I nodded, my eyes shut tight, and tried to open myself to his power. It was difficult, unlike just hours before. We had been intimate then, and my guard was down. Now, I had walls thrown up in reaction to the most excruciating physical pain I'd ever experienced. I cried out and panted, battling to force them down and let him in. It seemed the more I fought, the less ground I won.

"She needs to open, Ezren, and she's exerting herself too much," Jana said. "You need to join with her."

"No," Ezren replied.

"It is *not* enough just to send your Fae power into her, and you know it. You have to take hold of hers and join them; it is the only way she'll feel your strength," Jana protested.

"You know I can't do that, Jana," Ezren hissed.

"Oh, for the gods' sake, it's not a coupling, it's a joining, and it's the only way to end her pain," Jana shot back. "Unless... there is one other way," Jana said bitterly. "You could grant her request."

I was shaking now, my voice hoarse from screaming, my face streaked with tears. Ezren looked at me, and I looked back through hooded eyes as he brushed the moisture from my cheeks. "Forgive me," he said to himself, or to me, I wasn't sure. And then he bent his face to mine and tilted up my chin in his thumb. He kissed me, hesitantly at first. And though my pain remained, the rest of my body reacted, and I relaxed. At that opportunity, I felt all of his magic flow into me. His magic took mine into his, weaving them together in what felt like a more... deliberate way than before. It had been an accidental exploration of our magics when we kissed last. This was more intimate—like an intentional claiming.

I felt a disturbance deep inside of me, a small well of power that must have still been buried there. My mind seared with pain again at that power fighting for release, but I didn't scream or cry out or resist. I just kept focusing on Ezren's touch, his exploring tongue in my mouth, his arms tight around me, and his magic flowing through me. And I pulled on that magic more, needing his strength, which he gave willingly. I was giving and taking, and so was he. Our magics churned together, to the point I did not know what was his and what was mine. And then, as if they'd always been, our powers were one, and a shock reverberate through him and me. The pain was gone, just a small throbbing whisper of memory.

He held me there, our sweaty foreheads pressed together while we panted for minutes before untangling our magics. And when it felt safe to pull away, I saw more than my tears on his face. He looked at me in disbelief, like I'd changed somehow.

"You have," he whispered, and I was too confused to realize he'd answered my silent thought.

I scanned the group—everyone else stared at me, too. Ezren reached up, outlining the shape of my ear. My hand shot to the other.

And felt the soft but distinct point of a Fae ear.

WE RESUMED OUR DESCENT, but this time Ezren held me at his front, Blackjack tied off the back of his stallion's saddle. I ensured them all I was fine to ride, but he'd insisted.

Not just my ears changed. I could feel additional length on my limbs, and the strength they now carried. I never possessed a fully human body, just a constrained Fae one, Jana said, so the change was not so extreme that I grew a foot and multiplied my strength by a factor of ten.

But what Jana hadn't realized, she told me with an apology, was that during the cleansing, she should have freed more than just a Witch's Earth magic and memories. Fae magic lingered there, buried by Fayzien, which demanded release the moment we entered the Fae realm.

What that magic was, what it meant, remained unknown to us all.

I hadn't fully appreciated the advantage the Fae held over me when we fought, just because of their bodies, so being several inches taller and stronger than before made a vast difference. Ezren still stood a head above me, but he didn't have to bend more than a small tilt of his head for his eyes to meet mine. And there were my ears, which now formed sharp points. No streams of water presented themselves, nor pools, nor mirrors, so I had no opportunity to admire them. Ezren, however, indulged himself. Many times on our ride, I found him smiling at them, or reaching up to give them a gentle touch.

"What is the *matter* with you?" I demanded, half annoyed, half delighted, turning around as much as I could after the third caress. I was also being driven a bit mad by the hand that rested firmly on my belly, holding me close while we rode. That was the issue with a single saddle; given we shared it, my womanhood pressed into the pommel far more than it typically should have.

I sighed, attempting to think of anything to distract my mind from the massive male body pressed into my back. "Your turn to ask a question."

I could almost feel his smile radiate from behind me. "I believe I'm owed two questions, *Bellatori*."

"Fair's fair."

"What was your favorite thing to do in the human realms? In your free time, I mean. Chase boys? Knit quilts? Or perhaps you were a skilled carver, always whittling by the fire."

I snorted. "I think I was more likely to chase frogs than boys." I paused a moment. "I loved to read—stories mainly, but anything I could get my hands on. We were a small town, but so many passed through to buy our silver. The head schoolteacher knew I was one of the few girls whose family had bothered to teach her literacy, and he always found new material for me."

The arm that wrapped around me tightened almost imperceptibly. "A curious mind, then," he murmured into the back of my head.

I grinned. "Always."

"So you know—silver is a magic suppressor... it is made and spelled in the form of cuffs, chains, binds." The Dragon-shifter's tone darkened slightly. "You should know that if you don't already."

A breeze blew stray strands of hair into my face and I cleared them with a pff. "Jana thinks that's why Fayzien chose Argention—the town suppressed my magic. Even so, I don't think I could remove my necklace. It's all I have left of my mother."

"I would never let you, *firebreather*. In any event, it's likely too small to make a real difference in your power."

A minute passed, and we rode in silence, me leaning back into his warmth. "You have another question, Dragon shifter."

His chuckle wrapped around my ears. "I suppose I do..." He hesitated. "What do you desire most in this world?"

I considered. "If you'd asked me a month ago, I would have said to be free. Free of a life of boredom in Argention, an arranged marriage, and tedious labor. But now... I don't know. It seems silly to want safety, but after my family, after everything..." I trailed off.

Ezren's hold on me tightened more, his hand a protective grip on my abdomen. "It is not stupid at all to want to feel safe, Terra."

I pressed my eyes together, desperate to shift the topic to something lighter, something that didn't weigh on my heart as heavy as thoughts of my mother's hair slipping through floorboards.

"My turn. What's 'a coupling'?" The word still floated in my mind from my painful, exhilarating change.

I felt him still behind me, silent for a few beats of his horse's hooves. He cleared his throat. "It is like a joining, but ehm, more personal, shall I say."

"That does not *at all* explain what it is."

He shifted in the saddle, exhaling. "It would be a joining where one would, um, enter the other."

I cocked my head, confused. "But you did enter me."

"I did not enter you!" Ezren whispered. "With my magic, yes, but not in that way. I meant—I meant in the *male* way."

"Oh," I said, heat blooming on my neck. "Have you ever done it?"

"Once," he said, his voice low. "And I will never again."

"Why?"

"Not your turn, Terra," he said, forcing lightness into his tone.

His words sent a pang to my chest, a small wound. He didn't trust me enough to share the experience. I sensed pressing him would be futile.

"I haven't seen you use your magic yet," I said, changing the subject. "Which I guess isn't unusual, as Leuffen told me Fae usually save it for battle. Will you show me?"

His mood relaxed. "Mine is a light of sorts. Not sunlight. There can be a heat to it similar to my Dragon Fire, I've been told. It has a precision and breadth; it does not need to be one thing nor the other." He opened his tanned broad hand in front of me. "Like your power," he whispered into my hair, "it can be used for destruction or creation." A small glow omitted from his palm, a ball of moving light, more beautiful than any magic I'd seen before. It seemed to dance on his skin, not flickering like a flame but ebbing and flowing—pulsing. And then he closed his hand, the light vanishing. "Better not let Jana see," he said, his voice low. "She's rabid about us conserving our power."

"Mine does not feel like it needs conserving, though she keeps saying so. When I use it, I feel stronger. I know it sounds unusual..." I shrugged.

Ezren chuckled. "That doesn't surprise me. Can I run my power and strength dry, calling on my strange magical light? Yes—it's limited by what's inside me. But you? An Earth Witch has no worry of running out of Earth."

WE REACHED the tree line and made camp. Tomorrow we would cross the valley. We arranged the bedrolls in the usual way, six around both fires. Parson volunteered for first watch, and I lay on my mat, eyes wide open and listening for the breathing around me to become routine.

It did finally, and I rolled to my side. "What are you doing?" he breathed as I crawled in his direction.

"You know exactly what I'm doing," I replied hotly. He pulled me on top of him, and I let my hips rock slowly back and forth.

"Terra," he whispered, his hands skimming my waist. I felt a slight twitch from underneath me, and my insides stumbled. "Not like this."

My body tightened in anticipation, and I exhaled in frustration. "Why not?"

He smirked and something mischievous glinted in his expression, which had the unfortunate effect of making him more attractive. "Once you've lived more than a hundred and fifty years, you learn some things are meant to wait."

I gaped at him, seeing his face clearly under the night sky, given my newly enhanced eyes. Leiya had mentioned his age was above that of a Witch, but hearing the number cross his lips had me in awe again. "One hundred and fifty! But you don't look a day over twenty-eight... in human years, of course."

Ezren brushed the strands of hair from my face, and brought his lips close to my ear. "While I may have the looks and stamina of a young male, there are certain things in which I am *far* superior to a twenty-something." Strong hands pressed into my hip bones, pinning me in place, his tone turning lethal. "And when I show you them, you will scarcely be able to hold in your power, let alone your voice. So no, not tonight, nor any night until we get to Valfalla. No matter how much you beg." And then he stood easily, taking me with him—laying me on my bedroll.

"And feel free to beg, *Bellatori*." His whispered words tickled my skin, sending a shiver down my spine. "It will only serve to delight me more."

He kissed me on top of the head, like that was that.

But of course, that was *not* that—I was fuming with desire and mortified at the denial. In no world was I going to beg him, but I had a better idea. I almost lost the nerve to lack of experience, but I looked back at Ezren, eyes closed with a stupid smirk pasted to his face.

If you tease, I tease, Dragon shifter.

I unbuttoned the top of my trousers, noting the twitch in his ears. I slipped my first two fingers into my mouth, wetting them. And then, I ran them down the opening of my pants, making small circles on my point of pleasure, like Leiya had instructed me so many days before. A bolt of something foreign ran through me, and my body jerked. The feeling seemed to coil through my abdomen, all the way to a heat in my throat. I continued for longer than I'd planned—delighted by the unexpected lightness the new sensation conjured—before I remembered why I'd begun in the first place. I looked back at Ezren to find him staring at me with what I could only describe as murderous lust.

He rose, slipping underneath my blanket in the blink of an eye. He towered over me and drew my hand from my trousers. "Do not move a muscle," he growled into my ear.

Before he replaced my hand with his own, Parson appeared out of nowhere.

"Oh good, you're up," he said to Ezren. "We have to wake everyone. Fayzien is almost here."

CHAPTER SIXTEEN

NAMELESS VALLEY

*N*ot much could have killed my desire then, given how my new Fae body seemed to have needs I was *completely* unprepared to control. But at the mention of Fayzien, the heat in my veins turned to ice, and I leapt to my feet faster than I was used to, buttoning my trousers.

Ezren laid a steadying hand on my back. "Where?"

He's here, he's here, he's here. A primal charge surged through my veins—activating my every nerve.

"I saw some movement in the valley, so I shifted to get a closer look. It was Fayzien; I'd know those blue eyes anywhere. He has a full Viri company with him." Parson grimaced.

"Shit," Ezren muttered.

I forced air through my nostrils, blowing out the fear churning with a dizzying need for revenge. "What's a company?"

"A Viri company? Oh, maybe five hundred warriors at best, a thousand at worst," Dane answered from behind us. "Don't worry, sweet Terra, your lover here can probably kill a hundred Fae foot soldiers with a single fiery exhale."

My jaw loosened at the word lover.

"I will not slaughter Viri warriors, as I've told Jana numerous times. Nor will I expose my shift to a thousand witnesses. But thank you for the clear admiration of my skill in battle," Ezren shot back.

The blurring fury Fayzien's name dredged up in me ebbed for a moment. Viribrum was a Fae kingdom at odds with the Witches of Drakkar. So at odds, Jana thought them set to invade. My return was supposed to quell that tension.

"Why would Fayzien have the support of Viri warriors?" He had supposedly acted for the Nebbiolon Witch Queen in kidnapping me —and killing my sire—due to believing I threatened his position. *Why would he have thousands of Fae soldiers at his disposal?*

"I have no idea." For the first time, Dane was without an answer.

He's here. My blood sang for action, to demand why he murdered them, to gift him with the same fear he'd forced on my mother when he stole her life.

We woke the remaining slumberers. Under Jana's direction, we packed up and headed for higher ground. She wanted a full picture of Fayzien and the company before we made a move.

We crept through the brush. I did my part, thickening the wood for additional cover and parting the foliage when we advanced off-trail. And as I did, I inhaled every ounce of magic I could. Storing—building.

Today will be the last day he draws breath.

Eventually, we came to a clearing with a small rock overhang. We left the horses and a few soldiers under tree cover. Jana, Ezren, Parson, Dane, and I approached the edge, and I let the bushes stretch a little so that we could crouch behind them.

The sky wore a hazy bronze color, indicating the hour before dawn. Even from a mile out with no sunlight, I could tell it was Fayzien. I suppose the combination of my improved range of vision and intuition solidified the recognition, for a female can always sense the wrongness of a male who transgressed against her.

"Can we maneuver around them?" Dane asked. "Portal, perhaps?"

"Dane, you know how dangerous it would be to split up. And don't think for a minute Fayzien wouldn't sense the portal and intercept you. We have to be strategic," Jana replied.

I ground my teeth. "What we need to do is kill Fayzien."

"Direct engagement is out of the question. He has nearly a thousand Fae warriors with him. And he'll let every last one of them die before we can get to him," Jana said.

"You all swore to me that if we were to meet Fayzien again, you would do whatever it takes to help me kill him. You cannot deny me now." My voice was foreign—cold. I could barely hear it over the sound of my own blood pumping, ringing through my ears.

Ezren turned to face me. "I know you don't feel a strong connection to the Fae, but they are your father's kind, your kind. There may be cousins you have never known in that valley, family you should one day like to meet. I have relations I have not seen for a century, friends I have fought alongside in battle, that could lie in wait down there. I don't doubt you could raise the Earth and end them all, burying them in your rage and vengeance. But trust me when I tell you, it won't bring your family back. Only a heavier burden to carry the rest of your life."

I looked down at my hands, examining the point at which the flow of my power sprouted. My throat tightened. "I can't leave him alive," I whispered.

"I know," Ezren said to me.

"We need to lure him away from the group," he continued, addressing the others. "If we can separate him from his warriors, Terra and I can handle him. The rest of you will have to use your Witch magic to hold the company, to prevent them from swarming the mountainside."

"And how do you suppose we do that? What makes you think Fayzien will leave his warriors?" Dane asked.

"Me." A plan formed in my mind. "He won't waste a moment if he thinks I'm alone and unguarded. He'll come running."

Before Ezren could negate the idea of using me as bait, a loud cracking ripped through the early morning air, and we all nearly jumped from behind our brush covering. Fayzien's voice cascaded over the valley. "Hello, Terra and rabid band of rebels. It is lovely to see you all again."

My mouth flew open at the impossible amplification. The others looked weary but unsurprised.

"What a clever trick that was. I'm sure Janathia's dirty idea, to send a decoy. But don't you worry, I took care of the Casmerre easily enough," Fayzien's chilling voice boomed around us.

"Why is he talking about Casmerre?" Ezren directed his cool words at Jana.

"No," I breathed, fear twisting in my gut for Leiya, Leuffen, Sanah, and the others. "Casmerre is what I named the ship."

Dane swore, the words a cry of pain that stuck in his throat. The rest of them looked at me the way the twins had when I said that name. Ezren appeared as if I struck him. "What?" I demanded.

No one said a word. "When I told the twins what I'd named the ship, they acted like I'd designated it the devil's spawn. They said it was the name of a dog that had killed their parrot. Can *someone* tell me why my dog's name is so offensive?"

Jana relaxed just a fraction, still on edge, but not Ezren, whose skin neared the color of his eyes. I narrowed my gaze at him, but then Fayzien's voice rang once more.

"Terra, my dear, I have something of yours. Sweet, sweet Giannina was so distraught after your disappearance from Argention. What a minx you are to have left her and her handsome brother worrying after you! What a worrier, that one. Quite taken with you, I believe. What eyes he had! Clear as crystal. Just like Gia's. I had to leave him there, though—he was a nasty complication. But the lovely Giannina, well, she came oh so willingly after I told her I knew where you were..."

I stopped hearing him; my pulse drummed and my head swarmed with rage. Without thinking, my power flowed out of me like lightning from clouds. It rumbled down the mountainside, towards the valley, giving me a strange response from that place. It shook the peaks but left the grass-covered plain of the valley untouched. I felt only a vacuum of nothingness, dark and devoid of life—so unlike the pure existence of the surrounding rocky peaks. It made no sense. I should have heard the call of the Earth, answering to my magic.

Fayzien's voice cackled in response to my outburst, reverberating against the sharp mountains at our backs.

"Something is wrong." I shook my head. "There is no life in that valley; I could sense nothing."

Jana ran a hand through her silver hair. "Maybe it's of the dead after all," she murmured.

Before I could ask what that meant, she continued. "Terra, we go with your plan. Get as close to the plain as you can without actually touching it—there should be some Earth at the base of the mountain slope you can use to your advantage. Ezren, do not leave her side. Parson, see if you can get a better look in your shift to make sure he doesn't have the human with him. If he doesn't, give us a sign to show our position—a swan dive in your raven form. Once Fayzien sees us without Terra, it's up to her to get Fayzien to pursue. Parson can help unless the company is overrunning the rest of us. We'll try to hold them on the lower hillside for as long as possible to minimize casualties. They will undoubtedly begin surging towards us. Everyone must go on foot; mounts will be too slow on the cliffs. Understood?"

We all nodded, Dane struggling to keep the tears from his eyes. I swallowed my own fears, pushing back thoughts of Sanah drowning in the sea amongst our other friends. A moment later, Ezren and I took off in one direction, with Parson flying above us, while the rest of the group headed into the unknown.

I RAN FASTER than before in my new body, but I still willed the Earth to help us both. Within minutes, Ezren and I ran about a mile.

We panted when we stopped, attempting to slow our breath and train our eyes and ears.

And there it was, a swooping dive from a black raven, rising up and facing the mountain. Parson. Good. That meant Fayzien didn't have Gia with him. *He must have been bluffing.* The thought bloomed weak relief, knowing in my gut that it was unlikely. He knew the ship's name, and Gia's name, somehow.

Parson flew to the other group, signaling help needed on their front. *We need to make this fast.*

We pressed our backs together as if we were about to perform a dance we'd rehearsed a thousand times. I raised my palms and chose four trees around us, sycamores that peaked above the rest. I thrust my power into them, sending their tops higher. I asked their sparse leaves to rustle in an unnatural, eye-catching way.

Here, they whispered over the valley, carrying my message to Fayzien. *Here, she waits for you.*

We held our breath, every minute that passed thick with anticipation. I wished I could see the rest of the group, to know how they fared.

"He's not coming," I worried, nauseous at the inaction. My skin itched for a fight I'd held in, a battle I'd waged in my head for weeks now.

And then Fayzien appeared in front of me.

One glimpse, and the last time I'd stood before him rushed back. I was naked, exposed—violation seeping through me. I'd expected to think of my mother in that moment, of the family I'd lost. But even then, he ripped that honor from me, reducing me to the shame I felt and buried, the violation wrapped up in an expanse of grief so wide I'd forgotten all about it.

But of course, I hadn't truly forgotten.

After an eye's blink, I registered it was not actually him. Disappointment and relief washed over me. His image blurred as if it were merely a reflection on the water's surface.

"You really think I'm stupid enough to meet you on my own? My gods, Ezren, I know you have thrice the years of strategy, but how could you think me *so* novice? I didn't come to be the Manibu by playing into the hands of others." Fayzien's hair-raising cackle rang out, eyes sparkling as he taunted us.

"You monster—"

"My, my, my, someone has come into her Fae figure ever so nicely," Fayzien cut in, his gaze running down my body, his tongue running the length of his lips.

Ezren growled in response.

"Oh, I see," Fayzien drawled. "How delicious this is, two Fae lovers, both forgotten by Viribrum. Tell me, Ezren, do you think of Esmie when you feel her underneath you? Or rather, is it the image of the fine Pri—" Before he could finish, Ezren slashed his blade across the image, anger rippling off him like I'd never seen.

Fayzien's mirage reformed, now grinning madly. "Ah, don't want me to ruin the big surprise, do you... Well, that is utterly fine by me. I do love surprises," he crowed with a wink.

Focus, Terra. "You bore me with your gaming," I bit out. "Where is Gia?"

"Ahh, yes, Giannina. Such a delicate, lovely girl. Or woman, I should say, for are you a girl if your breast swells with milk for a babe? I will tell you, I have never enjoyed the human scent, but hers? So fertile, so rich. Almost *unnaturally* mortal. I nearly wish it was me that put the babe there," Fayzien chuckled to himself. "Well, never say never..."

If fire flooded my veins before, it turned to molten lava now. "You talk incessantly." I let out a rumble that shook the surrounding peaks, loosening rubble from above the tree line. The noise rang loud, and I let it build, showing him my power.

This is my domain. I am the Earth. Here, Fayzien bows to me.

I knelt in the dirt, taking joy in the feel between my fingers. I sent an image into the Earth, commanding, pleading for help. It rose around us, blurring out Fayzien's water mirage until it dissipated, hanging in the air like a paused dust storm. I could see very little, but I cared not. I raised the dirt everywhere on that mountainside. "Find him, take me to him," I whispered to every spec of Earth that dangled in the air around us. The dirt swayed at first, the building of a hurricane. Ezren placed his forearm around my middle, pulling me up into him.

The particles whirled away, surrounding us one moment and gone the next. We blinked our eyes open to see the rumbling storm heading northeast. Towards the valley. I looked at Ezren, guilty and pleading.

Every fiber of my being needed to follow that storm.

He nodded, soot coating his features, knowing my intention at once. "Okay."

"Will you be able to control it?"

"I don't know. I'll try."

"What about the witnesses?"

"Fuck it," he returned his blades to his back strap and unfastened it. "We need to move, turn around, and spread your arms."

I did, and Ezren tightened the leather harness around me. I felt the comfortable weight of the swords and he placed a hand on the back of my neck.

"If anything goes wrong," he said, his voice low, "if I lose control, one well-timed throw of your knife to my eye should do it. Don't hesitate."

I didn't have a moment to object—he ran more than a dozen yards away from me and began to change. I hadn't seen him shift into Dragon form before. It looked far less graceful and far more painful than the twins or Parson shifting. His Fae body seemed to fight his will—he screamed, his head twisting in unnatural angles, veins threatening to burst from his neck. Green scales emerged, his limbs contorted—until fiery eyes and a slowly swishing tail swung at me. I approached him, but he reared on his hind legs, flaring his nostrils and flapping his wings.

Roots sprang out of the ground and circled the Dragon's ankles, tightening under my direction. Distant screams, pitched and unnatural, rustled the trees. *No time for games.*

The Dragon did not like the restriction and roared alongside the sounds of the company. I darted behind it, dodging breaths of fire thrown haphazardly in my direction. A nearby vine tossed itself to me and I caught it. I was flung into the air and landed in a crouch on the Dragon's back, gripping the horns that sprouted from his spine.

"It's me!" I yelled at the Dragon as it reared against the restraints. My voice did little to calm him, and he continued to pull at the binds, so I loosened the roots around his feet. A moment later, we were airborne, the Dragon's long and mighty wings flapping, carrying us above the trees.

The Dragon bucked and twisted in the air. I thanked the gods for my new Fae body, which somehow had the strength to remain seated. I gripped the scaled beast with all the might my thighs could muster, my skin rubbed raw from clutching his spikes.

"It's me," I whispered, sending a tingle of my magic down his spine. "Just me."

A breath later, the Dragon settled into flight, no longer trying to throw me from him. I could see my Earth storm gathered in the middle of the valley. It whirled like a tornado now, Fayzien at its eye. He had no Water to aid him, so he held it back with his spells, firing slips of magic around him in a battle I knew he could not win. I reached out to the tornado, attempting to call it to further action—to neutralize Fayzien until I got there by filling his lungs with debris. But I received no response. The Nameless Valley sucked the life from my storm. The Earth seemed to only operate under the original intention I spelled it with.

I'd lost the advantage Jana told me to hold, but I didn't care. He was close—so close. I nudged the Dragon with my knees, as one would a horse, and he barreled towards the storm.

I gently pressed down on his spinal spikes, steering straight for the storm's center. *C'mon, Terra. For them.*

I stood on the Dragon's back, careful to keep my balance, and drew Ezren's blades from the harness he'd fastened to me. Right before I was above Fayzien, I leaped, landing in front of him, one knee to the ground. The Dragon flew off, roaring into the sky without any apparent direction. The Earth dropped, satisfied with the completion of its mission, the falling dirt forming a battle ring around us.

Moonlight gleamed off the blades out in front of me. Fayzien was covered in Earth, looking worse for wear, and my lips parted, the corner of my mouth tugging up in reaction to his struggle.

He looked at me with an unmasked hate. "You foul bitch," he spat at my feet.

I had dreamt of this moment many times since I'd seen him last. Now, none of my fantasies came to me—none of the fear and shame from minutes before. Only a coldness settled deep into my bones.

I twirled my blades in my hands, which to Fayzien may have looked like show but was meant to test the weight of my swords. They felt more natural now, given my new strength. He whispered, a spell of sorts, and two swords of his own appeared. I called to the Earth, searching for a root or a rock to trip him. But like I'd felt earlier, if life existed on that plain, it did not respond to me. Neither of us would have our elements, then. Blades it would be.

Fayzien lunged at me, like he knew I tried to draw upon my power and failed. I blocked his blow with ease. He struck fast but with less strength than I had faced against Leuffen or Ezren. Likely, he was drained from spelling.

I was not.

I quickened my pace, letting my blades fly, knowing I could afford the effort to tire him.

And he did. I knocked one of his blades from his hand with my left, and my right blade grazed his leg. He yelled out, and I sent my heel into his manhood. He bent over, crouching, as I approached him, my sword gleaming in triumph from his blood. I shook with a fury fueled by the memories of the last few weeks and the smugness on his face when he spoke about Gia.

Not Gia.

He stood as soon as I reached him, unhurt by my strike to his groin. When he did, a silver rope appeared in his hand, shimmering with magic. I dropped my left scim and placed both hands on the emerald hilt of my right blade, figuring I'd need double the strength to fight his enchanted whip. Fayzien raised his arm and sent the silver rope towards me. It collided with my blade in a loud snap that sung through my bones. He attempted to tighten the whip around my weapon to disarm me, but I yanked, and he skidded my way. I sent my heel to him once more, this time into the bleeding wound I had left on his thigh. He yelped at this, stumbling, but used the momentum to loosen his whip and swing it around while he spun towards me. The weapon connected with my back and sent me a good ten feet to his right.

My ribs crunched beneath me as I landed with a thud on the ground. I grunted, gritting my teeth against the stabbing pain radiating into my abdomen. Heat pricked my eyes, threatening to impair my vision, and I choked down a cry. I pushed myself onto all fours, spitting blood and forcing air back into my lungs. It was all I could do to keep hold of my blade when the enchanted whip cracked on my backside once more.

I groaned and Fayzien pulled back his weapon, laughing through his huffs. "Well," he breathed, "this is a demeaning position if I've ever seen one."

I spat another mouthful of blood and looked back at him. The fire burned inside me—hot, hot, hotter than I'd felt before. "I am going to kill you," I growled.

"No one will be killing anyone today, sweet Terra. I have no interest in your rebel friends, and it is time we go home. But first, I'm going to have my fill of fun." He winked and raised his whip once more, this time aiming it at my head.

I rolled onto my back, raising Ezren's emerald-gilded blade to protect my face as I sent my power through the weapon. It was a frantic move—I threw whatever magic I'd built up into it in desperation—in hopes it would strengthen my sword.

The emerald on the hilt glowed, a soft shimmer at first, and then blinding us in a moment of what looked like... Ezren's light. Power flooded from the blade to my veins in an ecstasy I had never known—and likely wouldn't come to understand for some time. It connected at once with Fayzien's whip, and instead of the contact reverberating through me, I felt the case of a clean cut. At once, the severed rope shriveled up, dissipating in the air.

I had no time to gape at my small victory or to wonder where the strange and foreign magic came from. My muscles felt an urgency my mind did not. In a fluid motion, I removed a throwing knife strapped on my thigh and flung it, sinking it into Fayzien's shoulder. I prowled to him as he fell to his knees, clutching at the blade. Before he could remove it, I clenched my hand around his neck, squeezing with enough strength to hurt, but not kill. Fayzien's eyes opened wide to mine, and his hands went to his throat, attempting to loosen my grip.

"I have never ended a life, but for this, I will carry no guilt. You will hurt no one else, you violating, murderous piece of *filth*," I whispered, willing the tears to stay behind my eyes as I raised my blade.

"Wait," he gasped laboriously. "Gia—if you kill me, she, she dies," he croaked. And if all he wanted was hesitation from me, that's what he got. He took the advantage and sent his fist deep into my abdomen, the blow connecting to the ribs I'd already cracked. I released him, doubling over, screaming at the sharp pressure.

I tried to rise to my full height, but pain lanced my core. My arms formed a protective cocoon around my midsection as I huddled there.

I am going to lose.

Instead of trying to land a killing blow, he took a step back from me, conjuring another weapon. He had no time, because the Dragon descended from behind me. And Ezren's neck coiled back in a deep breath, before he let out a lethal strike of fire, incinerating Fayzien in an instant.

The blue-eyed man was gone, leaving nothing behind but a smoking pile of ash.

CHAPTER SEVENTEEN

DESERT RAIN

"No!" I yelled—dread that Gia could now be at risk rising in my throat. I prayed he had bluffed, that he had never even seen her. He never showed any evidence of it, save the knowledge of her name. My eyes fell to the small pile of ash that appeared where the Fae had just stood.

The Dragon circled above me, letting out a loud roar of triumph, followed by more breaths of fire scattered in the air. Numb, I watched him for a few moments until he grew tired and landed on the barren ground. He shifted upon impact and tilted his head at me, his expression inhuman. I slumped, devoid of energy to deal with an unhinged Fae. He came over to sniff me curiously, perhaps my defeated posture posing no threat to his animal instincts. I looked up to see the slits that remained in his eyes.

"Ezren," I pleaded. "Please, don't fight me. Come back."

His expression remained blank. I touched my hand to his. He jumped back upon contact, but I held tight, letting his motion pull me up. I wrapped my arm around him, placing the back of his head in the crook of my elbow. And before he could do a thing, I buried my face into his neck and let out a sob. He stilled. I looked up, tears blurring my vision, nervous to see if the depths of his eyes were still slits. His pupils reformed circles, set in that gorgeous green.

His arms came around me at once, pulling me tighter into him. I wept without restraint. The catharsis was over, and my family was still gone. A part of me had always known it would feel like this, but even now, the rage stayed simmering inside me. Fayzien was dead. And it had fixed nothing.

"It won't ever go away, you know," Ezren murmured. "Loss is that way. It ebbs and flows. Sometimes, it has the power of a current trying to pull you under. But you are strong, Terra. You will fight it every day. You may not always win, but you *will* win more than you lose." He tilted my face up to his. I found a pain in his eyes that I hadn't noticed before.

"You killed Fayzien," I mumbled, unable to say anything else. "Did you mean to? How did you know I needed help?"

"Same as before," he said, disbelief in his tone. "I heard you scream my name."

The sounds of screeching from the mountainside ripped into our world before I could reply.

We ran.

THE SCREAMS GREW louder and more unnatural as we neared the edge of the plain. Fayzien had been alone, leaving his company to penetrate the mountain wood and flush out our group. The sun was rising now, not yet visible above the eastern peaks, but high enough to send a glow over the valley.

We were fast, but blind to where the group was, or how they were holding Fayzien's company back. The warriors did not know they were now following the orders of a dead man. *Who would command them now?*

At last, we reached the edge of the Nameless Valley. I flowed my magic into the mountain slope's dirt, running it upwards, hoping to get a sense of what unfolded in front of us. Dane and one of the other Witches appeared in our sight. We ran to them, and they each took one of our arms. A moment later, we were moving through space and time in the unexplainable way of the portal.

The group was north of where we had left them and at a higher elevation. I jogged over to Jana. "Fayzien, he is—"

"Dead, yes we know."

"How?" I asked.

Jana placed her hands on my shoulders and spun me around. "Look."

From our high point on the mountain, I could see the sun reflect off of hundreds of creatures moving between the trees in our direction, like cockroaches scurrying away from light.

"What the—"

"We ran from the warriors initially," Jana said, "evading and spelling them to confuse their direction or slow their pace. We figured once you killed Fayzien it would be like cutting off the snake's head. Maybe we could stop them somehow, convince them to turn around. But then, all of a sudden, they were no longer Fae. It makes sense; Fayzien would've never had the support of Viri warriors." She shook her head. "We should have known."

"Crona," Ezren breathed. "By the gods, I have never seen so many. He must have enchanted them."

"Exactly," Dane responded. "And masked their appearance with a glamor. I have never heard of a Witch creating a glamor so difficult without Fae help, but... he was part Fae, after all."

I peered down once more, looking at the small non-flying bat-like creatures that roamed up the mountainside. A thousand strong, scaled and fanged and web winged.

"What are they?" I whispered.

"Lesser Fae, some would call them. Easily masked and charmed. One alone is harmless, and they are rare enough. Some males hunt them, for their scales are known as... performance enhancers. But I have no idea how Fayzien herded so many together. They don't dwell or hunt in pairs, let alone numbers such as these," Dane explained, wonder and dread mixing in his words. "I would have thought they'd disperse upon Fayzien's death, given his spell ending. But they may be so deep in fear and confusion that they're still moving. He must have drawn on the valley somehow."

"Drawn on the valley...?" I echoed.

"A thousand years ago, the valley was said to be the source of a Death Witch's power. She either sacrificed something here, or, well we don't know for sure. It's mostly thought of as a housemaid's tale. Still, the valley has never been named. It seems to... lend and reserve power in abnormal ways. This phenomenon has been documented over the years, but the explanation remains a mystery. Some think it's what feeds the realm barrier, some have more... sinister beliefs."

"We should get the hell out of here," Parson chimed in, refocusing the group. "They're stupid creatures and have no direction now. We'll be able to elude them easily."

"If we leave," I asked hesitantly, "where will they go? Will they cross into the human lands?"

"It is possible," Jana said slowly. "There isn't near as strong of a barrier keeping the magic realm from the human, as there is the other way around. If they are confused enough, they may continue in the direction they were sent."

"And they could wreak havoc on entire human villages." My observation held a question.

"Yes," Ezren cut in. "They could."

The monsters were gaining ground fast now, nearly three quarters of the way to where we stood.

"We can't let that happen." My words were more of a plea than a statement.

"I could try a different spell," Dane thought aloud. "To freeze them, maybe for an hour or two at the most. It is a tricky one, like a counterweight to my fire. I've only done it once, and I'll need to link with someone. It should work, but I'm too drained to do much more than that."

"Do it," I said. "If nothing else, it will buy us time."

———

JANA SHARED WITH DANE, and together they sent a freeze down the slope of the mountain, which settled through the trees like an unforgiving frost. The Crona stayed fixed, contained for the time being. And thus began the debate.

Dane was hollowed out. Jana too, having forfeited the last of her reserves. Parson had shifted maybe six times in the hour; he couldn't put down a thousand rabid creatures with whatever Fae magic he had left. The rest of the group was tired, emptied, or lacked the skill to offer a solution. It seemed it would come down to Ezren or me.

"Ezren could shift again and burn the suckers," one of the other Witches mused.

"That would only work if someone controlled his Dragon form," Dane refuted. "And I do not have the strength to bend the will of a Dragon right now."

"He listens to me." I swallowed. "Well, sort of. I think my voice calmed him."

"That's not enough," Dane said. "Controlling his actions takes skill and practice, which we clearly don't have time to develop."

"I don't really remember the time in my shift. I fought to stay present, and I heard Terra's cry on the plain, but... it was distant. I didn't have control," Ezren admitted.

"Terra could split the Earth again, let the ground swallow the bastards whole," Parson chimed in. "Like when she trained with Dane."

"Far too risky," Jana countered. "If she too greatly disturbs what lies in that valley, well... we don't know the consequences. She could risk the collapse of the realm barrier entirely."

"I'm not sure I could do that anyway," I said quietly. "The valley does not respond to me."

"Could you suffocate them with your Earth storm?" Dane eyed me with suspicion.

"You mean raise up dirt from the mountainsides and individually asphyxiate each one?" He nodded, and I considered. "Maybe..." I grimaced. "I don't know if I have enough strength to do it."

Jana inclined her head. "The blood of your power is life. To cause death to a thousand creatures individually would be a tax."

"You need your damn Siphon," Dane muttered to himself, but then he looked at Jana in realization. She studied him a moment and then turned to Ezren and me.

"A joining might do it—but even that doesn't produce such a surge in power. But if you performed a coupling..." Jana trailed off.

In an instant, Ezren's face was alight with rage. "Absolutely not." Ezren's body tensed, his eyes blazing.

I felt a small punch in the stomach, now that I knew the coupling meant sharing power through... intimacy.

"Ezren, you *must* set your past experience aside. Terra is not Esmie. She is made of the Earth. She is far stronger than you give her credit." Jana's words had a gentleness to them, as if she spoke to calm a wild, cornered dog.

"You know Esmie isn't the only reason your suggestion is so foul," he growled.

Foul? Ouch.

"Ezren, please consider the alternative—hundreds, *thousands* of humans could be at risk," Dane begged.

"You've heard my answer." Ezren's voice was low.

"Leave us, please," I said, my eyes trained to the ground and my face heating. At once, they retreated, making to find the horses should we fail and need a fast escape.

I turned to Ezren when he spoke, "I'm so sorry, Terra, that they would suggest such a thing, truly, I would never—"

"How dare you," I breathed, "make this decision without my input, and while I stood right in front of you." My body felt alight with a myriad of emotions, including the ember of desire for him that never died out, even on the battlefield. "You didn't even ask me what I wanted."

He stared at me almost blankly and opened his mouth to respond, but quickly closed it.

"If I'm so revolting to you that the idea of being with me to save human lives is horrifying, well, I'll gladly ask Parson or Jin or *anyone else* to lend their services," I bit out.

"It's not only my involvement in a coupling that disturbs me, it's yours." His stare was wild. "A coupling is extremely dangerous for any Fae or Witch, but it is *particularly* so for females who have never lain with a male before."

The color in my cheeks intensified. "And what makes you so certain of... that?"

"Terra, I can scent it all over you. Not just desire, but... *new* desire."

I gaped at him, the heat singeing my face now. I nearly lost my nerve, but something more important than my embarrassment won out. Determination, fear of lost human life, and *need.*

"I want to do the coupling, Ezren. And I want to do it with you."

He came to me at once, his palms cupping my cheeks and his fingers running into my hair. "Terra, you will likely lose all control. And my magic—you've seen it. It's old and strange and unusual for a Fae. We have no idea how our powers will mix. It could kill you."

"But we do know, sort of," I breathed. "We've done the joining, and our magics seemed to combine instinctually when we kissed the first time."

He shook his head. "That is nothing like the coupling. Couplings are wild and unpredictable occurrences of power and magic. They can bring beautiful things or absolute destruction. Trust me on this."

I pulled away from his touch. "And you know so much, do you? Is it that you only want to couple with that female everyone keeps mentioning? Esmie? What, is she the one who left you and broke your heart?" I asked, bitter.

"Yes, she did," Ezren bit out, the words sending something sharp to my lungs.

He let out a loud sigh. "She was my wife. We were married two decades, and she wanted a babe more than anything. I persuaded her to do the coupling; I'd been told it could help one conceive, and only virgins were at real risk of death, anyway. So we did it. And..." He paused, taking another breath. "And I killed her with my power. So yes, she left me, just like everyone else," he spat. "And yes, it broke my heart. It was no one's fault, but my own."

I shuttered my eyes, feeling the loss radiate off him. So *that* was the source of pain I'd recognized in his eyes earlier, when he told me about the ebb and flow of never ending grief. "I'm so sorry," I said, wrapping my arms around myself as tears ran down my face.

"I can't have your death on my conscience, Terra, I can't."

I went to him, placing my hands on his chest. Sending one's power into another was an intimate act, as I'd discovered when Fayzien non-consensually did it to me so many weeks ago. After sharing with Jana, I knew how to do it right—only proceeding if I felt willingness from the host.

One probe of power and I sensed his intrinsic acceptance. So I flowed my magic into him, gentle but firm. He let out a low moan that vibrated through my core, a sound I'd sell my soul to hear again and again and again.

"Why can't you trust me," I murmured to myself.

"I do trust your strength, Terra. It's *mine* I don't trust," he murmured, eyes glazed. I dismissed his words by pushing my power further into him.

"Do you feel me, Ezren, in every inch of you?" I whispered.

He nodded, his head tilted back, his breathing labored. "Open your eyes and look at me." He did. "I am sorry for what happened to your wife, I truly am. But answer me this, honestly. Did her power feel like this? Could you feel her strength possessing you, like mine does now?" I searched his face for the answer.

Plain truth laced his words as he said, "No. No, it did not."

178

I withdrew my power from him, and he looked away. I didn't have to ask again. He knew I'd made up my mind, and he didn't have the willpower to keep denying me. Of course, his constant pulling away, the way he could not look at me now, hurt. But, I *had* made up my mind.

I walked to the middle of the clearing and sank my palms into the ground. I didn't have to do much, for the Earth was witness to our decision, as it would always bear witness to me. Immediately, trees and brush and root sprouted with the joy of fresh blooms, forming a private room around us. Flowers ran up the vines, and wisteria grew in a knitted canopy over our heads. My clothes were replaced, too; silkworms skated over my body, cleaning and leaving only the fine weaving of their proteins on my skin. In their wake, a sheer and loose shift pooled around my knees. Finally, four large trunks emerged from the ground, shaped into the posts of a bed, the mattress growing out of supple grass. I looked around at my creation, a splendid private garden, an oasis on a mountain, shrouded in soft morning light.

I beamed. "Thank you," I whispered.

My eyes met Ezren's, which sparkled in reflection of all that had grown around us. His clothes, too, had changed, his torn battle dress swapped for silken trousers that left little to the imagination. My gaze wandered down his body, lingering on his sculpted abdomen, and falling on what lay beneath his tunic. He swelled there, I could see, and the sight sent a buzz of adrenaline through me.

I remained still on the ground, kneeling several feet from our earthen bed. He stalked toward me. I tore my eyes from him, looking at my hands to steady my rapid breathing. Once he arrived, he stood silent. I felt his eyes roaming my body too, knowing he could see nearly all of me.

"I know you don't want to do this, so we can just get it over with," I mumbled, falling victim to insecurity. He bent over and placed two fingers under my chin, lifting it so that I peered up at him. I was acutely aware of his manhood now, just mere inches from my face.

"No," he said, his voice like gravel, not unlike the animal tone he possessed when the Dragon blood still flowed through his veins. "If you want this, if I'm to be your first male, I will do so by delivering you every ounce of pleasure you can take," he said, now in command. "So no, I will not just get it over with." He extended a hand, pulling me to stand. His face was grave and serious, yet the desire was there, plain as day. "Promise me you'll fight the power overtaking you, fight to control it, to set it out with intention."

"Okay," I responded, barely hearing him. The heartbeat in my chest rang in my ears as much as in my womanhood.

"Now tell me again, Terra, tell me you want this," he breathed, his lips a mere inch from mine. "Tell me you're sure."

I let my gaze run up the length of his body, landing on his emerald eyes, on fire as ever. He looked at me then, really looked. His stare was wild with unbridled hunger, mingled with bewilderment. He looked at me like he'd never seen a woman before. Like I was an oasis, and he hadn't had water in days. As if I could be his salvation— a spring well in the desert—or a figment of his imagination.

That look made me feel more naked than if I'd removed my shift. It said a thousand things and made a thousand promises. It undressed me and destroyed me; it coaxed a wetness between my thighs. Points formed on my breasts in friction against the sheer silk that covered them.

But mostly, the way Ezren looked at me woke me up. It made me feel something I hadn't felt in a long time, if ever.

Alive.

I nodded and realized I was starving, too. "I'm sure."

CHAPTER EIGHTEEN

SHARP REVERSION

*O*ur coupling was—and was not—a coupling. It was, in the way that we created a surge of power that kept the Crona from the human realm.

It was, in the way that a permanent heated longing had settled in my low belly.

It was, in the way that the little flame, which had started burning for Ezren the day we'd met, was now a full fire—carrying with it a terrifying truth that it would remain there, in some form, for a long, long time.

It was also something else entirely.

We'd been successful in diminishing those creatures, which—after the coupling—we'd discovered were more like magical figments than living, breathing things. They'd turned to dust with our surge of power, and as we walked through the forest to ensure none remained, my conscience was relieved to find out no real lives had been lost. Fayzien's spell had simply been broken.

By the time we neared Valfalla, Ezren had only just calmed down after several days of blind fury at Jana—apparently, for not telling him that our coupling would not only be a coupling, but a binding. I still didn't know what that meant, because he couldn't discuss it without flying into a fit of rage, and when I asked anyone else, they said it was Ezren's duty to tell me, and his alone. The only thing I knew for sure was that the mysterious binding left a slight burning sensation on my left hip.

I should have been afraid of what had built between us in such a short span of time—we'd known each other for just over two weeks. A rational mind would have feared it or questioned it at least. But I did not. I thought of nothing else but the wanting that possessed me. I was drowning in the need for him—I wanted his body, his mind, his heart. I wanted to know everything about him so badly it hurt. He denied me all three. Though he held me every night we slept, the skin-to-skin contact like a drop of water to quench a blazing thirst, he refused to do anything more. He was tense and silent when I asked him why. Most nights he woke covered in sweat, and it took nearly a half hour for his heartbeat to slow.

Jana decided to bypass Panderen due to Fayzien's remarks and sent Parson that way to report back on what he found of the Casmerre and her crew. Dane grew so sick with worry he didn't speak at all, and I couldn't say the rest of us fared much better. After four days of riding and a day and a half of portaling, which Jana now allowed due to the Witches recovery of magic and Fayzien's death, we approached the Fae capital of Viribrum. Valfalla—the imposing stone city built into ocean cliffs. When I first laid eyes on it, a memory hit me of that castle fading into the distance as I rode away in a bouncing cart.

Jana instructed us to wear our cloaks with the hoods drawn. The air stank of fish, excrement, and trash as we made our way through the winding cobbled streets, heading for the palace.

When we reached the gates, Jana withdrew her hood and requested an audience with the king, murmuring some Viri word that granted us access. I had to lean on Ezren for support, because nausea overcame me—memories buzzing in my head, trying to resurface. They had never come so fast before, and I could scarcely make sense of them. Just a swirling of images that meant little when blurred together.

"What's wrong?" Ezren asked me, concern threading his words.

"I'm fine," I bit out. "Just dizzy."

The guards led us into the throne room. The ceiling soared impossibly high, and bright light streamed through windows stained with the thick, foamy smear of ocean spray. Limestone and glass drenched every surface—from the tile floors, to the ceiling, to the furniture. It all matched the sleek cream aesthetic of the space. But I noticed the emptiness most—the cold that permeated the room.

We didn't speak, and the group was as tense as I, though they weren't fighting to hold in vomit, as far as I could tell. Eventually, Ezren transferred my hand to Jana's arm, stepping a few yards behind me. I felt much too sick to ask why.

And then an announcer entered, tapping his staff to the ground. "King Darlan of Viribrum, his son, Prince Casmerre of Viribrum, and the Rexi Neferti of Nebbiolo," he belted.

Our group stilled even further, the words echoing off the massive stone walls that surrounded us. My head shot up at the mention of Casmerre, and I knew right away that the name had never just belonged to my dog. They walked in, and my eyes landed on a Fae with jet-black hair—and a pair of striking, golden-rimmed, purple eyes. He was lean and tall and had all the grace of a grown male, nothing like the little princeling I remembered. I gaped at him as his name, and its significance, set in.

And then a fourth figure emerged from the darkness behind the thrones, with piercing blue eyes that bore into me. Blue-eyes of a Fae that should have been dead.

Fayzien spoke, the smuggest of smiles spreading across his face. "Your Holiness the Queen Rexi and Your Highness Prince Casmerre, may I present to you your long-lost daughter, and your long-lost betrothed, Princess Terragnata of Nebbiolo."

At Fayzien's words, memories erupted in my mind like a volcano. The buzzing in my head became a scream, the world spinning too fast, so fast that it felt like I was catapulted, physically moving through time. I wondered for a moment if I was experiencing what the healers in Argention referred to as vertigo.

I heaved over and vomited. The memories surged, brighter and brighter, and then all I saw was black.

PART II

VIRIBRUM

CHAPTER NINETEEN

HOME SWEET

I woke with a pounding in my head, a throbbing in my joints, and that strange burning sensation on my left hip. I peeked one eye open to see swaths of sheer cloth draped from four posters around me.

Bed, I'm in a bed.

A grand one, at that. Set in a mass of pillows, heavy duvets, and golden silk sheets. A matching sleep shift brushed over my skin. I stretched out my limbs, which seemed to ache with something more than the stiffness of sleeping too long.

I pulled up my shift to reveal faded bruises covering my stomach... as if I'd been beaten, but weeks before.

Strange.

I drew back the bed curtains and examined the room. It extended long rather than wide. Massive velvet fabrics parted from windows that must have been a half dozen yards tall, revealing a stark drop off to the cliffs a hundred feet below them, flush with a roiling sea. I peered out the window, looking at the long drop, remembering what had transpired before everything had gone black.

Cas. My childhood crush, best friend, and my intended husband.

He'd stood in front of me a man, so changed from the boy I'd known. The memories had not yet settled in my head—they swirled as if disturbed from a long sleep. But who Cas was to me, who he'd always been, was clear as crystal.

An impressive stone fireplace smoked between the windows, likely lit in the past hour. At the end of the room perched an *enormous* copper clawfoot tub with a thick water pipe overhanging the rim, and steam curling out from it. I had seen illustrations of those contraptions—that allowed for heated running water. We had nothing like it in Argention, and I vaguely remembered maids filling my tub—before I came to the human realm. It sat nestled in the corner next to two more opposing windows, a matching chamber pot, and a fine dressing station.

I relieved myself. Someone must have been in here recently, given the drawn curtains, crackling fire, and prepared bath. Before I could investigate further, the door opened.

A young Fae servant girl walked in, carrying a breakfast tray. My stomach betrayed my still untrusting mind and gurgled for all the room to hear.

"Oh! Good! Yer up, finally. Me tought ye would sleep tru anoder day!" she exclaimed. "Me brought ye brekkie, jest en case."

The many unknowns froze me on the spot, and at the top of the list was whether or not I had dreamt Fayzien to still be alive. A sneaking feeling in my gut told me it was not a dream. *I should have known the bastard wouldn't go down just like that.*

The servant busied herself with a cheerful attitude, setting up the tray by the seats across from the fire, and putting a kettle on the coals to heat. She had chestnut hair and soft brown eyes and looked no more than fifteen. "Ye know, m'lady, there ain't much en thes world that isna betta' than a fresh cuppa tea." She winked at me.

"What is your name?"

"Olea. Ef ye canna tell, I'm te be yer hand lady, ye see." She curtsied.

I closed my eyes and exhaled. "I have one question I need you to answer right now, Olea. It's very, very important. The Manibu, advisor to the Queen Rexi, the one they call Fayzien—was he here when I arrived?"

She giggled to herself. "Oh yes, the blue-eyed one, ye dinna remember? He es easy en me eyes, te be sure, especially after healin' from hes burns—he was a bet charred fer a day after he arrived. A powerful Wetch, 'at one. Everyone be talkin' a' hem now, cuz when ye soiled yerself weth yer vomet, well, he lost hes stomach, too. The Rexi was fumen'. So much so she sent hem halfway across the room weth her magic and left. She doesna take te weakness, from what I can tell."

I sank onto the rim of the tub, my knuckles turning white as my hands gripped the edge.

"So it's true," I breathed. *He must have portaled at the last second, only having faced a small lick of Ezren's fire.* "And the queen, she is my mother?"

"Why yes m'lady, she es. I ain't never seen her before. I heard thes was the ferst she set foot on Fae ground, though she was married to a Fae before a' course. But a mother knows no bounds, when et comes te a child, hey?"

My head swam with memories, but none of them were images of the Rexi. Now, I saw almost exclusively Cas. How could I not have remembered who the purple-gold-eyed boy was to me? He'd been my best friend, partner in crime, and confidant growing up. I had always known we would marry. He used to give me small tokens of amethyst or tanzanite, purple gems set in rings or necklaces, or beads on a dress. A promise of our future, he would say, just a boy of eleven when he did such things. My heart swelled at the memories, the fondness and innocence in them. I wondered what kind of male he'd grown to be.

"And my betrothal to Cas? Is that still... expected?"

"Aye, a' course. Ye two were betrothed a' berth, or so hath been said. I dinna know the full story, but ye two were supposedly inseparable as Faeries. The whole country knew a' yer engagement; many even speculated ye'd be Salanti."

Salanti. The word held no familiarity, another mystery of this world I'd been ripped from. I rubbed my temples. My mother was *not* a dead, nameless Witch from Nebbiolo, as Jana had told me. Not only was she very much alive, but she reigned as queen. Which made me a princess. And a betrothed one at that. Every last one of them had lied to me. Ezren. Jana, Dane, Leiya, Leuffen—the lot of them. They made me think I was just some famed warrior's daughter who could stop a war by showing I lived—not a political piece in some power game between kingdoms. I suddenly knew why Ezren was so hesitant to touch me, why he refused to lay with me again after that first time, why his face turned green when he'd learned what I'd named my ship.

He knew I was engaged to another. And he never told me.

Heat pricked my eyes and my throat ran dry, my pulse quickening. I'd always known Jana was using me and had accepted that. But she'd *sworn* she did not deceive me, and her words were empty. More gutting than anything, I hadn't anticipated this feeling of betrayal from Ezren. Perhaps his lies cut the deepest because I never expected them. The smallest voice inside me laughed cynically. Despite my efforts, I had started to trust Ezren.

I should've known better.

And on top of all of that, why didn't I remember the Rexi if she was my mother?

"Olea." I nearly growled at her, fighting to keep the tears back. "Where stays the green-eyed Fae, the tall warrior called Ezren? I owe him a sharp punch to the gut, or perhaps the groin, depending on how he grovels when I see him."

Her eyes widened at my question. "Dinna worry, m'lady, he es taken care of. Ye dinna have te worry about hem ever again," she said hurriedly.

"I'm not worried about *him*! In fact, you should be worried about *me* hurting him!" I snapped.

She looked frightened now. "Mess, I canna even imagine what me'd wanna do te me captors. Ye lekely wanna kell 'em all. But ye canna do that, ye see, they are the keng's property now. Take heart, me lady, Hes Majesty well seek justice." She said the last part so reassuring in tone, laying a comforting hand on my arm.

I looked at her, a slow realization dawning on me. We were having two different conversations.

"Captors?" I wanted to punch Ezren's teeth in for lying to me, absolutely, but... *kidnapping?*

"Yes, m'lady. An' the prince nearly beat the male te hes death, the one ye spoke a', when he scented hem all oer' ye. But they've all been charged weth treason an' threatenin' the crown. Dinna worry, mess. The keng well try 'em as traitors. They'll likely lose their heads for et, an' ye'll never have te see them folk again."

A pit formed in my stomach, imagining Cas laying a hand on Ezren. And then frustration flooded my gut. *Traitors?* I knew they lied to me, but they'd returned me to Viribrum, they'd righted Fayzien's wrong. How could Cas not know Fayzien's evil, that *he* took me away in the first place?

I stilled. *Did they lie about that, too?*

"Olea," I breathed. "I still need to see Ezren. Can you take me to him?"

"Naye, I dinna know where he es. And even ef I ded, I'd not take ye to a' dungeon. They ain't no place for a princess. But I can take ye te see yer friend."

"My friend?" I cocked my head in confusion, but then I gasped in understanding. "Gia?" I breathed. "She's here?"

Olea nodded, excitement opening her face. "Aye, an' she's the ferst 'uman me seen up close!"

FAYZIEN HAD NOT BEEN BLUFFING about his possession of Gia in the Nameless Valley. And while I knew her presence at the palace could only mean one thing—they would use my dear friend to control me somehow—I refused to see another soul until I laid eyes on the woman and confirmed her well-being.

Olea promised to take me to Gia, on the condition that I ate and bathed first. Those were certainly not my priorities, but my stomach wouldn't stop grumbling, and Olea said she'd be beaten if I were seen leaving my room looking anything less than a princess. So, I ate by the fire and then let her wash me, let her work through the knots in my hair as my thoughts swirled.

I didn't know how I felt. I was angry and hurt, confused and with no faith in any truth.

And I worried. What had happened to the Casmerre? Had Fayzien been bluffing when he'd said he'd 'taken care of' the ship? I imagined Leuffen and Sanah struggling amongst rolling waves, Leiya flying high above, unable to do anything to save them.

I imagined seeing Ezren's head rolling away from his body, severed by the executioner's blade, his green eyes devoid of life.

The images sent tremors of terror through my body. I might not have been able to do anything about the Casmerre and her passengers, but I couldn't let Ezren die.

When Olea finished, I was sparkling clean, and my incredibly long, sandy hair fell in waves around me. It seemed my new Fae body affected even the rate at which my hair grew.

If she saw the bruises on my abdomen, she said nothing while forcing me into a corset. I realized how unaccustomed I'd become to wearing them, after nearly a month in breeches and a simple brassiere. She bound the strings as tight as bows, and pulled my breasts toward each other in the front so they sat upright and full, close to touching my chin.

Olea painted my face, put ash on my lids, and stained my lips. She let my hair dry around me. For a wilder effect, she said.

I tried to object when she pulled out an extravagant gown, but she only clucked her tongue at me, saying this was appropriate princess daywear. She chose red, she said, because I should seem as ripe as an apple when I saw my betrothed for the first time again. The comment made me grimace.

The dress consisted first of a 'corset cover,' red lace that fit snug around my breasts and mid-section, extending down, buttons fastening between my thighs. It covered very little of my rear, matching the lines of my undergarments. Then came the red sheer slip. It was sleeveless but cuffed at the neck with a band of gold, and the hem touched the stone floor. Finally came what I prayed was an actual dress, but it was merely an open, sleeveless robe of layers of red chiffon that she belted at my midsection. When I stepped into the heeled slippers Olea placed in front of me, I had the bizarre feeling that all of this was just to prevent me from running away.

Finally, she adorned my wrists with matching golden cuffs and snapped dangling gold chains onto the lobes of my ears.

I examined her work in the mirror. One could see all the way down to my lace undergarments, and when I walked, the chiffon layer fell to the side, revealing the outlines of my full legs. Only the sheer slip covered my chest, which meant at each rise and fall of my breath, my breasts replicated the movement. My drying hair fell in waves around me, blonde whorls that neared my abdomen. All of this, paired with the dark paint on my eyes and the red stain on my lips, made me an image of sex incarnate.

"Olea, this is absolutely ridiculous. I look like I am soliciting invitations for something I am most *certainly* not."

But she responded with some rambling that the prince's betrothed must look like a goddess, for that is what I had to be: formidable and fertile to warn other courtiers away from him. She pushed me out the door, leading me to Gia. The thought of anyone seeing me so scantily clad was horrifying. In fact, I could have sworn the guards posted outside my door blushed when I passed, but the promise of seeing my friend outweighed my shyness.

Olea led me through winding stone halls, and I did my best to be alert, to let the layout of the palace return to my memory. I made note of small details or abnormalities in the stone and cracks on the floor, marking each turn we made. Finally, when it felt like we had traveled at least a mile of winding passageways, we arrived at another large room. A different wing for guests. They must have housed me either in the wing for dignitaries or family of the crown. Which one they considered me I did not yet know.

Olea curtsied to the posted guards, her eyes batting at one of them for a moment too long. She gave a quick knock, and the door swung open at the hands of another serving maid. And through the door, I saw Gia standing before the fire, looking by all measures... unharmed.

Despite the chiffon floating around me, I ran to her, pulling her into an embrace. She returned the gesture and breathed into me, "Terra, thank the gods." We released our hug, both examining the other for any harm or injury. Her eyes fell to my wrists, darkening a moment before she blinked, and the shadow from her face cleared. "Your ears!" she exclaimed. "So it is true then, you are ... Fae?" She struggled to say it, as if it was a foreign word.

I nodded, tears threatening to streak the ash on my eyelids. "Well, half," I choked out.

I pressed my hand to her belly, and sure enough, a small but firm bump protruded from her waistline, almost noticeable on her otherwise petite figure. And the distinct swell in her usually light chest hadn't been there before. I turned to the maids. "Leave us, please." They curtsied and left.

"How long?" I whispered.

Now it was Gia's turn to hold back tears. "Four, maybe five months. The midwife here says closer to five." She shook her head. "At least I still have a small piece of him."

I exhaled in realization. "*That* is why he proposed just months before Spring Day! You knew then, didn't you? Why didn't you tell me?" I asked, a tiny sliver of hurt slipping into my voice.

"I only suspected. My cycles have never been regular, so there was no way to know for sure without visiting a healer, which I couldn't risk, of course. I told him my suspicions. He was overwhelmed with joy and said that he'd never wanted to wait to ask for my hand, anyway." She wilted at the memory. "The next day he spoke with both our parents, and they agreed to forgo tradition. I still don't know how he got them to agree without telling them I might be pregnant. Our wedding would have been just a few weeks from now," she said, tears defying her now, running down her face.

I felt the familiar pang of guilt and dread.

I hugged her again, not wanting to let her go. "I will get you out of here, Gia. I promise," I whispered. "I don't know what Fayzien did to you, but I swear I will find a way to kill him for what he has done."

Gia pushed me back. "Terra, what are you talking about? Fayzien saved my life."

I gaped at her. "Fayzien is the one that killed my family, Danson included. He kidnapped you and brought you here."

"He did not! The band of rebels who took you are the ones who slaughtered your family, Terra. One moment we were sitting in our secret spot, and the next, they were all around us, taking your unconscious body away. I wanted to fight so badly, but one of them put a spell on me that made my legs walk back to my house, and lay down in my bed. I was stuck like that, paralyzed, for days. If Fayzien had never come and freed the spell, well, I would still be frozen there right now!"

My mind tried to explain her words. "But Gia, I *saw* Fayzien kill Mama. I saw it with my own eyes..." I trailed off.

She swore under her breath. "He said this might happen."

"What?" I demanded.

"He said they might try to... to confuse your mind. He warned me you might say all these things. And then, when you arrived a few days ago, the Fae prince could scent that male on you, the large Fae with green eyes. Fayzien said he seduced you, manipulated you to trust him, or maybe even took you against your will," she replied cautiously.

My head was exploding, and I paced her room. "Ezren most certainly did not take me against my will," I forced out, earning a curious eyebrow raise from Gia. "He did lie to me; they all did—and that I will not forgive. But they did *not* kill my family. That was Fayzien, I am sure of it." They'd shown up days after Mama died; no way could it have been them. *Or could it?*

Gia took my hands. "Did you lay with him, Terra? The green-eyed warrior?"

Her gaze was always so penetrative; my dearest friend could see right through me. I crumpled, nodding, an old shame creeping into my throat.

Gia looked at me with an understanding sadness. "I'm guessing you thought you loved him?"

I released a shaky breath. "I don't know, maybe," I whispered, afraid my voice would crack if I spoke at full volume. "All I know is that when I'm around him, I can't fully breathe, I can't fully think. It feels like being burned alive from the inside out, no matter if we're close or apart."

"In love with a real-life Fae male? Giving her body willingly to a stranger just weeks after meeting him? Well, that isn't the Terra I know—and anyway, what you described sounds more like a hex than love."

"I... he..." I sighed, a familiar fleeting feeling of heat washing over me. "It did feel like a spell, in a way. I was drawn to him instantly, like I've never been to any other. But it was real. So, so, cripplingly real. Ezren saved my life on multiple occasions—and it was *me* who pursued *him*. He did what he could to deny me, but, well, like I said, it was real. I will not forgive his lies—he failed to tell me about Cas and so much more. But I know he'd never hurt me. I think he..." I trailed off, unable to complete my sentence.

What did I really know about Ezren's feelings? What could I trust from his actions, given so many of them were part of some elaborate scheme to fool me about my identity?

"Terra, look at the facts. Fayzien came to bring you back here, to reunite you with your birth mother. He told me everything. But he came in peace, bidding for your hand at Spring Day, with no violence. There are a hundred witnesses to that. He found me, freed me, and offered to take me with him to find you. He never forced me. But the rebels? Your so-called Ezren? They took you by force. I watched them drag away your unconscious body! And after they did so, how did you wake? Were you a prisoner?"

I looked at the floor. "I was in chains," I recalled softly.

"Yes, you see? Somehow they tricked you into thinking Fayzien killed your family. They wanted you to believe him the enemy, to trust them instead."

My mind swam. "Gia, I battled Fayzien, first in the Argen forest and again in the Adimon Mountains. He, he tried to hurt me, he taunted me... he violated me! He even threatened *you*. I know all of that was real," I whispered.

Gia's clear eyes bore into me in earnest, yet an unfamiliar desperation lingered there. "Terra, Fayzien says some Witches can put memories in heads that did not exist before," she offered in explanation.

I flinched at the word *memories,* a small inner voice reminding me how my memories had been altered before. And the unanswered question of how I'd not remembered who Cas was lingered in my mind, as well as who my birth mother was, hell, who *I* was. How had memories of my sire come back flowing freely, but the rest evaded me like eels in a pool? I didn't know which memories to trust anymore and nearly doubted the reality of my life in Argention. But Gia was here, standing in front of me. Surely, those years were real. *They had to be, didn't they?*

I let out a slow breath, attempting to quell the budding nausea swirling in my belly. Realization set in, ringing clear in my mind. I'd have to find the truth on my own. I could trust no one, not even Gia. For her memories, her thoughts—just like mine—could have been altered by Fayzien. Or someone else.

I eyed Gia. "He never touched you? Never harmed you when you traveled with him?"

"Fayzien? No, of course not. He was very gentle, actually. Portaling while pregnant is *quite* heart-burn inducing," she replied.

"Did you both portal all the way back here?" I asked.

"Yes, after about two weeks of riding around looking for you. He said one of his scouts had found you, but you were a prisoner of a large group of rebels. I begged to come with him to find you, but he said there could be a battle and that, as a pregnant human, I would be in grave danger. So he took me here and promised he would bring you back safely. He kept to his word, Terra," Gia said gingerly. "For here you are, safe and unharmed, in front of me, though dressed in a way I thought I would never see." She giggled at her last words, and I giggled, too.

I softened. "I look ridiculous, don't I?" I shook my head. "This is what a princess should look like, according to my handmaid."

Gia chuckled again. "My dear, you're dressed like you could make other females pregnant just by *looking* at you. Thank goodness I'm already with child, so I will be in no danger of spontaneous conception," she said, finishing the joke with a wink.

I laughed once more and squeezed her hand. "Gia, I feel there are things we both have not been told, truths that have been withheld from us. Something isn't right about these creatures, they deceive. But promise me this; trust in me. I will find the truth about my family's murder. I will seek justice for them, for Danson."

At this, she nodded in agreement, but I sensed her holding something back. I gave her hand another squeeze. "All right, time to get to work."

CHAPTER TWENTY

OLD FLAME

I left Gia's room to find Olea waiting outside the door. I wondered, not for the first time, who she reported to.

"Me lady, ye canna delay longer. Ets time for ye te see yer future husband."

An image of Ezren's face flashed in my mind, and I squeezed my eyes closed and opened them again as if it would make the picture disappear. It did little to quell the turmoil of emotion his face conjured—rage, longing, hurt. His lack of honesty might not have been a true betrayal, but it felt so. Like I could no longer trust him.

But any confrontation with Ezren would have to wait. Olea led me down more twisting stone hallways until we reached the grand staircase of the castle. It opened to a large foyer, and I marveled at how the space triggered memories of life in Valfalla. Clear as day, I could see Cas chasing me for a pastry I stole from his plate. I could see my father instructing me to be still as we stood in the foyer, receiving distinguished guests alongside the king. I could see a white-haired girl pinching me as we walked to our lessons, making me turn back and stick out my tongue to her—an action that earned me the stick.

Before I could lose myself in recall, Olea led me outside. The crisp air was ecstasy on my skin. Cool, but not cold, and full of salt and sea. I sucked in a deep breath, the smell triggering even more familiarity and nostalgia. It grounded my fresh childhood memories, making them more vivid and feel *real*.

We made our way around the side of the castle to a large, pale stone patio that jutted out of the palace onto a rock cliff. *A training ground.* The roiling sea provided a stark backdrop for two Fae in the middle of an artful duel, both wearing practice masks. Groups of courtiers gathered around watching the spectacle, most of them female. Anxiety coiled in my belly as we approached them, for I knew their shrewd glances would pick me over. The Fae continued sparring. When we drew closer, the taller one lifted his palm in the air, and his opponent halted. The crowd fell silent and followed his gaze, which landed on me.

He strode over to meet us, and my breath quickened. I was an image of red chiffon whipping in the wind, set against a picture of pale palace stone and an unlimited ocean horizon. The prince removed his training mask, letting his jet-black hair fall around his face, no longer pulled back at the base of his neck. When we were fifty feet away from each other, I could no longer stand it. I kicked off the stupid slippers Olea forced me into, and ran towards him. He did the same, lifting me up in his familiar but unfamiliar arms, twirling me around with one forearm on my waist and one hand tangled in my now wild blonde hair.

His scent hit me first—almost exactly like I remembered, but more grown, more masculine. A musky cinnamon and clove, indicating he still carried a fondness for the spice-filled soaps he'd loved as a boy. And when he pulled me in close, I felt the oddest sense of comfort, like I'd come home. Experiencing that feeling in the arms of someone who would have been a stranger to me just days ago—days I was in the arms of another—felt... bizarre. It made me question the realness of the moment, of every moment before it. I winced at my lack of trust in reality, praying my reaction was not perceivable.

199

He set me down and cupped my face in his palms, his thumbs rubbing back and forth on my cheeks. "*Mi karus*," he breathed, and I smiled at the use of his old pet name for me. "I have thought about this moment every day for seven years. I nearly lost hope." He shuttered his eyes and pressed his forehead to mine, pulling me into him once more. He re-opened his eyes and ran them down my body. "You are no longer the little warrior I remember," he said, a mischievous smile forming on his face.

I blushed, which made him burst into a deep chuckle. "But still equally shy with compliments, I see," he teased.

I met his eyes. "*You* are no longer just a little Fae boy, leaving me purple-stoned trinkets as love tokens," I shot back, the familiar banter returning to us.

This sent his smile wider, and his eyes shone, no doubt pleased I remembered such a detail. They were just as I recalled, shimmering gold rims around deep purple irises—streaked with flecks of something that recalled stars. He turned and faced the crowd, which had grown larger during our embrace.

"Fellow Viri, as you have discovered by now, my childhood friend and companion, Princess Terragnata of Nebbiolo, has been returned to us!" he bellowed. Cheering erupted from many, but not all. A few courtiers leered at me with narrowed eyes.

"I plan to uphold a promise I made to her many years ago," he continued. He turned to me and removed something from his breast pocket: a sizable, roughly cut tanzanite gem set on a thin gold band. I had never seen a jewel so captivating; it looked like a bright evening sky decorated with a thousand sparkling stars. He knelt, and I froze, aware of the many eyes searing my skin.

I didn't hear what he said next. I just remained still as he lifted my left hand and slid the ring on my finger, a perfect fit. More cheering ensued, but I couldn't hear it over the pounding in my ears. He turned to lead me back to the castle, my arm linked to his. As we made our way, my eyes brushed over a small set of windows at the base of the stone place. Silver bars covered the openings, and I swore I saw a flash of green from behind them.

———————

CAS LED me into a small sitting room. My mind reeled from the display—from the shock of it, for one, and from the singeing thought that a certain Fae warrior witnessed it.

He placed a glass of amber liquid in my hand, and I stared into it.

"Drink," he commanded. "You look like you need it."

I took a gulp and sat on the couch, the fiery liquid burning my throat.

"Terra, I'm sorry for the spectacle, truly, but I had to put some rumors to bed, for your sake. Prying eyes are never friendly here, which you may remember."

I chewed my lip, and he took my hands in his, turning them over as if to remember their lines and curves. "Terra, *mi karus*, are you okay?" he asked, genuine concern in his voice.

I shook my head. I could barely distinguish true memory from lie, which left me utterly confused about how I should feel—towards Ezren, Jana, or the situation as a whole. What I did know, was that I didn't feel okay.

"I don't know, Cas." It felt so good to say my friend's name once again, and it undid me. I wept, and he pulled me onto his lap, pressing my head against his chest, calming my heaves by tracing letters on my back. He kissed the top of my head numerous times. Finally, when I quieted, he said, "I will *kill* the bastard for laying a hand on you. That was never part of the deal, Terra. You have to know—"

I jumped back. "Deal? What deal? Are you talking about Ezren?" I asked, now on the defensive.

"Yes, I'm talking about the deserting Dragon filth that raped you!"

I gaped at him. "Raped me? What gave you that impression?"

"I could scent him all over you when you arrived. And not in the way of two lovers, in a claiming way. And you looked so ill, so abused, you keeled over almost immediately!"

I sighed, exasperated at the territorial bullshit he spewed. "Cas, that's because my memories were swarming my head like bees. And for what it's worth, Ezren was barely willing to touch me."

He quieted for a moment. "My sense of scent has never been false. It is unparalleled. The *only* other possibility is if you did something called the binding—" He stopped, his eyes widening.

I just looked at him, guilty and confused. I still didn't know what the binding meant—only that the coupling we'd done to kill the Crona had accidentally led to it. Cas's gathered, prince-like expression turned to pure rage as he read my face.

He shot to his feet and walked with such intensity it wouldn't have surprised me to see steam pumping from his ears. I gripped my chiffon skirts, running to keep up with him, grateful I had shed those ridiculous shoes earlier.

"Cas, wait, please, can you just stop for a second!" But he kept moving, and I kept on following him through more twisting halls. Finally, he stopped at an iron door guarded by two Viri warriors. I caught up to him and grabbed his arm.

"We did it to save human lives, to prevent these horrible creatures Fayzien created from breaking into the human realm. I didn't even remember who you were then. And I don't even know what a dammed binding *is*!"

Hurt flashed in his eyes. "But he did. And he does." He turned to face the guards. "Keep her up here." And just like that, he disappeared down the stairs, the iron door clanging behind him.

Whatever anger I had felt towards Ezren paled in comparison to pure fear for his life. He was a formidable warrior, but he was likely chained and helpless in a cell. Cas would injure him severely at best and kill him at worst.

I turned from the door that Cas had slammed in my face. I whipped around, drawing one of the guard's swords. As expected, they were unprepared for my wild action. I sent my knee into the groin of the one whose blade I stole, while jamming the hilt of the sword into the other's temple. Before they had time to react, I slammed the other into the stone wall, hard enough to knock him out. They both slumped to the ground in front of me. Less than fifteen seconds after Cas had descended the stairs, I again ran after him.

The dungeon dripped with a cold and dreadful aura, but I didn't let my bare feet dwell on it as I flew down the hall. It came to a T shape, but I heard a jingling off the right side. I veered towards the noise. Sure enough, a guard was fumbling with a ring of keys, Cas behind him. In a moment, the door swung open, and I darted into the cell, whipping around to slam the bars shut after me. The guard and Cas gaped at me as I stormed in silently thanks to my unadorned feet. Ezren stood almost naked, wearing only a small cloth covering his manhood and a collection of chains. They circled his neck, wrists, and ankles. I noticed a smattering of unhealed bruises and cuts that danced over his muscled body.

"Terra," Cas bit out, "what do you think you're doing?"

"I will not let you kill him, Cas," I breathed.

He rolled his eyes. "Oh, for the gods' sake, I wasn't going to kill him. Even before I knew you two were bound! He's a Dragon shifter. There's no way my father would condone him being wasted. But Terra, he has to pay for what he did. If not in body, then at least in mind."

"And what exactly did he do?" I shot back.

Cas looked at me, evaluating. "You really don't know what the binding means, do you?" he whispered.

My blank expression offered answer enough. "Ah, *now* this all makes sense. You don't know what he took from you." Cas shook his head in disbelief.

Ezren cut in, his voice strained and dry. "She took from me, too, Princeling. And if you're too young to remember, one does not *know* when a binding will happen. It just does."

"Well, you still chose to couple with her! How did that make you feel, warrior? To know you were claiming an untouched female betrothed to another? Did that excite you?" Cas growled at Ezren. "Or did you just want a second chance, with any poor unsuspecting female, to redeem yourself after your last attempt?"

I turned around to face Ezren, pressing my back to the cell door. His eyes were blazing with a rage directed at Cas, doing his best to see if looks could truly kill. I searched them, looking for some ulterior motive, an answer to *why* he'd chosen to couple with me. He'd certainly been resistant at first, but Cas's vague accusations fell flat. No words could shatter what we'd experienced. It had been etched on my body, and his.

But, no matter the connection we'd shared—it did not change the fact he'd lied to me.

"Look at me."

His eyes pulled away from Cas. They traced my body, lingering on every inch of exposed skin. He had never seen me in a dress, save for the silk shift I wore during our coupling. Hell, he had rarely seen me *washed*. His expression seemed to brighten ever so slightly as it followed the lines of my figure.

"Why?" I whispered, a tear escaping down my face. "Why did you lie? You may not have spoken complete falsehoods, but you took advantage of my trust. You let me believe the crap Jana spewed about my Witch mother being dead, let me believe my memories had been restored when you *knew* there were key details missing. I could take it from anyone. *Anyone.* But not you," I breathed, my voice hitching on the last word.

His gaze fell, landing on the new ring I now wore on my left hand. I shook my head, knowing he would say nothing in front of Cas. And though I still raged at the warrior, I wanted Cas's focus elsewhere. I didn't know what kind of psychological torture he had in store for Ezren, but I wasn't about to allow it. Any verbal weapons used against him would be wielded by me, and me alone.

So, I turned on my heel, exiting the cell and slamming the door behind me. I slipped my arm in Cas's, steering him back towards the exit. "Come on, Cas, he's not worth it," I said, my words sending a slice of pain to my chest, nearly breaking my resolve. Cas hesitated, but then I looked up at him, batting my lashes, playing wounded princess. It wasn't difficult.

"Please?" I breathed. He regarded me with concern and nodded. And then we left. While I knew I had spared Ezren whatever torment Cas had planned for the time being, I had the overwhelming feeling that he was not safe there.

CHAPTER TWENTY-ONE

LITTLE DOVES

$\mathcal{C}$as walked me back to my chamber, silent the entire way. I sensed I should not press him, that his rage kept him ensnared, dangerous. I didn't remember him like this. He was always the calm one, never riled, never had anger bubbling under the surface like many males did. He was a carefree boy when I knew him.

Things had changed for both of us.

"Have your maid dress you in dinner-wear," he said when we reached my door. "I assume you don't want to meet your mother with your breasts out." He said the last part with joking intent, but I flinched anyway. Then he brought his lips to my hand, brushing them over my skin, a whisper of a kiss. He made to let go, but I held on. So much felt the same, yet so much changed in the boy I'd known. I wanted to know why.

"What happened to you after I... left?"

His guarded eyes seemed to soften. "It was a long seven years, *mi karus*. You may remember me sweet as a dove, but that's because *you* balanced me. When I had to accept your death, well, I certainly fought that idea for a time. I was young. I didn't understand why someone would want to hurt you. But eventually, I did. I came to see the evil that weighs against the good. And my world changed. I lived in a world where you no longer existed, and that made it feel like my place in it was... well, different. I didn't want to be the dove anymore."

I don't know if it was the nostalgia of our childhood or the brokenness in his voice, but I reached up and laid my palm on his smooth, clean-shaven face. I searched his eyes, and I kissed his cheek, soft and hesitant, like we were still kids in the woods. And he kissed mine back for a moment, but then pulled away, his guard up once more. He shook his head, a wry smile spreading over his face, and murmured, "I'm not a little dove anymore, Terra. Remember that."

And then he left. I stood alone at my door, wondering not for the first time about *my* world and *my* place in it.

OLEA STOOD READY, a plethora of evening gowns laid out on the bed in front of her or hung from the armoire and other creative places. I paid little attention to them.

"Olea, what's a binding?" She threw me a suspicious glance as she busied herself laying out the jewels that matched each dress. "Et esna a common theng, te be sure. Why'd ye ask?"

"I heard some courtiers talking about it, and if I'm to be a Fae princess, don't you think I should know what everyone is talking about...?" I ran my fingers down one of the bodices, hoping to seem interested in the clothes more than the binding.

"Aye me lady, aye. The bindin' only happens durin' a couplin', which es when two Fae join their magic durin' intimacy. The couplin' doesna go wrong, per-say, but them magics like each other too much, ye see? They're too powerful together, so the magics decide te never part. They *bind*. And then the couple—their very souls—are bound fer eternity. For ef one en the bindin' es hurt, so es the other. And ef one en the bindin' dies, well so does the other," she said, giving her last few words the drama of a folklore reading for small children.

So it's... a death bond? What in the bizarre Fae-Witch world—

"From what I've heard, et can only be a High Fae, one w' real old magic, that can bind. Ets also been said et can only happen between Salanti, but et happens so rare, ye see, I dinna know for sure."

My head swam. "How *do* you know for sure when a binding happens? And what is... salami?"

She laughed out loud, deep from her belly. "Well, salami es a cured cut a' pork, ver' good w' cheese. *Salanti*," she emphasized, "es a title. Et means *Match*—like yer soul's twin. Ye canna know ef yer Salanti without a blood sharin', which es part a' the Matchin' cere- mony. Ef yer blood grows stronger together, then yer Match es true— and yer Salanti. Usually, ets quite romantic and ends en a marital pact, but not always. Et gives the two special abilities, ye see, te share thoughts an' senses and the like."

I furrowed my brow. The concept of romantic partnerships blessed by special abilities and cemented in sharing blood was unfa- miliar—I didn't think I learned about it as a child. *Had Viturius and the Rexi been Salanti?*

"Do you have a Salanti?"

Olea shook her head, her eyes wistful. "Ets rare. Not near as rare as a bindin', but rare. Many search fer a proper Match an' never find em'."

"And the binding," I prompted, directing her back to my unan- swered question. "How do you know for sure if it's done?"

"They say ye'll know because each well have a little bet of the other— a special mark a' some kind," she answered. "Oh, me almost forgot! Stay where ye are, I'll be right back. Me hath a surprise for ye te wear tonight."

Olea scurried out of the room, and I stood there, one hand on the bedpost, one hanging on my stomach, breathing in and out as slowly as I could to remain calm. I bunched up my chiffon skirt in one arm and folded the lace undergarment back with my other hand, extending my left leg forward. And sure enough, though I'd started to doubt my memory, one shimmering green Dragon scale lay imprinted there, right on top of my hipbone.

That explained my unnatural bruising. What Ezren felt, I felt. His pain was mine.

Now that I knew its significance, the slight burning from the scale turned into more of a gentle searing sensation. I wondered how Olea hadn't seen it before, but I guessed she wasn't watching me all that closely when I stepped naked into the tub.

Olea put me in a gown of green satin, long-sleeved and simple, to my relief. It still pushed my breasts to my chin and nearly suffocated my waist, but at least it fully covered my midsection and legs. She wiped my face and recast the paint on my cheeks and lips, leaving my eyes with less kohl than before. She brushed my hair out long and let it fall in waves around me. Finally, she placed a simple crown on my head, not much more than a band of gold two fingers wide. As soon as it rested there, I felt a gentle vibration. Olea turned me to the mirror, and I watched flowering spill out of the crown. Vines and blooming buds traveled down my hair and all across my dress, adorning the fabric. The pattern swirled and moved with my breath against the swish of my gown. The largest blossoms gathered at the hem, but other than that, the image never appeared to still. I was a living garden, the Earth incarnate.

"How?" I didn't normally enjoy dresses, but this one warranted appreciation.

Olea shook her head, admiring her work in the mirror. "I dinna know, lassia. I only heard that Cas brought et back after one a' hes great adventures. Supposed te display the wearer's power, should he or she be worthy. Et looks splended on ye."

I took one last look at my image and exhaled. Flowers streaked my hair, and hues of orange, fuchsia, and deep red traveled around my green covered body.

"Olea, what is the queen like?" I asked, fiddling with the large purple rock that sparkled on my finger. When I first met Olea, she mentioned the Rexi had never been on Fae land before—maybe that's why I didn't remember her.

"The Rexi?"

I nodded. If she thought the question strange, she didn't show it.

"I dinna know much, mess. Formidable, te be sure. She only arrived but a few days before ye, and she rare attends banquet."

The Rexi arrived a few days before me. Having never been on Fae land in her life.

She knew I was coming.

OLEA LED me to the top of the grand stairs that emptied into the foyer. Cas waited there, casually leaning against a stone pillar. He'd tied his dark hair low at the nape of his neck, and he wore a simple black warrior's jacket with a few buttons undone, revealing the contours of his chest and a few swirling lines of a tattoo. His eyes glinted upon my approach, admiring the gold on my head and the purple on my finger. He bowed, hinging low at the waist. Before I could attempt a curtsey, he reached up to my hair and plucked a purple iris. He fastened it to his jacket and a dazzling smile stretched over his features.

The prince turned and extended his arm to lead me down the staircase. I placed my hand on his biceps, signaling a pause.

"We need to talk."

"Oh dear, that sounds ominous," he said back casually.

"I asked Olea what the binding is."

He closed his eyes and inhaled. "You don't need to worry about that. I have the best minds in Viribrum working out how to undo it.

And until then, Ezren won't be going anywhere. Nothing will happen to you, *mi karus*. I promise."

I shifted my weight. Though he'd intended his words for comfort, they addressed the wrong concern. "That wasn't really what I meant, Cas. Olea also told me about the Salanti thing. That the binding may only happen if the two are... meant to be Matched, or whatever."

Cas's face turned serious. "Salanti is an antiquated concept—one that cannot be proven without blood sharing, which is now a *choice* for females in this court," he snorted. "There was a time when it was not, when each suspected Salanti would have been forced to blood share and Match to see if their blood strengthened. Be grateful we live in more modern times, *mi karus*. While the binding is something completely out of our control, choosing to Match—choosing to cement that partnership—is not."

"Is there another way to test it? Without choosing to 'cement the partnership'? If I am *supposedly* meant to be Matched with someone, that feels like important information for us..." I drifted off, feeling transparent. A primal part of me needed to know if Ezren was my Match, even though I understood little of what it meant. But what good would knowing do? If we weren't Salanti, then the blood sharing would do nothing. And if we were...

Cas interrupted my spiraling thoughts. "There is an imprecise way to tell. It is said when Salanti find each other they omit a... potent smell to attract the other. Supposedly, the scent is fairly undetectable to the couple, almost subconscious, but god awful to those around them. There another matter of Salanti being able to communicate mind to mind that is a tell, but it typically manifests after the blood sharing."

A memory of Leiya commenting on my scent flashed through my mind. A moment later, I saw the image of Ezren standing in a river, his shirt sticking to his skin, telling me I'd *called* for him when the Earth split.

If I had been unmoving before, I was a statue from the palace halls now.

"But," Cas continued, "I scented nothing of that nature omitted from either of you earlier in the dungeon, and I'm pretty sure you'd know if he could read your thoughts." Cas lifted my chin, his fingers just grazing my skin. "I would put it out of your mind, *mi karus.* Likely your heritage wanted to bind, nothing more."

I chewed my bottom lip, unsure if that sentiment confused me more or less. Putting the Ezren thoughts aside, I refocused on the immediate issue. Dinner.

"Also... my mother. The Rexi. What is she doing here, Cas? She never bothered to come to Viribrum before, as far as I can remember. What does she want from me?"

Cas's snort rang hollow. "Now *that* I don't know. You'll have to ask her." Something more lingered in his gaze.

I did my best to look afraid and timid rather than the angry and confused I felt. "And what about Fayzien? No matter what Gia says, I know he hurt me, Cas. In Argention, he stripped me naked and sent his power through me. And I have strong reason to believe he killed the family that raised me."

Cas's mouth formed a grim line, the lack of shock on his face leaving me stunned. "Yes, don't worry, I'm dealing with him, too." The confirmation that it *was* Fayzien who murdered my family sent a burning trail down my throat. But before I could say another word, he took my arm in his and led me down the stairs. We veered to the left, the doors of the great banquet swinging open before us.

As WE WALKED into the hall, a mustached servant tapped his staff to the ground, and the reveling quieted. He announced us by name and title, and we walked through the crowds of courtiers that were bustling with excitement a moment before. This transported me right back to Spring Day. Except instead of the Matron guiding me through the chaos, Cas did. This time I was even more picked over, like a prized mare being led to auction. The hall glittered with rows of long candle-laden tables that led up to one horizontal head table facing them all on a dais. Cas noticed me eyeing it and whispered in my ear, 'The table of the crown.' In the middle sat the king, Darlan. And next to him, his honored guest. The Rexi Neferti, Queen of Nebbiolo. My birth mother.

The silence became near deafening by the time we approached them. Cas unwound my arm from his and bowed deeply, shooting me a look on the way up. I took the hint and curtsied, extending my right foot far behind and touching my knee to the ground. I dipped my head in deference and let my emerald satin skirts pool all around me on the stone floor, at which point the magic running over my dress developed a mind of its own. The vines that traveled down my skirts extended beyond the hem in an instant, parting slightly at the root and hissing like dozens of forked snake tongues seething at a threat. My mouth fell ajar at the malice of it, and I stood in a hurry. The silence grew louder.

The queen regarded me with shrewd study, revealing nothing on her face. But then, in a relieving moment, the king laughed, said something to welcome us, and gestured to the band to resume playing.

I let out a breath, and Cas guided me up to the table. The revelers acted preoccupied, complying with the king's subtle order to sway with the music, but I felt hundreds of eyes on me. The queen rose, her iridescent silver gown swaying as she stood. She brought each of her hands to my cheeks, pressing her unnaturally long, gleaming chrome nails into my face.

"Terragnata, at last, you have returned. What a joyous moment it is when a mother can look upon her grown daughter, a sight I thought I would never be blessed with," she said, her voice full of warmth and soothing calm, which did not meet her eyes. Before I could open my mouth to speak, she drew me into her, and placed her lips to each cheek, leaving a sticky sensation that indicated the red of her lip stain remained.

The awkwardness and wonder of meeting her overwhelmed me.

She was the woman who bore me, who brought me into the world. But beyond the softness in the curves of her face and the color of her hair, I could sense no genuine connection between us. She had not raised me, not as a child nor an adolescent. I felt a wrongness in her I couldn't place.

Cas pulled back my chair, and I sat on her right. Cas joined the king on his left, and we were two children again, at the elbows of our life-givers.

"Mother," I said, looking at her out of the corner of my eye whilst surveying the room. "How long has it been? Over fifteen years?" I asked, feigning innocence in my tone. If she hadn't ever been on Fae land, I guessed the last time I saw her was when I left Nebbiolo as a child.

Her saccharine smile dripped with contempt. "Yes daughter, fifteen exactly, I believe, as I recall your birthday is soon. Twenty, you will be, and I last saw you when you left Nebbiolo, just a few days into your fifth year."

The king chimed in. "Oh, Terra, it is *good* to have you back! So splendid that you will turn twenty soon. It is not usually a day of marked celebration, you may remember, due to its insignificance in the context of a Fae lifespan. Fifty, now that is a celebration year I will never forget. But since you have just arrived, I would relish the excuse to throw a gala in your honor."

"How sweet an offer, Your Majesty. But I am afraid we will be departed by the day. It is time Terra returns to her birth country," the Rexi said with false regret.

I bristled at her audacity, but before I could protest, Cas jumped in. "What a lovely idea it is to allow Terra the opportunity to explore her homeland. But, I am afraid that won't be possible, given she must stay here to plan the nuptials. And the Skøl, of course."

"You can't be serious," the queen said, gaping at Cas, an expression I guessed she didn't wear often.

I furrowed my brow, ignoring the word *nuptials,* something needling at my memory. "What is the Skøl?"

"I'm afraid he isn't joking, Neferti," the king said. "We had origi-nally agreed to forgo the Skøl, I know, as a favor to secure our alliance. But that was when we thought Terra would mature in this land. Terra has been gone a long while, in terms of her formative years. The people don't know her; she is not much more than a foreign Nebbiolon Witch. And many vied for Cas's hand in the time she was gone. Custom must be upheld," he said firmly.

"What is the Skøl?" I repeated.

King Darlan turned to me. "The Skøl is an ancient tradition where Fae females compete for the hand of the future king. It is a wonderful competition of might, beauty, and skill. It is how my beloved late wife, Agustina, won my hand. May she rest in peace. Don't worry, Terra, I have no doubt you will best them all," he finished with a wink.

"And if I lose, then I don't marry Cas?" I asked, attempting to hide my relief. I could barely tell truth from lies, and I certainly was *not* ready to commit my life to someone I no longer knew. And there was the matter of my green-eyed Fae, whom I'd yet to forgive, but also yet to forget.

Cas narrowed his eyes at me, no doubt reading my expression, and replied, "Yes, assuming you lost in a way that left you *alive*. Some of the events are quite brutal. Not all the competitors survive, and many eliminations occur by... physically besting the opponents."

I stared at him, recovering after a moment. "You mean killing," I said flatly.

Cas nodded, looking only a little regretful and not nearly as perturbed as I knew I did. The thought of having to slaughter others for Cas's hand made me ill. "And what if I am not ready to be married?"

At that, the three of them gaped at me like I'd spoken blasphemy.

My mother cut in, her voice low and sharp. "Terragnata, it is not a matter of being ready. It is a matter of duty. It is time Witch and Fae unite. Wouldn't you agree, Darlan?"

"And what of the matter that I am bound to another?" I said before the king could reply.

The king choked on his food, and Cas's eyes enlarged with swift, unforgiving rage. But the queen looked unruffled. "That will be dealt with, my dear; it is not of your concern."

The silky way she said those last words sent a shiver down my spine. An idea popped in my head, unannounced. "Why don't *you* just marry King Darlan if you're so eager to cement ties between Fae and Witch? Are you not both widowed? What a powerful match it would be," I said, fighting the petulance that worked its way into my tone.

Once again, the king choked on his food, and Cas's eyes threatened to bulge from his head. The Rexi just laughed and said, "Child, your naïvety betrays you. It is not simply your union with Cas that is required; it is the heir that you will produce, the heir that will be of both bloods. While I would be honored to accept an offer from King Darlan, I am afraid I am much too old to bear a babe once more."

She smirked at me, so dismissive in response, so satisfied in expression. I rose, pushing my chair back, and the noise of it drew some eyes to me from the crowd. I descended to the front of the dais and curtsied just short of kissing the floor. This time, the vines, which had roiled around me, stilled. "I beg your leave, Your Majesties; I am feeling tired after such an eventful day." Before I turned to go, I caught Cas's eye. Pure bewilderment had replaced the anger on his face.

Good. I wasn't the only one who was no longer a little dove.

CHAPTER TWENTY-TWO

EMPTY CHEST

"*E*t esna proper te walk out on a queen or king, *especially* durin' a' banquet, lassia," Olea said as she readied me for bed. "I suppose ye'll be needin' trainin a' the ways a' the court."

I didn't reply and Olea fell silent, dressing me in the gold satin shift once more, and wiping my face clean. She braided my long hair in twin plaits that touched my mid-back. I then bid her to take me to Gia's room, for she had not been present at the banquet, and along with Fayzien's absence, I noted it. I wouldn't be able to rest without checking on her.

When I arrived, Gia was already asleep, and I crawled into bed with her, sending the maids away. I told Olea to fetch me in the morning. Gia mumbled upon feeling my presence, as if she had expected it. I tried to relax into her steady breathing, my eyes fixed on the sliver of moonlight that shone through the window.

But I could not sleep, for the Dragon scale continued to pull at me from my hip bone. The overwhelming feeling radiated into my low belly, and it oscillated between a pulsing and a slow burn. I let the moon travel lower in the window, waiting for the almost dusk hour when I knew most of the revelers would either be in bed or too drunk to remember if they encountered a wanderer in the halls. Once late enough, I slipped out through the door, clicking it shut behind me.

I yawned next to the guard stationed by the door, feigning exhaustion. "Even the soft snoring of a woman keeps me up," I said groggily.

"Will you need an escort back to your room, miss?" the guard asked.

I shook my head. "I know the way. Thank you for the kind offer."

I ambled at first, making sure I rounded several corners before I took off in a silent run. My Fae sight let me pick up on the cracks and markings I had noted before. And within a few minutes, I peered around a wall, looking down at the main staircase. There must have been another less conspicuous way to get down, but it would have likely been a passage used by the servants, and I was in no position to wander through servant quarters without being noticed.

But as luck would have it, I found the foyer empty. If any guests still reveled, they had moved to private quarters. I crept down the staircase, mustering all the stealth I could. Only four more passageways, five turns total, until I reached the entrance to the dungeons. I hurried forward, planning my distraction of the guards. When I began to take my last turn, the sound of a familiar voice reached my ears, and I froze.

Fayzien—with a companion I could not identify. They spoke in drunken, hushed tones.

"Well, now that Cas knows he's bound to the bitch, we can't hurt him. At least not physically. But in a way, mental torture is that much more delicioussss," Fayzien slurred. "And Cas is perfectly supportive of that." His cackle raised the fine hairs on my arms.

"And how do you do it, then?" the unknown male voice asked, probing.

"Ezren doesn't know Cas lets me see him. So I describe in detail what I'm going to do to the bitch now that he's locked up. I tell him that by the time he's let out of the cell, I will have made her scream my name so many times she will have forgotten his. I don't know if he fully buys it, but the image hurts him all the same." Fayzien snickered.

I vibrated with rage, for myself, for my family, for Ezren. And though I directed the bulk of my anger towards the vile Fae-Witch I'd overheard, I couldn't help but think of Cas, too. How could he cooperate with such a monster? I cursed myself for not having a blade, for I would have given anything to shove a dagger into Fayzien's sickened throat.

A small part of me remembered how it felt when I'd thought he'd died. How the grief hadn't budged an inch.

"I heard you killed the collaborators, as well—the ones that sailed for Panderen," Fayzien's companion said, their voices growing nearer. My heart at once sunk with pain and got swept up in a fresh wave of fury. I was close to doing something stupid. But I darted two hallways back, hiding myself in the shadows of an alcove. I waited for them to pass, hoping the ale that clearly lingered in their veins would dull their Fae senses.

Fayzien laughed with a darkness that made me cringe. "I made the North Sea swallow that ship whole. What happened to its passengers, I neither know nor care."

They continued their walk, their conversation turning to a dull recounting of the night's festivities. "I am going to kill you, Fayzien of Nebbiolo." I breathed the death vow when they were well out of earshot. *For Sanah, Leuffen, Leiya, Danson, Javis. Father. And Mother. Not. One. More.*

My whispered words hung in the air, burning with more hate than I'd known I could feel.

———

WHEN THEY WERE GONE, and I'd composed myself from the trembling shudders that wracked my body, I restarted my journey. To my relief, only one sentry guarded the dungeon door, lounging against the wall. I snuck into the hall and pressed my body into the side of another alcove just a few yards from where the guard stood. I needed to neutralize him without him recognizing me, or registering who disarmed him. I made a small bird noise, a sound I learned to create when we hunted grouse in the forest. He started at that, looking for the source of the call. He walked right past the alcove where I lay in wait.

I jumped on him from behind, covering his mouth with one hand and placing his neck in the crook of my other arm. He struggled for his sword, but given my legs wrapped around his midsection, he failed to reach his weapon. I tightened my grip, pressing my forearm harder into his air pipe. It only took a few moments before his body softened. I placed my feet on the ground once more and lowered him into the alcove I had jumped out from. He would wake up in a few minutes if I did nothing else, so I hit him on the head with the hilt of his dagger. And then I took the key ring from his belt and scurried down the wet stairs.

In moments I reached the T again, and I veered my jog right. In less time than that, I reached Ezren's cell. He sat in the corner, eyes closed, his head tilted back to rest on the stone wall. I stood there a moment, just watching him, knowing I had approached in silence. Eventually, he would get a whiff of my scent, but I no longer rushed.

He jumped to his feet, easy and smooth, the warrior in him showing. Anger and feelings of betrayal coursed through my veins, combining with desire and the discomfort I had from seeing him this way. Filth covered every inch of him, but the bulges of his abdomen, the sloping lines of tension in his arms, remained visible. It took me right back to that day in the Adimon mountains, blinded by the image of light and flowers and his hands all over me.

"Terra," he said, waking me from the memory.

I snapped my gaze back to his. Dull no longer, his eyes blazed into me in the same way they had when I first looked into them, him hovering over me in the Argen forest. I entered the cell, walking over to him. And then, with a silent prayer, I slipped the smallest key from the ring into his chains. I almost cried out in relief when I heard the click, and I undid the balance of his chains. He remained still as the last of them fell to the floor. His eyes landed on the ring I'd neglected to remove from my left hand.

"It seems you have accepted the prince's betrothal offering," Ezren said, his voice stiff and unreadable.

"I'm not here to discuss the prince, Ezren," I replied coolly.

He flinched almost imperceptibly at the use of his name. "Then what would you like to discuss?"

"Why?" The same question from before, yet unanswered. "Why didn't you tell me about my mom, my title, and Cas?" I whispered. "Why lie?"

"I didn't lie, Terra. I just couldn't tell you. I wanted to—many of us did—but we couldn't."

"Why!" I demanded, choking back tears. A sudden realization hit me like a slap. "My memories. Jana didn't free all of them, did she?" I breathed. "She withheld them from me on purpose. Why?"

He said nothing.

Anger bubbled in my voice. "Answer me, Ezren. Did she plant fake memories in my mind? Tell me the truth."

He looked at me again, his expression alight with the same hunger that woke me up mere days before. "You want the truth? Here it is. I *murdered* my wife. I've had to live with that guilt every day of my gods damned existence since. I could barely remember what it felt like to *hope*, let alone care for another. I've lived in a shadow—half asleep—wandering alone from one place to the next as a low-level warrior for coin.

"Until I met you. Half wild and covered in days of filth... brimming with fight and fire. You were so *alive*, and it was intoxicating— the first time I'd felt anything in a long time. In one hundred and fifty years, I have *never* met anyone like you. I didn't think anyone like you even existed. I knew you were betrothed, and it killed me not to say anything. So I tried to stay away, I really did. But then you made me *breathe* your wanting scent and..." he trailed off, a part of him twitching in my periphery.

I didn't move a muscle. I didn't dare glance away from his face.

"Believe me, I regret my actions. I should have never laid with you, not until you knew everything. And if I'd known the binding would happen... I would have let those Crona walk right into the human realm. But here we are, bound. And while they may try to undo it, so long as there is breath in my lungs, I will be bound to you, whether you like it or not."

My stomach twisted, like I'd just been punched. *He regrets lying with me, but not lying to me?* And all those words... Though not exactly a declaration of love, he'd spoken things I'd craved to hear deeply.

My wounds went deeper.

"I will never be bound to someone who deceives me, who lies to me. I've been lied to too many times in my life," I spat, barely able to get the words out without feeling physical pain in my chest. "After losing my family, I was so vulnerable. I let myself *trust* you. All of you. I won't make the same mistake again."

I made my way back to the cell door, swung it open, and stepped to the side to ensure some distance remained between us when he left.

"But right now, our binding is the one thing keeping my mother and the king from shoving me down the aisle to marry Cas. So you need to leave, Ezren. Go far, far away, and don't fucking come back," I choked out the last part, unable to meet his gaze. I fought the moisture threatening to streak my face, and I feared a look at those burning emerald eyes would undo me.

I didn't know if sending him away would prevent them from breaking the binding, but I knew he had to leave. Not only could I no longer trust Ezren, but I would never have a clear head to seek the truth—about my memories, my kidnappers, or how I felt about Cas—with him near.

Ezren stood before me, not too close, respecting my obvious

request for space. I bit my lip to keep the tears at bay and raised my head, willing myself to look at him in the end.

His expression grew soft. "Terra, I'm sorry. I should have never let things go as far as they did. Just know that even though I may never be able to give you what you deserve, I will always be there for you. Break your left small toe, and I'll know you want me to come. At any other injury, all of which I will feel, I promise not to interfere."

And he walked past me, turning once more from the end of the hall. "Should you choose to one day marry Cas, or should you not, I think you'll make an inspirational and revolutionary queen, whatever region is your domain."

And then he was gone, and my heart broke, which shocked me, for I had thought it was already broken.

CHAPTER TWENTY-THREE

TATTOO LESSONS

I let myself cry for a long while, huddled in a ball on the floor, arms wrapped around my sides, not caring if the guard woke and found me. Eventually, I realized it had been quite some time and that the sun would rise soon. I made my way up the stairs and eased the dungeon door shut. When I went to the alcove to check on the guard, he still slept, naked and bound with small remnants of his clothing. Ezren would have needed something to wear out of the palace.

My eyes had swollen, and my head pounded. While I wished to go back to my room to sleep, I also wished for some semblance of comfort. I considered returning to Gia, but that would raise questions with the guards.

So I sought out Cas. Not for intimacy, but he was still a friend, and I knew he would hold me if I asked him. I returned to the wing where my quarters were and walked in the direction he had left my room the day before. It was a gamble, but I suspected they housed me in the East Wing—that of the crown. If my memory of the palace layout didn't fail me, he should be nearby.

I passed several doors, but they were unguarded, so I assumed they weren't his. Finally, I came upon two massive wooden doors that would open away from each other, a pair of burly guards flanking them.

"Is this Cas's room?" I asked from beneath lowered lashes, attempting to defer suspicion by looking like his to-be bride shyly paying him an early morning visit.

One of them cleared his throat. "Ehm, yes, miss, but I don't think he wishes to be disturbed—"

I cut him off by swinging one of the doors open.

And there stood Cas, naked by the moonlit window, smoking some sort of pipe. His hair hung unbound and wild, and I could now see the full extent of the swirling lines of tattoos that snaked up his body. Thorned vines tangled with fir sprigs and aspen leaves, running from his outer knee, up the side of his buttock, up his lean abdomen, and then culminating in a cluster of buds and branches on his pectorals. And even from my vantage point, I could see the word formed by small letters floating amongst the flora and fauna that decorated his chest.

"T E R R A," it read.

I gaped at him, and he returned with a casual incline of his head, as if he expected me to be there, unashamed of his bareness. "Do you like it? I got it the day I turned fifteen. It had been over a year, and I'd finally accepted you weren't coming back. I got it to keep your memory alive, to never forget you, and to remind myself to never love again, to prevent another experience of such... loss. We were so young, never married, and yet I felt I knew the pain of my father when he lost my mother. Such dramatics, are we not, when we're young?" He chuckled to himself. I stood there, gaping a moment before I realized I had not sensed the other presences in the room.

My eyes shot to the chaise by the fire first, which had a white-haired Fae female draped over it, very passed out, very naked, and very covered in welts that ran the full length of her lean backside. And then I looked to the bed, and blinked several times, for I almost did not believe it was Fayzien that I saw there, a sheet partially hiding his manhood, his breathing soft and relaxed.

I looked back at Cas, my eyes wide with confusion, shock, and anger. He smiled at me once more, this time with sadness. "I told you, *mi karus*, I am no longer a little dove." And with that, he guided me to the door and sent me through with a gentle push, shutting it with finality.

As I walked back to my room, a numbness descended over me. I was too stunned by what I had just seen and the significance of it all to feel any real emotion. The image of Fayzien asleep in Cas's bed was one I'd not soon forget, but also one I had *no* fucking clue what to do with. The mixture of the unexpected revelation on Cas's love life combined with the pain of Ezren leaving was a dull ache in my body I knew would throb for a long time.

I collapsed in my bed and stared at the ceiling of my canopy. When sleep eventually claimed me, I slept dreamlessly.

THE SUN STREAMED through parted drapes the next morning, but instead of Olea bustling around my room, Cas's head peaked out over the armchair in front of the fireplace. I shut my eyes and pulled the covers above my head. The philandering Fae heard me stir and parted the bed curtains, sitting down next to me.

"I know you're awake in there." I moaned in response, and he drew back the duvet. "Good morning *mi karus*. Tired today, are we? Did you get up to any midnight mischief last night?" he asked, his tone lighter than expected.

I knew he wasn't referring to my visit to his chambers, but I said anyway, "I was thinking about it, but the lucky lad ended up already having his hands—and his bed—full."

He chuckled. "I didn't mean that. As you may or may not know, Ezren escaped last night."

I rolled over, facing my back to him. "Ezren's whereabouts are not of my concern," I grumbled.

"Ah, I see then. Well, the one that freed him may be of concern to you. For freeing a traitor, under Viri law, is punishable by death."

"Hmm. Well, did the guards see who did it?"

"Apparently, they did not."

"How unusual. What a mystery."

Cas chuckled again. I turned towards him, my head still lying on the pillow.

"What's got you so cheery this morning, then?" I demanded. "I can't imagine it's the time in the sack with that murdering bastard."

My insult didn't land. "I just forgot how feisty you are, Terra. Regardless of everything that's happened, I am truly glad to have you back," he said, his eyes glittering.

The image of Fayzien naked in Cas's bed flashed in my mind, curdling my empty stomach. I sat up, bringing my face closer to his. "Why him, Cas? He's a monster. He murdered my family in cold blood; he violated me. He sank a ship full of Fae and Witch kind who were just trying to protect me. He should pay with his *life* for what he's done. How can you be intimate with someone like that?" My guts twisted at the thought, acid bubbling up my throat.

He snorted. "Well, for one, I hardly call what Fayzien and I do intimacy. Secondly, I've known him for a long time. He came to Valfalla as the Nebbiolon emissary after your disappearance. He opened my eyes to a new world—a world that has helped me deal with some of the uglier sides I'd developed since losing you. I never trusted him; he worked for your mother, for the gods' sake. But he's not as evil as you might think."

I gaped at him, not knowing if I should press further on *when* Fayzien's lessons began. Cas had only been thirteen when I was taken.

The thought almost made me lose what little remained in my stomach.

"The fact that Fayzien began to broaden your sexual horizons—

when you were still a *child*—is not at all a reason I shouldn't kill him," I spat.

Cas rolled his eyes. "I'll have you know, I was a consenting age when those lessons started. And regarding his violation of you—I have punished him greatly. I guarantee he will never do it again. If it's his life you think he owes, well, that's not up to you. Do not take revenge into your own hands, Terra. Murdering another in Viribrum, no matter your quarrel, no matter if you are a *Nebbiolon princess*, is also punishable by death. Anyway, as for his killing of those humans or Jana's collaborators, I don't know if you can really blame him. He likely just followed orders from the Rexi."

I bristled at the way he said *those humans.* "What do you mean? How could *she* have ordered him to kill my human family? She would've had to have known..." I trailed off.

She would've had to have known I was alive.

"Cas," I breathed, "Jana made it sound like Fayzien kidnapped me and killed Viturius of his own volition, because he was threatened by my existence or something. But he did it under orders, didn't he?"

He exhaled through clenched teeth. "I believe so, yes."

"Why?" I whispered, fear blooming in my chest. *Why would my birthmother have my birthfather killed... and me hidden?*

"I'm still working on that, *mi karus*. It took me long enough just to *find you*; it will take me a while to figure out the evil Witch queen's master plan," he said, attempting to inject humor into his tone. "And I can only push Fayzien to reveal so much at a time."

His joke did little to penetrate my focus. "You sent Jana and the others, didn't you?" I asked, remembering his *that was never part of the deal* comment about Ezren. The pieces started to form a picture.

"I did. I couldn't leave Valfalla without raising suspicions with Darlan—he'd long forbade me from continuing to search for you. He was convinced you were lost forever and that I'd go mad if I didn't stop looking. But we'd finally found a solid lead, so I sent Jana and whatever rebel regiments she'd been operating with to get you. She was a good friend of your father, and I had grown to know her after his death. She, too, had suspected there was more to what happened than the bullshit 'Drakkarian Witch kidnapping' story your mother sold to Darlan and our kingdom."

"Why did Jana lie to me then? She said my mother had died when I was young and never mentioned my title. She kept my memories about who you were hidden."

He closed his eyes for a moment. "I may have given her too much liberty—I was so desperate to get you back. I told her to do whatever it took to persuade you to go with her. It's possible that she thought bringing everything back would be too overwhelming for you. I have questioned her, of course, and that's the story she tells."

My mind buzzed with questions, processing the knowledge that my birth mother had been the one to kill my sire and place me in the human realm. "How did you find me in the first place? How did you even know I was alive?"

Cas kicked off his shoes and sat fully on the bed, causing me to wiggle over and make room.

"A few years into my travels, I found myself in a tea den in the Hafian desert. I overheard the strangest story. A wanderer, a practitioner of the ways of the old gods, talked of a Fae girl that he'd met in the human realm. The girl, not more than fourteen, appeared human, given she lived with humans and her scent was that of humans. But he knew she was Fae because one day, he saw her fall from a forty-foot tree, a fatal crash that should have crushed her human ribs, punctured her lungs, and killed her instantly. But she lived.

"I pressed him on the tale, to tell me details of the girl. He shared enough of his knowledge that I firmly believed it was you, but in the end, he wouldn't tell me where you were. He said the code of the wanderer, the old ways of the gods, demanded he not reveal such things. I would have killed him right then, but I didn't want to interfere with the gods."

"I remember that fall," I whispered, a tear running down my cheek at the memory of my brothers and the way they'd rushed to me. "No one could explain how I'd lived."

Cas rested a hand on mine. "After that, I enlisted Jana to help my search. Things were getting worse on the relations front—the Rexi had used your death as a catalyst to ripen tensions between Viribrum and Drakkar, and Darlan had fully taken the bait. After another two years, we found one of your original abductors, who confessed you were alive, living amongst humans in Argention. Jana left immediately to find you—to bring you back to Viribrum."

I nodded, feeling some relief. His story of how I was captured, hidden, and ultimately found at least lined up with Jana's.

"I never thought the Rexi would catch wind of it, let alone show up in *Valfalla*. I mean, she's never even left Nebbiolo since she was Siphoned at age thirteen."

Siphoned. The word snagged in my mind. Dane mentioned it before Ezren and I had coupled. I still didn't know what it meant exactly—Jana had only told me it was "a sacred bur oak that fed her power." Before I could ask, Cas continued.

"But I suspect she discovered we'd found you, sent Fayzien to collect you, and then waited for us to bring you here in the case he failed."

A numbness descended over my flesh. "So... what now?"

"The Rexi arriving has been a... complication. She pressured Darlan to jail Jana and her crew immediately, claiming they were involved in your abduction. I'd planned to reveal the Rexi's guilt to my father when you returned, but that went out the window the moment she arrived. Her power is not to be underestimated, Terra—the stories I've heard..." He shuddered. "It would be a serious risk to challenge the Rexi's integrity whilst she's here. I need hard proof before I tell Darlan, before I make my next move."

"We. Before *we* make *our* next move."

The corner of Cas's lips twitched. "So last night didn't scare you away too much, then?"

"I still don't know what to think about last night." *Half-true.* His dismissal of Fayzien's behavior enraged me, but I needed Cas's help.

He turned towards me more directly now, the golden flecks in his eyes illuminated. "Terra, I have to say this. You were my first true love, and you will be my last. I have never opened my heart to another, and I never will. In that way, it will only ever be you."

"But in body?" I asked quietly, unable to meet his eyes.

"Like I said, a lot has happened in the last few years. I have developed... tastes. Needs that you can never satisfy."

"And you would never let me try? To satisfy your... needs?" I asked, not sure if I wanted to try, but needing to know where I stood.

He paused. "Some of the things, well, no. There are some desires I have that I would never, ever involve you in. But they need to be filled... Filling those desires is how I maintain control of the things inside of me that I would rather you not see."

I eyed him and exhaled. "I get now why you made that whole display of proposing to me, having Olea dress me up like a harlot. You have a reputation, don't you? You needed to extinguish the rumors that you wouldn't uphold your commitment."

His lips formed a tight, guarded line. "No matter what you think of me or what you saw last night, I will always, always protect you."

While the pang of Ezren's departure still pressed heavy on my chest, Cas was here—he was real. He was the only thing from my old life that made sense, the only thing I could believe in. "I want to know you, Cas. All of you," I whispered.

His eyes searched mine, and I could tell he was unsure.

"May I see it again?" I asked. He cocked his head in question, a wicked smile appearing on his face, and I rolled my eyes. "Your tattoo." I gestured to his chest.

He nodded but made no effort to remove his shirt. I sat up more, the sheets falling away from me, revealing the thin shift that did little to hide the curves of my body. He rested with his back against the headboard, and I leaned over him, undoing each button. And then I drew the sides of the shirt away from him, exposing the artwork on his chest.

I let my fingers run along the ink, tracing the letters of my name, the displays of the Earth. Cas closed his eyes. "It's beautiful," I murmured.

His gaze grew foggy—distant. "There was a time when I thought you'd never see it."

I paused a moment, letting my fingers continue to roam the lines of the image on his abdomen, remembering the closeness we shared as kids. He must have felt an utter lack of control when I was taken. While the image of Fayzien in his bed remained ripe in my mind, as did the pain of Ezren's departure, a desire wound through me I could not completely deny.

I kissed each letter, lingering my lips from one to the next. He drew in a sharp breath, and I saw the whisper of movement in his trousers.

"And now that I have seen it?" I breathed.

His voice turned to growl. "Are you trying to tease me, Terragnata?"

I smirked, feigning innocence. "What*ever* are you referring to, Prince Casmerre?"

At this, he pulled me on top of him, his hands firm on my hips, raising his own into mine. Invisible ropes tightened around my wrists, raising them above my head as if they were fastened to the beam above me. I pulled on them, and a gentle but firm tug responded.

I narrowed my eyes at him for the use of magic.

"You have *no* idea what you're doing, Terra."

He put his mouth to the crook of my neck, a kiss that ended in the gentle tug of my skin with his teeth. I whimpered in reaction, unthinking, my whole body wrought with tension. Cas's hand crept up my shift until his palm lay flush between my thighs. He dipped his two fingers into my opening. I cried out, craving nothing but the wild ignorance of release. An invisible rope tightened around my mouth, stifling the noise. I was panting now, my nostrils flaring in and out at the speed of my heartbeat.

Cas lifted his two fingers for me to see, extending them apart, revealing a wetness from deep inside me. "I would be lying, Terra, if I said there weren't many times when I wondered how you would taste," he murmured, rubbing the wetness of me between his two fingers and his thumb. I moaned in response, the sound strangled by the invisible rope that separated my lips. He brought his fingers to his mouth, tasting me, his eyes shuttering for a moment.

Moisture crept down the skin of my inner thighs. Cas ran his hands under my shift, making to lift it above my head. But his fingers found the Dragon scale imprinted on my hip, and he stilled.

"Ahh, Ezren's mark." He ran the tip of his finger over it. I shuddered, struggling against my invisible binding. He furrowed his brow and cocked his head. "Interesting," he said, his thumb brushing the moisture that had slipped onto my inner thigh. "I wonder if this is for me." He examined my wetness once more. "Or for him."

He paused. "Or, I wonder if it's neither, and your desires are simply a result of settling back into your Fae form. It is ironic, though, that while I am marked for you, you are marked for him."

At that, he swung his feet over to the ground and stood, his open shirt parted. "I cannot tell you the satisfaction it brings me to see you like this, *mi karus*. If I were a less seasoned male, I would have my way with you right now, without a second thought. But not yet. I need to know it's really me you crave, and not a simple physical reaction, or the need to replace what you feel you have lost." And then he tilted my face up, letting his invisible rope on my mouth fall away, and kissed me, his lips brushing mine in a whisper that contrasted the firm grip on my jaw.

"One day, *mi karus*, I so hope." He slipped on his shoes and walked out. When he shut the door, the balance of the ropes fell, and I collapsed, a motionless heap on my bed.

CHAPTER TWENTY-FOUR

RELUCTANT ROYAL

I lay on the bed, unmoving, for a time, the phantom of desire still in me. Defeat and an overwhelming sense of loneliness clung to my skin. I considered attempting self-pleasure, but I was inexperienced and dejected.

Eventually, Olea came in and started the water for a bath. She coaxed me into it and gave me tea and biscuits and wouldn't stop her jabbering until I'd eaten half the portion.

My thoughts drifted as she discussed proper court etiquette. *What's the point of any of this? I should just take Gia and leave.*

If I remained here, I would be the object of endless gaming and scheming. Though I loved Cas in a way that would never cease, I still didn't know much about who he'd become, or what he wanted from me. And there was the matter of my longing for another.

"Terra, wallowin' doesna do much for ye," Olea said, her hands on her hips and a frown on her face.

I rolled my eyes, and she continued. "How're ye gonna prepare for the Skøl ef ye jest set here, as a wounded pup?"

"I have no interest in that absurd competition. I will not *kill* just for the chance at Cas's hand."

She clucked her tongue. "Well, ets lekely there'll be more death should ye not participate."

"And why do you say that?"

"Well, accordin' te tradition, the Skøl es only open te five challengers, should there be a favorite selected by the king. That would be ye, en thes case. But ef there es no favorite, none chosen, well then the competition es open te any Fae female that wishes te join. Ets only happened a few times, the last bein' Darlan's Skøl. Ets how he came te wed Agustina, a daughter a' common Fae. En that Skøl et was about a hundred Fae females that perished."

The thought of a hundred Fae females fighting to the death for a chance to marry Cas made my stomach drop. "In my case, should I decide to compete I mean, how are the five females chosen?"

"Each High Fae House family submets a female te compete. Ets te show the king's pick es the best, an' she canna be outwitted or beaten by even the top a' each House. The Five High Fae Houses can be traced back thousands a' years. Te be a' one a' them families, well, ets a great fortune."

I huffed. "Have there always been this many traditions and archaic rules in Viri culture? They are *extraordinarily* difficult to keep track of."

Olea only chuckled. "Yes, mess."

AFTER OLEA GOT me out of the bath, I dressed in training clothes, simple, soft leathers that allowed for free movement. And she redid my braids, winding them together in one large plait down my back. I asked her if I could get hold of the blades that I had on me when I arrived, and while she said she had not seen them, she promised to seek them out.

Olea deposited me at the training grounds, where I was to meet an instructor. The grounds were separate from the spectacle platform on the cliffs, where I had seen Cas again for the first time. These were proper warrior arenas, with spaces for conditioning, gravel pits for sparring, tools for archery, lanes for dagger throwing, and more.

My trainer had not yet arrived, so I walked around, feeling eyes follow me as I examined the spaces and weaponry. I watched a pair of Fae males spar in hand to hand combat, sizing up their techniques and comparing them to what I'd been taught in my early years, and re-taught by Leuffen. They were fancier, but also less scrappy and practical. I fingered the points of throwing knives and tested the weights of various swords. My sight landed on Cas in the conditioning arena, which sent a pang through my chest. He alternated from pushups to pullups on a metal bar set in the notches of two posts. I had not expected to see him again so soon after our morning encounter. And to make matters worse, the white-haired Fae I saw naked in his room the night before stood next to him, eying him as she struck a hanging flour sack. A wash of territorial possession came over me, though I knew I had no right to it. For a moment, I considered ignoring them.

But then, she looked my way and laughed.

Oh, this will be fun.

I made my way to the bow and arrow station and examined them. Finally, I found one with the right weight and balance and contour of shape. I stretched it out several times before I set out against the target. I knocked an arrow back into the bow and let it fly.

I could feel the searing stares as I not only hit the bull's eye on my target, but as I fired again and again at the targets surrounding me. To my delight, the white-haired female paid me no more attention, her gaze still fixed on Cas's glistening body while she struck the bag. In an instant, I sent my final arrow in her direction. It landed square in the middle of her flour sack, mere inches above her head. The small rip in the tension-loaded bag caused the whole thing to explode, flour shooting out all over her white hair and fair body.

She sputtered, clouds of flour puffing out of her mouth. She whipped around to look in my direction. Cas ceased his pullups and stared at me in disbelief, in good company with the rest of the trainees in the room. I saluted him with a smirk and left the arena.

THE WALK back to my room turned into a run. I didn't at all feel myself. Who was I in the first place? A part of me still wanted to kill Fayzien—a desire that had been driving me for the last month—but that part was wilting. I'd taken no pleasure in his death the first time; it absolved none of my grief and anger. If I was being honest with myself... I simply wanted to never see him again. To ensure he'd never hurt someone I loved *ever* again.

So unless I killed him, which Cas made clear could lead to my own hanging, I had to leave. I had to grab Gia and bolt. However, nothing but sea surrounded one side of the palace and miles of cobblestone maze blocked the other. And even if I *could* find a map to navigate the tangled city center, there was the matter of Gia's human fragility. I had no idea how long the journey back to the human realm would take without portaling—a skill I'd yet to learn. I could hunt and find clean water and shelter. But could I safely navigate thousands of miles of land inhabited by unknown magical creatures? With a pregnant human for a travel companion?

We were stuck here unless I could find someone to enlist for help.

The thought fired a synapse in my head. *Jana.* While she'd lied to me about my mother and my title, Cas seemed to trust her. And though I certainly didn't plan to forgive her actions anytime soon, I needed her. At minimum, she owed me the truth, but I also had a feeling she might be able to offer more.

Help to leave Viribrum.

I FOUND Jana with ease by stopping a lone, skinny-looking Fae in the serving quarters and passing him an unremarkable gem from my wardrobe for telling me where the king held the traitors.

Although determining their location came easier than expected, the access proved challenging. First, they were held in a much more secure location than Ezren had been, which puzzled me. The only way to access their cells, completely underground beneath the palace, was through tunnels leading from the guards' quarters next to the stables. Second, it seemed my prison break from the evening before had put the palace guard on notice, because about ten of them stood around where the young Fae pointed when I asked him to show me the entrance.

I bid the servant thank you and stayed lurking behind the corner that turned to the guards' housing and stables. I considered another late-night break-in, but they would expect that. Distraction seemed the best option, and one that didn't have my signature all over it. I would need help.

I found Gia in her room, staring out the window, and requested that she come with me for a walk. She was easy to motivate, and her lack of characteristic stubbornness bothered me, the abnormality prickling my senses.

But I was mission-focused. I tucked her arm through mine and led her around the castle, trudging through the muddy ground to approach the stables nearby the guards' quarters. We passed a group of guards gossiping about the poor soldier found tied up naked in that fateful alcove. And then we walked up to one of the stable hands grooming a recently ridden mare, brushing her sweat. I batted my eyes at the two of them in admiration.

"My, what an impressive steed. How lucky you are to be charged with her care," I said.

The young Fae met my eyes in surprise. "Y-yes, miss, mistress," he stuttered.

I placed my hand on his forearm as it continued to run the brush down her bright chestnut flank. "I would just adore the chance to help groom her," I purred.

He looked at me in alarm, as if assessing whether my request was a test. I could feel Gia's eyes of suspicion on me, but she said nothing.

"Do you have a prick?" I asked with an air of innocence, and he blanched. "A pick," I raised my brows. "To clean her hooves."

His cheeks flushed, and he handed me the tool. I went around the mare, crossing her at a distance from behind. Gia remained on her side, facing the guard quarters, jabbering with the stable hand about the types of horses they maintained and their training regimens. I knelt beside the chestnut and leaned into her. She shifted her weight and bent her knee, giving me her hoof in routine. I took it in one hand, but instead of picking it out with the other, I bent down and placed my palm on the ground. The mare's large body hid mine from the rest of the stable hands, and, more importantly, the guards.

I may have not been a Water Witch, but I had learned to bend the Earth. So, I coaxed the dirt, squeezing it together until every inch of moisture rose to the surface. It moved slow at first, but then the water from the ground pushed to the top. And in less than a minute, the ground grew slick. Another fifteen seconds, and half an inch of water pooled beneath my feet. It built around the semi insulated stable and guard keep, causing a mild panic. Some Fae ran around shouting, others just lifted their boots in disbelief. The mare beside me stomped, prancing in reaction to the rising water level. I chuckled to myself, amused at the ease of arousing chaos and confusion.

Time to find Jana.

But then someone grabbed the collar of my leather vest. I was pulled to standing, my hand no longer commanding the ground beneath it. Cas looked over me, fuming, his eyes more heated golden than cool amethyst.

"What. Are. You. Doing." Cas ground out, his words more threat than question.

I leveled a look at him and said nothing. In my peripheral, Fayzien waved his hands around, swirling the excess water in the air, forming shapes of animals that galloped into a well a few yards off. At that, Gia clapped, along with many other Fae. My stomach turned over at the sight.

Cas grabbed me by the shoulders and turned me to face him. "Terra, answer me."

"Is that an order, Prince Casmerre?" I said, venom lacing my words.

"What was that about? And your display in the training arena? Why did you nearly shoot the head off Xinlan?" Cas demanded.

I only blinked at him.

"You know Terra, you're behaving like an absolute *child*. Not at all like my future bride, let alone the future Queen of Viribrum." His voice dripped with a condescending disdain that made my blood boil.

"Perhaps," I said, my voice low, "that is because I neither want to be your bride, nor the Queen of Viribrum."

Cas released me and pain flashed across his face. "I would not say such things lightly if I were you," he growled.

"Does it really matter what I say, what I think, or what I want?" I whispered.

"Do you even know what you want, Terra? Just this morning, you were begging for me to have my way with you. And while I don't know if it's the binding or how you actually feel, you still clearly yearn for Ezren. What do you want in life? If you don't want to be queen, what then? Do you have any aspiration for greatness at all? If you do not, tell me now. I'm sure I can set you up with a nice, easy, country-Fae husband. I have no doubt that, with your skill-set, you would be a *legendary* farmer."

I froze for a moment, mouth ajar. His words settled, pressing an uncomfortable weight on my chest. I turned on my heel, not bothering to look back, not even for Gia.

CHAPTER TWENTY-FIVE

BLADELESS WEAPONS

*T*he sun slipped from the sky, reflecting warm colors on the pale palace stone, as I ran back to my quarters in denial of the tears streaming down my face.

I flung open the double cherry-wood doors leading to my room, disregarding the Fae guards already posted on watch. I was a prisoner and a pawn. It seemed I had been the entire time I was 'home', every *single* day since my father tried to take me to Nebbiolo, perhaps even before then. Liberty, the thing I had always craved in the human realm, was just as out of my grasp as it had always been.

Thankfully, Olea was not in the room when I arrived. I knew she would come soon, to prepare for whatever dinner-banquet-torture waited for me that night. But I didn't desire to see my mother, Cas, nor the reveling group of courtiers, all waiting for me to make a mistake. No, I would practice an age-old human trick. I would fake sick.

Fae couldn't catch a common cold nor a fever like humans, but I remembered something Dane said to me. *"Faeries and Witchlings mature similarly to humans. First bleed for females is typical between the twelfth and fourteenth year."* He didn't explicitly say Fae experienced the pain of flow, but they did feel the pull of the moon. I hadn't had a cycle yet in my new body, so I'd have to take the chance that Fae females suffered the same consequences as human women. Something in my gut told me they did. Being a female was never easy, regardless of species.

I rummaged around the wardrobe, looking for sharp crystal earrings or a scrap of metal I could draw blood with, given my lack of weapons. I found something better. A half full bottle of brandy.

I smirked and tossed back much of the rest of the bottle. The rest I poured into the chamber pot, topping it off with my own relief. And then I opened the window and smashed the bottle against the side of the palace, below the sill, until only the shard of a handle remained.

I undressed my bottom half and then I ran the broken edge of the bottle the length of my underfoot, wiping the drawn blood with my worn undergarments. The brandy muted the pain, and still I grimaced at the vulgarity of my act. My resolve hardened, knowing it would save me from banquet torture. And maybe, if I felt up for it, I would again attempt to see Jana late in the evening.

I left my undergarments on the ground next to my bed, praying Olea wouldn't make me remove another pair for further proof. Then, I dressed in bedclothes, curled up under the massive canopy, and prayed for sleep.

I FELT the tug of sleep and a soft picture came into focus. I was back in the Adimon Mountains, before our coupling. I stood facing him— the green-eyed warrior—sheer silk draped over the curves of my body, lavender and soft pink wisteria flowing from the canopy ceiling atop the room of my making.

Ezren stepped closer, still towering over me despite my newfound height. My breath grew heavy with anticipation, acute awareness of my bareness beneath the silken garment lancing my core. His eyes searched mine, and I stared right back, unable to move.

"You have no idea how much I want you, Terra," he said, his voice low.

He took his middle and index fingers and placed them on my lips, gentle in his touch. I intuited his meaning and parted my mouth, tracing them with my tongue. After a moment he pulled them out, trailing his fingers across my lip, dragging on my chin. His fingers moved to my neck, traveling down the center of my chest, and lingering on my abdomen. And then, when they were just below my stomach, he leaned in and whispered, "Moan, when you like something, squeeze my shoulder if you feel pain."

He let his finger brush where I parted, and I convulsed, nearly falling, but Ezren's forearm wrapped around my waist, steadying me. And then he let his fingers slip into my opening so slowly that I writhed, standing in the position he held me in.

The moan came whether I was commanded to or not.

I raised my hands to his neck, gripping him for stability while I felt the pressure of his fingers inside me, his thumb drawing circles on my spot of pleasure. "Ezren," I half breathed, half groaned. "I. Can't. Stand."

He chuckled and nipped my ear. Then he withdrew his fingers and squatted down, tossing me over his shoulder and making his way towards our grassy earthen bed.

My fingers pressed into the Dragon scale that pulsed from my hip bone, sweat and the gods knew what else drenching my shift. They'd allowed me to sleep through the night, and soft light peeked through the drape cracks. Predictably, Olea busied herself around the room, preparing the fire and bath. I sat up, strings of disrupted hair framing my vision.

The realization that I'd awoken in this bed for only the third morning sat heavy on my chest.

"Ye were moanin' quite a lot, en yer sleep, miss. Te be sure, et sounded more like... pleasure, than pain, but are ye alright?" Olea's cheeks colored with a faint flush.

I slumped back into the pillows and sighed. The question conjured the image of Leiya, and it sent a pang to my chest. "Good morning to you, too," I grumbled, staring at the canopy above me.

She busied around, fluffing chair pillows and dusting surfaces I knew she'd cleaned the prior morning, before turning to face me, hands on her hips. "The prince—he wilna satisfy ye? He has a reputation 'at one. But me suppose he'd be more proper wi' hes bride." She looked at me as if about to share a secret. "Dinna worry mistress, me hath somethin' for yer problem," Olea whispered, winking.

I covered my face with a pillow and groaned into it. Cas's words rang through my head, the truth in them searing. What did I want?

Fayzien dead, Gia safe, Leiya and co returned, my family back, Cas's respect.

Ezren's naked body tightening around me, his soft co—

I stopped the image before it consumed me, removing the pillow to see Olea hovering over me. "Yes?"

"Here ye go," she extended her hand towards me. In her palm, she held a long and round glass object, resembling a small cucumber.

My face scrunched. "What is it?"

She raised her brows, and then it dawned on me—a tool to pleasure oneself. My cheeks reddened.

Olea giggled. "Ah, yes, I forgot yer former ken es 'uman! And they dinna value female pleasure."

I just looked at her in disbelief, and she continued. "Though, I dinna know ef the Fae would either, ef there wasna need for et. But et isna like 'umans—ye canna bed a male once an' swell weth a babe. For the Fae, they say et takes an average a' *five hundred* times. The males realized them females had te enjoy et, ef they were gonna get em' te do et 'at many times! Many a couple use thes fer... how shall I say, starten' the fire. Dinna worry, thes canna crack, the glass es the strongest made. And, et es spelled te move weth vibration when ets en ye."

At that point, Olea must have been tired of my gaping at her extended hand. She put the glass object into a table drawer next to my bed. "Yer nervous, ets okay. But I'm tellin' ye, ets normal for a female te take her pleasure en her own hands. Ye canna think straight unless ye relieve yerself. I'll leave et here, ef ye wanna try."

With that, she winked at me and pulled me up from the bed, bringing me to the bath.

"Do the Fae always insist on bathing this frequently?" I asked, hiding my wince at the hot water on my still-healing foot. "Or do I just particularly smell?"

Olea giggled as she brushed my dry hair, which fell out of the copper tub. "Naye, te either. But ye've been a bet down since ye came here, and my ma' always said baths are key en settin' the mind right again."

"Olea, where are you from? Your accent... reminds me of someone."

"I'm from the North, miss! Panderen born n' raised. Me voice es akin te the, ehm, well the lower classes. Ets got a' bet more grit n' es a bet less refined."

"I'm not sure if this is a personal question, but do you have magic? Like some Fae do?"

"No mess, I dinna have Fae powers. They say only the Fae weth the ol' blood have the magic en em. But, ef yer askin' me, et seems to be random," she answered, resign in her words.

"I see." I sensed she didn't want to continue on the subject. "I have a favor to ask, a bit of an odd request. Is there a way for me to go underground? As you know, I spent the last few years in a forest, surrounded by Earth. The Earth calls to me, and here, well, I'm surrounded by stone and sea. Even if it's just a dirt pit in the ground under the castle, being closer to the Earth would comfort me, I think. It would help me to, em, how you put it, get my head right."

I closed my eyes and prayed to the gods that she wouldn't see through my request. She stayed quiet a moment, either considering me or evaluating any ulterior motives. But she huffed and said, "I dinna know ef et will work, but me thenks there es an old chamber, deep under the palace, 'at was used by practitioners a' the old ways. I dinna know ef ets blocked off now, but I've 'eard of Faeries playin' down there in the dirt. Ef ets not blocked off, et could work for ye. But what're ye gonna do there? Just sit alone en the dirt fer hours?"

I smiled at the convenience of her question. "Hmm, now that you mention it, perhaps I could read? Is there a library anywhere around here?" I asked, feigning all the innocence I could muster.

OLEA PUT me in a simple riding dress, not free of a corset, but at least complete with a set of britches beneath the skirt, which I could tie at the hip if needed. Several layers of gauze also padded the britches to catch the flow. I faked a grateful smile when she gave them to me, cursing my choice in illness, for I realized I'd have to sacrifice a bit more blood if I were to keep the ruse up.

Apparently, the prince had requested I be dressed and delivered to him when ready, but since I awoke much earlier than usual, I would have a few hours until he expected me. And while the thought of speaking with Cas again made me see red, my mind wandered elsewhere.

Olea waited for me at the library entrance, which was marked by sweeping brass doors, citing that serving maids were not permitted to enter. I frowned at the rule but didn't spend much time considering it. It only made my task easier.

I breathed in the scent of the parchment, and a wave of nostalgia came over me. I hadn't been in a library since I'd come here last, and like typical Faerie children, Cas and I used to play hide and seek amongst the stacks. I would chase him around, trying to plant kisses on his cheeks, and he would run solely for the purpose of making me pursue him. The memory sent an ache through my chest.

Quiet stillness commanded the library, given the early hour, which meant any noise echoed through the large hall. The wide room housed maybe a dozen rows of books that ran towards the back of the hall, which quickly went from light-filled to dark, as the upper levels covered the back half of the room. Massive stained windows that told stories of the old Fae, casting prisms of color over the bookcases, adorned the front half of the library. In the middle of the room, separating the front from the back, a spiraling wrought-iron staircase wound up to the second and third floors. And if I remembered correctly, a trapdoor hidden somewhere in the library led to the lower levels.

I had spent much more time here than Cas. Books had been an escape for me even then, as they later were in Argention. I climbed to the second floor, sensing an undisturbed layer of dust upon everything. Luckily, I found a lit torch I could take to the back of the level. Just like I remembered, a sign marked the final shelf. *Maps.*

I let my fingertips brush the fading spines. Bunches of maps on parchment were bound and organized by region or topic. I found the Valfalla section, the largest booklet labeled *City Layouts Over the Years.* I opened it and flipped to the last page, the most recent city map. I ripped it from the string binding and tucked it into my corset. I kept looking, letting my eyes run over each spine, each section-marker, but nothing near what I needed appeared. I almost gave up, wandering through the other aisles, not sure what to look out for. Eventually, another section-marker caught my eye: *Architecture and Buildings.*

I picked out my next target—*The Palace of Valfalla and Its Thousand-Year Transformation.* The booklet had many iterations of palace blueprints, but I settled on one from the mid-millennia, when practicing the old ways was commonplace. I scanned the parchment, finding three underground chambers similar to what Olea described, connected by a series of tunnels.

I tucked the paper under my corset with the other map and made my way through the stacks. As I turned the corner, I ran smack into a firm body I identified right away by the sinking feeling in my stomach. My blood went cold, and I looked up to piercing blue eyes.

"Well, hello there, Princess," Fayzien purred.

I stepped back from him. "You," I growled, attempting to shove down my desire to wipe the smug look off his face with the curvature of a dull knife.

It didn't work.

"I will kill you." My voice was gravel.

"Oh? I'm assuming that won't be for some time, given I *know* Cas has advised against something so foolish."

I wanted to tell him he wouldn't see it coming, that he'd finally know peace one day, and on that day, I would take everything from him. But the thought only brought my mother's dying face to the front of my memory.

"Why did you do it?" I whispered, fearing my full voice would crack. "You *made* them my family, *you*." I jabbed my finger at his chest. "And then you *murdered* them. They were innocents."

Fayzien's smug face turned serious. "Listen to me, you privileged, complaining whore. I picked your mother and father up out of a *gutter* in Laharam. Two boys and no money—I paid them handsomely, and they knew the risks. They knew I'd have to alter their boys' memories. And I *always* told them if you were discovered, I'd clean house," he sneered. "They agreed anyway. Humans can be so... desperate."

I launched at him and he portaled out of my path. He was fast, his dodge so instant I had no time to recover before colliding with the opposing stack of books, sliding to a pathetic lump on the floor.

My head pounded from anger and the impact, but I could still hear Fayzien's laugh ringing out. "Fell for that little trick again, did we? Here's a tip—I have the fastest portal in all of Nebbiolo. It makes me *exceptionally* hard to kill."

If I'd hated Fayzien before, I didn't have a name for the emotion I was feeling now.

"What are you even doing here, lapdog?" I spat blood. "Are you following me, a glorified babysitter now?"

Fayzien laughed, a humorless mocking sound. "You really do think of yourself as highly important, don't you?"

I rocked back on my heels, peering up at him. "No, but I think *you* see me that way. It must be distressing to see the letters of my name inscribed over the heart of your lover. Am I in your head, every time you see Cas bare? Do you wonder if he's thinking of me when he lies with you?" I revealed my teeth painted with fresh blood in a murderous smile.

Fayzien's face contorted. My blade-less weapon had struck true. I laughed out loud, delighted in his reaction, which only angered him more, and he grabbed me by the throat with one hand, hauling me up, tipping my head to his.

"You little bitch, think you're so smart, do you?" he whispered, his hand tightening on my airway, spit flying from his mouth and landing on my cheeks. "You're an overvalued twat, with no aspiration, and little more talent than raw magic. Raw magic means *nothing* if you don't have the skill to use it. And unlucky for you, I do. I am coming for you, Terra of *nowhere*, of *nobody*. We'll see who sits beside Cas at the end of this."

He released his grip, shoving me into the stacks, and stormed away.

CHAPTER TWENTY-SIX

WHITE LIES

I stroked the bruises on my neck, rinsed my mouth with water from a jug that had been set for visitors, and grabbed a readable-looking novel on my way out so I'd have something to show for my time in the library. Olea's eyes widened at my throat and face, and I shook my head in response. "I'm fine. Had a small run-in with Fayzien."

She gaped a moment, but then fell into step with me. "Ye jest let hem get away wi' 'at?" she asked quietly, leading me through the serving quarter.

I clenched my jaw. "I wanted to rip out his eyes for laying a hand on me. But he was angry, and angry people tend to reveal things they ordinarily wouldn't. He's not mine to deal with, anyhow. At least—not yet."

She didn't press further.

We walked through the kitchen, and for the first time, I saw those that had been behind closed doors. These Fae were not like the ones I had come to know. Some were horned, with hair covering their faces, some smaller with ears even more pointed than mine, though I knew they were mature. Jana once told me of Elvens and Gobbles, which many referred to as lesser Fae. They looked away from me when I gazed in their direction, in deference, shame, or hate I could not tell. Something about them didn't sit right with me—like they were there by force. I wished I could tell them that I, too, was forced to be there. But I knew it didn't compare.

We approached a smaller wooden door at the end of the serving rooms, and Olea tugged it open, rust squeaking on the hinges. She grabbed two torches from an opposing wall and handed one to me. We made our way down, traveling far beneath the palace. Maybe I imagined it, but I thought I heard running water. We must've been lower than Ezren's cell, for his had a small, barred window at the end of it that looked out of the palace. We were deep underground by the time the staircase ended. And as Olea had predicted, dirt made up the floor.

The room she mentioned was just a few paces from the bottom of the passage, and not concealed by any door. Cold emanated from the circular space, and it smelled of mildew. Frescos of the old Fae decorated the walls, but the colors had faded and a thick layer of dust and grime lined them. A small ledge ran the circumference of the room, like a trough. Instinctually, I dipped the flame of my torch to it and the fire caught. In an instant, a ring of flame encircled us, save for the open entrance.

I knelt on the ground and sifted dirt in my palms, sighing in satisfaction, putting on a display for Olea. She tapped her foot with a nervous rhythm, perhaps disturbed by the eeriness of where we were.

You can wait for me in the kitchen if you want," I offered. "I'll be at least an hour." She looked hesitant but relieved, and she nodded before making her way to the stairs.

I remembered little about the lessons of the old ways of the Fae I had been taught as a child. Rumors of ritualistic sacrifices, both animal and Fae, came back to me. The history of what likely occurred in this space, thousands of years before me, hung heavy in the dense air.

Once Olea's footsteps faded, I untucked the blueprint from my corset and smoothed it out over the dirt. The blueprint showed several sections, each representing a different level of the Valfalla palace. But instead of the three rooms on the underground level I'd seen before, there was only one. The circular shape of it swelled before my eyes—as if the ink bled from the script. I blinked, wondering if I was hallucinating. And then, it burst into flames, a controlled burn outlining the room on the paper, mimicking where I sat. The flame traveled outside the room, turning right and following a passageway to what appeared to be a closed wall. But it tore through the drawn barrier and continued on, snaking through several more turns and then stopping, marking an X. I looked at the image of the ground level and swallowed in realization. The flame placed the X on the map directly below the guard's quarters. Where they held Jana, according to the servant I'd paid the day before.

I ran my hands over the parchment, sensing the magic in it now, wondering how a blueprint could have known my intention. "Thank you," I whispered. And the flame responded, drawing a message back to me. The flames snaked and circled, burning in a swirling script that read: *Anything for the daughter of the Mother.*

I didn't have time to puzzle over its meaning, because a moment later the paper erupted into full flame and reduced to ashes. I panicked for a second, wondering if I could remember the path it showed me. But the image had burned itself into my mind. I got up and ran.

———

I CAME to the first wall in a matter of minutes. The flame had just gone through it, so I attempted to do the same, thinking it was some sort of illusion.

My nose cracked against the stone, and I fell back. I almost laughed out loud, wiping the blood from my face for the second time that morning. I pushed myself back up and felt the wall with one hand, my torch still in the other. One of the stones felt hollow to my touch, thinner, and I pushed it in. The wall turned, as if on an axle in the middle. It revealed an opening, and I ran through. Two lefts, one right, and another left. And then I faced a dead-end once more.

I pressed my ear to the dark brick. If the map directed me correctly, the holding cells were on the other side. Muffled sounds echoed through the cracks. I ran my fingers around the wall pieces, and one of the bricks wiggled in its place. Slowly, I drew it out, and set it on the floor, willing my breath to quiet. Distant words came into focus.

"You know, I tire of your visits, sister," Jana's voice said. I peeked through, attempting to see to whom she spoke, but the lack of light obscured the curved passage. Even with my Fae sight, they were too far away.

"You forfeited calling me that long ago, Janathia. You will address me properly," the other voice said and my insides turned cold.

Jana cried out in response. "Yes, Rexi," she breathed, her voice dripping with resentment and pain.

My jaw loosened. *Sister? That would make Jana my—*

"You are a pathetic excuse for a Nebbiolon. Did you really think I wouldn't know you went for Terra? A traitor, that is what you are," the Rexi said.

Aunt. I pressed my lips together, continuing to suppress the sound of my breathing.

"You may have been fine to let the Drakkarians and Viri feud for centuries over her disappearance, killing countless innocent in the process, but I was not," Jana shot back.

"I was protecting the queendom, you simpleton," the Rexi spat in rage, sounding more unhinged than I thought I'd ever hear her. "Yes, I am a mother, but I am a queen first. I could have killed Terra, you know. There were many who believed that to be the only way to protect Nebbiolo from her."

Though I'd already stopped moving, her words stilled my heart. The Rexi worried about her queendom's protection. *From me.* The image of flying debris that had almost killed Dane danced in my head. Was my power what she truly feared?

"But I sent her away," the Rexi continued. "To protect my people, our people. To protect *her*. I had to fake her death—the Elders wouldn't have rested any other way. And you, you ruined that! Many more, of our own kind for that matter, *her included*, will suffer because of your actions."

Jana made a huffing sound, as if she wasn't buying the story her sister sold. "And what about Viturius? What of *him*? Do you think of him at all? Or is he simply collateral damage to you?"

I furrowed my brow at the mention of my birth father.

The Rexi was silent a moment. "We both know it wasn't me who killed Viturius. That burden is on you, dear sister."

With that, footsteps on the cold, wet stone grew faint with distance. Then, no sound remained, save for soft weeping from Jana.

I DIDN'T HAVE endless time before Olea would return to find me, but I waited as long as I could, both to ensure the Rexi had gone, and to give myself a moment to process the information their conversation revealed. Jana was my aunt. She was family. I didn't know if that knowledge made me trust her more instinctually, or more furious at the lies she spun to her own blood. *And what about the 'danger' I supposedly posed to the Nebbiolon people?* I gazed at my fingertips, wondering what wreckage the Rexi thought my hands would cause.

I found the wall lever and pulled it, the gentle scrape of stone against stone echoing through the halls. The cells were not empty, but neither did they house true life. The prisoners were largely immobile in their chains, unaware of me as I passed them. And then, I came upon Jana's cell.

She sat on the ground, covered in filth. Her back pressed into the wall, her hands and feet bound in silver to suppress her magic. And while I'd been harboring anger and resentment towards her, it melted away seeing her like that.

"Jana," I whispered, placing a hand on the bar of her cell.

"Terra." She blinked her eyes open and looked at me. "How much did you hear?"

"Enough."

"I suppose you feel betrayed," she murmured, looking toward the other end of the cell.

"You lied to me." My cool voice bounced off dripping stone walls. "You told me my mother died. You swore you didn't speak falsely to me."

"Terra, the mother that bore you, the mother that swelled with you inside her—she is dead. She has been for some time. I did *not* lie about that. But," her voice hitched. "But she is dead because I killed her."

I narrowed my eyes. "What do you mean?"

She cleared her throat. "I suppose I should start at the beginning." She exhaled in preparation, pausing a moment. "Your mother, several decades my junior, was a brilliant Witch growing up. Siphoned so young, so full of life—"

"What is a Siphon? I keep hearing that word."

Jana smiled, resting the tips of her fingers on her clavicle. Her smile disappeared when they did not meet the wooden necklace she usually wore. "Every Witch of generational power has a unique object that can amplify their magic. Mine is the ancient bur oak that is normally tied around my neck. Upon coming of age, a Witch will start his or her search for such an object. There is a draw between Witch and Siphon, an unmistakable pull. It is an honor to find your Siphon quickly, though some search for decades."

"Do I have a Siphon?" I asked.

"You do. Someday soon, it will be crucial for you to seek it out. I know you'll find it quickly, just like your mother did hers."

I paused, wondering if it would be something of the Earth, like Jana's. When I said nothing, she continued with her story.

"When Neferti met your father, Viturius, well, I had never seen such an instant pair. She was wild, and he reveled in it. Part of the reason she was so free was that she did not grow up with the burden of a future crown."

"You were supposed to be Queen of Nebbiolo," I breathed.

She nodded. "I am the eldest. I had seen what happened to the Queens of Nebbiolo, our mother included. They were all... changed after being crowned. I grew up knowing that one day, I would be the one changed, stone-cold, and unrecognizable atop a throne. So I shut everyone out, swearing to only breed after I assumed the role.

"But the universe's plans are rarely of our own making, and fate is full of surprises. My surprise was Reece. My chambermaid. I thought nothing of her; she was simply a servant. But she showed me unconditional kindness and shouldered the pain of my burden, though I never asked her to. It happened without me realizing... one day, I just knew I couldn't live without her. But a Nebbiolon Queen marries only for breeding. And Reece couldn't give me a babe. So I left a letter abdicating the future throne to your mother. It was a few years after you'd been born.

"Our mother died shortly after I left. Neferti took the crown and sent you and your father to Viribrum. She was always stronger than me; she did what she had to without a second thought. And as they all do, she changed. She is not the same, not even close. So, it's my fault your mother is gone, Terra. My fault your father is dead. My fault the Rexi so coldly cast you out to the human realm. If you are looking for someone to blame, blame me."

Any resentment I'd held for the Witch before me evaporated. I suppose I could have been angry with her, for she caused my family's separation. But she did what she did because of love. And I was no stranger to resenting one's birthright.

"What did she mean when she said she was *protecting* Nebbiolo from me?" I asked, chewing my lip. "She thinks I can't control my power? Am I truly so dangerous?"

"I honestly don't know what she meant, Terra. I don't think it would be a fear of control—control can always be taught. And you have already come a long way; you are no danger unless you want to be. Ever since she accepted the crown, she has spoken in riddles. I have long stopped trying to decipher them. But I had to find you, Terra. Thousands of innocents would have died if she allowed you to remain hidden, blaming Drakkar for your disappearance. I already have so much guilt to carry, I couldn't bear more. And Cas had figured out you lived, anyhow; he wouldn't have rested until you returned."

I met her gaze. "Speaking of Cas, why did you never tell me about him? You left memories of my mother, of my title, caged in my head—when you'd unlocked my memories of Viribrum and my sire. Why?"

Jana sighed once more. "I thought the knowledge of your title would confuse and frighten you. I worried you'd think we were ransoming you or using you for your position or something twisted like that. And I couldn't conceal the memories of your title without concealing Cas too, for he is the prince and you two betrothed. As for your mother, I didn't conceal your memory of her; you simply didn't have any. I swear on Reece's grave, I never planted a fake memory in your mind. Terra, I am truly sorry. I thought I would have time to explain; I didn't think your memories would erupt upon seeing Cas, and I certainly didn't think Neferti would be here upon our arrival, ready to order me away in chains."

The four weeks since Fayzien first set foot in Argention had been filled with confusion after confusion, horror after horror. I scarcely knew what or who to believe anymore. But sitting there, in front of my aunt, an overwhelming feeling of reassurance flooded over me.

Cas trusted her. He'd trusted her to find me.

And I knew I trusted her too. I only prayed I wouldn't regret it.

I held my aunt's gaze. "I believe you."

Her mouth wobbled, a glint in her eye. "That is enough for me, niece. I only hope I can one day also earn your forgiveness."

I swallowed, preparing for the final question I felt compelled to ask. "Did the Rexi order the death of my family in Argention?" My voice croaked out of me.

"I don't know, my dear. I wouldn't think her so cruel, but I scarcely know any longer."

I squeezed my eyes shut, forcing back tears, and exhaled. "Jana, I need to leave this place. I can't be around Fayzien without wanting to kill him, even if he doesn't hold the ultimate blame. I don't trust a word that *queen* says. And Cas, while he may care about me, he wants me to compete in this ridiculous contest for his hand. I'm a pawn here—I've always been a pawn. Can you help me get out of the castle, out of Valfalla?"

She looked at me, her eyebrows pinched. "And where will you go, dear?"

"Anywhere. I don't know. I'll go back to Argention to return Gia to her family. And then, perhaps, I can search for Leiya and Leuffen, to see if they survived Fayzien..."

"And then? What will you do? Live on the run? If you learn anything from my story, it should be that one cannot outrun their duty without consequences. I suppose you know what will happen if you refuse to participate in the Skøl. Hundreds will compete, and many will die. Are you prepared to live your life with that knowledge, that burden?"

"That's their choice to compete," I murmured, but it sounded like a weak excuse, even to my own ears.

"True," she admitted. "And I thought the same thing of my younger sister. She made the choice to serve, to not abdicate. But I will tell you this: the guilt and the pain come anyway. She would still be the loving and wild Witch I knew, if I hadn't left. You can't deny who you are, Terra. It always catches up to you."

"So what am I to do? Just marry Cas? Become some bred mare to unite the Fae kingdom and Witch queendom? Forget about all that Fayzien has done, never to think of Leiya, Leuffen, and Sanah again?"

She sighed. "No, that is *not* what I'm saying. Fayzien is not worth your time—he is the Rexi's dog. And Ezren went to search for any survivors of the Casmerre with Dane. As for competing in the Skøl— it will simply save the king and Cas embarrassment and prevent the unnecessary loss of life. You won't be married right away; there's a victory period between the Skøl and the wedding. It will give you time to figure out what to do next." Jana paused. "Have they found a way to unbind you two yet?"

I swallowed, the tightness in my chest loosening a little when I heard someone was looking for the twins and Sanah. "No, but Cas says he's working on it. I suppose it will be harder for him now, though, since I let Ezren go."

Jana winked, as if she already knew I'd been the one to free him. "Smart girl. How'd you do it?"

"Oddly, they kept him in an above-ground cell. It was much easier to access than this one. I freed him the day I woke."

"It's called a spectator cell. They must have wanted him to see something."

A slice of pain hit my chest. I looked down at the purple stone Olea insisted I put on my left hand this morning. "Cas proposed to me in front of a large group of courtiers."

"Ah, I see." She paused. "Do you miss him?"

I shook my head, trying to clear the tears that were forming. "I shouldn't, I know. He lied to me, too, withheld *so* much from me. And I've only known him a month, such a short time compared to Cas." I whispered the last part.

Jana considered a moment, only a *drip, drip, drip* echoing through the cell. "Well, it is that way for some. It wasn't like that for Reece and me. Our love was a smolder that burned for a long while until my eyes opened to it. But for Viturius and Neferti, it was like two waves crashing into each other. It doesn't always take time for great swells to build, only the right conditions."

I closed my eyes, numb from the overwhelming amount of information. "He said something to Cas, when they talked of the binding. He said that I had taken something from him. What did he mean?"

"Terra, you must understand, Ezren has been a warrior his whole life, one of the best in history. He grew even fiercer on the battlefield once he lost his wife. It has been his identity, his release. But now, well, I imagine he will think twice before risking his life ever again. Now, he will always be risking yours. Any injury he ever sustains will be one you not only feel but could die from."

I stroked the bruises that formed on my throat. "And he feels every injury of mine, even a stubbed toe?"

Jana eyed my neck but didn't mention it. "Perhaps not a *stubbed* toe, but every injury that requires significant healing, like a broken toe, sure."

Something sharp twisted in my chest. "I need to go. I've been away a while now. Should I come back here? To free you?"

She shuffled over, and reached through the cell bars, her cold hand grasping mine. "No, I have accepted my fate. Ezren offered to release me when he came for Dane and the others, but I asked him to leave me here. I hoped you'd seek me out, that I would get the chance to explain everything. I am *so* glad you came, Terra." She shook her head almost imperceptibly. "My beautiful niece. You remind me of her, you know. The best parts."

I squeezed her fingers in farewell and turned to go, but hesitated. "What happened to Reece?"

"She died nine years ago. We were blessed with a decade of freedom together. While I can't say I live without regret, I will always be grateful for the time we shared."

I stared at her a moment, memorizing the lines of her face. "Goodbye, aunt," I said, wondering if it would be the last time I'd see her—if she would end up like the dusty corpses that dwelled in the neighboring cells.

CHAPTER TWENTY-SEVEN

GOLDEN HOPE

Olea waited by the passage entryway, staring through a pane window at an off-duty guard exercising. I was confident she hadn't moved a muscle in the time I was gone; she couldn't look away from the same handsome soldier that stood outside Gia's door days before.

She led me through the kitchen and out to the stables. Cas stood next to two large Andalusian geldings, their coats a watercolor of creamy gray tones adorned with warm brown manes. Despite the potential distraction, I floated back to our conversation the prior afternoon. Swallowing, I approached him.

Cas's black hair swayed around him in the mid-morning breeze. "Good morning, Terra," he said, his voice soft and cheery.

I eyed the prince and the steeds that flanked him. "Good morning, Your Highness."

He grimaced at the coolness in my voice. "Are you feeling better?"

I tilted my head in confusion, but then recalled the excuse for my absence at last night's banquet. "Oh, yes, thank you for asking. I am."

He stepped closer until we were inches apart, bent his head a little, and took one small inhale. He retreated, his eyes sparkling. "You don't smell like a female bleeding."

I scoffed. "Well, you're mistaken."

"An exceptional nose is one of several gifts from my bloodline. I am never wrong when it comes to scent." With that, he winked and then cocked his head to the side, his eyes catching on the bruises circling my throat.

"Those marks on your neck. It looks like someone choked you," he said, his voice low.

I shrugged. "I had a run-in with a certain blonde lover of yours," I said casually. He narrowed his eyes, and I laughed, the sound pitching too high to be genuine. "Oh, so sorry, I forgot there's more than one! The male."

"Is that true?" Cas asked.

I nodded, picking idle flint off my jacket.

He mumbled something to himself in rage and then gestured to the horses.

"I didn't ask you here to discuss your courses, nor Fayzien's behavior. I have a present for you, and his name is 'Romeo.' He is a proud seventeen hands and a wonderfully clean ride. Unlike some of us around here," Cas said, throwing another wink in with his last comment.

I rolled my eyes and approached Romeo. I showed him my hand, letting him warm to me as I stroked his face down to his velvety muzzle. "You've winked entirely too many times for this early an hour. And don't think this makes me forget yesterday." I paused. "But I will say, he's a beauty." I said the last part more to Romeo than Cas.

He moved behind me. "I'm sorry, Terra, truly. My words were cruel."

Heat pricked my eyes. "Cas, I have no one to trust here," I whispered, still facing away from him. "You are supposed to be my oldest friend, my partner in crime, my confidant. But you give me half-truths—you didn't even tell me Jana was my aunt. And yesterday, you treated me less than—less than *you*. Like if I didn't fulfill the purpose you'd laid out for me, I was worth nothing." I choked on my words.

If my revelation about Jana surprised him, he did not show it. He only placed both hands on my shoulders and brushed his lips against my neck. "I'm sorry, *mi karus*. I'm sorry," he whispered into my skin.

I let my eyes shutter, tilting my head back into him, but I snapped out of it a moment later. I shrugged him off and turned around to face him. "That might work on you lovers, Cas, but it will *not* work on me. I don't want gifts or murmured 'I'm sorrys.' I want a genuine apology."

He chuckled, and I shot him a menacing look. He raised his hands in guilt and said, "Okay, okay. I'm sorry for speaking so cruelly and wrongly to you. I didn't treat you as an equal. You deserve much better from me, Terra. I will... do my best never to address you that way ever again."

I almost rolled my eyes. Something told me to have little faith in what 'his best' would translate into.

I FOLLOWED Cas on horseback through the winding cobblestone streets of Valfalla.

"Is it usual to be unaccompanied by guards?" I asked.

He shrugged. "I have a shadow, always. You probably haven't noticed him. But other than that, a lot of those who live within these city walls are Fae. I fought alongside them in battle. They have my respect, and I theirs. I've never had a serious issue."

After what felt like hours, we exited the city perimeter and reached open farmland. He kicked his horse into a gallop, and Romeo followed on instinct. Whether or not Cas intended it, simply allowing me space to run a horse out of the palace made my anger toward him slip away.

By the time he slowed, we had come upon what looked like a small, abandoned farmstead with a clear pond on its border. I recognized the place, remembering it from our youth. If we behaved, and if the heat of the day peaked to unbearable levels, our tutors would bring us here for morning studies. In the afternoon, Cas and I would swim in the pond.

It wasn't quite mid-summer, and on the coast the temperature never rose to such heights, but here the air had heated up. The leather-corseted riding jacket stuck close to my body. A part of me longed to strip down, to feel the cool silky water on my bare, sweaty skin. Cas looked back at me with a devious smile, as if he thought the same. But instead of diving in, he walked around to the other end of the pond and knelt at the base of a large oak tree.

I lowered myself beside him. He ran his fingers over the bottom of the trunk, landing on a carving. He traced a line straight down to the ground from the marking and dug in the soft dirt.

I watched him in silence. He parted the dirt, making a mess of himself and getting nowhere. After a few minutes, I placed my hand on his. "Want me to help?"

He looked up at me in confusion, which then dissipated into a grin. "Go right ahead, Princess."

I removed my riding gloves and rested my hands on the Earth, sensing the target of his digging. I found it in a moment and curled my power around it, a root pushing it to the surface.

The root rose, placing a worn leather pouch in his hand. He looked at me, awe creeping into his purple eyes. "What's it like?" he asked after a moment. "Having power over something alive?"

"Some days, I think the Earth has power over *me*." I chewed my lip. "But it's not really like that—having power over something. It feels like a part of me... as essential as my breath or heartbeat."

The side of his lip quirked and he turned back to the pouch. "Do you know why I always gave you purple stones when we were young?"

"Because they matched your eyes?"

Cas offered a rueful smile. "That's part of it. Once, maybe a year or two after you arrived at the palace, you told me you liked my eyes because they were your favorite color. After that, I bought every purple stone I could get my seven-year-old hands on." He laughed at the last part.

"But though I loved bestowing tanzanite and amethyst upon you," he gestured to my left hand, "I never meant to propose with it." He tipped the pouch into his palm, and a clear-stoned ring, set on a golden band, fell out.

He blew on it, clearing off the dust, but it scarcely needed it. Even in the tree's shade, the stone reflected prisms of rainbow-colored light all around us. I couldn't tear my eyes away.

"Seventy years ago, my father gave this to my mother when she won the Skøl. It belonged to an original High Fae Viri queen but had been lost for centuries. Darlan found it during his youth campaigns and swore he would give it to the female that proved to have the fiercest heart. The myth of this ring is that only the fearless can possess the power of the unknown stone. On her deathbed—my birthbed—my mother requested it be given to me as soon as I could close my fist. I had nearly nothing of her growing up, save for tales of her greatness. And this ring. Though I was young, I knew from the moment I met you that you, and only you, would wear it. When you were gone, I buried it and told my father I lost it. He beat me with a wet rope for that. It was worth it. Even if you never returned, Terra, I would have never placed this ring on the hand of another."

Cas finished, and I realized my cheeks were wet. "Cas," I whispered, "I don't know what to say—"

"I know you don't want to get married yet; I know you still have many questions and doubts. And possibly feelings for someone else. That's okay." He met my eyes. "We'll take it one step at a time, figure it out together. I just wanted to show you."

He rose, extending his hand to mine, pulling me to stand. "But will you wear it? It doesn't have to be a promise of anything. I've always wanted to see my mother's ring on your finger. Especially now, after so many years thinking I would never get the chance."

I paused for a moment. I hadn't said yes to his public proposal, not really—he'd slipped the ring on my finger before I knew what was happening. And though this wasn't a proposal, it felt significant. My stomach clenched, the image of Ezren seeing yet another ring on my finger sending a pang to my chest. But Cas had mourned my disappearance for so many years, and if wearing this ring would give him solace...

I met his gaze. "Yes, Cas, I will wear it."

At that, he slipped the ring onto my right ring-finger, and a zing went through my hand. I jolted slightly, my eyes shooting up at Cas to see if he noticed the reaction. He only gave a quick brush of his lips to my cheek. And then he turned to go, taking my hand with him, leaving me to wonder if the ring was more than just a gift.

My heart broke as we ran the geldings back to the palace, and away from the forest. Cas guided his horse next to mine once we slowed to a walk.

"You're apprehensive about the Skøl," he said flatly.

I sighed. "It isn't just the competition, per se, though I do find the concept *completely* archaic. It's what comes after. The marriage. In Argention, I spent years dreading the village's matching ceremony, knowing it might end in my engagement. I've always wanted more than that, Cas. It doesn't always feel the same—sometimes overwhelming claustrophobia, and sometimes a slow burn. But it always comes back to one thing." I paused. "I want freedom."

"I don't know if freedom is possible for people like us. Whether we like it or not, we were both born with the weight of a crown. It is our duty, and our honor, to carry that weight as best we can. For the sake of our people."

Though I didn't like his words, they rang true. The problem was, I didn't know who *my* people were. Cas felt a clear responsibility for the Viri folk, and the Rexi *seemed* to care for the Nebbiolons. But since I was ripped from my life so early... did I feel a responsibility to the Fae? To the Witches? I matured in a human land—Argention, the only community I knew. In a way, I felt more human than Fae or Witch.

I chewed my lip, Jana's advice tugging at the back of my mind. "I will compete in the Skøl. But I want there to be an understanding between us. I still don't know what wearing a crown or being a leader means for me. I'll do my best to figure it out—whether it means standing beside you, or not. But I need time to figure out what *I* think, what I feel."

And who I feel for.

"Can you delay the Skøl as long as possible?" I asked.

"For you, *mi karus*, anything."

I lifted my brow. "Anything?"

Cas groaned in mock sincerity. "I have a feeling you're going to make me regret saying that."

I laughed. "There has been one thing on my mind. Jana told me I had family here—relations from my birth father's side. Well, I just wondered... can I meet them? Would they... want to meet me?"

Cas's expression was unreadable. "They live north. I... suppose we could arrange a visit, but it'll have to be after the Skøl, given you'll be training nonstop between now and then. And then there's your mother. I'm not sure she would approve."

"Speaking of my—" I hesitated, the word *mother* stuck in my throat. The image of my mom laughing in the kitchen after one of my brothers made a joke popped into my head. "The queen," I said, my tone careful.

"What of her?" Cas asked.

"Who does she expect to rule Nebbiolo, if I marry you?"

"We would rule jointly," he said simply. "Just as we would over Viribrum."

"But then, why did she send me away in the first place?"

"As I said, I'm working out her motives. Likely, she only supports our union publicly but will seek to undermine it behind the scenes. What she wants from you or any of us, I cannot say."

I paused, considering his words. Our horses swayed, snaking through the narrow Valfalla alleyways, the rhythm of their hooves a metronome on cobblestones.

"Maybe I should talk to—" Firm hands yanked me from Romeo's back. Before I could scream or resist, someone shoved a cloth in my mouth and bound my hands behind my back. And then the light slipped from my view as a black sack covered my head.

CHAPTER TWENTY-EIGHT

ROLE PLAY

I bucked and struggled against my captor's grip, Cas shouting in the background.

"Fight more, and he dies," a voice said. An oddly familiar voice, but I could not place it. Cas's yells faded to silence, so I cooperated.

Just minutes later, I heard a door open and the cool, damp air of a cellar settled on my skin. The bag still covered my face as someone shoved me down and tied me to a chair, making my breath swarm hot all around me.

Footsteps neared, and the sack was pulled off.

I blinked, my vision adjusting to the empty, dimly lit stone chamber. Parson bent over me, his light brown hair pulled into a low bun.

He stared at me, betraying no emotions. A sinking feeling swelled in my gut.

"Parson," I said, my voice low. "What am I doing here?"

He remained silent, just watching me.

"You, you *snake*," I hissed. "Who do you work for? Another of Neferti's lapdogs?"

He stood unmoving and said nothing. Another conclusion dawned on me. Jana had never figured out how Fayzien knew my location in Argention was compromised—how he knew Jana was coming to extract me. It had left her to wonder if she'd had a mole in her ranks.

"You told the Rexi that Jana had found out I was alive, didn't you? *You* are the reason my family is dead," I growled.

Recognition sparked in his eyes. It looked like he wanted to say something but couldn't. And a moment later, voices echoed through the room.

Dread sat like bricks on my chest at the prospect of seeing the Rexi. But my mother did not appear in front of me. King Darlan did.

He looked jubilant as ever, his cheeks rosy and a twinkle in his eye. One would never guess he was a captor approaching his prisoner.

The king took a deep bow, extending his arms out. "Princess Terra, hello! I *do* apologize for the regrettable circumstances of this encounter. I promise you, they are absolutely necessary. I would never do such a thing without utter cruciality." He rested his hand on his heart.

"Your Majesty, why am I here?" I fought to keep my voice even.

"Yes, of course. We might as well get on with it." He sat in an empty chair his companion set out for him. I did not recognize the other male, a tall and slender Fae with a sallow, distant expression.

"I need you to do me a favor, my sweet Terra. I need you to compete in the Skøl."

I rolled my eyes. "Is that what this is all about? I told Cas this morning that I would compete in the absurd competition."

The king's face contorted in an instant. "I will allow your petulant interruption this once, Terragnata. If you roll your eyes at me again, I will remove them from your skull. Now, back to what I was saying. I need you to compete in the Skøl, and I need you to lose. On purpose."

My insides went cold—at more than just his graphic threat. "I *am* still a bit unclear on the mechanics of the competition, but isn't it a fight to the death?"

"In some cases, yes," the king replied. "But not all. Will you face competitors who want to kill you? Most certainly. However, some contestants disqualify for performing the tasks slower than others. I truly cannot tell you more than that without spoiling the surprise. I trust you're clever enough to situate a scenario in which you neither win nor perish."

I shivered. "And may I ask *why* you request this? I can't agree if your motivations are unknown to me."

"Well, it should be in your best interest, no? You said yourself you don't want to marry," Darlan said.

"While your deflection is much admired, King, I won't alter fate intentionally without knowing why. And it would crush Cas. Why would you want to do that to your son?"

"Cas may speak beyond his years, but at his core, he is a besotted young male. He is much too naïve to understand certain things, though he believes he understands them better than I. He says he wants to marry you for the advantage of our kingdom, and certainly, that was the idea in the beginning. But much has changed. The needs of Viribrum have changed. And he is blind to those changes, for all he sees is you. I, however, do not. I see *everything* that goes on in Viribrum. Even what goes on in backwoods silver mining towns, deep in the human realm."

"You knew," I spat.

"That your mother was the one that sent you away? That you were never, in fact, dead?" The damp perspiration of the cellar beaded on his brow as he squinted at me. "Of course, I knew. I knew from the beginning! Such fools they are, the lot of them. To think I have no idea what goes on in *my* kingdom. I was not happy about it, initially, for she meddled in an agreement we had without consulting me. But my young boy had become so smitten with you, so weakened by emotion, I nearly thanked her for it. I hoped he would become stronger in your absence. And for a time, he did. But then he discovered you were alive and became obsessed with finding you. Now that he's got you, he's fixated on the image of you two sitting side by side, ruling over Fae and Witch alike. The fantasy of a child."

"What do you mean, the needs of Viribrum have changed?" I murmured, knowing I could push my luck too far with the cantankerous ruler. *If the king no longer wants to unite Nebbiolo and Viribrum through marriage... what does he want?*

The king sighed. "I have no obligation to answer you, my dear, but it *is* better you learn this hard lesson now. Witch and Fae are not meant to coexist, at least not as equals. Fae live longer; we're stronger and wiser. Thousands of years ago—millennia before Nebbiolo was even a twinkle in the first bitch queen's eye, Witch served the Fae in Viribrum. In my younger years, I thought it prudent to align with Nebbiolo, to hurry along the transition back to the old ways. Change starts at the top, they say. But your mother's display with your abduction proved the unreliability of your kind. Cas believes he will remain in command of himself, but he is weak. I know he'll fall to your will—a Fae male becoming subservient to a Witch," the king sneered. "The thought makes me sick."

"You think the Witches will one day... serve you," I whispered, more to myself than to the king.

King Darlan's chest bobbed to a deep chuckle, and he clapped himself on his round belly. "Oh, my Terra, I am not saying Fae will be restored to greatness in one century—it may take many! Anyhow, it is not your concern. Focus on one thing. The Skøl."

I swallowed the urge to roll my eyes at *my Terra* again for the sake of them remaining in my skull. "So, I lose the Skøl, on purpose, somehow I survive, and then what? Cas marries someone else?" An image of Cas's white-haired lover in a white dress flashed in my head, but I shooed it away. "What becomes of me?"

"You go back to where you belong. Your home. In Nebbiolo," he said definitively.

"Your Majesty, I was raised in Viribrum. I believe I have relations here on my father's side. I matured in the human lands. Nebbiolo is not my home."

"Well, although your mother and I can agree on nearly nothing, that is one area we see eye to eye on. Your duty is to the Nebbiolon people, whether you like it or not. You will one day be their queen." Darlan's eyes gleamed with something that said, *though not for long.* A shiver danced down my spine.

"And if I return to Nebbiolo with the Rexi, what will happen here? I've been told the tensions with Drakkar should cool with my return, but you talk as if there will be no peace..." I trailed off to goad him. I grasped the gist of his desires but knew little of his plans.

Darlan grinned. "A curious one, you are. Just like your father. While my plans are of no consequence to you, I will say this: Your mother used your disappearance to increase those tensions, hoping the two kingdoms would destroy one another. And if it is a war she wants, it is a war she'll get. The decades of hate she has sewn into the hearts of the Witch and the Fae did not simply *dissipate* upon your return. I can promise you one thing—if there is a war between the Fae and Witch, the Witches will stand no chance."

My stomach curdled. "Won't many die," I breathed, "if Drakkar and Viribrum go to war?"

"You are naïve, child, to think you would not do the same to protect your own people."

I struggled in the chains, physical and not. "And the purpose of this display? Why did you have me kidnapped and bound?"

"Well, for one, you will not be let out until you agree. And secondly, your abduction will be positioned... how shall I say, advantageously for my cause."

"If you think I won't tell Cas about this, you're—"

"Be very careful, Terragnata. This conversation stays between the two of us. *Only us.* And if it does not, and if you fail to comply with my request to lose the Skøl, well, I would fear for your aunt's safety. Accidents can happen in prison cells. They do all the time, in fact. They also happen to young pregnant humans, so *delicate* they are."

I shook my head, looking at the ceiling. If it wasn't clear he was threatening me before, it certainly was now.

"I agree," I huffed, praying to the gods that one day I wouldn't be a pawn in a massive chess game, one I hadn't the slightest idea how to play.

———

PARSON DEPOSITED me in a heap outside the castle gates, the sun already making its descent. He told me to stay put until someone found me. I did, thinking of Ezren—wondering if he'd felt the injuries I'd sustained. The king ensured that I looked worse for wear, a part of his antagonism plot, I guessed.

And then there were guards fussing over me. Cas arrived in under a minute, folding me into his arms and carrying me back to my chambers. He'd looked better himself, with several bruises smattering his face. They'd heal in a few hours, since strong Fae blood coursed through his veins.

He walked in silence. No doubt, Cas wanted to wait to interrogate me until we were far from prying ears. As we neared my room, my mind wandered. "What is your shift shape, Cas?"

He barked out a laugh. "You may find it amusing. While I was blessed with superior scent and unusual magic, my shift is, shall we say, less admired."

"I could use amusing right now," I murmured.

"A cat. A black cat with purple-golden eyes. Though I can be very ferocious in my shift, should I need to be." He winked.

I giggled, imagining him in his feline form, snuggling against me.

He set me in a large chair in front of the fire. *Why did I let him carry me the entire way?* My legs still worked just fine. The question dissipated with Olea bustling around, preparing tea for us and a bath for me.

Cas knelt in front of me, taking my hands in his. "Terra, I'm so sorry. I should have seen them. I was distracted, and I didn't protect you. I am so, so sorry," he whispered.

I pitied him at that moment, wondering what demons my being

274

snatched under his nose brought up. I cupped his cheeks. "It's okay, Cas, I'm okay. I'm here."

He shuddered and leaned into my touch. "My guards are investigating, doing everything they can to figure out who the attackers were. They will have to question you at some point. But right now, I just want it to be you and me, *mi karus*. If... if that's what you want, too."

I knew what he offered. I could not deny the comfort, nor the fact that Cas and I had a bond of some kind. It didn't compare to what I had with Ezren—unpredictable, a wild flame. The connection between Cas and me was old, based on history and mutual understanding. It was safe.

"Olea," Cas said, still gazing up at me. "Please finish preparing the bath and then leave us."

She complied. And when she left, Cas pulled me to stand. My hair hung in a matted mess around me. Cas pulled off my riding gloves first, checking to make sure both rings still remained on my fingers, and kissed each one. He undid the outer layer of my riding skirts next, letting them fall to the ground, then pulled out the laces of my leather corset, which ran up my front. He was slow and deliberate in his motions. My breath stuck inside my lungs. I couldn't exhale, knowing what came next.

The leather fell to the ground, and I now stood in a simple cream shift with breeches beneath it. His eyes ran down me, lingering on the shadow of my chest, which was visible beneath the sheer fabric.

"My turn," I whispered. He was still in his riding wear. I unhooked the fasteners of his jacket, spreading it, and then I pushed it off him. His tattoo stared back at me, and I let my eyes and fingers trace the outline of it once again. He exhaled, tilting his head back as my fingers made their way down his abdominals, which flexed with his deep breath. They landed on his waistband, and I undid his trousers. I tugged on them, and they fell to the ground, revealing nothing but his manhood beneath.

He swelled, and I froze, my eyes widening, still unused to such a sight. He noticed my trepidation and uttered a laugh, turning to walk to the tub. Cas lowered himself in and rested his head against the lip of copper. "When you're ready, *mi karus*, the water is warm."

I took a steadying breath and slipped my hands beneath my shift, shedding my trousers, leaving nothing beneath the sheer fabric. I went to the tub and climbed in after him, my shirt sticking to my skin as it saturated with water. He lounged on one end, I on the other. I splashed some water on my face and arched my spine, tilting my head back and letting my hair soak. Cas watched me, the heat of his eyes burning into me.

I sat straight up, my knees folded beneath me, and looked at him, unable to move.

His gaze met mine. "We don't have to do anything you don't want to."

I remained still for a moment, unsure. But the desire was there, whether it was a product of the trauma, my new Fae body, or pure need. I nodded, my eyes not leaving his.

That seemed to be enough for him, and he reached forward, pulling me on top of him, the water sloshing all around us. I was dangerously close to his manhood, looking down at him. He brushed my hair away from my face, placing his hands on my neck, his thumbs pressed to my jawline. "You're okay, Terra," Cas said, more to himself than to me.

Before I could think further, I brushed my lips to his. He kissed me back, running his hands down my sides, raising bumps on my skin despite the warmth of the water and the thin layer of wet cloth shrouding me. And then he thrust into me, holding my hips while he moved. I cried out, losing myself in the joining of our bodies.

I WOKE IN MY BED, shrouded in silk, with Cas nowhere in sight. I could only hear the rhythmic crash of waves beneath my window.

I lay there, listening to the sound of the water, remembering the sensation of Cas inside me. It felt good to lose myself in the pure physicality of *need*—to revel in the comforting touch of someone familiar.

But I could not shake the guilt. Ezren's face lingered in my mind, even in those first moments Cas was inside me. It felt... dirty.

I resented that notion, the self-loathing that seemed to have been schooled into me. We came together in the inevitability of the moment—the stress of the day, the closeness we'd shared for so long. It didn't feel wrong, the act. The wrongness came from thinking of another. Perhaps it would fade with time.

I fell asleep to those thoughts, stubbornly ignoring the buzzing from my hip bone.

A SHAKING of my shoulders ripped me from my sleep. "Mestress, me hates te wake ye, but ets urgent," Olea said. "The Rexi. She's asken' te see ye."

I peeked an eye open—barely dawn. I'd slept a mere two or three hours, and I moaned in protest of the disturbance.

"Please, mess," Olea pleaded. "She said ef ye didna come, I'd have me personal hours suspended fer a month."

I didn't know what 'personal hours' were, but the desperation in Olea's voice roused me. I sat up, rubbing my eyes, my body aching from the previous day's manhandling. "Where is she?"

"Her guards are waiten' fer ye outside the door," Olea answered.

I stuffed my feet into the slippers next to my bedside and grabbed a matching silk robe.

"Wait," Olea protested when I made to exit. "Ye really should be dressed, te see the queen. Et isna proper—"

"Did she specifically request me to be dressed?"

Olea shook her head.

"Very well then," I said, knowing perfectly well that the bruises I'd earned the past few days would be visible.

I⊤ was a long walk to her quarters, which were not in the wing of the Crown but in the wing dedicated to distinguished guests. She was fully dressed, of course. Her hair, the color matching mine, was tightly piled atop her head, revealing the soft curves of her face that I also possessed. But we were not alike in every physical way. Where my eyes resembled the Earth, all life and vibrance, hers were an inky pool of black. They were death.

She tapped her chrome-colored nails against the window ledge on which she perched, her deep purple velvet gown draped all around her. "You're late. I thought the delay would at least mean you bothered to dress," she said, her eyes still trained on the hazy morning outside the window.

I stood motionless, wondering how to address the female who bore me for the first time in private. "Hello, Rexi. What have I done to earn this coveted early morning summons?"

She was silent a moment. "How are you?" she asked, her gaze dragging towards me.

I shifted on my feet, assessing the authenticity of her question. "You mean, how am I, after being pulled from my horse, strapped to a chair for interrogation, beaten, and dumped at the palace gates?"

Her eyes narrowed at me. "What did the king want from you?"

I stilled. "It wasn't the king," I replied. "It was a group of men, with—"

"Let me guess: shaved heads, imposing face tattoos, and long dark robes?" She raised her eyebrows in boredom.

I closed my mouth, weighing my options. The king had made it perfectly clear what would happen if I revealed anything about the nature of our conversation to anyone.

Before I could respond, she spoke again. "Let us change the subject, my dear. Have you chosen to compete in the Skøl?"

"I have."

"I see. And do you plan to lose?"

I nodded once, almost imperceptibly, and said, "I don't know what you are talking about, Rexi. I have no plans to lose."

"Good," she said, flicking her wrist. A whoosh of air shot out from the Rexi in all directions, as if to coat the walls. "We can speak freely now. I've sealed the room. If any stray ears were on us, they will report your denial."

I blinked, wondering what spell she just used, and how I could learn something so handy.

"It's easier for all of us if you lose that blasted competition. The sooner you do, the sooner we can return home."

I flinched at the idea of going anywhere with the cold stranger who sat in front of me. "Do you no longer approve of my match with Cas?" I asked carefully.

The Rexi sighed. "That match was always Viturius's idea—never mine. It would have had advantages... the heir, in particular, could have been used to control Cas. Darlan, too. But the king no longer supports it. Publicly, he does, of course. The bastard can't stand to lose face. But if the match is not supported privately, then it is doomed to begin with. It is far more advantageous for us to return to Nebbiolo. It is why I hoped Fayzien would retrieve you *before* you made it to Valfalla—we could've returned to Nebbiolo and avoided all this Skøl business entirely. But we are here now, and I do not think it wise to reject the prince outright." The Rexi paused, thinking for a moment, while my stomach boiled at her casual mention of manipulating Cas.

"It is time, Terra, for you to get to know your home so that you may prepare for your role as queen. It may come sooner than you think."

White-hot anger mixed with terror flashed through my body—at her callousness, her arrogant assumption that I would follow her orders without question. "And what makes you think I have any interest in ruling? After what you did to me? To my father? To my Argenti family? You have no idea who I am. You don't know me at all! I am no daughter to you, no future queen," I spat.

In an instant, my body was hauled across the room until I stood before her. The Rexi's thin fingers wrapped around my throat, her chrome nails pressing into the bruises left by Fayzien the morning before. I choked, gasping for air, my toes fighting to remain on the ground as she raised me up with a strength I did not know Witches could possess. I grasped for an ember of my power to call to any nearby earthen object, but the flicker of magic sputtered out like a damp rag had been put over it.

"A Witch queen's strength draws from her people," she purred, answering my unspoken thought. It is nearly unlimited. If you fear the power Darlan has to harm your little human friend, then listen carefully. I could end Prince Casmerre with a mere thought. Lose the Skøl, as Darlan instructed. And then we will leave. I will hear no more whimpering or whining. The queen's bloodline means a duty to the Nebbiolon people, above all else."

She released me, and I dropped to the floor, choking on new breath. I could've laughed out loud at my earlier thought to wound her with the sight of my bruises—when she had just added to them herself. The door flung open, and a guard walked over to me, pulling me to stand, while the Rexi resumed her staring out of the window. I followed him, numb, not looking back.

"Terra," she said, pausing us as we exited her room. I turned my head over my shoulder, hate roiling off me. "We all have our role to play. It is best you accept that."

And then the door shut in our faces.

CHAPTER TWENTY-NINE

SIMPLE INTENTION

*A*fter those hectic first few days, I slipped into a routine in the palace. Per Cas's request, two guards trailed me at all times. I would wake up and have breakfast with Gia. We would take a walk around the gardens, where she spent most of her time. We talked about pleasant things: the herbs she helped to grow, what she learned from the midwives about birth. She seemed happy enough, and curious—asking me questions about the Rexi and the king. I stressed over my friend, for she was herself, yet not. Every so often, she would grow distant, pensive. But even after multiple discussions with the midwives and palace healers, they all assured me she and the baby were perfectly fine.

I sometimes spent a few hours exercising, either sprinting on the track in the training hall or practicing hand-to-hand combat with Cas or members of his personal guard. While he had limited experience in battle, he was still a strong fighter, excelling past the average man in training, but I matched his fancier combinations with my scrappiness and surprise. I held back a few times, letting him pin me and win. I didn't know why I did it, for he was never in a foul mood when I bested him and won occasionally by his own merit.

After a break for lunch, I would resume my training. Skill practice for an hour or two, either with a bow, sword, or small blade. The afternoon finished with lessons in Witch magic. Cas was adamant about this, for I would need to leverage all my abilities to win the Skøl, he said.

Cas rotated my instructors. I trained under an Air Witch for element control, to ensure I did not call on the Earth during the Skøl. Darlan had announced it would be a disqualifying act due to the unfair advantage it gave the favorite. But as Fae could use Fae magic, I would be allowed to spell. As long as I refrained from leveraging my element, cantrips, task spells, and portaling would be acceptable.

So, I also trained with a skilled speller, followed by an expert in portaling. The latter took me weeks of lessons, for the concept was simple but completely intangible. I had to envision a window opening, letting me out the other side. But even after dozens of lessons with the grumpiest portal-maester, I could only travel a few yards.

"Focus," Sabnae hissed, hunched over his cane. "If you drain yourself, girl, you will be stranded. Or worse—lost to the in-between."

This day, Cas had directed me to meet my instructor outside the castle. He'd portaled us to a large rock off the coast, the palace in the distance. I clutched my woolen coat, the damp air whipping my hair across my face and chilling my teeth.

"I am *trying*, maester Sabnae," I gritted out, spreading my hands again, doing my best to outline a portal in front of me.

"Pretty hand dancing will do nothing for you, girl." The waves pounded the rock we stood on, ocean foam spraying the old male's woolen coat. "It's all up here," he said, tapping his temple. "Take us back to the palace."

"I know I can, I just need a moment—"

"Your enemies will not give you a moment, girl. They will give you no mercy. The portal is a Witch's immediate escape route, her instinctual response when the battle turns from fight to flee. It is one advantage we Witch have over the Fae. But—you *must* know your limits, at the back of your mind, always. If a Witch is too drained, she may be lost to the in-between forever."

"And how will I know if I'm too drained?"

"The portal may not come. And if it does, it most often will sputter. If you've just released a large swell of Witch-power, that will likely be the case. However, it's an important limit to know—if you're drained. More than once, I've seen a Witch lost to the in-between, even though her portal didn't clearly sputter."

The ocean wind lashed at Sabnae's robes with a vengeance, and he revealed a crooked smile. "I happen to know you've not been training with your Earth powers, given you'll not be permitted to use them in the Skøl."

"Right, I'm not *drained* now, per-say, I'm just having trouble visuali—"

Sabnae portaled. Leaving me stranded at least a mile from the palace.

"You've got to be *kidding* me," I swore, nearly sobbing in frustration.

It took me hours, and I had to portal from rock to rock to return, an excruciatingly slow process. But that experience finally settled the lesson in me. While I could still portal only a quarter mile, and I had to either be able to see or have previously seen my destination, it was a useful distance.

I spent the evenings in banquets, a different dress each night, a different slow torture. Tensions ran high between the Rexi and me—she had not summoned me again after that first time. During the dinners, she spoke in riddles and harped to the table about the importance of my Siphon—or ignored me entirely. When I was unlucky enough to receive her direct address, she spoke of our return to Nebbiolo. How she would show me our queendom, how I would know our people. I wondered if she planned to kill me on our way there, maybe dump my body into the Dusked Sea. Maybe she would wait, letting me see the land of my birth first. I began to see her lack of motherly attachment, her deep desire to be rid of me. She never asked of my years in Argention, or Valfalla for that matter. She had been clear in her words to Jana—I posed a threat to her and the Nebbiolo people. I could imagine that the threat she considered me at age twelve had only amplified with time.

The king droned on about how I should train in shifting, which sent the Rexi into a fit of silent rage every time, as she believed Witches were above it. He rambled about the bride I would make, about the luster of our wedding, about the heirs we would have. Formidable warriors. *No* warrior boy would match that of the blood of my sire, the great warrior Viturius, and the great King Darlan. His words curdled in my stomach for more reasons than one.

Of course, I told Cas nothing of my conversation with the king, nor the Rexi, for they had both made their threats plain. I thought again about freeing Gia and Jana, but the risks were more than I wanted to take. So, I continued to train for a battle I would eventually lose. I had answered Cas's guards' questions after the incident, reciting what the king had dictated to me. They weren't Fae, I said. Shaved heads, swirling tattoos on their faces. Asked me about the king, the prince, and the Rexi. Cas's guards seemed to know who my account implicated and left me alone after that. And of course, Cas shared nothing with me.

We hadn't been intimate again after that first time, which I came to realize was a product of the day's intensity and triggering circumstance. Cas was shaped by my loss when we were children, and I think he needed me then to reassure himself I hadn't gone away again. He never returned to my bedroom, which to my surprise did hurt a little, but was just as well. My dreams of Ezren hadn't subsided, and I *had* taken to using Olea's gift in the mornings, recalling our coupling. It stuck in my mind like honey on the fingertips—when I closed my eyes and pleasured myself, it was all I could see. I tried to think of other things, fabled princes of stories long forgotten, but if I wanted the release, I needed Ezren's image, green eyes and a golden muscled body. Dark auburn hair, in tendrils, framing his beautifully harsh face, decorated with male scruff. And when I thought of him, my scale turned to scalding hot ice, sending a tremor through my body, as if it knew where my pleasure came from. Afterwards I would lie in bed and hold in tears, for Ezren was *exactly* what I needed and exactly... wasn't.

After just short of two weeks of training, the king announced the date of the Skøl. He made the proclamation at a banquet one night, without informing any of us ahead of time. It would be in ten days' time, he said. He also announced that the next night would be a grand celebration, for the day marked an important milestone.

"What is he talking about?" Cas muttered, and then reddened once the king said the ball would be in my honor, for tomorrow I'd enter my twenty-first year. A special gala to not only celebrate my twentieth birthday but also my return home, which represented a deliberate blow to the Drakkarian campaign against Viribrum. I rolled my eyes, wondering how much of it was celebration, and how much was politics.

The next day, I finished my training early, per Gia and Olea's requests. They awaited me in my chambers, both dressed for the event, still hours away.

I walked in, already exasperated by what I knew would be extreme fussing over my birthday look. It surprised me to find no myriad of gowns strewn around the room, no trove of jewels opened up and on glittering display—only a steaming tub and two giggling females. I narrowed my eyes at them. They just gestured to the water.

"I don't know if I like the two of you teamed up," I grumbled, lowering myself into the bath. Gia smacked my head lovingly and said, "Oh Terra, when are you going to learn to trust someone?"

Her tone was light, but the words hung on me as they combed through my sweaty braids and scrubbed the dirt from beneath my nails.

They dried me with a thick cloth and wrapped me in a robe. I sat in front of the open window, the sea breeze blowing through my hair while they applied shadows and pigments to my eyelids, cheeks, and lashes. I fought the urge to fidget, nervous about what the night had in store, but when I asked, Gia only tsked at me to stay still.

After they finished and my hair dried, they worked together to braid it, pulling it wide, leaving strategic pieces out to frame my face. It had grown so long it neared my rear when unbound. They said the result was regal, and after looking at their intricate work in the mirror, I couldn't disagree with them.

"Alright, what terrifying dress will you two be putting me in tonight?" I asked. They giggled. "Oh, my dear Terra, tonight you will be dressing yourself," Gia purred.

I cocked my head in confusion, just when someone knocked at the door. Olea admitted four guards, each carrying the corner of a large pallet covered in dirt.

"The other day you coaxed a full rose bed out of a barren, dried garden patch. It got me thinking. I wondered what you could do with fertile soil." Gia winked at me.

"And ye'll have thes, te' help ye," Olea added, retrieving the golden crown from the chest. I hadn't worn it again since that first night in court.

The servants set the pallet in the middle of the room and left. My brows furrowed together. "You two just spent an hour removing every spec of dirt from my body, and now you want me to roll around in soil to make a dress?"

Olea clucked her tongue at me. "Ets jest a hunch, Terra, ye see? We thenk et'll be, err, different."

"Humor us, will you?" Gia batted her eyes.

And so I did. I let my feet sink into the silky soil, remembering the luxurious feeling of connecting with the Earth. Gia removed my robe, leaving me bare, and Olea set the golden band on the crown of my head. The power of it thrummed against my skull, but this time it only stirred, rather than exploding in action. I reached out to the energy from where I stood, calling the Earth in a language that was ours, and ours alone. It sang back to me, whispering my full name. I tented my fingers by my sides, and the dirt rose from the pallet, floating mid-air, drawn to my fingertips. Instead of giving it a thread of a picture, an intention to follow, I tried something different. I spoke a spell, a simple cantrip that would dress someone. "Sero-ores," I commanded to the Earth and crown.

As I spoke the words, a piercing light burst from the Dragon scale on my hipbone, not hot to the touch, but blinding. It hung in the air for a few seconds, and we all cried out—Gia and Olea for the brightness, me for the surprise force on my leg. And then it was gone, as was the dirt I stood upon. I blinked my eyes open, searching Gia and Olea for injury. They only stared back at me, mouths ajar.

"What is it?" I demanded, panicking at their expression.

"Terra, you're going to have to see this," Gia whispered, taking my hand, gently leading me to the mirror.

I gaped. I wore a dress of layered emerald chiffon, a color that reminded me of Ezren's eyes. A jewel-toned sash just above my belly button belted a deep V neckline. Long billowy sleeves synched at my wrists with golden engraved cuffs. The skirts gathered all around me, different shades of green blending together in a fluid way that changed with the air or movement—the hues ebbed and flowed upon the fabric, clearly a product of magic. And of course, small colored buds clustered on my waist, spreading out from there and thinning in quantity as they did so. The gold crown was no longer a simple band —it remained, but also bled into my braids, weaving tendrils of gold through my hair. My eyes, normally an earthy color, shined an even brighter green, more illuminated than Ezren's—so bright I guessed one could see them in the dark. And if all of that wasn't enough, the real change came from my skin. It glowed, a soft warm hue of light, shimmering like diamonds reflecting the sun's rays. The effect was not just breathtaking; it was *otherworldly*. I looked no longer even Fae —more like one of the old gods.

As if Olea heard me, she whispered, "Ye look te be the Mother, herself." And then she dropped to her knees, pressing her head to the floor. "Hail, Creatrix," she chanted, and Gia and I stared at her as if *she* had changed.

Luckily, Gia took charge. I was grateful for the Gia I knew to be shining through in a moment like this. "Olea," she murmured, "get up, please. Go tell Cas that Terra will not need an escort tonight."

Olea curtsied and scurried off. Gia looked back at me once more, inclining her head.

"Well, no one will be able to deny that you look like a queen," she said.

I cocked my head. We'd barely discussed the politics I'd been swept up in—potential royal duties included—but the knowing in her eyes made me wonder if Gia observed more than she let on.

But before I could ask her, she turned, made her way to my door, and looked back at me. "Wait fifteen minutes, then come down. I'll be waiting for you," she commanded, leaving me with a wink.

I spent those long minutes with my head out of the open window, breathing in the salty air, basking in the sliver of shining crescent moonlight. I would be more on display than ever before, and a part of me hated it. Another part of me reveled in it. If the king and the Rexi were going to threaten me, use me for political advantage, well then, I would play by the same rules. I would use what I had to give myself every advantage. I shut the window and walked out.

THE ILLUMINATION of my skin and eyes grew even more prominent in the low light of the banquet hall. Before the doors opened, I heard the announcer tap his staff to the stone floor, a quiet settling over the revelers. And then, I entered. The Fae that had spent weeks picking me over stared with open jaws. The only audible sound came from my slippers striking stone, and out of the corner of my eye, I could see the golden shimmer wafting off my skin, creating a soft halo around my body. At some point in my procession, a set of hands slammed on the banquet table. They were followed by another, and another, until my feet moved to a slow beat that echoed through the hall.

I turned to face the party-goers when I reached the table of the crown, which I was to be placed in the middle of, given the banquet *was* in my honor. I extended my arms out to the side and closed my eyes, feeling the glow on my skin intensify as I worked my magic. The buds on my dress bloomed before the crowd, bigger and bigger, until the flowers could no longer stay. I whispered to the blooms, a spell of life that was a cantrip and the Earth woven together, just as I had made the dress. When I did, the thousands of flowers transformed mid-air into a kaleidoscope of butterflies, bursting away from me and soaring through the hall.

"Creatrix!" a female voice cried out. Countless cries followed until the hollering and clapping drenched us, drowning everything else out.

LATE IN THE EVENING—OR early in the morning—I collapsed in my bed, exhausted from the hours upon hours of dancing with Gia and Cas, and the many other Fae that *now* vied for my friendship. Cas was kind, introducing me to many of his warrior companions who had come just to meet me. A traveling fiddler bunch, renowned on the continent, played for hours, and we danced until our feet hurt. I allowed myself too much wine and thought little of the king and Rexi, who both fumed at my winning display, and then retired early.

Gia and I bent over in chortles when we pushed Olea toward the guard we'd caught her eyeing the past few weeks. Gia knew him, because he was posted to her, so we arranged for them to dance, and then lost our composure when her face reddened at our intervention. It must have gone well, for she asked me late into the evening if I could undress myself. I cackled once again and bid her to go.

Cas left before Gia and I did, and I wondered who warmed his bed that night. But Gia pulled me out of that thought spiral by dragging me back to the dance floor, and I marveled at the energy in my pregnant friend.

After the music began to dwindle, we walked with arms linked back to our chambers, and I deposited her first. Only one guard remained at her door, and we giggled once again.

I made my way back to my chamber, feeling a sense of peace for the first time in a long while. My skin prickled at the sweet sea breeze in my room when I entered. I collapsed into bed, not bothering to remove more than my shoes, a smile spreading across my face.

Something prodded me from under my back, something hard and out of place. I flipped over in an instant, throwing the pillow to the side. And there lay a package wrapped in cloth, with a note on top labeled *Terragnata*.

My insides warmed. Cas was always such a lover of gift-giving. I sat on my heels, my skirts all around me, opening the note first. It read:

> *Happy Birthday, Bellatori.*
>
> *If you want me close, as more than just another sword in your defense, you only need to wear this ring, and it will be so.*
>
> *Your choice. I cannot wait to see the things you do, no matter if up close or from afar.*
>
> *- E*
>
> *P.S. You looked radiant tonight. I find it impossibly hard to not smile when you do.*

I froze, the breath catching in my lungs. Slowly, I pulled the cloth apart, as if the contents might jump out at me. The inside revealed a curved dagger with a blazing emerald pressed into the engraved hilt, rather like the cuffs on my dress. Wrapped around the blade was a piece of ribbon with a delicately braided golden ring, specked with emeralds, fastened to its knot.

I picked up the blade, sending my magic through it, and the stone glowed, thrumming with power like Ezren's sword had when I fought Fayzien in the valley. I looked around the room, imagining him climbing through the window, standing above my bed, laying the gift beneath my pillow. I rolled onto my back, holding the dagger flat on my chest, letting the tears slip down my cheeks as the wine pulled me into a restless sleep.

CHAPTER THIRTY

PERSISTENT CONTACT

*M*y head pounded when I woke to a dim room, Olea nowhere in sight, which was little surprise, given the way she left the ball the evening before. Thankful for the extra rest, I undressed, noting that the glow had faded from my skin. I put on my silks and stared at the gifts I'd clutched all night long, wondering what to do with them.

I found a loose board under the bed and pulled it up, revealing the unfinished floor beneath. I laid the dagger there and closed the wood on top of it.

The ring I was less sure about. I considered putting it with the dagger, but it didn't feel right. I certainly was not going to don it on my hand—the thought of wearing two rings from two different males made my head spin.

I rummaged through the jewelry collection Olea maintained on my behalf. I found a pendant attached to a long, fine, gold chain that dipped below my chest. I detached the pendant and put it with the dagger, then threaded the braided ring through the chain. I slipped my new necklace around my head, tucking it under my shift. It hung inches below my silver dragon.

I climbed back into bed and curled up beneath the sheets, willing away the throbbing in my head and praying for sleep to come. But my mind drifted elsewhere, and restlessness nagged at my low belly. I sighed, rolled over, and opened the drawer of the small table next to my bed. Grabbing Olea's gift, I let my memories lull me into the reliving of pleasure.

MY MIND TRAVELED BACK in time—to the memory of a garden amongst craggy mountain peaks. I had become addicted to this memory.

Ezren tossed me onto the grassy bed and it curled around me in response to the contact. He plucked several of them, soft green blades. He knelt before me, running them up my leg, starting at my feet, making his way up my calf, and lingering on my inner thigh. The anticipation was unbearable, and he dragged the grass blades under my shift, over my womanhood, which sent a series of convulsions through my body. I opened my eyes, expecting to see him laughing, taunting. He was looking at me with an intensity I'd never seen, an intensity that had *never* been directed my way before. I was burning up from the inside out. "Has anyone ever told you how attractive you are," he murmured, almost to himself. My breath quickened—I was near gasping now, my chest rising and falling with barely contained violence.

The canopy seemed to exhale when we did, the flowers blooming and contracting with us. Ezren ran the blades of grass up the rest of my body, up my abdomen, circling the peaks of my breasts. The soft contact on the thin silk shift sent a shudder through me, and he pressed my hands above me. As if the Earth now responded to him, or perhaps my secret desires, vines circled my wrists, rendering me helpless.

I arched my back, and he pulled my sheer shift upwards, letting it rest on where my wrists were now bound. He hovered above me, supporting himself, staring. I searched his eyes, panicked for a moment that he would change his mind.

But then he pressed his mouth on the silver dragon that hung around my neck, the tempo of his breathing matching mine. "I have never met anyone like you, Terra," he whispered, wonder on his lips. And then he kissed me deeply, and I arched into him, attempting to hold him in place, my thighs wrapped around his torso.

He rasped a laugh. "Patience, *Bellatori*." Ezren kissed my neck, licking and nipping me strategically. He paused on my breasts, closing his mouth around them. He made his way south, pausing again above my womanhood. This time, I could feel his breath, and I cried out in frustration. He slipped two fingers inside me, his tongue making small circles above my opening. Only moments passed before I exploded in pleasure, for it had built up so long, and Ezren certainly knew how to release it.

I submitted to the breath-stealing bliss, not worrying about the sound, nor the power that echoed around me. If a canopy draped above us before, we were in a palace of flora and fauna now, an expression of my surrender. The vines released my wrists, becoming part of the display. My eyes welled with tears, and I pressed my hands into them, my breath short and fast. Ezren came atop me again, his hands framing my face, thumbs brushing away the tears that had escaped.

"What's wrong?"

I only shook my head, laughing silently at myself, at the overwhelming nature of pleasure I'd never known. I placed one hand on his neck, dragging his lips to mine. And the other I put on his backside, attempting to guide him into me.

"Wait," Ezren pulled away from my kiss. "Are you absolutely sure?" His eyes searched for any doubt, any hesitation. "You can always change your mind," he said, his usually gruff voice full of tenderness.

The feeling of anticipation threatened to burst my chest wide open. "I have *never* been more sure."

He kissed me furiously then, not requiring another ounce of confirmation. His thrust into me was slow, but firm. I'd become thoroughly wet, so I felt no pain of friction, but was unused to the size of him. His deliberate kisses grazed my lips, my chin, my throat, as he rocked back and forth, letting me adjust to the sensation.

Desperation grew in both of us. Though naked and joined, we somehow weren't close enough. I wanted to devour him, wanted him to devour me. We became one body, one soul. I would have drowned myself in his skin if I could have. I came undone once again, this time opening myself fully to him, sending my power out and accepting his. He did the same, and then our powers melded into one, surging through us as we both found our climax. Ezren shuddered violently when he finished, grunting in pleasure. His light exploded out in every direction, and my Earth exploded with him. He lost himself completely, and it looked like his now Dragon-slitted eyes could no longer see as he thrust into me the last time. The image of him, undone completely by my body, caused my womanhood to tighten around him once again.

Ezren moaned, twitching inside me as we remained connected. His magic and more were still flowing into me when he groaned, "It has to be now."

And though I'd lost myself in the moment, in the orgasm that reverberated through us both, he grounded me. I sent our magic mixture down the side of the mountain, raising every speck of dirt to drown every Crona. I felt their heartbeats, strong beneath their frozen exteriors. And then I felt the life leave them, slowly at first, and then in a snap. I cried out once more, exertion mixing with sadness, mixing with residual pleasure. And in an instant, I knew it was done, and Ezren collapsed atop me, holding me to his chest.

It was over, but it was not. Our powers continued to magnify, hanging in the air, and a shimmering green light blinded us, searing our flesh. I shrieked at the excruciating pain, as if my skin was being peeled from my body and my heart was being ripped out. It lasted for a few terrible moments longer, and then it stopped, the magic sucked back into our bodies, quiet settling all around us.

We looked at each other in worry, and his eyes roved over me. "Are you hurt?" he panted.

I shook my head. "The end, with the magic, it... it was painful. Was it for you?" I asked, unsure.

He tilted my head to search my face. "I didn't know it would hurt. I mean, I've never heard of that. And... are you okay, otherwise?"

I nodded, a shy smile forming on my lips in remembering. "Is it always like that?" I murmured, searching his face, no longer talking about the pain at the end. "Your... finish. Is it always that intense?"

He looked at me for a few moments, his breathing still heavy. "No. It has never been like that."

I half laughed, half choked in relief, and he tightened his arms around me, giving me a little squeeze. "I felt like I wanted to be more than one with you. Like I wanted to *be* you," I whispered into his chest.

He nodded in agreement, and I propped myself up to see his face. It was relaxed, sated, but something churned just below the surface.

I poked him. "What are you thinking? Your thoughts are quite loud."

He let out something between a murmur and a sigh, as he traced his fingers the length of my body, sending shivers over my pebbling skin. "Nothing escapes you, does it?"

I poked him again. "Now I really must know."

"I was just thinking about when we met. I know this may sound crazy, but from that moment on, I knew—" He stilled, interrupting himself with silence, his fingers stopping on my hipbone, which had a small, shining, green Dragon scale imprinted on it.

"What is it?" I asked, looking down at where his touch rested. But he did not move, and he did not speak. He only deepened his breath, his nostrils flaring in anger. A moment later he was up, out of bed, shrouded in nothing, pacing in our little garden, shaking.

THE END of the memory almost prevented my release, but I replayed the rest of it like a revolving door in my mind. I cried out into a pillow, feeling the cool metal ring pressed against my chest and wetness streak my face. I knew Ezren couldn't set foot in the palace again without being imprisoned, but I let myself think of another life, one where we dwelled in a forest far away with horses and a cottage built of pine. And then it set in, the pressure on my chest that I had simplified to loneliness. He'd been gone less than three weeks. And a part of me felt broken and a part of me felt stupid and a part of me felt like I'd imagined the whole thing.

THE NEXT SEVEN days I did not attend banquet per tradition, which I took no issue with. I had nine days left to prepare for the Skøl, which meant rising early and training until I collapsed on my bed in the evening. Cas and I would begin the day by running sprints before breaking our fast together. Then, he would watch as I drilled in armed combat with at least two of his warriors at once, while he barked out critique or approval. His guard was well trained and experienced, but somehow still, my practice blades always found ways to meet them.

When Cas was satisfied with my swordsmanship, he forced me to duel Fayzien. I was furious and delighted by the suggestion. It offered me the chance to inflict some suffering on the Witch—or so I thought. We weren't allowed to use our elements, since it would be prohibited in the Skøl. It proved difficult to separate my Earth magic from simple Witch spells; they'd always been inextricably linked in my mind. Fayzien was, unfortunately, a formidable fighter, even without his element. It made me realize how drained he'd been in the Nameless Valley—how much magic he'd used to create the Crona.

At first, Fayzien out-spelled me every time. It might have bothered me, but I learned the most effective spells—tried-and-true magical tricks that non-element Witches had used in battle for thousands of years. I could conjure a magic whip or bend the light to blind him. I could summon a hive of bees to swarm him, and of course, I could portal strategically during a spar.

"When are you going to learn you cannot out-portal me?" Fayzien purred as I stumbled, having tried to portal right up to his unguarded side, only for him to vanish the moment I appeared.

I caught myself before hitting the ground, resuming my fighting stance. "When are *you* going to learn that hurting others will *never* make you hurt less," I spat.

He laughed, a light sound—the sound I knew he made when I scratched the surface of his skin with my words, *so* close to a puncture. And then he conjured that magic whip of his—the one he'd made in the valley. "You are mistaken. I feel very little, actually."

I didn't flinch at the whip. Instead, I conjured my own.

"Oh, really?" I said, twirling my weapon. "I think you do. I think you feel love—for Cas. And I think you feel hatred—for yourself."

Blue eyes bulged, and then he lunged for me. *Bullseye.*

I waited, one breath—two—until he was upon me. And then I portaled, to right above his head, so that I fell onto his back, my whip wrapping around his neck.

I pulled tight—so tight that we were one body. He could try to portal, but I'd only go with him.

He struggled, stumbling to his knees, his hands releasing his whip and grasping at my makeshift noose.

If he wanted to yield, he'd need to tap the ground. Rules were rules, after all.

He only clawed at my iron grip.

"You are simply a pawn," I whispered into his ear. "And you hate yourself for it. I used to be afraid of you, to crave nothing more than revenge against you. But now," I barked out a laugh, "I pity you. You're a sad, lonely, angry creature—who Cas could *never* possibly love."

He struggled even more, gasping, portaling us all over the arena. I held tight, going with him, until his movements slowed.

One heartbeat, two. He didn't yield.

I could end him—right then. It would have been fair, completely within the Viri sparring rules. Unless he yielded, I could kill him and hold no blame.

I could deliver the death vow I'd sworn.

But I'd already thought he'd been killed once... and it had done absolutely nothing to take away the pain of losing my family. It had done nothing to absolve my grief.

In truth, I thought of Fayzien less and less. He was not the mastermind I once considered him. The day after Fayzien choked me in the library, I saw him in the corridor, turning his bruised face away from the light. Cas had punished him. Despite my feelings towards Fayzien, it didn't sit right with me. I didn't like the idea of one lover punishing another.

Fayzien's struggles stopped; his body grew limp beneath my grip.

And I knew, with surprising clarity, that I'd regret killing him even now.

So, I released the male who'd wronged me, who'd violated me, who'd murdered my family.

And when I released him, the last shred of anger I had towards him was released, too.

Fayzien slumped to the ground, passed out but not dead, his chest heaving.

I bent over him, knowing he couldn't hear me.

"I forgive you," I whispered, a tear slipping down my face.

For Mama, Papa, my brothers—I would not kill. I would forgive.

A thought lanced my mind. *He did not yield.*

I only wondered if he could forgive himself.

After sparring with Fayzien, I transitioned to studying. Cas and other experts taught me about the history of Viribrum, evolving political alliances, and the events of the Skøl. I pressed Cas on the happenings in the kingdom, who the men with swirling tattoos and shaved heads were. He always hesitated in answering, saying he wanted to keep me away from it all. But sometimes, the instructors would acquiesce and make an admission before Cas could say otherwise. My 'abductors' were presumed Drakkarian Witches. Ironically, the tensions between Drakkar and Viribrum had grown regardless of my return to the kingdom.

Darlan's words itched at the back of my mind.

Witch and Fae are not meant to coexist.

If it's a war she wants, it's a war she'll get.

I hardly had time to unpack the implications of my learnings, for after history, I endured lessons of the court. The Five High Fae Houses of Viribrum could trace their existence back multiple millennia. Saxoni, Brisk, Daini, Nepos, and Odacer—each distinguished by its own specialty. According to Cas, the blood of all houses had been mixed through the royal line over generations. Cas's mother had not been of High Fae blood, and Darlan was part Brisk and part Odacer.

I would face one female of each house. I asked Cas which I should fear the most, and he shook his head. "Terra, you should fear them all. They will kill for a chance to wear your crown. Remember that."

There would be three events of the Skøl. The details of each event were unknown to all, save for the competition maester. However, each had a theme or a goal, Cas said. Those never changed. The first was a test of Beauty. The second a test of Strength. The final a test of Honor. And without being told, I knew the interpretations of those concepts would be vast.

"Tell me about the previous events," I said to Cas one morning at breakfast. "Tell me about your mother's Skøl."

He looked at his plate. "Hers was much more gruesome than yours will be. An open Skøl is like... trapping a hundred wolves with a single fawn. The events are also more lurid, for the competition maester has more to eliminate. I'm not sure you want to hear about her Skøl."

"Even if mine will be different, I want to know."

"Agustina trained in combat. Unusual for Fae females, unless they're from the House of Daini, or they're identified young for the Skøl. Her family dwelled in a southern town, near the border with Drakkar, where raids were not uncommon. So, she begged the soldiers in town to teach her the ways of the sword. Most shunned her, but one of them was sweet on her younger sister and acquiesced. And she improved.

"Her reputation grew, for she would fight anyone in the street for a penny or a chance at approval. But the soldiers would not welcome her in. Then, the King of Viribrum died suddenly and mysteriously. And Darlan was crowned. Darlan's father had not yet hosted a Skøl for his son, so no favorite had been chosen. Thus, the Skøl was open to all Viri females who wished to compete. Agustina traveled to the capital alone, facing thieves and bandits, and gods know what else along the way. By the time she reached Valfalla, she was one of a hundred that planned to compete."

Something warm tightened in my chest at the pride in his voice. "She sounds fierce."

Cas lifted his chin. "You have no idea. The first event, the test of Beauty, eliminated two-thirds of the competitors. A hundred human men were deposited in the arena. The competitors had to convince as many of the men as they could to... erm, castrate themselves, using their beauty and tools of persuasion. And, of course, competitors may eliminate their competition at any time. Agustina supposedly killed fifteen competitors on her own during that first event, whilst winning nine castrations. For the event of Strength—"

"Stop," I breathed, nausea swirling in my belly. "Cas, I will *not* harm innocent, helpless humans. You have to know that."

He looked at my pleading face. "It won't be like that, Terra. There are only six of you—and none of them innocent humans.

301

There will be less collateral damage *because* you are competing. And if worse comes to worst, just focus on staying alive. Even if you can't eliminate anyone, you can secure victory through winning individual events. But prepare yourself—most do not leave the Skøl without at least killing in self-defense."

I swallowed, thinking about the faceless competitors that could lose their lives at my hand. Even if they weren't human, they were still daughters, sisters, and loved ones. *I couldn't even kill Fayzien— how am I supposed to kill strangers?*

"Don't forget," Cas continued. "If there are two of you left standing at the end of the third round, whoever has won more events will win."

"What if there are two, or even three remaining contestants, but each won a single event? How does the Skølmaester account for the tie?"

"Fae detest ties," Cas muttered. "They are viewed as a cursed thing, producing two inauspicious losers of a draw rather than a pair of winners. But they have happened. There's a legend that goes back thousands of years, to the 14th and 26th Skøls. After both, the future king was forced to visit the temple of Abnithe far north, near Panderen, to consult the gods, leaving the result to stand before their judgement."

I examined my fingers, the wheels turning in my head.

"Don't you dare let there be a tie, *mi karus*; I have *no* desire to visit that ghastly place." Cas's mouth twisted into a wry smirk. "And even if the gods chose you, a tie would cast a dark shadow on our union."

I leveled my gaze. "What would happen, Cas, if I lost?"

He met my eyes. "Besides the fact that I will be heartbroken?" He shook his head. "I fear if you don't win, I won't be the only one to suffer. You are the key to unite Fae and Witch, Terra. Tensions are brewing, and many call for an invasion of Drakkar, namely the House of Conquering, Odacer. You're not Drakkarian blood, of course, but you are their kind. Witch kind. Our union could one day bring all kingdoms under one banner, one ruler, peacefully, without blood-shed. Think of it—Viribrum, Drakkar, and Nebbiolo united in one strong kingdom."

I considered him, wondering if his father was right when he said Cas was more dreamer than ruler. His idyllic fantasy seemed impossible.

"I fear we are on the brink of something—an invasion, or worse," he continued. "My father does not trust the Drakkarians. The borders are becoming dangerous. A war between our peoples could prevent an alliance for many generations. Memories of Fae and Witch are not short."

"But does Darlan want that? A union between Witch and Fae through our marriage? Does he actually want to keep the peace?" I asked, my voice low.

"Yes, of course. Our match was your father's idea, but Darlan has always supported it."

I nodded, wishing I could say more. "And you would give up marrying for love? For the heart?"

"I *am* marrying for love, Terra. I am marrying for love of my country, of my people, my warriors. And as for my heart, it is also yours," he whispered. "I know I don't act conventionally, seeking you out each night. But you are dear to me in the highest way, you *must* know that."

I frowned. I *did* know that—and I knew that to Cas, duty came first. I could see a life with him, one we'd imagined as children. He would protect me—he'd care for my every wish. Still, a question bubbled at the back of my mind. *Is that what I need?*

A pang of guilt lanced my chest. By losing the Skøl, I could save Gia and Jana. I'd regain a sliver of freedom in choice in the absence of forced marriage. If I could forgive him, for the lies and deceit, I'd be free to at least explore what existed between Ezren and me. But all of that would be at the cost of my duty. Cas would have no support in uniting Witch and Fae. I was sure the king would make good on his intention to invade Drakkarian land.

Could I forgive myself if thousands died and I'd done nothing to stop it?

I cleared my throat, speaking low. "Cas, how many of your guard do you consider truly loyal?"

He cocked his head at me. "All of them. They all have fought alongside me, some of them I have pulled from trenches, covered in—"

"How many of them would you bet, with my life, could not be bought? With gold or silver, or the promise of power and reward?"

He narrowed his eyes. "Five. And another five warriors that are not in my official guard but act on my behalf in... other ways."

I leaned across the long table toward him. "Could you arrange for them to take Gia and Jana out of here before the Skøl?" I whispered.

He lifted a brow. "Why would you ask such a thing?"

I shook my head. "I can't tell you. Please just trust me, Cas. I need to know, no matter what, that they are away from here, safe. And no one can know they are gone until the Skøl is underway."

"What aren't you telling me, Terra?" Cas ground out, his voice low.

"You don't tell me anything!" I whisper-shouted. I exhaled. "I'm sorry, please, just, can you do this?"

"Okay," he shook his head, his body language contradicting his words. "I'll have three of my best take them out of the city—inland. They can wait out the Skøl in a small farming town. But Terra, the request worries me."

I tucked a stray piece of hair behind my ear, avoiding his eye. "Thank you."

CHAPTER THIRTY-ONE

GREAT PRESENTATION

*T*he night before the Skøl, the competitors stood at the front of the banquet in presentation to the court. They'd all trained in private, so I didn't gain any advantage by watching them or learning their strategies. This night's banquet took place on the large patio platform by the sea. The air had grown warmer, and the area allowed for commoners to spectate. The onlookers gathered outside the patio, opposite the ocean, surveying the competitors they would follow so closely over the next three days.

The sun still shone when the banquet began. I arrived first, as per the custom. The cheering from the crowd that followed my name being announced made me jump. I hadn't realized I'd garnered that type of support—or *any* type of support, for that matter.

I'd insisted on wearing battle dress, rather than a flimsy gown, which I was thankful for in the end, as two of the other competitors had chosen similarly. Like House Daini, I wore a leather ensemble. House Odacer flaunted full chain-mail.

The most formidable was House Saxoni—the House of the Defender. She wore a gown, yes, but it was crafted from what looked like one thousand blades, the hilts of the daggers removed, the points jutting out from where they were fastened in place. The seamstress arranged them so that she could use her arms without being pierced. And she glittered, too, a moving mirror. I stared at her, her black hair piled atop her head, pinned with more blades. Her eyes sparkled in a cat-like yellow, daggers in their own right. She was called Tey.

Brita of House Daini, also known as the House of Glory, was plain featured but looked fearless and battle-tested in her worn-in leathers.

The Odacer was called Livia. Her full chain-mail dress blocked most of her body, but her hair was a muted blonde and cropped at chin length.

Cleo of House Nepos came clad in a tight sheer gown, a tribute to her clan's alignment to truth and her tall, curved figure. The gown hugged her body and trailed on the floor behind her. Her full breasts sat upright, pointed from the sweet sea breeze that no doubt crossed them. Her bare legs were long and striking. Not even her womanhood was covered by anything more than her own growth, which made me blush, but made many in the room stare in her direction. She had shining brown hair that fell in textured curls all around her. Her cheekbones were sharp and her eyes even sharper, a deep serene blue. It reminded me of the old tales of a Siren on a sea.

The last to be announced was House Brisk, the House of Judgement. The announcer boomed, "Xinlan, of House Brisk," and I stilled at the familiarity of the name. Surely enough, a pale, lean female with white-blonde hair and dark eyes appeared, more clothed than she had been when I saw her lying naked on Cas's chaise lounge. My stomach knotted, for I imagined she had not forgotten when I shot an arrow into the flour sack right above her head on the training field. Her simple black gown was more of a satin sheet of fabric, pinned on both her shoulders, draped so that it revealed most of her back. She embodied black and white, pure judgment, as her house demanded. Her clan cheered when she entered, as all the others had upon their announcements. And then, the king summoned the six of us, to profess our intentions for all of Valfalla to witness.

Luckily, in this activity I went last.

Livia of House Odacer—the conquering house—went first. She promised that as queen she would help Cas lead Viribrum into its Golden Age, driven by grand conquests that would bring prosperity to all.

Next, Xinlan of House Brisk. Her voice projected over the waves with more strength than I would have guessed from her. She said that she would serve the future king more faithfully than any other, that she would be the balance needed to maintain peace for the kingdom. Fitting, for the House of Judgement.

Then came Cleo of the House Nepos, who claimed she would be a voice for the small, the weak. For the disenfranchised, for those who could not speak their truths. She seemed to inspire love of all kinds, and I wondered if it was genuine.

Brita of House Daini knelt before them, bearing her blade, and said that she would be a warrior for the people and for her king, bringing honor or protection, whatever was in the best interest of the Viri people.

Tey of House Saxoni stepped forward next, and she put on a display that left the other competitors seething. She flung her arms to the sides and dozens of blades left her dress, piercing the sky and then diving into the sea. The crowd erupted, and she shouted she would die before letting a drop of Viri blood shed; that she would protect her people, her king, with her own heart. The other competitors huffed at her display, but I did not, for it gave me two things: knowledge of her magic, which seemed to be control of the forces of gravity, and an idea.

A hush fell over the crowd as they waited to see what the favorite would say, what she would do. Even the ocean seemed to grow quiet in anticipation.

"Many of you do not know me." I spoke firmly, yet I sounded unsure to my own ears. "Many believe me an outsider, with Witch blood and human rearing." Some murmured in agreement, and I almost faltered. "But I am no stranger to you," I shouted. "I am the daughter of Viturius of Viribrum, the great warrior of the North, of no house, of no clan. He was of no alliance to anyone but his people. He fought alongside many of you in battle. He showed you strength, cunning, and, most importantly, loyalty. Loyalty to you and to no one else. Not to a house, not to a select few, nor to himself. I cannot say that I deserve to be your queen more than the others that stand before you, willing to die for the position. Only the Skøl will decide. But I can tell you that if I am crowned, I will be loyal to the Viri people and will spend each day serving them in the best way I can, as my father did."

And with that, I knelt on the stone, sending my power down through the thick rockery beneath us. I let a rumble loose, just enough to shake the platform gently at first, and then a bit firmer, letting it build. I bid the Earth beneath the stone to shift, ever so slightly. And it obeyed. A small crack formed in the middle of the stone patio, releasing pressured water that had roiled beneath, built by swelling waves. And water *exploded*, shooting up into the air. Before it came down, soaking the crowd, I spoke a simple cantrip Fayzien had used against me once to knock me off guard. "Vapor-ropav," I murmured, and the water turned to snow midair.

Flakes of glittery, salt-filled crystal floated down around us. And when they landed on the stone floor, little flowers bloomed in their place. Salt, water, and small specs of dirt were the basis of my concoction—just needing some silent urging from me to take shape. I hoped it'd show the Viri that even when there seemed to be nothing, I could bring life.

The crowd stilled in shock for one long, painstaking moment. Relief washed over me as cheering and shouting replaced the silence. I had debated if I should show them my element, for it was a branding of my Witch heritage and difference. But in the end, I decided to listen to Ezren and Jana's words that had begun to beat within my heart. There was no point in denying who I was.

The snow dissipated, assisted by the gentle summer wind and sea that breathed in the air. The ceremony commenced with celebrating, which was, of course, augmented with drink, food, and dancing.

Cas approached me once the gathering was underway, standing by my side, turning to admire the revelry.

"Quite the display, *mi karus*. Fairly, ehm, dauntless of you, shall I say," he winked at me.

I didn't turn to face him. "Well, I couldn't have them thinking I was boring, could I?"

Cas chuckled. "I dare say, Terra, you'll never be in danger of that." And then he took my hand, discreetly, giving it a slight squeeze. "Please be careful tomorrow," he whispered.

I exhaled, steadying my nerves. "Is everything in place for Gia and Jana?" I said back, my voice low.

"Yes. They will be taken care of."

I nodded, doing my best to act unafraid of what lay ahead. Then I looked up at him. "Cas, if... if everything goes well, if I win, what happens next? What does that future look like? For me, for us?" I asked, unsure if I wanted to know his answer.

He fixed his gaze to the roiling sea in the distance. "We will be wed fairly quickly. You will have to go back to Nebbiolo, for a time, to appease the Rexi. And I won't allow that before we are husband and wife. Our union would afford me much greater reign to ensure your protection. I don't know if I'll be able to come with you—Darlan may not allow it—but I will send warriors sworn to you. Then you will return to me, and you will prepare for queendom. And one day, we will rule all of Viribrum and Nebbiolo. And possibly more."

My stomach tightened at the 'fairly quickly' bit, which contrasted with the victory period Jana had foretold. I wondered if his plan factored in the minor detail that my life—my body—was still bound to another. But not wanting to speak of Ezren, I whispered, "Cas, I don't know if I want to rule. I don't know if I should."

"Terra, we've talked about this. It's your destiny, whether you like it or not."

I nodded, unable to say more. But a thought pricked my mind. I wondered if Ezren's comments about not denying oneself extended to the queendom. Did I hesitate to accept becoming queen because I didn't want that life for myself, or because I felt unworthy?

Or did I know somehow, deep down, that destiny had something else in store for me?

———

GIA ENDED up by my side for the rest of the night. Cas, by honor, was bound to spend time with each competitor. My eyes became sharper when he lingered next to Xinlan. I couldn't help but observe the way she grazed her fingertips on his forearm, or how she leaned too close to him when she spoke. He had not made promises to me. In fact, he had been honest from the start about his intentions. And I desired another. But watching their interaction seemed to burn a hole in the lining of my stomach. I couldn't distinguish the jealousy of wanting him from wanting something he had, whether that was power, or freedom, or the love of another.

We walked back to my room when it was acceptable to leave, though the banquet was not quite winding down.

"Neferti was not present tonight," Gia noted.

I huffed out a breath. "She doesn't approve of the Skøl."

"Have you tried to spend much time with her?" Gia asked. "She is your mother, after all."

I shook my head, trying to block out the memory of her chrome nails pressed into my throat. "She is not my mother."

"What do you know of her?" she pressed. "Have you interacted with her alone, even once?"

"Gia, she's not like that, and you know it. I don't want to talk more about this," I said, my tiredness and stress letting my tongue cut sharper than I'd wanted.

She grew silent as we approached my chamber, and I turned to her, pausing before we were within earshot of the guards posted at my door.

"Tomorrow, Cas will arrange for you to go somewhere safe. Maybe it seems a silly precaution, but I don't know what will happen to me in the Skøl, and I won't be able to check in on you. I will be much better focused if I don't have to worry about your safety," I said, a lie disguised with truth.

She narrowed her eyes ever so slightly but nodded.

I returned her nod with a tight squeeze, feeling the swelling bump in her belly that now separated us. She cupped my cheek and stared at me. "Do not forget who you are, Terra. And do not for a *second* hold back. Especially if your life is on the line—you give them everything you have."

I winked, fighting moisture from surfacing in my eyes, the corner of my mouth quirking up. "You got it, Giannina." And then she kissed me on each cheek, and we parted ways. As she disappeared around the corner, I prayed that hadn't been the last time we saw each other.

A TAP on my door woke me at dawn. Guards delivered what looked like a standard uniform, and Olea dressed me. Canvas trousers, fastened high at the waist, decorated with purpose-built pockets. I tucked my long-chained ring necklace into the leather corset, which sat over a loose blouse. Lastly, Olea slipped my arms through a worn leather jacket. She secured my Skøl approved blades, including a backsword, a thigh-strapped knife, and a boot shiv. Olea braided my hair in long sweeping plaits and painted kohl on my lids for "intimidation," she said.

I cleared my throat. "Olea, I want you to watch over this for me." I took out the clear engagement ring I'd kept in my pocket since the day Cas had given it to me. I hadn't worn it once after my abduction, not wanting to draw more of the king's attention by showing off his late wife's ring. I had only kept it in my pocket, hidden, just as Ezren's ring hung hidden around my neck.

The serving maid gasped, her eyes wide at the gem. "M'lady, where ded ye get such a stone?"

"It belonged to the late Viri Queen. Hide it in my floorboards and watch over it. And if... if I don't make it back, sell it as covertly as you can. Make a life for yourself."

"Why me, m'lady?" she asked, still blinking at the ring.

"Even though I know you've likely been directed to report on my movements, to at least the king, you've stood by me. You always ensure I'm prepared for whatever battle I'm walking into. I'm grateful for your kindness."

We beamed at each other, understanding passing between us. I'd considered giving the ring to Gia, but she'd have no idea how to sell it in the Fae lands, not in secret anyway, and I trusted Cas to take care of her.

Olea? She would be forgotten.

I slipped the jewel inside her pocket. "You can hide this later. For now, may I have a moment alone? Just to clear my head."

Olea squeezed me, murmuring her thanks, and joined the guards outside my door waiting to escort me to the Skøl. I released the loose floorboard from under my bed, drawing out the emerald hilted dagger. I wasn't sure if they would scold me for bringing my own weapons, but it was worth a try. So I unbuttoned my outer layer and strung the blade up on my chest, fastening it in place with the laces of my corset. I closed my jacket and gave my appearance a glance in the mirror. I looked neither Fae, nor human, nor Witch.

A tap on my door disturbed my silent consideration.

Time to go.

WE WERE to make our way on horseback to the competition location, a large arena close to the city called the Convallis. All the contestants came together in a long procession through Valfalla with the king and the prince at the front. The contestants were scattered throughout the line, and I brought up the rear. To my relief, I saw no sign of Gia waving me off. Cas gave me a slight nod, which I took to mean both good luck, and a sign of success in removing Gia and Jana from the palace. I didn't see Fayzien, but to my surprise, the Rexi was there, mounting her own steed and joining the procession. She pulled her horse next to mine, and we followed the group in silence.

I rode Romeo, the beautiful gelding gifted by Cas. He was strong and proud, which gave me much needed solace and strength as we paraded through the city. Fae onlookers and Viri subjects cheered and jeered, and all in between. I was the favorite of the king—and perhaps even of some at court—but certainly not of the people. My tricks and displays may have won me favor and the nickname 'Creatrixi' amongst the courtiers, which, according to Olea, was an ode to my Earth magic, but on the streets, I was a nobody who belonged to no house, and no people.

"Why did you join me?" I asked the Rexi, my voice low but audible.

She didn't bother looking at me. "Every competitor is accompanied by a large group of their kin, representatives from their Viri House. I am your only kin here."

Not my only kin. I pictured Jana in her cell and the faceless relations of Viturius I had yet to meet. But despite myself, my heart squeezed—it was the closest thing to maternal sentiment she'd offered since our reunion. Once more, we resumed our comfortable silence, accustomed to the weight of what hung between us.

We reached Valfalla's gates by late morning, and while the open space and unsaturated air should have provided me comfort, my stomach only clenched tighter. I clucked Romeo into a soft canter, in unison with the rest of the procession. We rode west alongside the forest, away from the coast to our right. Within an hour, we slowed to a walk. The caravan veered left, curving around something I could not see. The queen and I arrived last, just before the guards and warriors posted at our back. I sank my heels low in the stirrups, pushing myself to stand, peering over what had become an edge. It was an enormous pit, a crater of unimaginable size—I'd never seen anything quite like it. Even Neferti exhaled beside me. The entire procession of over a hundred lined only a tiny portion of it, shoulder to shoulder, facing its center.

We all stood, waiting.

I turned to the Rexi, attempting to distract myself. "Has there ever been a male Skøl?" I asked. "In the case there is only a female heir to be wed?"

The Rexi snorted, an undignified act on her always dignified facade. "Yes, once. They all killed each other." She snickered to herself. My face contorted at the disturbing thought, and the even more disturbing reaction from the Rexi. She shot me a look of disdain. "Oh, don't look at me like that. I only chuckle because it is so predictable. I promise, you will come to know what I mean in time, especially once you see the civility of a queendom."

I nearly laughed myself off my horse. Whether from the chatter of my nerves or the lack of emotional control, my mouth moved against my better judgment. "Oh, is that so? Is murdering husbands the civility you speak of? Or, perhaps you refer to the kidnapping of young girls, erasing their memories, hiding them away with strangers, allowing them to love those strangers as kin, and then killing them? *Hmm?*"

The Rexi's face twisted into pure disdain. "Terragnata, as a Princess of Nebbiolo you may *never* address me that way," she whispered, venom dripping from her words. "And beyond that, you have no gods damned idea what you speak of."

"Oh, don't I?" I hissed back. "Why don't you educate me then?"

But before she could respond, a loud horn sounded.

The Skøl began.

PART III
SKØL

CHAPTER THIRTY-TWO

UNWELCOME IMPOSTER

*T*he horses reared while the hoard of warriors whistled and cried out in high-pitched battle calls. The king and the prince led the charge, galloping around the Convallis, descending through winding dirt ledges that swirled down the pit like the lining of a funnel. While Cas could not offer details of the beginning, I knew the first horn meant time to pay attention. The spectators would descend until they had a bird's-eye view of the arena, each stopping in a designated viewing spot. The contestants, who were mixed amongst them, would go all the way down. How the observers could see anything in the sprawling arena miles below, I had no clue.

Ahead of me, Tey stood on her galloping horse, balancing effortlessly with her arms spread wide, her black hair tightly bound on her head as it had been the evening before. In one swift motion, she sprung up and into the pit in a backward dive, shifting mid-fall into a soaring bearded vulture with a ten-foot wingspan—a Lammergeier. The bird dove until I could see her no more.

To my relief, the rest of the contestants did not turn into a flock of birds flying away. That didn't mean their shifts weren't useful—they could have been conserving energy.

I entered the descending spiral and saw the prince and the king as small dots far below me. The procession became primitive. Warriors shrieked and beat their chests. Horses galloped with no fear down the narrow ledge, nostrils flaring. I lost sight of Cleo, Brita, and Livia, but Xinlan's white bobbing head remained in the corner of my eye.

After several revolutions, Romeo became skittish. He bucked and reared and I tightened my thighs to hold on.

"Woahh, boy, settle," I murmured, keeping my breath steady despite my heart pounding.

He continued to spook, and I got the disturbing feeling he would jump off the side of the cliff. "Romeo, settle," I soothed, patting his neck, attempting to hide my anxiety from the animal, knowing it would only worsen things. My heart betrayed me, thundering so loud in my chest I wondered if the Rexi could hear it.

Further down the sloping path, I saw Xinlan's white hair sailing into the pit, her painted stallion beneath her. So my instinct was right —Romeo was about to leap. I attempted to throw myself from the beast in hopes I would not drag him to his death.

I moved too slow. A moment later, I fell through the air, strapped to a horse that jumped to his certain death.

I looked back to see the Rexi's blank face, devoid of all emotion, dark eyes pulsing. Her mouth formed a word, but I could not hear it— my heart had stilled, and everything went quiet as we fell through the open sky. Romeo whinnied and thrust his head up, confused and panicked. I wrapped my arms around the horse's neck in an iron grip, my face tickled by his mane as we made revolution after revolution, somersaulting.

"It's okay, boy," I whispered, pressing my eyelids together, praying it would be. I shoved down the nausea building in my gut and envisioned my window, a portal through which I could take us both to safety, to the grass meadow that looked like a spec on the ground.

The portal pulsed strongly in my mind's eye, and I reached out to it. There was a whoosh feeling—the impact of still air, and in an instant, we were through. I held onto the beast for dear life, praying he would not collapse and crush me. But he did not, for my portal was gentle enough, and he only stumbled, disoriented by the ordeal.

I let out a small sound of relief mixed with triumph. I looked around, allowing Romeo to regain his footing while I swallowed the bile that built in my throat. We'd landed on a grassy plain, no other contestants around. But a whizzing noise pulled my attention up to see the rapidly approaching figures of Xinlan and her painted horse.

I kicked Romeo into a run to remove us from their fall path. I looked up and locked eyes with Xinlan, desperation and fear marking her face. I didn't think this time; I portaled to her without hesitation, grabbed her in less than a second, and then portaled safely to the ground in another. I landed with her in my arms, my bent legs absorbing the impact, several yards away from where her mount met his unfortunate end. I winced at the gruesomeness, its blood and flesh painted on the Earth, and a brief pang of regret struck me for saving her rather than the innocent animal. If it weren't for the restrictions of the fickle magic, limiting me to transport only one other living thing, I would have at least tried to save them both.

Xinlan looked at me with awe and confusion. "For the flour sack," I mumbled, shocked at not only my decision to portal, but the speed of it. Not as fast at Fayzien's, but faster than I'd ever portaled before. Before she could react to thank me or stab me, I ran, leaping onto Romeo's back, urging him to a gallop into the trees.

––––––––

My first step after entering the forested arena was to find proper food and shelter; Cas's words rang in my ears. Three challenges over approximately three days, no break. The victor would be whoever won the most events—and was still breathing at the end. I swallowed hard, the reality of the situation hitting me. I fought the urge to look at my hands, to wonder how I would handle it, how I would feel if...

If I looked down to see them covered in blood.

I shook the morbid thought from my head, shifting my mind elsewhere. *How could any of the spectators see us?* We landed so far down I could barely make out the point at which we'd entered. The Convallis was fathomless and thickly wooded. More like a pit than an arena. Fabricated though it was—trees I did not think could easily grow this deep in a rocky hole—the smells and vibrations of the dense forest tempted me to flex my element magic. A part of me considered it, for it would disqualify me. Since not only my innate power but also the natural environment of the arena fueled my Earth magic, they deemed it an unfair advantage over the non-Witch contestants. And since this was the *Fae* Skøl, I had to play by Fae rules. But just as Fae could shift, I was permitted to portal. And just as Fae could use their natural magic, I could spell.

It would be a justifiable enough explanation for my loss, not being able to resist the Earth. And the king would be pleased. But my moment of weakness passed. I would not loosen my grip on control. Not because I intended to win, though. Regardless of Gia and Jana's safety, I had no intention of winning and being forced into a marriage I'd yet to accept.

I smiled, remembering Cas's offhand comment about how the Fae detested tied outcomes—how they viewed them as producing not two victors but two losers of a draw.

The king said I had to give up the win, but he did not say I had to allow a victor. It would have to be a draw.

THE FIRST CHALLENGE instruction arrived close to sunset. I crouched around a small fire, the smoke bound by a simple containing spell, eating roasted roots that took me no time to find, even without my Earth magic. It comforted me to know that my years as a human clung to me. As if I always had something to fall back on.

Romeo remained alert, and I thanked Cas for such a reliable

steed. Maybe it was better I hadn't flung myself from him in the end. His presence made me feel a little less alone.

He began hacking, and I got up to check on him. He'd been grazing before—perhaps he choked on some fibrous roughage. But when I opened his mouth, a thick, crumpled piece of parchment fell into my hand. I removed it, and he snuffed in gratitude.

It read:

WELCOME, CONTESTANT OF THE THIRTY-THIRD SKØL IN RECORDED HISTORY. VIRIBRUM THANKS YOU FOR YOUR SERVICE, FOR YOUR DEDICATION TO THE FAE PEOPLE. TODAY, SIX OF YOU WILL COMPETE IN THE CONTEST OF BEAUTY. THIS IS THE FIRST TEST OF YOUR WORTHINESS OF THE KINGDOM.

BEAUTY IS IN THE EYE OF THE BEHOLDER, BUT WHAT MAKES THE BEHOLDER REGISTER BEAUTY? IS IT THE COLOR OF THEIR EXPERIENCES, OR THE RHYTHM OF THE TIMES?

THERE IS A CREATURE INTENDED FOR EACH OF YOU IN THE ARENA, SIX IN TOTAL, AND YOU MUST SEEK IT OUT. YOU MUST CAPTURE IT AND MAKE IT SEE YOUR BEAUTY. IF YOU SUCCEED, YOU WILL HAVE WON ITS HEART.

THE FIRST TO DO SO WILL WIN THIS EVENT. THE LAST TO DO SO, AND THOSE WHO FAIL TO DO SO BEFORE SUNDOWN TOMORROW, WILL BE DISQUALIFIED. REMEMBER, CONTESTANT, YOU MAY ELIMINATE YOUR COMPETITORS AT ANY TIME.

SKØL!

At that, a sound erupted, and I nearly jumped a foot in the air at the thunderous cheering from faceless watchers above us. I swore, fighting the urge to roll my eyes at the inscription's vagueness. *How in the gods' name would I prevent a victor with such rules?* I shuttered my eyelids, twitching my Fae ears to listen for movement. I only had to prevent myself from disqualification, which meant protecting my life, finding whatever creature I had to enchant, and making sure I was not the last to do so.

Incessant chirping from swallows and magpies in the arena filled my head. The spiral down-ramp was no longer visible; it looked like only sheer cliffs lined the crater. A crater big enough to be the *entire* Argention forest. And even though I resisted calling to it, the Earth still called to me, which was a test and an advantage, for though I could not respond, I could observe and listen. I sniffed out a running stream and mounted Romeo, nudging him in its direction. I didn't know what creatures were placed in the arena, nor how to find one. And if I did find a creature, how would I know if it was mine?

The only thing I could guess was—if it was a living, breathing thing, which the word creature implied—it would likely be a drinking thing. Meaning it would need water.

When we were about thirty yards away, I slid off the saddle and bid the unusually obedient horse to stay put. He did, and I crept through the high grass, which turned into a marsh as I neared the sound of running water. I shivered at the cool, thin sludge soaking my boots, moving up to my thigh and then reaching my navel. The marsh pulsed with muddy fragrance, but I didn't mind, for it served as a dense cover.

As I approached the stream, I bobbed and weaved my head, staying low to protect my position, but also attempting a look at the bank. And sure enough, life was there. But it was not a gaggle of Gobbles, nor a clan of Elvens, nor a flock of unknown mutants that could be considered 'creatures.' It was four of the contestants, all but the stunning Cleo.

The muddy water reached my ribcage, and I slid lower, in to my neck, tilting my hair back to wet it and mask my scent completely. Not making a sound, I stood once more, training my ear on them.

"Our number one goal should be to kill her," someone said. "Screw the event. We don't know her magic, and the king said it was the priority. If she lives, we have no shot, and more importantly, no gold."

Bastard. Fighting the urge to react, I became a marsh wraith—invisible and still. My ears trained harder on their conversation.

"Aw, is the Daini scared of a little Fae girl? I say we compete in the damn competition and off her during the events. Of course, if anyone has a clean shot, then for the gods' sake, take it. But I'm sure as *hell* not worried about her ability to make it through an event, let alone harm me in the process," another shot back. *Tey.* I would know her razor voice anywhere—as sharp as the blades she wore.

"The king said she's pretty much useless without her element. What a fucking disaster! A Witch in the Fae Skøl! I bet that's why Cas won't lie with her. Imagine, a mixed breed in your bed!"

My cheeks heated underneath the muck. Several of the contestants cackled, and I bit my lip to keep in the words—and Earth—that threatened to burst from me. I imagined sending rocks into one end of their orifices and out the other.

"I don't know if we should kill her," a soft voice said. I didn't dare move to see the speaker, but I had a guess whom the guilty comment came from.

"Oh, and why's that?" someone else said.

"Did any of you wonder why the king asked us to cooperate to kill her? He must think it a difficult job, or he would have paid just one of us. And besides, what's his motivation? He *said* protecting the bloodline. But his royal line was sullied with that common Fae wife he had. I have a hard time believing that's his reason." The voice grew stronger. "And anyhow, she only needs to *lose* for the bloodline to be protected. Not die."

"His wife is *exactly* why he wants her eliminated. He doesn't want the disgrace of his blood sullied once again! Don't you find it unusual that his Fae wife died in childbirth? Have you heard of such a thing?"

They continued like that, arguing back and forth about the king's motivations, his orders, how they should follow them, and when.

Why would the king tell me to lose just to have me murdered? To make the hit easier, I supposed. But something wriggled in my mind. That couldn't be the whole story.

For the first time, sitting there in that marsh as the sun dipped behind the edge of the Convallis, I wished for my father. Not Ravello of Argention, the sweet-eyed man that rubbed my head as a girl. I missed him with every beat of my heart. But now I wished for my birthfather, Viturius, wished he could tell me what I overlooked, why nothing made sense. My memories of him were neither warm nor plentiful, but they were laden with respect. He had raised me to be tough and to come to him with any problem. I needed his strength, guidance, and clarity.

I stayed still for a long while in the marsh, unmoving as they left to pursue their creatures and the sky turned a glowing deep blue. They seemed to follow Tey's plan, which was to kill me whenever one caught sight of my trail.

"I wish I had my father, too," an unfamiliar voice said from behind me, and I clenched my entire being to avoid a loud, physical reaction to the surprise. I turned with caution, doing my best to ease out of the water in silence. Not an easy task. My stomach leaped into my throat as I looked into Ezren's blazing green eyes.

My mouth fell ajar, and I blinked several times to confirm I wasn't hallucinating in the twilight. "I imagine you miss him a lot," Ezren said in a voice that was not his. But the image was uncanny, and I could not move.

"What in the..." I whispered, my gaze locked on the warrior.

Ezren cackled in an unnatural way. "Beauty is in the eye of the beholder, is it not?"

My blood grew cold. "Show me your true form."

It laughed again, the sound like the scrape of nails on unfinished metal. "I would, m'lady, but you control what you see. Life, it is."

"I know what you are," I said louder. "You are a Talpa. You are a creature of the wood, of the Earth. Part Fae and part Gobble. You cannot lie. You shift and change—transform to reflect your surroundings," I stated, reciting my lessons. "This can include reflecting the desires of others. But, pray tell, what desires are your own?"

At this, the creature shifted its weight, almost imperceptibly, and I wondered if Ezren was my true desire. For if he was, it meant this creature was mine.

"I have no reason to answer you. But I can see you struggle to identify yours. *Pray tell*," it said, mocking me, "do you doubt the fire that burns inside you for the warrior called Ezren?"

"I barely know the warrior called Ezren," I ground out.

"Is that so?" the Talpa probed as he approached me, the water level at his mid-torso, oddly undisturbed by his movement. "Do you truly believe that, child?"

My breathing grew labored, for whether or not it was Ezren mattered little. The Talpa was the exact image of his body, and mine had no choice but to react.

The creature tittered to itself. "I think you know the truth, for you have seen his soul. Perhaps not for the first time. And by seeing, you have been seen, human one."

I fought the dueling urges to flee or leap on the non-Ezren Ezren. And then it was a foot from me, towering in the way he always had. While my female instincts roared, my Fae senses also sniffed out the creature's underlying scent. It was not Ezren's smell of piñon and strength and damp forest. It was a mix of burning fear, and underlying suffering. My longing turned to concern. I took one of its hands and it jerked back, but I held fast.

"Whom do you serve?" I knew it was not a free being. It stank of fear and misery—and I'd read the Fae often forced the lesser Faeries into servitude.

"I, I am bound to no one, peasant," it snapped, snatching its hand from my grasp. At once, I knew I had gained ground.

"How long?" I asked again, not breaking its gaze, willing myself to see beyond the blazing green eyes that sent flames into my low belly. "How long have you been captive?" I searched there, latching on to the string of pain I found behind the fire.

Its eyes darted once more, and for a brief moment they were no longer emerald or Fae but large dark orbs, terrified. But then he was Ezren again, resolved to regain the upper hand.

"You know nothing of what you speak. I hope it will bring you great pain, to see your death brought 'round at the hands of your lover," it hissed.

But before he could draw his blade, I said, "Tell me how to free you, and I will do it."

It froze, unmoving in Ezren's form. "That is no small offer, Princess. You know not what you suggest." His voice was dead quiet, his eyes flickering between his true form and his Fae figure.

"Enlighten me, then." My heart pounded, sensing this would end either in battle or something worse.

"Only my master can free me," it said, its voice thick with an unnatural lilt. "However, a new master can replace my old one. Should someone wish to take the place of my master, they must transfer me their lifeblood in more quantity than what I currently feed on. This is difficult and requires much suffering. It will also likely result in loss of several years of life, the exact amount unknown."

I pushed out a deep breath, tempted to fight the creature instead. Something inside me said the sacrifice was worth it, for flesh pain is fleeting, and the true feeling of freedom is not.

"I know as much as anyone the importance of liberty," I breathed. "I will do it, Talpa, and then I will release you. But before I do, I would like to see your true form."

It stared at me in disbelief at first, but then it shifted, beginning with large, shining eyes. The rest of its body changed, and it shrank to half the height of when it took Ezren's form, its neck just peeking out of the water. It had thick leathery skin, wide pointed ears, and might be considered ugly if not for the large innocent eyes of extraordinary depth that peered up at me.

And then Ezren suddenly returned, for it seemed to be pained in its original form.

"How do I give you my lifeblood?" I asked the creature.

It blinked. "I just need to drink from a vein."

I waded back to shore, the creature following me. After a quick surveying of the moonlit surroundings, I undid the front of my leathers, removing Ezren's dagger.

I turned to face the Talpa, and it gasped. "What?" I whipped around, palming the dagger and searching for whatever surprised the creature. But I saw nothing, and when I looked at Ezren's form once again, it fixed its gaze on the hilt of my weapon.

"Where did you get that?" it whispered.

"It was a gift. Why?"

"I have not seen a Dragon's egg in a millennia. I thought they were all lost."

"A Dragon's egg?" I cocked my head.

"Yes, on the hilt," the Talpa replied, as if I was the oblivious one.

"You mean the emerald," I corrected.

"No! That is no emerald! Can you not see it blazes with the fire of a Dragon? That, right there, is a petrified Dragon's egg. There is no shell, it likely dissolved over many thousands of years. I imagine you have kept such a possession hidden from other Fae folk. For if you had not, it likely would no longer be yours."

I searched for some unborn Dragon embryo inside the gem. When I examined it, I only saw a shining flame within the green stone that wasn't really a stone after all.

"Well, I suppose I owe you a debt for the education," I muttered.

An eerie grin spread across its features, like it knew I was about to repay that debt ten times over. I ran the dagger across my palm. I made a fist, squeezing hard to draw the blood to the surface of the skin. And then I raised my hand to the Talpa.

"How much will you need?"

"A fair amount," it said, eyes trained on my already dripping palm a few inches from its face.

I nodded. It brought my hand gently to its mouth, and my body shuddered at Ezren's lips, his tongue that ran along my palm. And then it sucked, drawing the blood from my veins.

At first, it was just a tug, as if a string ran through my body to my chest. But a few moments later, the tug turned into a pull, and then a yank. And then the yank did not remain isolated to my chest but came from everywhere. And I could no longer describe it as discomfort, but sheer pain. The essence of my flesh was being sucked out, leaking through every pore. I bit so hard on my lip, stifling my scream, that iron tang coated my tongue. My body shook, uncontrollably, and I remembered that Ezren could feel my suffering. But then the Talpa stopped, staring at me in wonder, and the pain disappeared.

"Did it work?" I asked, breathless, reeling from the ordeal and surprised it ended so soon.

"You, you are bound, child?" it asked softly, now gentle with me, still holding my palm.

I shook my head. "I still don't fully know what that means, but yes, I am bound to the warrior Ezren."

Familiar green eyes sparkled back at me. "Well, you have lost less life-blood today because of him. He sent me much of his, rapidly and with intention, so I needed no more than a few drops of yours. The process is not usually so... brief."

I gaped at him, wondering how Ezren could have done such a thing. "Does that mean Ezren is your master?"

"No, no, it was your skin that was pierced. You have the power to dismiss me," it replied.

"Well, then, Talpa, I release you of service to me or any master previously."

And then it cried out, overjoyed, hopping some wild dance in Ezren's form. It picked me up and twirled me around, and I got so lost in its jubilance that it took me a moment to register when it collapsed, gagging.

I rushed over, opening not-Ezren's mouth. Carefully, I removed the lodged parchment, thick and crumpled like it had been the first time.

It read:

Competitor! Congratulations. Not only have you made this creature see your beauty, but you were the first to do so and have thus won the first contest. You have now moved to the contest of Strength.

Strength comes in many forms. There is strength of mind, of will, of resolve. There is corporal strength, the strength of skill and body. You must show all forms, as you must kill the Talpa standing before you.

The first to do so will win this event. The last to do so, and those who fail to do so before the next sundown, will be disqualified. Remember, contestant, you may eliminate your competitors at any time.

Skøl!

We both stilled, our arms placed on one another, and I looked into the creature's eyes that were not its own. My gaze flashed to my wrist, where a shimmering gold tattoo snaked from one side to the other, leaving a gold band. If I'd been the first to complete the test of Beauty, I could guess what it meant. This was the winner's mark. I pressed my eyes together in exasperation, drawing a slow breath. If I wasn't a target for the other competitors before, I surely would be now.

I looked back to the Talpa, peering down at me. I shook my head. "I—I can't. Even if you did not look like him, I cannot," I whispered, slowly untangling myself from the creature. I took a step back, shaking.

I expected the Talpa to shift, to turn and bolt. But it did not. Instead, it leaped on me, knocking me to the ground.

Saving me from a whirring arrow that soared right over our heads.

"Crawl!" it shouted at me in a whisper.

But I did not follow its order. Instead, I wrapped my arms around it and I portaled us both.

We landed on hard ground, next to where I'd left Romeo. I panicked, wondering if our pursuers had caught my steed. But he whinnied on our arrival, appearing from behind a large oak.

"Thank the gods," I muttered, jumping on his back. "Go Talpa. You are free. Leave this place and save yourself."

The creature, still in Ezren's form, turned to run but hesitated. "When were you born?"

I blinked at his question and Romeo danced, wanting to move. "We hardly have time for—"

"*What. Date.*" He ground out urgently.

"Uhh—fifteen days after the last spring new moon, ninety-two days after the Spring Equinox in the old Fae calendar. My twentieth was mere days ago. *Why?*"

"On the Full Moon of the Creatrix," the Talpa whispered, so softly I almost missed it. "Twenty years ago."

Romeo hopped and struck the ground with a hoof, begging to go, and I had to clench my thighs to quiet him. "What is the full—"

"Let us leave this place, and find somewhere safe," the Talpa interrupted, shifting painfully back into its true form. It took off in an unnatural run, bidding me to follow. I didn't have to kick Romeo into action. We galloped after the creature.

CHAPTER THIRTY-THREE

FAIR DEALS

"It's simple. Just kill me, then revive me. Perhaps you can use your magic to slow my heartbeat and then speed it back up again?"

I paced around the cave where we made camp—a rocky hole in the perimeter of the Convallis. "I'm not a healing Witch, you know that, right? I'm just an Earth Witch," I responded to the inane solution the creature had proposed.

"Ha! Merely an Earth Witch! Well, *those* are not words I thought I would hear in all my millennia," the Ezren imposter replied.

"Do you have to remain in his form?" I asked, heat climbing to the tips of my ears. "It makes it harder for me to think." I rubbed my thumb and index finger over my brow.

"Yes, your mind is quite deafening at the moment," the Talpa said, apparently privy to my thoughts. "Unfortunately, not only *can* Talpa shift to show the desire of those around them, we are highly encouraged to do so... given we are cursed to feel acute pain in our true forms. I've spent little time in my natural shape because of that. So, I have few options other than the reflection of my surroundings. Though you may not like it, what you desire is *most* undeniable."

I sighed, plopping down on the cold stone next to the fire, staring into the flames. "I have never brought someone back to life with or without magic. What makes you so confident I could do it now?"

"I am not. I simply trust, as you trusted me. How were you so confident that I did not deceive you when I told you of the lifeblood?"

"Talpa cannot lie," I said weakly.

"Yes, but they can deceive. It could have been a trick. I said the gift of lifeblood would grant me freedom—but I didn't say *only* my freedom. I could have been taking more than you knew."

"Well, it certainly sounds like you have experience with crafty wording," I huffed, rolling my eyes. "I don't know. I suppose I sensed more fear in you than malice. I also have been afraid, many times. You felt, familiar, like me. I guess... I guess I did trust you."

"But *why?*" the creature pressed. "You've had your trust violated many times in the past, no?"

I threw my hands up in admission. "I don't know why—perhaps, in here, everything is stripped away. There is no room for self-doubt in the Skøl. I have only instinct to rely on. And my instinct was to trust you."

"Exactly. You could say I have that instinct now, too," the Talpa said.

I paused, loosening a breath. "What's your name?"

"Talpa do not have names, you know that," it replied tartly.

"No, if my recollection is correct, Talpa do not have names they *share*. However, a trusted confidant, trusted enough to kill and bring back life, should know. Am I wrong?"

The Talpa eyed the flames. "I'll make you a deal. You succeed, I'll tell you my name thrice over. *And* I'll explain the Full Moon of the Creatrix."

Though my stomach roiled again at its proposal, my pulse quickened at the potential information. The way the creature said it felt weirdly *personal,* and it had refused to share more after we'd found a safe resting place. I curled myself into a ball on some soft ground I had gathered, letting my eyes shutter.

"Fine. I agree. No need to attempt it now. It's the middle of the night, and we have until sundown tomorrow. We must rest," I said through my yawn.

The Talpa rolled onto one side and fell into rhythmic breathing almost instantly.

I eyed the sleeping creature. *Why help me? Why not run?* I stared into the dwindling fire, little more than glowing embers, looking for answers and finding none.

HE CAME to me in my dreams once more, a soft touch here and a firm press there. It felt just as desperate, raw, and real as the first time. A time when we needed each other so badly we became *one*. When I was him, and he was me. That I could relive the moment in my head —the memory alone conjuring the same physical reactions—stunned me. Even though I knew it was a dream.

I rolled over on that grassy bed, Ezren moving with me until his eyes locked with mine. And he leaned over me, taking my shoulders in his large palms, thumbing them gently. "Terra," he said. "Terra," he said again, urgency in his tone. I stirred, blinking my eyes open, and I froze when I saw Ezren in the flesh, his face leaning over me. A jolt of hot lighting ran through my body.

It wasn't really Ezren, I remembered. It was a nameless Talpa, waking me with worry. I didn't move for several heartbeats more, recovering from the shock to my insides, taking small sips of air to calm the pounding in my chest.

"What is it?"

"I smell something," it whispered hurriedly, Ezren's eyes wider than I'd ever seen them.

"Okay?"

"Talpa can smell nothing, nothing at all—unless death is near." It released me and paced.

"So you smell death, then?" I asked, pushing myself up and raising a brow.

"No, no. I don't smell actual death. I smell 'something.' Anything. But only when death is near."

I rolled my eyes. "Well, what do you smell?"

"Iron. Metallic. It is hard on the tongue." It squirmed—an unnatural action to see on Ezren's form.

I squinted at the Talpa. "You smell iron? I expected *something tangy* or *something cooling,* but how do you know what iron smells like, or anything for that matter—" I was cut off mid-sentence by a dead Talpa flying through the cave's opening, landing at the foot of our fire.

The Ezren impersonator shrieked at the limp creature, mangled in its true form. It howled and sobbed, and I wondered if they had known each other. But the thought did not stop me from leaping up, drawing my broadsword from where I'd kept it strapped to my back.

Tey sauntered in.

"Tey," I said, nodding casually, noting the ring of gold on her wrist. She had won the second event. "What can we help you with?"

I angled my body to block my Talpa as I spoke. It stood a few feet back from me, and I knew if I let one of the other competitors kill the creature, it would disqualify me. Three, maybe four steps back, and I could grab it and portal.

Before I could launch backward, Tey spoke. "If you even *think* about portaling, she dies."

I froze as Brita appeared, dragging Xinlan into the cave, a blade stuck in her thigh.

Xinlan fought the grip, but Brita snickered and pressed a knife to her throat. Blood soaked Cas's lover's leg, dripping down her ankle. To her credit, she did not whimper. But she didn't meet my gaze. She looked defiantly past me, as if she wouldn't acknowledge the situation at hand.

I stared. A heartbeat passed. I was tempted, *so tempted,* to let

Xinlan face her fate. I'd already saved her life once, what more could I owe her? But Tey's blades hovered in the air, and I knew what the threat implied. The two seconds it would take me to turn, grab the Talpa, and envision the portal could be enough for one of Tey's flying blades to sink into the soft spot of my back. And more than that, something inside me couldn't leave Xinlan alone in the cold, dripping cave with no hope for a way out.

Half a breath had me drawing a large semi-circle in the cave's dirt floor with the tip of my boot, and whispering "clypeus" to it. In an instant, an iridescent green flame erupted in a shield from where the line lay on the ground.

Tey lost her composure, and the blades from her armor flung themselves in our direction. Fury marred her face as they bounced harmlessly off the shield and fell at my feet.

"Come out and fight us, you coward half-breed!" Tey shouted, midnight hair swirling around her. Brita's knife pressed harder into Xinlan's throat, blood beading at the sharp edge. "Or I swear to the *gods* I'll have Brita gut this whore in front of your eyes!"

Xinlan shook her head slightly, despite the deepening of the wound it caused. Maybe she didn't feel worthy of a second rescue. I swallowed, weighing my options. "There's no reason to involve Xinlan in this," I said, fighting to keep the calm in my voice. "We can work this out, the two of us."

"Oh, the saint act again—what bullshit," Brita said, venom dripping from her words. "How do you plan to win the Skøl? Does the princess see herself above the rest of us? Clean hands, unlike your dirty competitors?"

"Can't you just speak a spell to stop their hearts or something?" the Talpa whispered behind me. I shook my head. Even if I could, I wouldn't have wanted to.

Tey launched another attack, attempting to curve her flying weapons around my half-tower, but the flames licked them away, snaking and extending where needed. She growled in fury. "You have three seconds before my knife sinks into her neck. Drop the shield, *now*."

"I'll make you a deal." I narrowed my gaze on the black-haired female shrouded in sharp points. "Hand-to-hand combat. No magic. No Brita. Just you and me and our swords."

A sneer crossed her face, and I did what I could to remain unaffected. "A fight to the death then, eh?"

"You could say that," I replied.

"Deal," she said.

I smirked, unsurprised at her agreement. Above all else, she wanted my life.

The Talpa moaned behind me in quiet protest. Xinlan's eyes were dull as she slumped to the ground, Brita no longer holding her up. Blood trickled down her leg, staining the dusty floor.

"Lower your shield," Tey said, stepping towards us.

"Blades first," I replied.

She acquiesced, her armor's cover flying off and landing in a pile at her feet.

I stepped through my wall of flame, which parted momentarily for me to pass.

Tey's face contorted. "I said, drop. Your. Shield," she ground out.

It was a gamble to leave the shield up while fighting. The spell required a steady feed of magic from me, which would impair my skill in combat. But the alternative meant leaving the Talpa vulnerable, which seemed like a worse choice.

I shrugged. "If you kill me, the shield will drop. Our deal was hand-to-hand combat. Perhaps you doubt your abilities to win fairly?"

Tey's face twisted into something feral, and she launched into the spar. Her quickness and lightness of foot drew me in. Her now undone black hair, a violent contrast to her pale skin, whipped around as she danced and twirled. Our blades met briefly each time; she was relentless, her next attack came while I defended the last. I grew tired fast. Her rhythm was too swift for me, which was new.

I had to slow things down, force her to match my pace. That was how the slower, bigger opponents usually won against me. But I didn't have the experience with that, and before I could figure out my next move, her blade slashed across my face. I saw it come out of the corner of my eye, but my dodge was too slow, and the tip drew a line parallel to my cheekbone. The resulting wetness tickled my cheek, a slow stream of blood.

Tey bared her teeth, but did not relent. She had been training her whole life for this and knew not to revel in any small triumph. She gave me no ground, and in fact used my faltering against me. Her body spun around, and Tey sent a sharp kick of her leg backward, the heel of her boot meeting my stomach with wild force. I hit the dirt hard, landing right outside my spelled wall, my sword ricocheting out of my hand.

My head tilted up to see the green flames licking out above me. I half grunted, half wheezed, the wind knocked from my lungs. Tey's black hair swarmed in my vision.

She grinned but remained silent, raising her broadsword. When it came flying towards my neck, I felt the tug of a blade raising my hand. Ezren's dagger had somehow appeared in my palm, the emerald shining on the hilt. I had no time to wonder how. My arm rattled with the impact of her large sword against my smaller dagger, reverberating through my body. I struggled to hold, her blade sliding closer and closer to my chin. I gritted my teeth when her eyes locked in on mine, swirling with a violence that roused my own anger.

"Can you see yourself, your reflection, in my eyes?" Tey hissed. "Look closely and see the face of a coward. Look closely, and you will see your own death."

She made to push harder, her final blow, but I flung my other hand up to the dagger. It glowed again, blindingly bright, and in one push, I shoved her up and back away from me. Tey flew through the air, hitting the ground with force. I barely had time to blink at the unnatural strength that push would have required—strength I didn't have.

"How in the—" She spat blood as I forced the heels of my palms

into the dirt. We rose to meet each other, well-matched dancing partners. She lifted her blade, ready to strike once more.

Before she could deliver her next blow, a voice echoed through
the cave, moving closer to us.

"*Tsk tsk tsk.* Such violence in you females!" Fayzien's
disturbingly delighted face appeared from the shadows, and our jaws
went slack.

CHAPTER THIRTY-FOUR

CURSED TIES

"Ｗhat are *you* doing here, Fayzien?" I asked at the same time Tey said, "You shouldn't be here, outsider filth."

Fayzien smirked. "I am half Fae as well, darling, just like the princess."

Tey gave him a look of murder and said, "She isn't welcome, either, if you can't tell. The Skøl maesters will come for you in minutes, and you'll be executed for interfering."

"Tey of House Saxoni, how *lucky* is it that I'm the most powerful Witch you will ever meet," Fayzien responded. "Shielding myself from the eyes of others is child's play."

I felt my heel touch the green flames that remained in place around the Talpa. I had no idea why Fayzien was here, and I didn't really care. I knew better than to waste a good distraction. So, I stepped through the shield, my back connecting with the Talpa, who then gripped me with the fierce strength of Ezren's body. As we portaled, my eyes narrowed pointedly at Fayzien, before I glanced to the near-dead Xinlan. As much as Fayzien hated me, I prayed he cared for Cas enough to get his lover out of there alive.

I WENT AS FAR as my memory and ability would let me, and we soon landed in that soft grassy clearing amongst tall trees. I gave the Talpa one look, and it lay on the ground, for it knew we could wait no longer. My heart tightened at the sight of its eyes closing, my mind repeating "this is not Ezren" as a mantra. I sat on its mid-section, my knees bordering its ribs. I pressed its shoulders to the ground and coaxed the air from its lungs. The sensation shocked me. It felt like I called to the air as I did to the Earth, and for a moment, I thought I'd broken the rules. But nothing rang out above me. I had not summoned the Earth, so I continued my work. Bringing two fingers to the place on its neck, I could still feel a slight pulse. Amazing that the Talpa did not struggle at all, such a feat against basic instinct. Eventually, I felt no pulse, and the creature shifted back to its small, leathery body, its withered hand clutching a piece of paper.

I didn't care about the parchment right now—I cared about reviving the lifeless being in front of me. I clasped my fingers together and began to compress and release its chest. I felt stupid, using the human tactic taught in Argention. But I was no healer, and though my magic searched the creature for a spark of life to ignite, it found nothing.

So I continued to press my hands into its chest and blow breath into its airway, attempting to inflate its lungs. After seconds that felt like minutes, I saw a soft rise and fall of its chest. Its black eyes looked up at me in wonder.

I cupped its cheek and pushed the tears back. "You are in your true form, friend. Shift if it saves you pain."

"Cobal. Cobal." It beamed at me. "You may call me Cobal. And for whatever reason, Terragnata of Nebbiolo, it no longer hurts to be in this form."

I relaxed into the grass for a moment, my legs stretched out, and looked down at my forearm. Unlike before, no new thin gold band appeared. It didn't surprise me, given the dead Talpa we'd seen, and what I noted on Tey's wrist. I had lost the second event and had to kill the Talpa simply to remain in the Skøl.

Cobal dumped the parchment in my lap and bounced up and down. "I knew you could do it!" the Talpa exclaimed, skipping around the small meadow. It looked joyous, with orbed eyes that beamed as it took in the world, finally comfortable in its own form.

I unfurled the paper.

COMPETITOR! CONGRATULATIONS, YOU HAVE TAKEN THE BREATH FROM THIS CREATURE, AND WERE NOT THE LAST TO DO SO, PREVENTING YOUR ELIMINATION. THE REMAINING COMPETITORS HAVE UNTIL SUNDOWN TO COMPLETE THEIR TASKS. REST AND AWAIT FURTHER INSTRUCTIONS FOR THE TEST OF HONOR.

REMEMBER, CONTESTANT, YOU MAY ELIMINATE YOUR COMPETITORS AT ANY TIME.

SKØL!

So it was tied then—one victory for me, one victory for Tey. I pressed my eyelids together, praying there would be another competitor besides the two of us to compete in the final challenge of the Skøl. If there was, I'd only need to ensure they won, and the draw would remain.

And stay alive. *That* I would also have to do.

"So... YOU HAVEN'T FULFILLED your bargain," I said to Cobal over a mouthful of nuts and berries. We'd spent the morning gathering provisions and tending to my various cuts and bruises. I'd been waiting for the creature to offer the information, but my curiosity overpowered my patience.

Cobal grunted. "I'm surprised you waited this long to ask."

"Well?"

"I swore I'd tell you about the Full Moon of the Creatrix *after* you succeeded in bringing me back, not *how long* after."

I narrowed my eyes at the Talpa. "Are you serious?"

The creature sighed. "Fine. I will tell you the meaning of the day, and nothing more."

I nodded. "As you vowed."

"The Full Moon of the Creatrix, the day you were born, is—how shall we say—an auspicious day to be born. The Creatrix is thought of by both Witch and Fae as The Original."

I cocked my head. "The original what?"

"The Original Creator. Original Fae. Original Witch. The Seed of Life. The Mother of All. The Beginning of Everything."

I chuckled. "You know, the Fae and humans aren't so different from one another. That sounds an *awful* lot like human folklore and religion."

Cobal bristled, which made a tinge of shame sting my cheeks for laughing at its customs.

"So, what is the Full Moon of the Creatrix, exactly?"

"It is the day the full moon intercepts the summer solstice. It is a day of honoring, celebrating, and generally giving thanks, for the interception only happens once every twenty years or so. Fae and Witch alike give thanks to the Earth and her goddess for what has been created, and for what will be. There are many sacrifices to the Creatrix herself. I believe your next birthday will be such a day."

"And why did knowing I was born on the day of this festival make you follow me?"

"For an Earth daughter, the likes of which has not been seen in a thousand years, to be born on this day... well, it is an auspicious sign, as I said. I could not abandon you. I can offer nothing more than that."

I thought to press the creature, but its expression was weary and warning, as if it had already shared more than it wanted. After filling my belly, boiling water to drink, and applying a makeshift salve to the slash on my face, Cobal offered to take the first watch. Resting seemed unthinkable, but the many portals and the duel with Tey had exhausted me. The next event could come any time after sundown. So despite my initial protest, I slept. The mossy clearing curled around me, and I sunk in. The mid-day sun warmed my core and I drifted into a sleep so strong, so enticing, I had the passing thought it could be magic.

And then I dreamed.

THE DETAILS and edges were blurry. First, I saw a flash of lightning. And then another. And another. Six Witches stood on a rock under the night sky—connected somehow. Sharing power. The lightning struck again, this time touching all of them. They fell, not one by one, but as a unit, save their leader. She roared, blood trickling from her eyes. And then her scarlet dripping gaze turned to me.

I fought and fought to focus on her face. But I could not make it out. The scent of a female filled my nostrils as she moved closer, her likeness still hidden from my mind. It wasn't until her face drew close enough to mine—so close I could feel the tickle of her breath on my skin—that I saw my mother's eyes. The blackness in them threatened to swallow me whole.

"It's time to go."

I couldn't move.

"I said, it's time to go."

This is a dream. Just wake up, and you can move.

"Terra, Descendent of the First Earth Daughter. It's time to go."

And then she raised her hand, as if to strike.

I SAT UP GASPING, my hand clenched on my pounding chest, the sweet scent of a female—old, ancient almost—pricking at my nostrils, like it had in the dream. I jumped to my feet, preparing for the next surprise from the competitors that had found me last time. But it was not Brita, nor Xinlan I scented. It was not Tey's smug, condescending face that emerged from the thickness. Swaying dark chocolate hair gleamed in the dusky light that filtered through the trees surrounding the meadow. It framed a rich brown face, with eyes of the deepest blue set atop cheekbones that could cut glass. Her beauty had been obvious when I first met her, but now she looked sad and tormented, somehow all the more striking for it. *Cleo.*

I drew my blade, though I noticed she was unarmed. She approached me, her long legs in a melodic saunter. By all measures, she seemed to come in peace, but her magic was still unknown, and I wouldn't be caught unprepared.

Cobal crouched behind me. My chest rose with anticipation as she neared, my eyes dancing around in assessment, searching for co-conspirators lurking in the distance.

"You did not kill your Talpa," she said, cocking her head at me whilst she approached, her gaze lingering on the ring of gold on my forearm. She had none.

"I did, but then I revived him," I answered.

She quirked her brow. "Ah, a healer Witch too?"

I shook my head. "I used a human method, just breathing air back into the lungs."

She gave me a distant look I couldn't quite place. "I could not kill mine."

My eyes narrowed, wondering if this was a distraction ploy. "You will be eliminated soon," I said flatly. "It will be sundown any moment. So, what use do you have for me? Do you plan to kill me, too? For the king's coin?"

She tilted her face to the sky, absorbing the last bit of sun that peaked through the opening of the Convallis. "I am not here to kill you, Terragnata. I am here to help you win. As I always have been."

I opened my mouth to object, to question, but she continued. "You won the first event, for you made your Talpa see your beauty within minutes. However, you wasted precious hours contemplating how to kill it, while Tey and Xinlan found their Talpa, completing the first and second tasks. Though I slowed her, Tey was the first to kill her Talpa and won the event of Strength. Livia was eliminated from the first round, and Brita and I..." she paused, looking at the sky again for a moment. "Will be following that path shortly. You know this, I assume, but I'll say it, anyway. You must be the one to complete the task of Honor first. That is, if you *want* to secure victory."

I narrowed my eyes. "What is your magic? And why do you want to help me?" The words came out more like accusations than questions.

"I have sight. Not in the way of The Sight, like some Witches have, but I can see the truth clearly. It's not very forward-looking, nor is it always evident, especially if I see a concept I don't understand. But I know this much is true. If Tey wins the last event, she will win the competition. And I know *that* is not an outcome you would desire."

"She is also preoccupied with another effort," I said, and Cleo looked at me with understanding.

"Aye, it's slowed her progress. She has gone mad..." she trailed off slowly. Recognition flickered across her face. "Terra, you *must* do what needs to be done in the contest of Honor," Cleo rushed her words as if she was running out of time. "It will be difficult, but much depends—"

The Fae fell silent. I looked around to see what halted her breath; there was not even a flicker of movement in the meadow.

Until there was.

I could tell we were still in the meadow, because the scent and feel of grass beneath my feet remained utterly unchanged. A glamor had slipped around it, altering the scene, bringing the spectators I hadn't seen or scented closer, so much closer. All of a sudden, their faces blurred together in a distorted illusion of jeering sport fans in stadium seats, and their cheers were louder, louder; they filled my ears. A blazing-blue line encircled the clearing in which we stood, making it an arena within the arena. And then a gong rang, a sound so intense it reverberated in my chest. I imagined it signaled the sun had slipped beneath the horizon, and the last event was to commence.

Cleo vanished—as if she was portaled away. What kind of Witch power would be required to apply a portal to another being without touch? I guessed the magic was also used on Brita, somewhere within the Convallis. The Talpa remained by my side—apparently a part of the new stage the Skølmaester had set.

And then they appeared, the final contestants. Xinlan and Tey portaled into the ring of blue, which separated our final battlefield from the spectators. I unsheathed my sword and took a few steps backwards to feel if any magic held us within the perimeter. A small shock to my left shoulder confirmed my suspicion.

Tey looked about ready to pounce on me when a swirl of black hair, whipping around in front of her, forced a to pause. Two young girls had appeared before Tey. I could not see their faces since their backs were to me, but they clung to each other, trembling. Tey's face turned ash white as she retrieved the message from one of their mouths and let out a cry. She wailed so unnaturally I could only imagine what the paper commanded. Sisters, perhaps. I swallowed, trembling a bit myself.

Xinlan, too, watched the scene, her wounds no longer visible, as she waited for her test to come. And just a few moments after Tey's, it did. An older couple appeared before her—I could see their features from the side. They had hooded eyes like her own. Parents, I guessed.

I pressed my eyes shut, my own shaking intensifying at the tenor of Tey's sobbing, terrified to see who'd be standing in front of me when I opened them. And then I felt the whoosh of the portal and knew they were there.

———

My eyes flew open to see Jana and Leiya standing before me, and the unnatural screeching from the spectator illusion barely registered in my mind. I swore under my breath. Though I was relieved to see Leiya alive and well, my gut twisted in anticipation of what their presence meant. Pure rage lined Leiya's face as she opened her mouth, extending a crumpled parchment from her tongue. Jana's paper-thin skin revealed the jut of bones—a whisper of the full Witch I'd known before her days in the Viri dungeon. Despite her now hollow face, she offered me a nod of reassurance, directing me to take it.

Leiya's expression screamed *wrong, something is wrong!* But of course, it was all wrong. My hands shook as I retrieved the message from Leiya's mouth, spreading the sides of the paper wide, and my heart thumped violently in my chest.

Competitor! Welcome to the Contest of Honor. A queen faces many difficult decisions in order to honor her king and her kingdom. Before you stand two traitors of the Viri crown, one of which will not leave this arena with their life. You must honor Viribrum and the king's wish by choosing which will live, and which will die. The first competitor to complete this task will win this event.

Those who fail to choose will be disqualified and watch both traitors die. Or you may decide to forfeit your own life to spare those who stand before you. This is the way of honor.

One dies, two die, one dies.

Remember, contestant, you may eliminate your competitors at any time.

Skøl!

Jana smiled at me—a smile full of a warmth so bright it beamed like love. "I am ready to reunite with Reece, to move on. You have many here that will help guide you." She glanced sideways at Leiya.

"And I have no doubt you will stand bravely against anything you face. Finish what you have started here, and then chart your own path. Seek your Siphon. It will help guide you to your destiny."

Her cryptic message hardly registered over Tey's ever increasing wailing, over the roaring in my head. Jana and Leiya had lied, yes, and perhaps used me. They'd withheld the truth about who I was to get me to cooperate with them. But seeing them stand before me... I felt no lingering anger or pang of betrayal. Only admiration and respect. My face grew hot as I fought back the tears that welled. I looked at Leiya; she met my eyes stoically, a true warrior who would accept any fate dealt.

"I don't think I can," I whispered, to them, to myself. I shook my head. "I don't think I can."

Before Jana could protest, a buzz filled the air. Tey's blades had left her armor and were soaring above her. *She will win if she kills one of them,* I thought numbly. *She won the second event. This would seal her victory of the Skøl.*

Tey extended her arms out, her face to the sky, red and puffy. The knives reached their apogee and came diving down, with a force so immense that when they punctured their target, blood exploded in every direction.

It happened so fast I blinked to make sure of what I saw. The blades had sunk into Tey's body, not the girls'. They burst out into tears themselves, coated in the remains of their sister. And then they vanished, portaled away, as if they had never been there.

The phantom crowd went wild.

Xinlan and I locked eyes. If she felt as sick as I did, she did not show it. She simply turned to the couple in front of her and bowed deeply. The male stepped forward and drew the sword strapped to his side. But before the edges of their metals could even collide, she lifted her weapon in the air, and sliced his head clean off.

I fought the urge to look away. The female next to him did not make a sound. She did not look at the rolling head that bumped against her foot, with eyes still open, nor did she flinch at the blood that sprayed across her chest. She only bowed deeply to Xinlan, and then was whisked away along with the body, vanishing through the depths of a portal.

As Xinlan turned towards me, a shimmering gold ring appeared on her forearm—matching mine. It would only be a matter of moments before she'd take her shot at eliminating me. We were tied, each the winner of one test—a draw in the eyes of the Fae. But to her, victory could still come if my life ended, or if I failed to complete the final task.

"Terra, dear, it has to be now," Jana urged.

"I can't kill you," I whispered while racking my brain for an alternative. I needed a loophole, some solution to this problem. But before I could string a conscious thought together, Xinlan's blade slashed towards me. I rolled out of the way and unsheathed my own sword, finding my feet quickly.

"His death cannot be in vain, Terra," she said plainly. "I'm sorry."

Our blades collided. She didn't fight as fast as Tey, given her injured thigh, but she certainly was just as strong. We parried and danced. Out of the corner of my eye, Leiya flinched at every clash of metal. The distraction cost me—Xinlan's leg found my ankles, sweeping my feet from beneath me. I fell, and she leapt on me in an instant. Without thinking, I portaled, leaving her fumbling on the ground, and appeared behind her, my dagger pressed to her throat.

"I'm sorry too, Xinlan. I don't want this... this fight," I choked out, pulling her up. "Drop your sword and forfeit. We will be tied."

"You have to finish the task for that to be true," she spat. She did not release her weapon.

"Please," I whispered, digging the edge of my dagger into her skin just slightly. "Please don't make me do something I'll regret."

Jana stepped in front of Xinlan, lifting up the tip of the contestant's sword and resting it on her own breastbone. Xinlan froze. "Terra, by honor of the king, do you choose me to die, to pay for my sins against the crown and otherwise?" Her voice was firm, confident, a contrast to her decimated state.

I shook my head, all words dying in my throat, as the tears broke whatever dam I'd tried to maintain against them. "Jana," I warned. "Don't."

"Daughter of the Earth, it is time. Look at me! I am withered to a ghost. I have many sins to pay for and souls to reunite with. It is *time*." She began to lean into Xinlan's blade, drawing blood.

Xinlan's muscle twitched, as if to take the choice away from me.

Before she could complete the kill, I whispered, "I choose you."

Jana leaned full force into Xinlan's blade.

And the gong rang again.

"Two final contestants! What a delight!" the Skølmaester's voice rang out above the mirage of spectators' unnatural cheering. It was the first time we'd heard him speak—his hair-raising tone carried across the dusky sky. Xinlan bucked against me, releasing herself from my grip, which had weakened anyway. My attention focused only on the Witch lying at our feet. A moment later, her body disappeared—Leiya too, was spirited away. Only Cobal remained near me, alert, sensing.

My gaze lingered on where my aunt's blood stained the ground. I'd barely known her, yet she'd sacrificed herself for me.

At least we'd tied.

"But we will not accept a draw in the thirty-third Skøl, per decree of the king!"

No, no, no—I had gambled on this. The draw had been upheld in the 14th and 26th Skøls, giving the future king time to consult the gods on the auspicious result. That would have bought me *months* to figure out the king's plan, the Rexi's motivations, to come up with a—

"One of you will leave this arena a victor today," he continued. "And one of you will not leave this arena at all."

So, I would die. Or I would win, and Gia would die at the king's hand for my disobedience. Jana's appearance at the Skøl proved she was not safe wherever Cas had hidden her.

"And that," he finished, "will not be a fate decided by your opposing competitor, but by your own self."

Xinlan and I looked at each other in confusion. I detected movement to my left. First, I saw Cobal sprinting out of the arena, clearly not bound by the magical perimeter. Something else moved. They were hard to see in the dusky light, but small black specs on the ground scurried towards us from the right. I looked left, and more came. And more from behind Xinlan. One second, I was squinting, trying to make out their nature, and the next, the arena was full of thumbnail-sized spiders—small enough that alone, I wouldn't think twice about crushing one with my boot. But together, the effect was terrifying. A second later, they came within reach of our feet. I portaled immediately, my instincts screaming at me to get out of there, but instead of safely landing elsewhere, I collided with the blue-edge perimeter and bounced back into the spider-filled arena.

I hit the ground. And then they were on me—the most unpleasant, hair-raising, terrifying tickle I'd ever experienced. But it soon turned into excruciating pain. They scurried under my leathers, into my nose, and through my hairline. Tiny fanged mouths bit and bit until welts appeared everywhere, approaching the most sensitive parts of my body. I kicked and screamed and jolted, attempting to fling them off me, but they were too small and too many for my fighting to be effective. I spelled, an expulsion cantrip, which shot them off in every direction—even out of my mouth, but that only provided a second of relief, and then more came.

"The first to perish loses, the longest to survive wins. Skøl!"

The Skølmaester's words brushed by me, and I found it hard to process his meaning. I pressed my lips and eyes shut, silencing my screams, not attempting another spell for fear of opening my mouth to them once more. I reached out for my Earth magic, not caring if I earned disqualification—just wanting it to stop. But there was no response, no zinging call back. Perhaps the mini arena had been spelled against the fight they knew I'd put up. And then they filled my nose again. With my mouth shut, I could feel the air slipping from my body as I lay in that meadow.

I just need to outlast Xinlan, I told myself. But in those moments, I couldn't think about tactics, or strategy, or the Skøl. I couldn't think of Gia or Jana. I couldn't even think about Ezren. I only thought of death. I begged it to come.

CHAPTER THIRTY-FIVE

VENOM SMOKE

*J*t could have been minutes or fleeting seconds I lay there. But at some point, the torturous demons scurried away— fleeing in all directions. Like it was *their* turn to be afraid.

I stayed on the ground, not moving. I wasn't sure I could. Everything burned, stung, hurt—but slowly, I started to breathe. *In and out, Terra. In and out.* Spiders no longer plugged my nose, and I peeked one eye open to take stock of the scene. The lid puffed so thick from bites I struggled to open it.

Did I win? If so, why isn't anyone cheering? Why didn't the Skølmaester announce my victory?

Or... am I dead?

Stillness settled all around me. I lifted my hand and sunk it into the ground—sending a jolt of hot pain up my arm. *Not dead, then.*

I fought to push myself up, every nerve ending roaring against me. My skin burned with the heat of a thousand suns. I could sit up enough to look around the meadow, now shrouded in moonlight—the blue perimeter and illusion of jeering fans had vanished. *Where is everyone?* The eerie quiet unnerved me. And only Xinlan remained. If she was breathing, I couldn't tell.

After a moment, my arm buckled, collapsing beneath me. I hit the grass hard. My eyes closed, the exertion overwhelming.

"Terra?" A familiar voice—not from the prone competitor who lay some paces from me, but further away.

I blinked, trying to clear the sting from my eyeballs, but the movement was slow, pained. *That voice... bad... or sad? So familiar.*

I tried to call out, but my voice died in my throat, a product of the bites I'd received, I guessed. *They must have gone pretty far down my esophagus... I almost don't remem—*

"Terra!" the voice called again, closer this time. *That voice, from dreams, nightmares... but who, who, who...*

My mind wandered, muddy and rambling. The only shred of logic left in me ignited the briefest of thoughts. *Could the bites have been poisonous?*

"TERRA!" Louder, closer. "TERRAAAA!"

I fought to open one of my blistering eyes. Someone rushed towards me, then right in front of me...

Him. Murderer. Cas's Lover. Rexi's lapdog.

"Fayzien," I croaked. The word came out so strangled that my ears did not recognize it.

He labored to breathe as he hunched over, placing his hands on his thighs and cursing, regaining his breath. I fought to keep my eye open, attempting to scan the thicket for other disturbances. I saw one cropped red hair contrasting against pale skin. In a moment, Leiya stood next to him, equally winded, but somehow still composed.

I beheld Leiya in disbelief, confusion, and uncertainty. She had just been portaled away—minutes or hours ago. And why was she here, with *him*?

"Lassie, tell us yer injuries," she commanded.

The world swirled in my mind. *Think, think, think*—but nothing came. My head pounded, a steady drumbeat, the thrumming of blood rushing upwards through my temples.

Cool, soft hands cupped my neck. A jolt went through me—they had no hard callouses of a warrior's palms. Fayzien. *Get away, I* hissed in my mind. I could not move. I tried to lift my arm again, but my limb didn't respond.

"Terra, ye must try, try te tell us, what happened?"

I screamed again in my mind, but not at Leiya's question or Fayzien's touch. I screamed because I couldn't move. A word started repeating in my head to the rhythm of the pounding blood that rushed through my veins—my body trying to fight whatever venom the spiders had gifted me.

Paralysis, paralysis, paralysis.

"Terra," Fayzien urged. He almost sounded concerned for me. "You *have* to try and tell us. Were you burned, with fire? Was it blue or orange?"

I did not move. He waited.

"She's breathen," Leiya said clinically. "An not bleedin'. Her skin looks like et was devoured by somethen' rotten, poor lass, but not flame. What could cause thes?"

"She could have been knocked in the spine, rendering her paralyzed," Fayzien said, his voice distant. "But her Fae blood would have healed an injury like that by now, and it doesn't explain the blisters."

I grew more desperate as they debated, pounding my inner walls, searching frantically for some movement. Nothing budged. Not a finger, nor a twitch of an eyelid. It had to be venom.

Would the poison eventually stop my lungs from inhaling air? Could it do that?

Breathe, think, breathe, think, I repeated, trying to slow my heartbeat. Panicking would do nothing to help.

A strangled groan floated from across the meadow. Footsteps sounded in the opposite direction from me. Someone running. More running. And then a thud.

"Xinlan, can ye say that again?" Leiya commanded.

"Deeghsie," her voice rasped. I knew it would dry up in a matter of moments, like mine had.

"Deeghsie? I dinna understand!" Leiya yelled in frustration.

Fayzien swore under his bread. "Dinghisenie beetles," he said.

"They look like spiders. Deadly if not followed by the antidote within a matter of minutes."

"What's en the antidote?" Leiya asked.

"A whole combination of things... spindle flower, up-root, ground truffle bone... and Faerie blood. Either Golbin or some close relation. It would take hours to make."

My heart sank. So this is how I would die. *Where did Ezren lie, unmoving?*

The venom seemed to seep into my heart—slowing everything. No need for panic now. Everything felt slow, slow, slow.

"Move over, you fools!" A third voice rang out of nowhere.

In an instant, my mouth was opened, my chin tilted up, and cool liquid trickled in. I could feel it dribble down the sides of my face, but I could not swallow.

"Plug her nose, warrior," the voice commanded.

"I dinna take orders from a Faerie," Leiya growled. "What are ye given' her?"

"It's an up-root elixir, you imbecile. All that is required to treat Dinghisenie bites," the voice grumbled. "No Faerie blood needed."

If they argued more, I did not hear, because my nose was plugged and I began choking and gurgling, a bodily reaction finally ignited.

"There, there, Daughter," the voice I now recognized as Cobal whispered. "Drink."

The liquid slid down my throat, cold and soothing my burning insides. He held my head, rocking it side to side, swirling his concoction inside my body.

My mind cleared. The panic returned with a vengeance, and my eyes flew open. I kicked immediately, sitting up with a force that made my burns *scream*. But I moved. *I could move.*

Fayzien used the rest of the antidote on Xinlan next to me, and Cobal beamed. "Debt paid," the creature winked. "Though it was not difficult. If these so-called protectors of yours knew anything of the forest, they might actually be useful."

I made to give Cobal a rueful smile, but its words triggered questions that the poison had suppressed.

"Leiya, what are you doing here with *Fayzien?*" I rasped. "Where are Leuffen and Sanah?"

She stood up, extending her hand towards me. As she lifted me to stand, my eyes caught on my forearm, which now lacked the faint shimmering line that had signaled my first victory. "Terra, we need te go, now."

I glanced at Xinlan, still in a heap on the ground, but finally stirring. Her golden tattoo was also gone, and my brows furrowed. Something wasn't adding up—had the Skøl ended? I could have sobbed at the sight of Leiya alive and well, but why come back, and why with *him?* I jabbed my hand through the air in Fayzien's direction, as if to re-ask my question.

Fayzien stood, moving next to Leiya. He only gave me a smirk and said, "We are here to take you to the king, dear Terra."

My heart constricted at the thought, however unlikely, that Leiya would betray me to the king. But before I could say a word, Leiya whipped around and landed her fist square on Fayzien's face, his nose crumpling under a satisfying crack. He bent over and started heaving, blood spurting all around him.

"To the gods, that was an overreaction to a joke," he wheezed.

"'At was fer the North Sea, ye worthless bastard," she replied, venom dripping from her words.

She turned and faced us, sighing. "I dinna come here *weth* Fayzien. I found Fayzien, who was also looken' fer ye. Though I'd rather eat knives than work wi' such felth, I needed hes help."

"Is Leuffen alright? Sanah?" I whispered.

"Aye, both are. They're awaiten' us en Viribrum a' the docks. Though the others... I dinna know how they fared. We lost the shep, ye see."

I stepped back from Leiya and moved towards Fayzien, no plan in my mind, only rage. But Leiya rested her hand on my shoulder, making me pause. Her look said *he's not worth it.*

"We dinna have time fer the whole story," she cut in. "Fayzien's storm was sweft, but she was naye small. I knew we'd be shet out a' luck, so I shefted and flew out en search a' land. When I made et back te the shep, She was gone. I only saw Leuffen and Sanah, clingen' te a piece a' what was left a' the Casmerre.

"An on our way here, we saw Drakkarians. A great many—maken' their way te Valfalla. I tried, *tried* te find Cas, te tell hem or the keng. But when I arrived, some dickhead Skøl maker found me and bound me throat wi' a spell, so I couldna speak. I was portaled ento thes circus, naye able te say a word about the attack. But I'm tellin ye now, we have te leave, *immediately.*"

So that's why the crowd disappeared, and the rings were gone. What happened to the spectators? Another wave of haziness swirled through my mind, my legs trembling. *Damn, that venom is strong.*

"Terra, snap outa' et!" Leiya shook me. "I saw a' least ten thousand Drakkarian Wetch warriors, comen' *here*. Te Viribrum. They'll have made et te the palace already. We canna stay."

At this, Fayzien inhaled sharply, his normally cavalier, debauching attitude replaced with an intense focus. "Ten thousand? Leiya, could you be mistaken? The only way that many warriors would have gotten here is through the Dusked Sea, or through the southern Viribrum border, which we would have known about weeks ago. And the queendom monitors the Dusked Sea diligently, as you know, for Drakkarian ships."

Leiya turned to face him. "Well, I was wonderin' jest that, Nebbiolon lap dog. The *why* es clear enough—the idiot Darlan has been threatenin' a Drakkarian invasion fer months. Even a novice warrior shoulda expected counteraction. An' even a novice warrior knows te use distraction te their advantage. What better distraction than a competition that occurs every fefty te a hundred years and leaves the palace unguarded! Idiots—the lot of 'em. The *how* es more interestin'. Perhaps Nebbiolo wants te return te ets Wetch roots, eh, an has allied weth Drakkar once more?"

"Never in our history have we been 'allied with Drakkar.' As you know, Nebbiolo was founded as a refugee state for persecuted Drakkarians," Fayzien ground out.

"Why," I rasped, interrupting the two of them before they ripped each other to shreds, "would all of Valfalla have abandoned the Skøl? Cas wouldn't have left me... or..." My eyes shifted to Xinlan. "Us."

"As soon as I heard of the impending invasion from Leiya, I portaled to Cas and told him. He asked if I'd personally evacuate you two." Fayzien's upper lip curled in disgust. "Just as well; I'm sure the Rexi would have ordered the same. Cas left to defend the city honorably, alongside the king and any able fighters, while I came to play rescu—" a screech pierced the air.

Cobal hunched over, dry heaving post outburst. I hobbled over and laid my hand atop its leathered back.

"Terra," the Talpa struggled to breathe. "I smell."

"Smell what, friend?" I croaked, protecting the creature's given name.

"I... can't... breathe," Cobal gasped and choked. "It... it is *ash*."

We looked at each other. A single flake of ash drifted in front of my face, illuminated by moonlight.

The smell of smoke filled my nostrils.

CHAPTER THIRTY-SIX

SHADOW FLAMES

I never thought I would be grateful for Fayzien's presence.

Over the past few months, my feelings for him had oscillated between pure hatred, pity, and apathy. But, in that moment, I was thankful for the Water Witch.

The Convallis had become a ring of fire, a storm of ash. A halo of embers rained down around us, lighting up what had been a night sky the moment before. It happened quickly; I comforted Cobal one minute, and the next, smoke stung my eyes and burned my lungs.

I counted heads—two half-breeds, two Fae, and one Talpa. The air grew so thick and suffocating that Leiya couldn't fly through the smoke and ash. And even if Fayzien and I *could* portal everyone out of there, which we couldn't without leaving someone behind, we had no idea what awaited us on the surface.

Fayzien ran away from the group, and for a brief moment, I thought he would leave us there. But he did not. He let out a small cry of victory and yelled at us to follow.

We ran blindly towards him, and his position came into focus by a small pond at the edge of the clearing we'd stood in. My eyes burned, and we began to choke, but seconds later, a bubble of

Fayzien's making shrouded us, the curved edges of it a thick lining of pond water. The smoke dissipated, and we blinked our eyes open, surveying our surroundings.

The scene we opened our eyes to was unlike anything I'd ever seen. The moon had been strong before, but now the fire illuminated the meadow like it was high noon. Burning trees cracked in half and thudded onto the charred Earth. Body parts flung through the air—maybe the Skøl watchers who'd failed to evacuate, their remnants soaring down and splattering on the arena floor. The air was opaque from the fire, and an orange hue coated everything I could see. A rip of pain tore through my chest and I held in a cry at the sensation of life leaving the plants and trees and turning over in the soil.

"I've never seen fire spread so fast," I choked. The smell of smoking flesh, even in Fayzien's bubble, threatened to turn my stomach over.

"Thes esna any fire ye've ever seen, Lassie," Leiya responded, dread and awe churning through her words. "Et's magic, te be sure."

"What do we do?" I wheezed.

"There is nothing we can do," Xinlan whispered. "Not against spelled flames. No one survives them."

Cobal let out a *harumph.* "Unless you're the one who cast the spell."

"And you let 'em walk right ento our kingdom," Leiya growled at Fayzien. "We should send ye to them flames ferst, see how the Water Wetch wilts."

"Oh, that's a brilliant idea. Send away one of two here who can portal. And don't forget, the protective mist around you would dissolve in an instant." He scoffed. "Good fucking luck. You wouldn't last a—"

"We don't have time for this," I croaked, my voice rough from the inhaled smoke. "We need to find a way to stop the flames. Fayzien could portal far from here, farther than I can. He could find safety, double back, and double back again—but I'm not sure we could survive the smoke long enough without his shield. And we don't know how the fire will spread."

Cobal nodded in agreement. "It would ravage the kingdom worse than the soldiers. If it hasn't already."

Silence held us at our throats for a few moments as the implications of my and Cobal's words settled on the group.

We had *no* good options.

"Terra could control it," Fayzien said, his voice so low it almost held regret.

We all looked at him, and I was unsure if I heard him correctly.

He winced and faced me reluctantly. "What is the Earth, if not the product of fire and water and air? The Earth is the intersection of the elements. Air, water, those might be trickier. But fire? Fire cannot burn—cannot spread—if there is nothing to ignite. You have been welling your power now, unintentionally, as you have not called the Earth properly in some time... you'd have to dig deep, but it *could* work. They say the first Earth Daughter could control fire with only a thought."

"Why would you tell us this? In fact, why help at all?" I rasped, uneasy about his willingness to collaborate. "You've only tried to wreak death and destruction on my life and the lives around me. Why not just portal yourself out of here?"

Fayzien's sculpted face contorted into a sneer, his blonde locks falling over blue eyes as he stared me down. "Don't mistake my current actions for some weakening of heart, Princess," he spat. "I'm simply following orders. I was sent here to keep you safe."

I did not have time to wage an internal debate on Fayzien's morality or motivations. "What do you think, Leiya?" I asked, keeping my eyes on Fayzien.

"I don't trust hem as far as I can throw hem. But I dinna see how et's not worth a try. We're setten' ducks en here, weth no way out."

I contemplated for a moment. "Okay. I'll try. Do you have an idea of how?" I asked Fayzien.

He pursed his lips. "I do not. But I *do* know how my element feels. Like it is my domain, stronger than how I command my own limbs. As if I have power over... its experience. The Earth is yours— it's your choice if the brush around us burns or not."

I looked at the group, and they gave me terse nods back. The Talpa whimpered from behind me, but there was no other protest. So I walked through the wall of moisture and into the inferno.

My bitten and already-blistered skin singed at the temperature in the air. I clamped down on my bottom lip to keep from screaming at the pain.

I had to work fast.

I ran a few paces back to the clearing, to keep some distance from the bubble, and fell to my knees. I balled my fists in the dirt, feeling the call back to me. The Earth responded in an instant, and inside me spread an immense gratitude that whatever spell had prevented me from summoning the element in the final Skøl challenge had dissipated. Cool Earth pooled to the top, snaking up my body, clothing me in a relieving layer of mud. The sting on my skin from flames and bites soothed. My lips—blistered and cracked—reformed. My hair and smoking brows smoothed. I knew I would only stay protected if my Earth armor remained—and that was not permanent. The heat threatened to dry out my cool shroud in moments.

The flames burned so unnaturally, as if under direction. Leiya was right—they must have been spelled. I reached out to the fire, my hands extended, searching for a familiar vibration. It didn't have the same tingle that came to me from the ground. So, I latched onto the call of the Earth, to the feeling of it being scorched, wilting under an unnatural heat. But instead of continuing to draw the life towards me, I sent my magic towards it—deeper, probing for the root of the fire spell. After a moment, a sharp zinging sensation hit me, an unfamiliar frequency. It was foreign, yes, but it also felt *wrong*. I pushed my magic harder, a dominating force, attempting to crush that seed of power, the strange spell from which the fire breathed.

If the spell was a stone wall, my magic was a battering ram. I stumbled back upon contact as if I'd collided with it physically. But I held my ground, digging my feet deeper into the mud, and closed my eyes. *The Earth is my domain. Nothing burns here, lest I allow it.* I sent my magic out once more, in a thousand tendrils, rather than the battering ram I'd tried the first time. They snaked around the spell's lifeblood until a web of me covered it. And then I squeezed, visualizing my magic as the living, breathing thing it was.

My threads of power tightened and tightened, though the spell resisted, almost squirming beneath my grip. I gritted my teeth, pushing harder until I felt a single crack.

My magic jumped, and my beautiful, strong threads of power surged through that crack.

The spell shattered.

Air whooshed through me—my power filling the sudden gap, a space of nothing where that writhing spell had been. I dropped my arms, panting from exertion, blinking the sweat from my eyes. I had subdued the fire, which lingered even though I'd destroyed the spell feeding it. By the way the burning swayed, by the way the tips of the fire licked, I suspected I would not be harmed.

I walked amongst the flames, testing my theory. They burned, but curled around me in deference, and I detected a strange residual magic... it wasn't a spell—no, I'd broken that. The flames were no longer under another's control, they burned without direction. But an unfamiliar power lingered in that fire—a sorrowful, tortured magic made of pain. I sensed cries of suffering amongst them.

My eyes still stung from the smoke and I looked back at the bubble. Fayzien did what he could from his cocoon, sending the rest of the pond water around them to form a moat. He spelled too, but his water magic could not match the fire that still raged. I did not have such constraints.

I extended my arms outward, flowing my power gently at first, little vibrations leaving my fingertips, exploring the curves of the flames. The fire itself resisted, fighting my control, as if it wished to return to the twisted magic that had created it. But I let my magic continue on its path, coercing the masterless power to follow. Without realizing, it was no longer a gentle vibration that left my palms. I felt every bend and snake of the fire, and I knew I could make it mine.

And then a voice entered my mind, female and unwavering.

Fire cannot be controlled, little one, only starved. Adding magic to a spelled flame is like treating an oil fire with water. You must starve it of its air. Seek to make it yours, and you will lose control—you will only set fire to flame. Deprive it of magic and set it free.

I whipped around, attempting to identify where the voice came from. But I saw nothing amongst the golden surroundings, no movement, nor did I hear a sound. If I was being tricked, I didn't know, but my gut told me to trust the words.

I raised my arms once more and my power flowed out. But instead of forcing control on the flame, I sought out the magic there, the power that lingered aimlessly in the burn. I pulled on it with swift force, sucking the life from the fire.

And then it came to me. And I saw what had made the fire feel so *wrong.* The embers of the fire's magic were shadows of the dead, and their suffering the fuel. I cried out, a guttural noise, for I was absorbing their pain. The fire waned, so I forged on, the bearer of the shadows' grief. My arms ached as the magic fire galloped toward me in blazing rings of agony. I stood, a beacon to the flames. My flesh remained intact, but I scorched within, an inferno of pain shredding me from the inside out.

I screamed once more, a scream with no sound. I could not stop the tidal wave of residual magic pouring into me, a steady stream that continued to run after the flames wilted. I collapsed, hearing voices, seeing images. Swirling tattoos and shaved heads and contortions of grief on their faces. An infinite weight pressed on my chest, and my vision went blurry.

The flames reduced to embers one ring at a time, rippling away from me at the center. I choked on nothing as I lay there, my hair spread out from me, decorated with white specs of fresh ash. The world grew blurry and the ground shifted at the gentle vibration of footsteps approaching me. What could anyone do to stop the magic I'd willingly absorbed? The strange power was devouring me from the inside out, and I had welcomed it—to starve the fire of its breath.

But when I looked up, it was not someone I recognized. I guessed she was a Fae female by the point of her ears, but she was faceless; only wisps of hair and body shape. She placed her hands on the dirt next to me, whispering unintelligible incantations to it. A moment later, I slowly sank as if in quicksand.

I submitted to the mud coating me, filling each orifice one by one. My ears, my nostrils, my mouth. I should have thrashed at the slow reminder of the spiders I'd faced less than an hour before, but I did not, for the Earth was my lifeblood, my haven. Soon, I was choking on the silky liquid, sputtering on my hands and knees in the clearing I had saved.

I blinked my eyes open, attempting to wipe some of the mud away. The others ran towards me, shocked faces watching me reappear painted in mud from eyelash to toenail. And the flames flickered in a swirling pattern that began with me in the center and extended out. Doing no harm. But my eyes didn't focus on the Fae that neared me, nor the curious shape in which the fire smoldered. They set on the dark hooded figures that emerged from the shadows of the surrounding wood, descending on the smoldering clearing, scims gleaming in the moonlight.

As if we trained together, the four of us turned our backs inwards to touch, Cobal at the center, peering out from between our legs.

Leiya, Xinlan, and I drew our blades, battle stances ready.

Fayzien whispered under his breath, no doubt preparing to form a lethal and complex spell.

"Terra, ye need te spell, now," Leiya said.

I couldn't move.

"She has never taken life from a living being, warrior," Cobal said. "At least not willingly. It will not be easy for her."

The image of Xinlan's blade sinking into Jana's chest flickered in my mind at Cobal's comment. I said nothing, squeezing my eyes shut, trying to block out that thought and the pictures of suffering I saw in the fire. I swallowed my nausea.

"Drakkarians!" Fayzien bellowed with a voice that was older, more robust and commanding than his typical sneering tone. "You have been told you fight for freedom, for a justice you and your people deserve. But you have been *lied* to! The magic you have is being wasted on frivolous pursuits. You feel the wells of your power run dry. Those that command you will see you starve. Stand down. Do not attack. Defy the regime and dismantle your true oppressor!"

The cloaked soldiers would have been invisible in the darkness if it weren't for the strong moon and flickers of a fire that had raged minutes before. Many halted their approach, startled by his commanding address, and exchanged glances. A few did not, but Fayzien's move found success.

He unleashed a spell. Magic burst out from Fayzien's fingertips and swept towards our attackers. About a third of the hooded beings paused in their footsteps and dropped their weapons. Their hands clutched their throats, gurgling in pain, choking on an unseen liquid. Still, dozens charged on, Fayzien sagging with exhaustion. "I'm tapped," he breathed. "At least for the next few minutes."

"Terra, ef ye dinna spell, now, we *well* die," Leiya barked out, eyeing Fayzien as he panted. "Me fighten es damn good, but fifteen te one odds are a wee bet much, even fer me."

I labored to breathe; a wall of gleaming steel barreled towards us. *Think, think, think.*

"You are an *Earth* Daughter," Xinlan's words sliced through the midnight air. "If you cannot survive, what hope do the rest of us have?"

"Think of your warrior," Cobal added softly.

Something inside me broke, and the cool separation of instinct washed over me. I walked out of the circle, letting my sword drag in the dirt while I twirled Ezren's knife in the other hand. The contact of my sword with the Earth sent a tingle through my body and left goosebumps on my still mud-shrouded skin.

One man parted from his group, matching my pace, signaling the running warriors to pause. They obeyed. "Daughter of the Earth! We have come for you," he called out, his hood still shading his face. "Your existence represents a grave wrong and has disrupted the balance. Come willingly and we will not hurt your friends or your loved ones. Fight us, and you will regret it."

I tuned out the confusion his words caused. "This is not your land," I called back. "Leave this place, and leave it unharmed, or *you* will be the one to regret it."

The only thing I could see from beneath his hood was a toothy smile. He raised his fist. Then he opened his fingers, and the warriors behind him rushed on.

I waited, unmoving, as they charged toward us. The Talpa cried out behind me, and Leiya shouted at me to spell. But I let them draw nearer and nearer, allowing my anger to build. I was sick of being threatened, manipulated, lied to, subjugated.

When close to fifty of them neared, I raised Ezren's knife, letting the Dragon egg gleam in the moonlight. The image of the blade raising itself in defense against Tey flashed in my mind. The Dragon egg had responded to me with pulses of power a few times before. Instinct took over, and I whispered a quick prayer to the gods before plunging the dagger into the Earth, sinking to one knee, and sending my magic through it. The Dragon egg illuminated, glowing even more brightly than it had ever before, and the ground broke in front of me. Dirt erupted in a wave, undulating towards the running warriors. It was too fast for them to react. They were either flung into the air or crushed in the undertow of Earth that ran their way.

The remaining soldiers, furious at the immediate loss of nearly two-thirds of their men, charged on, the toothy-smiled man at the front. He smiled no longer. He portaled and landed in front of me, just as I drew my knife from the Earth. The others had run to join me, and they protected my flanks as I locked my broadsword with the Witch leader.

His hood was back now, revealing thick eyebrows over dark eyes set in deeply tanned skin. I let myself get lost in the coldness of the combat that ensued. He was a good fighter, not as quick as Tey, but fast for a male, with strength to pack behind it. When I had fought last, against Tey, I had been spelling simultaneously. Not to mention I'd been fighting my nature, denying the call of the Earth. But now, I'd just unleashed a wave of magic, and it reverberated off me like an aura, powering each turn and blow I made.

To my left, Leiya cut through Drakkarians like they were butter to her spreading knife. Blood pooled in my opponent's eyes, and I sent a feather of my magic down the dagger. Enough to slice through his metal, like I had broken Fayzien's whip in the Nameless Valley. My broadsword slashed across his chest, and he stumbled. I sent the heel of my foot straight into his abdomen, and he fell back. And then I was atop him, raising my knife, the Dragon egg still glowing at its hilt. The Witch's eyes jumped between fear and wonder, and I faltered for a moment.

Cobal shrieked my name. My head snapped left to where the creature stood, unharmed, but pointing to the trees. And by the time I understood his warning, the arrow had pierced my skin, sinking into the base of my neck.

CHAPTER THIRTY-SEVEN

BOUND FATE

I gagged, choking on the blood that gathered in my airway. I fell to the right, my hand clutching my throat. The Witch beneath me yelled out in protest, a resounding "No!" I did not have the mental strength or clarity to process. He moved quickly, dragging me to my feet, making to portal me away. But as he did, the Talpa appeared at my side, standing proud at almost half the Drakkarian's height. Which worked just as well, for the Talpa sent a little fist right into the crotch of my would-be captor.

The Drakkarian released me at the last second, grunting with fury and portaling away. My legs buckled, but Leiya was at my side, draping my free arm around her neck.

My eyes sagged, and I felt life slipping from my body. I noted the soldiers' numbers had dwindled—only a few scurried away in retreat, departing along with their commander. Fayzien must have recovered enough strength to send a final blast of power.

"Leiya," I croaked, blood mixing with mud on my skin.

Leiya sat me down, resting my back on her legs, keeping me upright with a hand on my shoulder. "Fayzien, can ye heal her?"

He shook his head and I let my eyes close. But then Cobal spoke.

"Where is her blood mate?" the creature asked. "Her Salanti?"

Leiya shook her head. "Naye, she doesna have one. She hasna done a blood sharin'."

"No, but she is bound to him," Cobal replied, and their words floated around me, drifting more and more like I did.

"What?" Leiya hissed. "Te whom?"

"The warrior called Ezren," Cobal answered on my behalf. "He is also likely weak right now, for he feels the effects of her wound, though he may not bleed as she does. Their life forces can be shared, given they are bound. It may be enough to heal her. Is he near?"

Leiya shook her head, but Ezren's name sparked something inside me. Perhaps he was already on his way, having felt the pain I endured. But a small truth cracked inside me. He was a proud male, and I'd told him to stay away under all circumstances.

"Break my left small toe," I whispered, blood gurgling. *Now. Now that I've asked, he will come.*

Leiya and Cobal looked at me as if I had several heads, but Xinlan must have understood that I was serious and did not hesitate. She removed my boot and slammed the hilt of her blade into my left small toe without hesitation, and a soft cracking noise rang out.

I STARTED to slip from consciousness, despite Cobal's best efforts to keep me awake. Time passed in a swirl of eternity and split seconds.

"Thes es *mad*," Leiya hissed. "What ef the lad hemself es hurt? We have te get her te a healer," Leiya said, her voice more stressed than usual.

"He will be here," Cobal said.

A deep flutter filled the sky, and a large creature came into focus. Ezren soared down to us in Dragon form, his glimmering scaled body decorated with blood and ash.

My eyes wouldn't stay open anymore. I had only my ears. The ground crunched and yielded under his claws. He roared, the sound of something not quite Dragon, but also not quite Fae, likely a symptom of the Dragon blood that still ran through his veins as he changed.

"He esn't himself, after he shefts," Leiya groaned. "He's got a devel en hem."

"Bring him to her," Cobal commanded. "Her scent will calm him."

Leiya still held me tight to her legs, but then there was shuffling, and the clash of steel on steel. I heard a loud crack, a low series of grunts, and then the sound of a body being dragged in the dirt.

"Wait until hes eyes change," Leiya commanded.

Minutes or moments later, Ezren whispered, his breath close enough to tickle my face. "Terra?" He struggled to speak himself, and I knew the sensation of blood flooded his airway.

"Warrior," Cobal said. "Do you know how to use your binding to share your life source? It is similar to how you sent more of your life source to me when she freed me during the Skøl."

"I think so," Ezren rasped weakly from somewhere near me. "I remember the sensation. But how does it start?"

"Through blood sharing," Cobal replied carefully. "As you likely know, Fae's blood sharing with Talpa presents no risk of forming the Matching bond, given that Fae and Talpa could never be Salanti. But it will be different between the two of you. If you are indeed Salanti, she will forfeit her choice to Match."

"No," Ezren growled. "If there is any other way, Talpa, say it now."

"Hmm, show me your mark," the Talpa commanded. The words continued to float around me. "Interesting. There may be a way to share life without mixing blood. You will lose much strength. And we must try it fast, and if it doesn't work, be ready for the blood sharing."

Ezren grunted approval. "Where is her mark?" Cobal asked.

I fought to speak, to open my eyes, or to raise my hand. I could not. I only pictured the Dragon scale on my hipbone. A moment later, his rough hands slid gently down the side of my pants, running over my mark. Then he took his knife and sliced the pants from the top down, exposing my hipbone and the mark it bore.

I was slipping fast. I heard nothing else they said until Cobal directed Ezren to place the inside of his wrist on my scale. He then flowed not only his power and magic, but life source, into me. And it felt good, almost too good, like a drug numbing my pain. The arrow ripped free from my throat and Ezren's free hand pressed into my neck, stemming the flow of blood.

The tether between us existed no longer just in theory. It was not the whispering pull I felt to him when we journeyed east nor the conceptual bond I was aware we had after the binding. It was a ripcord, from me to him, a braided chain of metal, of ice, of fire, of all substances, of none. My heart was bursting as his life source flowed into me—liquid iron penetrating my veins. Ecstasy, pain, and everything in between flooded all corners of my body.

And then, quiet.

My eyes fluttered open. He kneeled, bent close, his wrist still pressed to my bare hipbone.

"Can you speak?" he whispered, his voice breathy but recovering from the strained contortion it had been earlier.

"Ezren," I rasped. The words came out and my hand flew to my arrow wound, which had closed now, only dried blood mixed with mud remaining where the shot had been.

"I'm covered in mud, aren't I?" I asked.

"Aren't you always?" he quipped back, and I choked on the tears bubbling up from shock.

That small noise broke him, and he pulled me into his chest, squeezing just slightly more than a typical embrace. "To the gods, Terra, I thought you were going to die," he breathed into me, trembling. With relief or exhaustion, or both, I could not tell.

"We," I corrected, pulling back from him to look at his face. "We were going to die."

His eyes—still rimmed with a panic that made a small part of my heart crumple—searched mine. "I can't lose anyone else, Terra. I can't."

"Ehem," Cobal said, clearing its throat, transporting us back to the smoking reality in which we sat.

I looked around, and so did Ezren, his body tightening when Fayzien's face came into focus. His muscles flexed, and I put my hand on his biceps, shaking my head. He raised his brows a fraction, but relaxed.

"We need to move." My attention floated to Leyia, squinting at the sky.

"Ten thousand Drakkarians must have taken Viribrum," Ezren said, his quiet words laced with fury.

"Aye," Leiya nodded. "'At was me count when I saw the bastards up north."

"They reached Valfalla during the Skøl, hitting the palace first, as it was relatively unguarded," Ezren continued, shaking his head. "In hindsight, this is no surprise. Of course, Drakkar would attack when the entire capital was distracted, with only a handful of palace guards on duty. From what I saw, a subset of the remaining ranks proceeded to the Skøl while the others pillaged the nearby country towns."

Leiya gave a slow, grim nod. "Aye, I had the same thought. I would say, we shoulda seen et comin', but the strange theng es, we would've. How can ye mess an army that size?"

"So the question is... how did they pull it off?" Fayzien muttered.

"No army has ever snuck up on Viribrum—ever—in the history of our kingdom," Xinlan whispered. "We are surrounded by sea. We have so many posts, so many redundancies, each with fliers to announce enemies." She went silent for a moment. "There is only one explanation."

My eyes snapped to hers. "They were invisible," I breathed.

"Ten thousand soldiers? Cloaked? Ha!" Fayzien snorted. "Even *I* couldn't manufacture such a spell."

"There es strange magic afoot... I can feel et. Somethen about the way the fire spread—et was spelled, te be sure, but somethin' felt... wrong," Leiya murmured, almost to herself.

Images of pain and anguish flashed through my mind. "I saw something in the fire." I pressed my eyes shut, remembering the screams and the suffering I'd absorbed. The memory was so fresh and alive in me that I had to shake my head to loosen its grasp.

Ezren's words interrupted the flashback. "What did you see, Terra?"

"Shadows," I whispered. "Shadows of the dead." I shook my head again, trying to shed the lingering tremor of agony I'd experienced from those people. "I felt their pain. What does that mean?"

Five blank stares met my gaze.

Leiya scanned the group to confirm everyone was as confused as she. "I have no idea, Lassie, but we'll figure et out, together."

"So, what do we do now?" My eyes drifted in Ezren's direction.

"We get you to safety," Ezren and Leiya said at the same time. They cocked their heads at each other, looking pleased to be on the same page, before turning back to me.

My nostrils flared, silent rage crossing my face. "Are the two of you serious?" I whispered, more shocked than angry.

"Aye," Leiya said. "Ye have significance fer stopping thes war, and ye know et. I have dreamt about et each night sence returnin' from the isles. I can feel et en me bones. And the Drakkarian said as much when they were tryin' te take ye! We canna lose ye."

"Agreed. The Rexi will have my head if you lose yours," Fayzien chimed in, though picking his nails in disinterest. "I'll go find the queen. You leave with them, find safety. If you flee to Nebbiolo, there will be a place for you."

"We have a Dragon." Xinlan narrowed her gaze at Ezren. "Why not *use* said Dragon?"

"He es not en control a' hes sheft—not fully. Hes awareness en the shape es lacken' an' he canna remain en the form fer long. Unless a trained Wetch es spellen' hem, he willna be a' weapon," Leiya said.

Ezren's eyes sharpened at the comment, but he gave a tight nod.

"And I am drained—from Terra's wound and healing. I'll need at least a day to recover my magic, let alone my shift."

"I am *not* going to abandon Viribrum," I said, my voice low. "I am *not* going to run while innocents perish at the hands of invaders."

"Viribrum is *lost,* Terra," Ezren emphasized. "Ten thousand soldiers caught us unaware—there is no way the palace guard of merely five hundred could have defended against them."

"We have to see if there are survivors," I growled. Names ran through my head. Olea. Cas would have gone back to defend the city. And where was Gia? The thought sent a pang through my chest, drawing Jana's image to mind. If Jana hadn't been safe from the king, I had to imagine he'd found Gia, too.

"I agree with Terra." Everyone's head turned to Xinlan, but she avoided my eye. "We cannot leave our people."

"*Your* people," Fayzien corrected.

"Let me be clear. I'm not leaving. Not without looking for survivors first." I held Ezren's stare, infusing myself with every ounce of confidence I had remaining, shoving down the grief and fear.

Leiya finally spoke again. "Okay then, Princess," she said, crossing her arms, a look of smirking challenge painted across her face. "What's yer plan?"

CHAPTER THIRTY-EIGHT

NOT ENOUGH

*T*here was blood everywhere. Streets, shop doors, storefront windows. Blood lined the cobblestones as it dripped through the grates, like a murderous micro-canal network. Like a wave of terror and punishment had doused the city by the hand of an angry god. I wondered if we *had* angered the gods.

It took until noon the following day to climb our way out of the arena. There was a reason the competitors entered via free fall—it was faster. *Much* faster. The spiral path that lined the Convallis stretched out in a never-ending ascent. Even with Leiya scouting in her falcon form, guiding us bit by bit to ensure we didn't run into any surprise threats, I was drained. Emotionally, physically, and even magically. I'd spent a fair bit of my power on not only erupting the Earth but keeping myself from teetering over the brink of death after a near-fatal shot to the neck. So, my portal was weak and limited to a very short distance. We portaled in bursts, Fayzien doubling back for Cobal since we could only portal one passenger at a time. After my portal sputtered so violently Fayzien thought I would get lost in the in-between, we decided to walk the rest of the way.

Ezren had accepted my plan, though he made a valiant effort to

376

protest at first. Severely weakened after sharing his lifeblood, he'd agreed to go with Cobal to the docks to find Sanah, Dane, and Leuffen, and attempt to secure passage from Viribrum should the city be lost indeed. Leiya and I would sneak into the palace, seeking survivors. I could only pray Gia hid among them.

If anything went wrong, Leiya could fly out undetected for help. Ezren grumbled at the logic, and my heart seized at the idea of letting the warrior go so soon after seeing him again, but he consented in the end.

Xinlan and Fayzien stayed quiet. I wouldn't have been surprised if they formulated their own plans, independent of ours. We were allies of convenience rather than allegiance. But one thing became clear—the Manibu would not be able to leave without searching for his queen.

Before we parted ways, the six of us camped in the forest. The sounds of the wood became so reduced it was as if the animals and faeries knew what tore through their kingdom and had gone into hiding. We had only the eerie silence to comfort us, and the far-off smell of smoke. If it came from the Convallis alone, I couldn't tell.

We'd regroup at sundown, by a city cargo entrance Leiya knew about. Should there be a way to take back the city, to save its inhabitants, we'd formulate a plan then. If not... well, we'd get to that.

Valfalla was quiet, too, not unlike the wood. Where I had expected to hear screaming, only the whisper of death lingered in the air. The fighting must have been swift and brutal for the city to have fallen in less than two days. Bodies—whole and very much not—lined the paths. I hadn't known what to expect, but it was horrific. And even more strangely, there were no Drakkarian soldiers in sight.

"Where are they?" I whispered to myself.

A woman curled up in a ball raised her head from her forearms. I hadn't even seen her—she was partially hidden by the shadows of the alleyway and covered in filth. "In the palace, m'lady," she said back, her voice weakened, but not empty. "I heard their orders—to take their prizes only from the palace."

My stomach curled. *Prizes.* I knew what that meant in the context of war. I pressed my nails into the heels of my palms, willing my eyes to stay dry, willing the contents of my stomach to stay put.

I knelt down next to the huddled figure. "Did you hear anything else?" I asked her gently. "Orders for soldiers to be stationed certain places or to look for... specific targets?"

Her tired eyes met mine. "Yes, m'lady. I mean, I didn't hear no stationing orders. But there was one in charge. He said that if the Princess of Nebbiolo was found, she was to be brought to the main hall alive. But everyone else was to take the blade. I think—" she choked a sob back. "I think the king may be..." She dipped her head. A moment later, she looked up towards the palace gates. I squinted, and eventually my eyes focused on something I hoped wasn't truly there. I swore under my breath. If I had to guess, we were looking at a severed head on a spike.

I swallowed. "You have to leave this place, do you understand? Run as far west as you can bear. There should be other Fae, Faeries even, hiding deep within the forest."

She nodded.

I stood, making to turn but cast a glance backwards. "What is your name?"

"Gemilane, m'lady," she responded. She blinked at me, some fire returning to what had been a gaze of fragility a moment before.

"Be strong, Gemilane. We all need to be. For the sake of Viribrum."

My plan wasn't terribly original. It hinged on my guess that at least *some* of the Drakkarian soldiers would have fallen in the invasion. We'd need only to find two of our size, with relatively intact uniforms.

For that reason, we agreed I would not attempt to portal directly into the palace—nor did Leiya shift and fly in her falcon form. We darted back and forth between alleyways, hiding behind pillars, searching for the right disguises. We had seen some wisps of black capes on the outer balcony of the palace—Drakkarian soldiers patrolling the entrance below them. Hidden from view, we couldn't count their exact number, but at least a hundred guarded the perimeter.

We continued to move in stealth, checking around corners for fallen Drakkarians—but had no luck. It seemed the Witch soldiers were precise about cleaning up their dead. I almost suggested pivoting plans when we came across an abandoned building near the palace gates. "En here," Leiya motioned downwards to a cellar opening, shaded from any watchtower view by a faded purple awning.

The Fae warrior heaved up the solid wood door and we slid through the opening, easing it shut with a near silent click. I chewed the inside of my cheek, remembering when I'd last been in a storage cellar below ground. That passage led me to find my mother at the hands of her murderer. I didn't want to imagine what I'd find at the end of the passage this time.

We came upon a stone wall and Leiya pushed a brick in. The wall opened up in front of her, revealing a dark labyrinth ahead. The light peeking in from the cellar wouldn't go far. She grabbed a dead torch from the wall and extended it towards me.

I took it from her, assuming she wanted me to carry it.

"Why're ye staren 'a me, like ye've been thumped en the head, too many a' time?" she hissed.

"What do you want me to do with this?" I asked.

"Light et, ye fool! We dinna have time—aren't ye a Fire Wetch now?"

I looked at the torch, unsure of how to proceed. I could feel no existing flame, no magic already called. I didn't know how to summon fire that didn't exist. When I called the Earth, I could already feel its presence.

Leiya let out an exasperated sigh and went back into the cellar, returning with two flints before I could think to follow her. She struck them over the torch, grumbling, and then the oil caught.

We moved through the tunnels at a pace that had me jogging to keep up. "I hate to point out the obvious here, but we still haven't found any uniforms to borrow from... disposed Drakkarians," I whisper-shouted.

"Ye thenk? We're jest gonna have te take them from the, er, less willing," she shot back.

"Maybe we should just portal," I grumbled—the idea of facing another Drakkarian in combat didn't fall high on my list. "I'm recovered enough—I shouldn't be at risk of the in-between, not at this distance. We can stay out of sight."

"Ye don't know what'll be waiten' en the other side of a portal, ye daft fool. I know these routes akin te the back a' me hand. Yer plan es good. We'll go tru the servants' quarters, an' listen te the other side. Where do ye thenk she'll be?"

She meant Olea, no doubt understanding the innocent maid would be my priority. While Cas would have returned to defend his home, he couldn't be my focus. *He was likely either already captured, or dead,* Leiya had said, when we debated the strategy of searching for survivors. Fayzien shuddered at the comment—I had the feeling his motivations for joining us in the return to Viribrum extended beyond just finding the queen. He'd opted to go in alone, given he was skilled enough to portal right into a broom closet, and seemed to be used to working solo. I bit the inside of my cheek harder, willing the distraction away.

"Servants' quarters, most likely. Unless... she went back to my chamber. I told her if anything went wrong, to take the ring I left under my floorboards. I meant for her to take it in case I didn't return, so she could care for herself... but, I suppose she could have thought I meant to guard it during an attack." My lips formed a silent curse. "I don't know if she would have fled right away or not."

"How loyal was she te ye?" Leiya asked, her voice still quiet.

"Very, I think." The words caught in my throat.

"Then she probably went back fer what ye promised her."

I nodded, more to myself than Leiya. "I stayed in the crown's wing, the east."

Leiya's head of fire-red hair reflected the torchlight. "Alright, Lassie. Keep yer knives raised and yer ears open."

As soon as the passage neared the castle, we could hear them— shouting, reveling, looting. The merriment of soldiers carried through the palace's grates into our subterranean route. There must have been thousands roaming the halls, searching for their rewards.

Leiya's Fae ears pressed into the stone wall, one I knew would move on a hinge with the right pressure into a hidden brick. I'd seen passages like this before, had used them myself when I visited...

Jana. My vision blurred, and my throat tightened. I'd barely known the woman, and yet... it was my fault she—

A shriek from the other side of the wall shook me from my spiral. It was female.

"Foul Drakkarian felth," Leiya muttered. "Thes—oh thes well be fun."

She pushed through the secret opening, and the door swung as if on an axle. Her hearing must have been incredible, for the timing was exact, and the door collided with a Drakkarian. But she continued pushing with a warrior's strength and unnatural speed. Before he could make a sound of surprise, the stone door crushed him, connecting with the adjoining wall and obliterating his skull.

I could see little of it other than the spray of blood and brain that escaped from the space between the two. I blinked, and then my head snapped toward another noise. A servant girl—her hair and blouse disheveled but otherwise unharmed stood in the middle of the dressing room. Leiya must have gotten us to the East Wing, but we weren't in my chambers.

"Know any cleanin' spells, lassie?" Leiya gestured towards the mess before dragging the body behind a dressing screen.

I swallowed the bile creeping up my throat. "Emundare." The gore on the stone wall and wooden floor evaporated.

"Can ye mind thes door?" Leiya asked the girl. "From the other side? Only open ef ye hear three quick knocks en a row. Ef we find others, we'll send 'em here. The passage leads outside a' the palace."

The girl sniffled, still gaping at us, but said nothing as she nodded furiously.

"Give us a few hours te direct others yer way. If we don't return by then—make a run fer et. Et'll be dark; shouldna be too much trouble to get outta the city unnoticed."

I gave her a smile of encouragement and she hid behind the secret door, Leiya pushing it back into place. I went to the dead Drakkarian and removed his cloak, averting my eyes from his smashed face. Blood stained the cloak, but mercifully, most had painted the wall rather than the fabric.

Leiya took it, fastening the dark cloak around her neck in one fluid motion. "Stay here," she growled.

I made to protest, but again, she'd already gone. Though my pulse hammered my throat, I froze, as still as a statue, waiting with a knife, ready. I didn't have to stand at attention long—less than two minutes later she crept into the room, another Drakkarian cloak in hand.

"Now, though every bone en me body es screamen fer a fight w' these fuckers, let's try te stay unnoticed, hey?"

WE WOVE THROUGH THE HALLWAYS, keeping our heads down and our pace measured. Occasionally, we lifted our eyes to check for survivors, but we encountered only a few warriors in this part of the palace—and they were either too drunk or high on celebration and spoils to notice us.

I prayed Olea would be there, hidden in my quarters, unharmed. *She will be. The gods cannot be this cruel.*

Minutes later, I pushed through the wooden doors of my chamber, Leiya flanking me.

The room looked exactly as I'd left it when I walked out in my Skøl uniform just days before. My bed was made, undisturbed, the curtains drawn, late afternoon light streaming in.

But something felt off. I couldn't place it. "Olea?" I called softly.

No answer.

"Something isn't right," I murmured.

I rounded the bed, continuing to survey the room. And as I did, my boot caught on a heavy obstacle.

A fat Drakkarian soldier lay face down on the ground, his body no longer obscured by the massive four poster. His trousers were down around his ankles and his breathing labored. To my eternal horror, beneath him lay Olea, lifeless eyes trained on the ceiling, a ring of black and blue bruises circling her neck, and a dribble of dark blood seeping from her mouth.

The world went silent.

And then it was very, very loud.

"You foul BASTARD!" I screamed at the top of my lungs, my head buzzing with a rage that made any logical thought inaccessible. I flipped the warrior off Olea, bunching his cloak in one hand, and struck his ugly tattooed face before his dazed eyes could even widen in surprise.

Crack went his nose. Blood trickled. *Not enough.*

Crack again. This time he screamed for help, and struggled to get free. More blood oozed.

Not enough.

Crack again. "*Terra,*" Leiya urged, and my gaze dragged to her. I'd forgotten she was there. I'd forgotten where I was, really. I only knew that in my hands I held the enemy, and perhaps pure evil itself.

I then saw why Leiya tried to get my attention. One by one, Drakkarian soldiers rushed into the room, until nearly ten of them filled it. They beheld the sight for a moment as if weighing whether the old soldier merited saving.

Bile rose in my throat, and I dropped my grip on him. Leiya's hand twitched towards her blade, but she did not dare move.

"Princess?" one of them spoke, his dark eyes gleaming, his tongue rolling over his lips. He made a step towards us, but I didn't care. I only looked back at my friend and imagined how cruel her last minutes were. I trembled violently. Time froze around me. I let out another cry, a wail that shook the Earth holding together the walls of the palace. The warrior paused and looked at me, genuinely confused.

"Why *her*?" I cried. "Why?" I pleaded with the gods. Why, *why* did their cruelty have no end? First, my mother, my father, my brothers. Then Jana. Then Olea. Death seemed to follow me wherever I went, having no mercy on the innocent souls who couldn't defend themselves against the havoc that trailed my path. The Drakkarian in the arena said it himself—they came for me.

Would Gia be next? Was she already gone?

My fault. My fault. My fault.

He made another step towards us, and said, "A serving maid? Why do you care? She is nothing."

I was a volcano, bubbling with a veritable magma flow of emotion that would wreak havoc on anyone or anything in its path.

CHAPTER THIRTY-NINE

INNER WORLD

I don't remember what came after. I must have lost consciousness. I woke up to hands pulling me out of my chamber, which crumbled with splintered wood and strewn stone, the walls no longer standing. Blood splattered what remained, bodies of Witch Warriors piled atop each other, shards of wood jutting out of them. Leiya was nowhere to be seen. And Olea... her body was left behind.

Two Drakkarians gripped my biceps so hard I thought they might pop. They dragged me away—away from the scene of death and destruction I'd created. Some hard metal—silver, most likely—coated their stiff leather, and I wanted to wretch away from it. I could feel their magic suppressing mine, like a damp rag on my soul.

I gritted my teeth through the gag they'd placed over my mouth. *Olea is dead.* I pressed my eyes shut, feeling the heat build behind them, wishing I could wake from this unending nightmare. *Jana, too.* At least she'd lived a full life. She'd made a choice—a sacrifice. But Olea... she was an innocent, caught in a king's war. And perhaps, if I hadn't given her a reason to return to my chamber, she would have made it out alive.

"I think we should take a detour, Gal," the one on my left said gruffly. "Show this princess a true Drakkarian welcome." He chuckled. "Besides, war is war. We *are* entitled to our spoils."

My insides turned cold as the Witch who'd spoken stopped and pulled me closer to him—he stank of mold and sweat. The Witch rested the tip of his nose on my head, and drew a long inhale. "For Nebbiolon trash, she smells quite appealing." I looked up at a wide grin, revealing a smattering of rotten teeth. Hate coursed through me and I steadied myself to fight, to break free of their unnaturally powerful grips. But I was frozen and my reaction time delayed. I could only see Olea's limp body, ravaged, her face blank.

"No." The single word came from the other soldier, but it rang through me like a call. It held so much familiarity, a feeling I could not place. The long hood of his cloak still covered his likeness, and though I peered toward him, he revealed nothing.

The brute huffed and just shoved me along harder. "Fine, later then."

We reached the throne room after several minutes of silence, and I squeezed my eyes shut. *Think, think, think*—I knew any chance of rescue I had would rely on my ability to signal my location to the others, or to escape and rendezvous at the meeting point. But I felt weak, helpless in their grips, my magic just a whimpering stir beneath their suppression. And I was tired—bone-tired. From being mauled by bugs, fighting an army of Drakkarians, and being shot in the neck. I was tired of seeing death, of causing it.

The heavily guarded doors to the great hall swung open, and I numbly noted how the tables had been cast aside to create a large open space. They were not empty, however. Swaths of Drakkarian soldiers pinned Viri females atop or against the tables, some still taking their pleasure violently, others in a slow, drunken way. My guards shoved me forward, down to whatever waited for me at the end of the hall, but my eyes could not leave those women. I sensed their screams had died, their whimpers swallowed. They were silent, retreated into an inner world I knew we all had.

386

My cheeks, now streaked with tears, felt a pinch, forcing me towards the front of the room. Another Witch standing close confronted me. I blinked. He was the one from the Skøl—who'd portaled away at the last second after I'd been shot. His fingers still gripped my chin where he'd turned me towards him.

He brought his mouth close to my ear. "You," he whispered, his cold fingers making their way from my face down my neck. "Killed many of my friends."

A shiver coursed through my body, but I didn't move. I wanted to fight, yell, kick—anything to resist. But I remained frozen, slipping into that place where I knew the Viri females had gone.

"And I am going to delight in returning the favor." His fingers found my collarbone, and he pressed down. At first softly, and then harder and harder. I could feel the bone splintering and cracking at his touch. The gag strangled my screams and though my body wanted to go limp, the guards held me firmly upright.

"Such strength in you, but also such softness..." He breathed hot on my ear. "I wonder if other areas of yours have similar qualities." His fingers left my fractured collarbone, traveling southward, and the grip from the hooded guard tightened, as if in anticipation.

"Enough!" a voice bellowed from in front of us—a figure upon the banquet dais. The warrior's hand retreated.

The room seemed to still as the speaker rose. He didn't bother drawing back his hood to address me. I could see nothing of him nor identify any unique characteristics save for the scraggly beard that tipped out from his chin, and the gleaming ruby that adorned his pinky.

"Ahhh, at last. The infamous Terragnata. We hoped you would join us. We've been waiting, oh so patiently," he sang, his voice booming against the stone walls, gesturing to the figures next to him.

And then I saw her. The queen sat at the table he had just sauntered from, the one we'd dined at together many times in the past few weeks. Her eyes were closed, her face pale and taut. Her normally shining dirty blonde hair was ashen. One cloaked Witch flanked her, tattooed but unshaven—a stark contrast to the shaved warriors that fought in the hall.

I set my jaw, drawing every ounce of strength I had left. "I can't imagine what you were waiting for," I said, my voice not much above a whisper. "I have nothing to offer you."

"Oh, my dear, but that is very much *not* the case. You are everything we have been waiting for. You are the key! And you are even more... so much more," his voice crooned, my skin crawling in reaction.

"Well, I would be happy to help in any way I can," I bit out. My face turned hot as I thought about the women enslaved all around me. "But you have to let her go," I said, nodding to Neferti. "In fact, you have to let all of them go." My last request fell to a firm, but barely audible whisper. I shook with rage now, and I feared speaking at a normal level would reveal that.

The Witch raised his head slightly, appraising me. "What would you want with an old crone set on your demise? Did she not send you away, banish you to live amongst the mortal?"

"What would *you* want with an old crone if I am the key?" I growled, still not knowing what that meant. The heat inside me grew, blocking out any doubts or questions.

He narrowed his eyes at me. "Young girl, you are so very at the beginning of your lifespan. Yet bold! Is it your lack of experience that makes you so? For you have had little time to know true sorrow, true failure." The Witch leaned forward, the swirling patterns of ink on his cheeks glinting in the light. "Tell me, dear child, do you even know who you are? *What* you are?"

The Witch laughed out loud at his humorless question, a guttural, menacing sound. The warriors still standing joined in until the hall became a chorus of mocking.

"No, you don't. She never told you. You are the key to restoring the balance destroyed by the first Rexi of Nebbiolo. If your *mother*," he drawled the word, as if to emphasize the irony of it, "wishes to see her people survive, she needs to do only one thing. Settle an old debt. With your life."

His words sent a jolt of betrayal through me that confirmed my suspicions about my mother. But it didn't compare at all to the overwhelming exhaustion that weighed on my bones. *Olea. Jana. My mother. My father. My brothers. These women—all around me. Suffering, suffering. Too much suffering. Because of me. Because of* me.

"I, however, want to *protect* you, to keep you safe. Which is why we came here—to save you from a king who plotted your death. And a queen who would sacrifice you for her own gain."

I no longer listened; I felt my inner world trying to swallow me whole—into a protective cocoon—into the abyss of dissociation. Before the Drakkarian could say another word, the palace stone floors shifted and exploded with water.

WATER BURST through the pipes that, unbeknownst to me, ran beneath the tile floor. A myriad of liquid volcanoes had erupted, inspired by my trick to woo the crowd before the Skøl. This time, it was not to please the guests. It was a tactical weapon, a beast with dozens of tentacles—individually drowning the Drakkarian warriors. Some spelled to cast the Water off, and some physically fought the element.

And then Fae rushed in—not from the grand doors—no, from shadowed alcoves, trapdoors, and floor grates. There were not many, maybe less than fifty, but enough to cause a serious distraction alongside the water. They must have been hiding, crouching in the unknown spaces of the palace, waiting to make their final stand.

One Water spear came for the ugly Drakkarian that held me, and immediately his grip dropped, as did the spell suppressing my magic. I lashed out at the proverbial chains and felt a whisper of my power trying to sneak through a blocked wall. It was so close I could see it— smell it, even—just not *grasp* it.

My joints remained locked, my mind growing more and more distant from my body. The other Drakkarian dragged me towards the exit, dodging the dangerous Water magic at every step and splashing through the debris. Though I could not see him, I knew Fayzien fought somewhere close. His magic would not kill me—he'd missed too many chances at this point. He wanted me alive. He wanted the queen alive.

My head jerked to the front of the room—where she'd been sitting before. The Rexi struggled to pull away from her guards, her movements whipping with such haphazard violence I knew she fought to prevent them from portaling her away.

My mother's lifeless face flashed in my mind again, sending a physical pang of regret through my gut. I'd stayed frozen when she needed me. Even if *this* mother wanted me dead, even if she'd been the reason the woman who'd raised me left this world... I had to act.

I turned towards the soldier who still gripped me and made to remove his hood. If I was going to battle another Drakkarian, I would look into their eyes. I brought my chained arm up to his face and he swerved back, startled—nervous even. I tried again, and he repeated the action, his stance even more defensive than before. I tried once more, this time yanking the arm he'd gripped towards me. But he pushed me back, turning away as I clipped the edge of his hood with my fingers. I could not see his face as my momentum carried me to the ground.

When I looked up, he vanished. I blinked, water dripping from my eyelashes. The strangeness of the interaction dropped to the wayside—I needed to find Neferti.

In the fray, I could no longer see her, could not see if she still battled on the pseudo-dais. *C'mon, Terra. No time for hesitation.* So I searched for a weapon—perhaps a felled warrior's sword.

In the chaos, I could see nothing but water and blood.

Until—a flash of green. Peeking out from under a ripped cloak.

My fingers knew as soon as I made contact. Ezren's dagger had somehow made its way back to me.

I clasped my still chained hands around it, not worrying about how—only thanking the gods for their gift.

"For Gemilane, for the Fae. For Olea," I whispered, letting a tear slip down my face.

And then I twirled and slashed, cutting through the wall of bodies like I'd done it thousands of times before—even with my hands bound. I only engaged when necessary, moving towards the table of the crown. And though I tried to withhold any lethal strikes, I fell into the hum of battle. But I did not ponder a single thought; my blade was a hand slicing through the mist, acting on instinct and training alone.

Water streamed down my face from the exploding geysers around us. Pandemonium surged, and it took me several seconds to register my surroundings. But then I saw her. The queen still fought her captors—not allowing them to get a solid grip on her. I knew she'd tire in seconds, not minutes.

A moment later, my dagger cut through air, striking down the warriors before they registered what was upon them. My gaze lingered on the bloodstains decorating the queen's skirts for a heart-beat, which was a mistake, for a Witch appeared next to me, grasped my hair, and slammed my head into the banquet table.

In the same motion, he yelled, "Sedric!"

I pushed myself up from the table and turned, dagger raised and clasped between my bound hands. But a Witch appeared behind the queen, shoving her into me. I had no time to react, or if I did, I was not prepared to seize it while still tied, for my blade sank into the queen's chest.

My mouth fell ajar and her eyes flickered in surprise. For all the evil and plotting I had smelled on her before, I saw only helplessness then. The world moved at a snail's pace, such slow motion, and I saw not only the Rexi at the tip of my blade, but Jana, a soft smile on her lips. And she changed again—into Olea, death on her face, a horri-fying emptiness in her eyes. Then I saw my mother's hair, peeking out from our floorboards, as the life escaped from her in front of me.

Before I could register what happened, before I could say a word or scream at the irony of her fate, the Witch that had shoved her into me pulled her back, my dagger slipping out from her chest.

The image of our last resentful interaction, just before the Skøl, flashed between my eyes.

Blood spurted from her wound, and she opened her mouth to speak.

But then, he portaled.

And she was gone.

CHAPTER FOURTY

TWO LANDS

I stumbled back into the table, my head reeling, and then I turned to my side and keeled over, vomiting the little food I ate on our journey from the Convallis to Valfalla.

I took in shallow sips of air, a thousand pounds weighing on my chest. Sinking to my knees, I looked around at the descending chaos of fracturing stone and exploding water. I was soaked head to toe from the uncontrolled blasts that continued to rain down around us, and I wondered if Fayzien used the nearby oceans to support his effort.

I told myself to move, to get out, but I could not, nor could I regain command of my breath. My head pounded, and I gasped as if the air that entered my lungs was not air at all.

A moment later, a hand cupped my shoulder. I expected to see a sopping Water Witch, but I turned to Xinlan's pale face. She looked about as bad as I did, her leathers ripped and tattered, scratches marring her arms and legs.

"Where is the queen?" Xinlan demanded.

"She's gone," I whispered between sobs. "I've failed. Again."

"Shit," Xinlan said. "Terra, we have to go. Now."

393

"I'm not going anywhere," I hissed. I knew sitting there put me at risk of capture, or worse. But I couldn't leave—I couldn't leave the women behind. I couldn't do anything for them, and I couldn't even save my own kin.

But I could stay.

"You have to *trust* me," she said, her eyes as urging as her tone.

That inner voice rose inside me, roused from slumber. It told me to listen, but I shoved it away.

A Drakkarian raised his blade to cut her down from behind, and I threw my dagger overhead, still wet with the queen's blood, sinking it in his eye, numb to the kill. "Trust," I said, the word unfeeling, a foreign concept I could not comprehend. And in a way, I couldn't—though Tey eventually turned on her, Xinlan initially had been a part of the king's plot. To kill me.

Beyond that, I barely knew her. My history of trusting strangers was blemished.

But I said none of that; my body tuned into the thrum of the battle around me. The roaring in my head screamed loud and deathly quiet. I looked around for the women I'd seen when they'd dragged me into the hall. But there were none. The Water magic had provided a distraction for their escape. *Good, that was good.*

"I have no reason to trust you. I'm not going anywhere." The words felt far away, like they belonged to someone else.

Xinlan yanked my hands from my lap and held my chains. They turned glowing orange, and she sliced her blade through them. I didn't have the energy to marvel at whatever magic made the cut possible. "Viribrum is lost. We have rescued every Fae we could have. We must go. *Now.*"

Before I could protest again, she dragged me to stand, pulling me after her so fast I barely had time to swipe back Ezren's dagger. We made it toward an alcove on the side of the banquet hall. Movement flickered in my peripheral and I ducked a left hook. Xinlan sent her blade into my assailant's neck, removing his head from his shoulders.

The image made my stomach roil, recalling the head she'd cut down in the Skøl.

"You cut his head clean off," I said flatly as she pulled me into the shadow of the alcove, away from the fighting.

Xinlan knew I didn't mean the Drakkarian she'd just saved me from. "I did."

"Who was he to you?" I whispered.

She made to protest; I could tell she wanted to urge me to run—but something in her face softened, perhaps at the grief she saw on my own. "He was my father. I did that so his soul could escape. In my house, that is a warrior's death. His soul will be free—to leave this body and this life. To rest in Requiem."

I looked at her in disbelief. In that moment, she'd had such clarity and strength. She hadn't hesitated a second. And neither had he.

"You have to *go now*," Xinlan begged. "Ezren is waiting."

Again, instinct swirled in my gut, that little voice my father spoke of gnawing at the back of my mind, urging me to listen. Still, I couldn't make myself move. My eyes wandered past her, landing on the blood that pooled on the floor of the dais. Blood that had trickled down from where I'd held the queen in my arms.

"Everywhere I go, death follows," I said bitterly. "My family, my sire, my aunt, my handmaid—all dead. And now, the Rexi... maybe she lives, but I also might have just killed her." I choked on those words, my throat constricting into a searing burn.

"You are so, so young Terra. But you will learn. You will learn to do difficult things, because you have to. Because so many *rely* on you. Right now—you have to make it out of here. Not just for this kingdom, but for yours, too."

Her words sparked something inside me, and another wave of distrust ebbed. I drew my eyes back to her face.

"We will survive this," she continued, her voice shaking with quiet anger as she surveyed the destruction in the throne room. "We will regroup. And we will take back our home." It seemed she spoke more to herself than to me.

And then I understood. She needed me—they all did—to go back to Nebbiolo, raise an army, and help the Viri take back Viribrum.

She needed me to trust her.

And I needed her. Though I had no interest in being queen, I could *not* sit back and let these horrors go unanswered. I could not. I couldn't stand alone against Drakkar. I'd need a court, warriors, loyalty. All resources based on trust.

That trust would have to start here. With a Fae who'd bedded my betrothed and had been paid to kill me.

"Where?" I bit out.

"East Tower." She nodded for me to go. "Your escape route will be clear. I've got clean-up." Her face held a sad smile. Despite all that had transpired between us, I almost smiled, too.

"Good luck," I whispered.

And then I ran through the hall, using the anonymity of chaotic battle as my protection. I only had to meet the blades of two Drakkarians before I slipped out the door and ran for the east corridor.

A distinct *meow* had me skidding to a stop. "Cas?" I called out.

The figure in the shadows changed. Cas lingered in the dark, his face puffy. "They put his head on a spike," he whispered.

I felt for him, I did. But the sound of Drakkarian footsteps nearing us squashed my sympathy.

"He said it was all to save me," he sniffed. "All of it—what he did to you, the price on your head, the lies—was to save me from some *prophecy*."

I stilled for a short moment, weighing the meaning of Cas's emotional drivel and how it changed the tilt of our world, but the footsteps continued.

I latched onto his arm, dragging him after me. "We have to go," I said, moving towards the East Tower. "Now."

"There is no exit that way," Cas mumbled as we ran up and up the spiraling servants' stairway. I ignored him, keeping my senses strong and alert for any threats lurking around the corners.

I maintained a ruthless pace. Up and up we went, until we

neared the top of the East Tower. I had only ventured to this place a few times, for it housed Gia's favorite reading nook, with a view of the gardens and the roiling sea.

I kept looking backward to ensure Cas was there and to keep an eye out for any pursuers.

I kicked open the thick wooden door. The familiar smell of leather and parchment filled my nose. It smelled of safety, of respite. But there was no Ezren. I paced around the room in a flash, searching under window seat pillows, as if he or a clue might appear. The sound of footsteps carried up the staircase. Not friendly footsteps.

That traitorous—what did I expect? Trust isn't cheap, nor easy.

My eyes caught on the horizon—a little pale dot on the ocean. A ship.

I gritted my teeth, thanking Maester Sabnae for stranding me out there during my training. I visualized the portal, a window opening in my mind, a door to take us there, pulsing, beckoning us forward.

And then it sputtered. *Shit.*

"Terra," Cas's voice grew worried, and the footsteps grew closer. "Can you portal us out of here?"

"I just tried," I said, fighting the panic from seeping into my voice. "I don't think I can, not without risking the in-between." *I must be drained from my earlier eruption, and those damned magic dampeners.*

"Terra! They're getting closer."

Think, think, think. Xinlan's words echoed in my mind. *Ezren is waiting.*

But he wasn't. I didn't know what to expect—Ezren here to defend me, or outside to catch me as I escaped. I checked through the window. Nothing. No Dragon in sight.

Not that a Dragon circling the tower in wait would be inconspicuous or wise.

I squeezed my eyes shut, knowing I had less than a minute to make my decision. I could either trust Xinlan with a literal leap of faith—or take my chances fighting our pursuers and regroup.

The second option seemed like a bad idea, given I was so drained I couldn't portal.

I turned to Cas. "Shift." I went to the curtains, ripping a long strip of fabric from them.

He sputtered. "*What?* No. Why would you ask that? I'm useless in my shift."

I fought my eyes from pressing shut in exasperation, the footsteps ominously loud now. "Cas, we don't have time for debate. Just shift." *I better be right about this.*

He huffed, making to argue more, but then the pounding on the stairs outside arrived at the door.

"Now!" I yelled to Cas. *Now,* I said to myself.

Cas jumped, but then did as I bid, leaping in his feline form into the swaddle I had prepared from the ripped curtain, slung around my shoulder. I tightened it, ensuring he was fixed there. I swung the furry cat from my chest to my back.

I stepped up on the reading bench and made to unfasten the window openings that overlooked the steep drop to the sea. But there were none. Someone had welded the window shut.

I padded back to the far end of the circular room, shaking my head. The creature on my back meowed in protest, but I had him snug enough that he could not move. Then, I ran full speed towards the window as the Drakkarians entered the room, their blades looking hungry. Before they could stop us, I burst through the glass, breaking the impact with my forearms raised in front of my face.

We fell, slivers of glass stuck in my hair, the wind whipping by us. My eyes closed on instinct the moment I passed through the window, but I forced them open now. I looked down to see nothing but swirling ocean and damp rocks beneath us.

We approached it faster and faster, the wind beginning to burn my eyes.

Fear flooded my veins. *Had I been wrong?*

My heart pounded so fiercely that I could feel it in my ears. I tried to reach out with my magic, to beg it to catch me, but I was *afraid* and had no command over the water. Closer and closer, the details of the rocks came into focus, sea foam caressing their jagged surfaces.

I had seconds, or less, to break the fall or to risk the in-between of the portal.

Terror rippled through me, and I wondered if the impact would be enough to break my Fae body. If Cas would splatter on the rocks.

Green scales appeared beneath me and I had but a moment to register the relief. I parted my legs, and the impact was brutal, reverberating through the fractures of my collarbone. I cried out in triumph and pain as the Dragon swept us forward and up, absorbing our fall to the best of his ability. My palms grasped familiar spinal spikes, and we were flying, away from the lost palace.

As we left the chaos behind, I sent a slip of my remaining magic toward that place—for the Fae I'd left there, the Fae to whom I owed my escape.

For Xinlan.

THE DRAGON DIPPED HIS HEAD, making a steep descent to the ocean. As he did, the ship came into focus.

It was only a mile from the coast, but far away enough that the Drakkarian armies would not notice the small, unassuming—and from the smell that began to fill my nostrils—fishing vessel that left the city. The sight of it confirmed what I'd hoped; Ezren had found where Sanah and the crew had been hiding by the docks. From the way the Dragon flew with precision, I could tell Dane spelled him, as he had many times before on reconnaissance missions. A nervous feeling of anticipation swelled in my gut. Upon landing I would find out if they'd located Gia. If Leiya had made it out of the palace.

"How will we land?" I yelled as we neared the vessel at an impressive speed. The cat on my back meowed in distress. I visualized the portal, but it sputtered and pulsed—clarity evading me even more than in the tower. "Shit," I muttered, gritting my teeth.

"Jump!" a voice on the ship called out.

I prepared to protest, but when I looked down, I saw someone had fastened a fishing net to the masts in a way that one could, conceivably, jump and safely be caught. I shook my head, grumbling, reminding myself to throttle whoever's idea this was.

The Dragon tilted his wings, and I knew what he meant to do. I reached behind me and swung the Feline to my front, cradling him to my chest with one hand, holding onto the Dragon's spine with the other. He tilted until he flew with his wings almost fully vertical, cornering around the ship. He got me close enough, and I launched myself out and to the side, turning my body mid-air so that I would land on my back. Seconds later, I hit the fish-scented net and bounced up, Cas nearly flying from my grasp.

A strong-armed Leuffen caught me before I catapulted off the side of the boat and set me on the ground. A small cry left my mouth, and I swung the cat behind me, pulling myself up to the Fae, pressing my head into his chest.

"Terra," he breathed into my hair, squeezing me back. "Yer alright."

I looked up at him, beaming. "And you're alive! Can he land?" I asked, searching the sky for Ezren.

Leuffen winked at me. "Dinna worry, lass. Dane's spellen' 'em."

The Dragon turned vertical once more, getting even closer to the net than he did before. He shifted mid-air, his warrior body hitting the net with grace. He launched up and landed in a crouch on the deck, as if he'd performed the stunt numerous times.

Leuffen dropped his arms from my sides, and I turned to face the fierce Dragon. He looked straight at me. Even now, the blaze of green eyes sent a pulse through my body.

"Purgo," Dane cast from across the ship, breathless from the exertion. Ezren stumbled as if struck, and the slits in his eyes subsided.

"Ezren," I whispered as he strode towards me. "You came ba—"

He cut me off, wrapping me in his arms, ignoring the passenger slung over my shoulder.

I crumpled into him, exhaling, the gravity of everything that had happened hitting me like a brick I'd dodged for too long. He squeezed me once, and then again so tightly I had the impression he thought I might slip from his arms. "You're safe," he breathed.

A moment later, the weight on my back shifted and I heard the sound of claws piercing fabric. The cat plopped onto the ship deck and promptly turned. I detached myself from Ezren to face a sopping, bloody Cas.

"Hello Ezren," he said coolly, brushing stray debris from his jacket lapel. "Thanks for the ride."

Ezren tipped his head back at Cas in acknowledgment, and the two of them proceeded to stare at each other in loaded silence.

"Well, I see ye've already managed te start a' cat fight," Leiya snickered, approaching the deck. "Thes well make fer one helluva' journey."

My chest tightened in relief at hearing her voice. Cas glared at Leiya but said nothing.

Gia appeared at Leiya's side, and my chest tightened further. "You're alright," I exhaled, pulling her into me gently, minding the bump that still swelled from her midsection.

Gia gave me a gentle squeeze. "I'm here, Terra."

A small sense of ease washed over me, clearing my mind. "What journey?" I asked, turning back towards Leiya.

She looked at me with a seriousness that I had not yet seen from her. "Well, Terra, ets time ye get answers, fer all our sakes, and fer the sake a' Viribrum. Lassie, we are headed te Nebbiolo."

I bit my lower lip, my brows knitting together as I surveyed the group before me. Dane looked like he'd slept on the dirt floor of an opium den. Leuffen wore armor covered in dried blood and muck. Leiya's leathers were still streaked with the ash that had rained down on the Skøl. Cas's face sagged, hollow bags drooping beneath his eyes. Sanah's hair was matted, though her eyes beamed. Ezren was also covered in gore, but looked at me like he always did, with wild adoration. And though she was the cleanest of the bunch—perhaps the only one who looked like they'd had a bath in the last few weeks—Gia's face was solemn.

Even Cobal had made it on the boat. And as it gazed up at me with those wise eyes, I wondered what the creature knew that led it to join us here.

"Why," I exhaled, suddenly aware of all the attention fixed in my direction. "Why do you all want to go? Viribrum may be lost, yes, but we don't know what awaits in Nebbiolo. It could be more dangerous —one of the Drakkarians implied the Rexi intended to sacrifice me to save the queendom. I don't know what we'll be walking into."

The group collectively held their breath. And then Sanah spoke.

"We might not all be Nebbiolon, or Viri for that matter," she said, her eyes sliding to Dane. "But, many moons ago, each one of us here was called by Jana to search for the lost Earth Daughter of both queendom and kingdom. And now that we found her..." Sanah trailed off, sinking to one knee. I stilled in anticipation.

"I think we know why," she whispered, her voice cracking. "I haven't been to my homeland in many decades. It would be the highest honor of my life to be taken home by a queen."

"We need ye, Lassia," Leuffen said, lowering himself as well. "Te breng the kingdoms together. Ye saw what the Drakkarians ded te Valfalla. Ye must unite the Wetch and the Fae te stand against 'em." My eyes fogged at the belief in his gaze. "Otherwise, we havena hope."

Ezren followed suit, his knee hitting the deck as the boat gently sloshed. The sight of him giving me deference sent strange waves of electricity through me. "Your power is unlike anything I've seen, *Bellatori*. You can defend, yes, and you can destroy, but you can also create."

Dane smiled. "In the darkest of times, it is hope that the world needs—hope that can only be found in the marvel and relief of creation."

Finally, Cas knelt, clearing his throat. "A week ago, I would not have expected to be here, kneeling before my oldest friend. I can't say I mind it." He gave me a devilish grin, and I felt Ezren tense, but he continued on, his tone turning grave. "But if there was a time for a prince to kneel before a princess, it would be when he has lost everything." He trailed off, choking on the words. My throat went dry. "It costs me very little to ask you this, Terragnata of Nebbiolo. Our king was slaughtered in his own palace, our females raped in their own homes. Do not abandon us." Tears flowed down his face now, and the sight of him begging—lowered on his knees—twisted something inside me. "Do not abandon me," he whispered. "Do not abandon us."

I bit the inside of my cheek, willing my eyes to remain dry. I did not think, I did not evaluate my choices, I could only react. I gave him a small nod and whispered back. "I will not."

"Te the future queen a' two lands!" Leuffen bellowed, beating his chest.

"To the future queen of two lands!" the rest cheered.

To the future queen of two lands.

I knew those words would ring in my ears for years to come.

CHAPTER FOURTY-ONE

DUAL LOYALTIES

*G*ia squeezed my hand, a violent wind whipping hair in our faces. The small fishing boat made good time, especially when aided by the Air Witch Dane had scrounged up from the slums bordering the docks.

I blinked at her. It was a wonder, really, that Gia made it onto the boat, that they had stumbled upon her by the docs. I still couldn't believe it—she'd somehow escaped the king's men when they came for Jana. And though I suspected Jana held some responsibility for that miracle, I wasn't in the mood to question the fortune. I just squeezed her hand right back.

"Can you believe only two months ago I fretted over Spring Day while we shopped the market?" I mused.

Gia shook her head. "It feels like a lifetime ago."

"This place is very different from Argention... from the human lands," I whispered, my words nearly stolen by the screams of the sea.

"You have no idea," Gia breathed.

I looked at her, cocking my head at the maturity in her voice. I didn't want to imagine the horrors she might've witnessed since I'd left for the Skøl.

Gia's expression remained distant for only a moment, and then it shifted back into concern. "Sanah and Dane found me a day or so back, during that competition—the Skøl, was it? And, well, they explained everything—Spring Day, Fayzien's involvement, how Jana, the woman who took you, is your aunt." She gave a small, somewhat guilty shrug. "I'm sorry I cast doubt over them. Sanah is truly lovely, and I trust their story. We're safe now. And we are together. Let that be a small victory."

I shook my head, suppressing the need to correct her *is* with *was*. "No apology needed, my friend. I'm only glad you are here."

She shifted her gaze back out to the sea. Her mention of the Skøl tickled something at the back of my mind.

"You know what's ironic? Jana brought me to Viribrum to show the public Drakkarians didn't murder me, to weaken King Darlan's support for an invasion. To *prevent* this very war. And turns out, bringing me here could have caused the invasion itself."

"What do you mean, you coming here caused the invasion?" Gia's brows scrunched together.

I let my oldest friend see the fear in my eyes. "Leiya and Ezren said, 'of course they would attack, Darlan forced their hand.' But, I'm not so sure. In the Skøl, when they invaded... it was *me* the Drakkarians were after. Their leader said as much at the palace."

Gia looked stricken for a moment, clearly weighing carefully what to say. She squeezed my hand once more. "That may be true, but we'll get to the bottom of all this. We're *safe* now, Terra."

She was right—we'd made it out of Viribrum alive—almost all of us. *Olea. Jana.* Their names repeated in my head, leaving little scores, etchings of regret and pain in my chest alongside the ones I bore for my human family. And for all I knew, the queen could be added to that list... at the very least, the Drakkarian's had captured her. Whether Fayzien or Xinlan had escaped, I had no clue.

But Gia was safe. So were Leiya and Leuffen. Cas. Dane. Sanah. Cobal. And Ezren. I'd lost so much, my own blood and not, but I'd also gained. And though I felt uncomfortable with the semi-royal treatment I'd received earlier, a familial atmosphere now lingered on the ship, a sense that laced every conversation and interaction.

That feeling was loyalty... and, perhaps, even family.

And my new little family was safe.

But as I uttered those words in my head, they rang hollow. I'd appeared safe for years in Argention, and that was an illusion. Had I ever truly been safe? And now... a sinking feeling wound tight around my chest. I didn't know how our voyage would go, or what our acceptance at Nebbiolo would look like. I didn't know how to save the queen, or even *if* she could be saved. Or how in the gods' names we could defeat a kingdom like Drakkar. I didn't know why they'd called me "the key," what that could mean, if the people of Nebbiolo would kill me for it, or call me to the throne. The one thing I knew, with chilling certainty, was a war had just begun. And for reasons still outside my grasp, I seemed to be at its center.

And if that wasn't harrowing enough—everyone on this ship seemed to believe *I* could save the world from conflict.

I shuddered, brushing off the constricting feelings of pressure and looming disappointment that always seemed to accompany thoughts of duty. "And you—you're okay with this? With coming to Nebbiolo?" I turned to face Gia once again. "I wish I had time to bring you home."

"Even if you could, I know traveling back to Argention pregnant is a fool's errand. You are my home now. And you are the queen expectant of an unfamiliar land—you will need as many allies by your side as you can get. These past few months have been... so unexpected. But no matter what happens, no matter what you face, you can *always* trust in me." A hint of a smile played on Gia's lips as she rested her hand on her swelling belly. I had the distinct feeling she wanted to say more, but I didn't push her. The gods knew it was a miracle she even made it here, carrying my brother's child.

"Your confidence never fails to surprise me." I chuckled silently. "But thank you. You are my truest friend." I rested a gentle hand on her round stomach. "My little niece or nephew could not be coming into this world to a better mother."

A sadness flickered across her face, but she only nodded and headed below deck, no doubt seeking respite from the biting sea air.

An unexpected couple of months, indeed. I'd been a human in a small mining town facing the sheer dread of conventional arranged marriage. If only I'd known what was coming for me on that Spring Day. If only I knew what was coming for me now. The cold air should have forced me to follow Gia below deck, but I remained still, frozen in time, anticipating what was ahead, my gaze fixed stubbornly upon a horizon that did not yet reveal an island.

Nebbiolo. My birthright. And perhaps, one day, my home.

EPILOGUE

WICKED QUEEN

*W*hen my daughter's blade pierced my skin, I knew it immediately. She had found her Siphon—or at least something close to it. Perhaps that was how she broke through my shield, though the thought was a trifle embarrassing. I'd been away from the Stone Throne too long. But indeed, that unique tone of power reverberated through her. A small, weak part of me grieved to think she might never realize it.

She looked young—so painfully young. She was brave and fierce, reminding me of a different self, one untouched by the Stone. Though she would likely never know such a sentiment from me, I played the part I always knew I must: the Wicked Queen.

And that bastard Darlan—the fat king had admitted to plotting Terra's end before he lost his head. Clever... manipulating her, throwing her off guard while he planned her assassination in that *wretched* competition. Claiming it served only to protect Cas from the prophecy.

Of course, he failed to mention that her death would undo a thousand years of progress, wreaking havoc across our queendom, and weakening those he viewed as rivals.

Ever the political mastermind. Too bad that lost him his head this round.

Still, a blunder on my part, underestimating him. I should've known he'd figured out what she was. Not that it mattered now.

I flashed back to that room where I birthed her—when the Elders visited. And everything had changed.

The Drakkarians called her 'the key.' *They* clearly had been misinformed.

If they truly knew our bloodline's ugly past, or what the Rexiprima sacrificed to form the island I'd inherited to rule, they wouldn't call her the key.

They'd call her the Undoing.

Terragnata, the first Earth Daughter in a thousand years, born on the day of the Creatrix Full Moon, to a future queen, was no *key*.

She was an impending explosion. She was the fulfillment of the prophecy delivered to the Witch Killer who'd formed our great nation.

I'd tried to stop it. To send her away. To eliminate anyone who might try and succeed at locating her, using her. I'd spared Cas, only a child, thinking naively he would move on.

Even Cold Hearts could make foolish mistakes.

My wound oozed, throbbing in a way that would kill me. Should they let it.

As we floated through space and time, I saw all their faces, in that great hall, tattooed and shaved—the faces of those I'd been taught for so many years to hate. They did not look so fearsome. They looked empty.

It took him many portals, the Drakkarian called Sedric, to bring us to where he sought. It was impressive that not only did he keep us from being lost to the in-between, but he kept us from being lost in *general*. The hours turned to days turned to weeks. He was not a healing Witch, but he clearly intended to keep me alive, clumping fistfuls of algae and moss to my wound in whatever field training he'd learned.

I laughed at his efforts, almost wishing he would just let me die. It would be fitting for Terra to take my life, as she felt I had taken hers. Maybe that would restore some gods damned balance the Elders droned on about.

I was not so lucky. Eventually, we made it to Mesha, or so I assumed. He brought me to some dreadful cell, dripping and cold, and a young healer came in to patch me up. They left me there for days, and I puzzled over my use. They hadn't bothered to torture me for details of Nebbiolon forces or the like.

Nor for details about the significance of my Earth Child.

On the fourth day, a hooded figure approached my cell. His scent was familiar, though he dressed as they all did, and swirling lines of ink on his jaw peaked out from beneath his hood.

Even with such deception, I knew, and I froze, huddled in a ball on the cool stone.

"Hello, Nef. It's good to see you," the figure said.

I held my chin high despite my pathetic position.

"Hello, Viturius."

BONUS

Did something feel... off about Gia to you?

Sign up for my newsletter at *cdmackenzie.com* and unlock a *free* chapter from Gia's perspective - for a limited time only.

And most importantly, don't forget to review Terra on Goodreads and Amazon. Reviews are my lifeblood.

ACKNOWLEDGMENTS

Writing a book is equal parts humility and hubris. It's a lonely endeavor, one millions venture into each year. I was very fortunate to to share it early and often along what has been a nearly five year journey.

I began Terra's first draft in February 2020 while living in Brooklyn with my two best friends. I remember thrusting my MacBook in front of my roommate, kicking-my-feet-giddy, as I pointed her to one of the first scenes.

After that, nearly fifteen people read this manuscript cover to cover. A huge thank you to my ride-or-die gals, my swath of dedicated beta readers, my dad repeatedly asking about what was going on with the book, and my mom telling everyone who would listen about it. Thank you to my partner, for inspiring me to become an entrepreneur. Thank you to my editor Elli, who was not only was dedicated to the story's development but also instrumental in getting the final draft over the finish line.

And most importantly, thank *you*, reader.

It's all for you.

ABOUT THE AUTHOR

C. D. MacKenzie is a 29-year-old emerging Fantasy-Romance author, living in the hills of San Francisco with her partner and a cockapoo puppy named Dobby.

While she works a day job, her heart has always been rooted in the world of imagination. She grew up reading Harry Potter, watching Vampire Diaries, and generally exploring excellence in the art of daydreaming. In 2017, she devoured her first Romantasy novel. She's been hooked ever since.

She is beyond thrilled to share with you her debut novel, Terragnata and the Heir of the Earth.

Printed in Great Britain
by Amazon

58310352R00239